Felony Warp

T.A. Csorba

Printed in the United States of America

First Printing, 2013

ISBN: 978-0-9841605-3-2 0-9841605-3-1 Felony Warp, ebook

ISBN: 978-0-9841605-4-9 0-9841605-4-X Felony Warp, hardcopy

Cybernetica Press Inc.
602 Massachusetts Ave.
Norfolk, VA 23508

www.barryclemson.net

Disclaimer:

This book is a work of fiction. Any similarity between the characters and situations depicted and places or persons, living or dead, is unintentional and co-incidental, and no offense is intended to professions or work forces presented fictionally in this work

There are satellite stations and colonies and there is faster than light travel and still there are people who drive around on city roads trying to make justice happen. Some of 'em even still wear badges. Not a lot has changed since the turn, but then the only people who thought it would didn't know a good thing when they saw it. Technology has not healed our ills. It only makes them easier to catalogue.

I.

Victor Friar

My partner told me I had to buy the coffee that day or go without; It was my turn. I argued that it wasn't and gave all sorts of examples why, but he just nodded with one eyebrow cranked in disbelief and sent me to the coffee machine. And here I thought it took longer than four months to break in a new partner.

Nothing spectacular had deprived me of my old partner: The guy retired finally after a long and thankless road, same road we were all walking. This new kid, well, he was fittin' in okay, but he'd lost his own senior partner to a shoot out on his 31st day on the job. Rough. The kid wasn't taking it so well, but I was trying to help him past it. It wasn't like he even liked his first partner, but it's a shitty thing to happen to a rookie.

But things change as you go, which I guess means you're still alive, so it's a good thing. Already, I had ceased to be a part of the old unit and was now part of the new. You know how your names become one when you work in a team, like "Fred-and-Ginger", "Laurel-and-Hardy," like that, well, partners are like that, too. So here instead of Kay-and-Friar, I was part of Friar-and-Sherrow, just like Unit 17 was Dally-and-Johnson.

Sherrow cursed me out about the coffee, then insulted the taste, like it was my fault the coffee machine turned out cat piss in a cup, and the shift got rolling. It would start with a 240 frying pan and end with a mess in road tavern, but that wouldn't be out of the ordinary. I cursed Sherrow back and decided he wouldn't get me killed out of depression today by the look of him. It really was a shame when a rookie lost his partner right off. Screwed 'em up good. Look at what had happened to me.

Max Canon

Darkness, as usual. He never seemed to wake up anymore when the sun was out. He sat up, still tired, kicking the covers aside with a meaningless curse, and rubbed his eyes. They'd be red, of course: He couldn't remember the last time he'd shaved to clear eyes. They were always bloodshot, always red. Dry and tired in the blue-white mirror light, the hot metal stink of the late summer city night leaking in through the little window over the toilet, the razor tugging across weary skin like sandpaper across that last raw nerve.

Maybe he'd skip the shave again today. No one noticed the difference anyway. No one ever looked at him properly, except maybe the cops and an occasional associate, and most of them only looked again after getting a glimpse of the hardware suspended at a reach-friendly angle in a use-blackened holster under his right armpit. The holster had cost too much too far back to belong to a cop, and the hardware was so technologically advanced that even the assassins and the maf didn't have 'em. The military had, once, and now Max had what was probably the only one left in existence. He hadn't met another one, at any rate. Made the nuke batteries awful hard to come by.

Frank Skills knew about it, of course, but then Frank Skills was the police chief, or whatever it was they were calling him these days, the department being the latest prototype of colony policing, and he'd had it off Max at least six times after cases that had gotten a little messy and required court time to clean them up.

The town was the usual mix of trouble and victims, and Frank Skills had his work cut out for him keeping it all sorted out enough to prevent spontaneous combustion. But civilians were exactly like the civilians in every other town

Max had ever been in and the cops were just like cops. There was no comfortable niche for an ex-soldier turned privately licensed investigator for hire. The profession was about as understood and accepted as assassination. Hell, assassination had a mantel of tradition to lend it respectability, or at least a flush of romance. People simply didn't trust a cop without a badge, never had, never would.

Not that there was blame in that. The badge was the only identification in the world that allowed the bearer to take undue liberties with the civilian populace. Some of the things you could do with a badge were crimes without it. Tossing somebody's apartment, for example. Or taking a man's weapon away.

The face in the mirror under the blue-white zombie light had never walked behind a badge. This face had no legal excuse to do any the things the job required. The only reason this face wasn't standing over the shaving sink at the local lock-up waiting for the sentence to be passed was that it had a low profile, a paranoid nature, and a long-standing relationship with Frank Skills.

And every time the sirens brought the private license to Frank Skills, the chief of police would sigh, shake his narrow head and say,

"What were you up to this time, Canon?"

And the private investigator would smile his crooked smile and say,

"Nothin' much, chief. Just thought I'd drop by to see how you were doing. Hope it's not a bad time for you," there in the hard wooden chair in front of the scarred steel desk, with the handcuffs cutting into his wrists and the bruises from the arrest still coming up fresh baby red on his face, smart- assing to the only man in town on the department level who had a say on whether or not to lock him up or have him shot. Legally, at any rate. There were a lot of people who could have a man like Max shot or locked away, but a man learned who he could piss off with impunity and who would fight back pretty quick in a city like Alaman and Max Canon had done the finding out before his left foot even touched dirt off the transport that brought him in.

It was a lesson half-learned, though. He was constantly finding more people to piss off in the course of the job. It seemed to be what investigating was all about: Getting into people's faces and pissing them off.

With a face like this, it wasn't too hard. Stubble over a jaw-heavy, hollow-cheeked face, cold blue eyes half-masted with exhaustion and too much of other people's tragedy, a hard mouth that couldn't smile without that first cup of coffee and nasty, sarcastic eyebrows that could carry on a conversation all by themselves and never say one nice thing.

And the romantic streak. Never forget that well-hidden, hyperbolic romantic streak.

A smart man also knew when to skip town. W. Maxwell Canon had done that, too, a few odd times, a step and a half ahead of the local thunder, with a dime in his pocket, a gun on his hip and his hat in his hand. But a man could also get tired of the race. Even dogs got too old to run, and Max thought maybe he was getting there fast. Certainly his knees weren't what they used to be, and every new town seemed meaner and dirtier and just a little more desperate.

The only thing special about this one was that his sister lived there and Frank Skills, and there were men like him in every town; fair men trying to do thankless jobs for no reward, no recognition and a pittance salary that just might stretch beyond retirement with very careful management. Frank only stood out from the long line of gray and beaten faces because his old partner had married Max's sister, which almost made him family.

Almost, but not quite. He was still a cop, like Eddy Archer was still cop, even when he was a brother-in-law, and Eddy had still run Max in for B and E on the Baldwin case. How strange to be arrested by your brother-in-law, booked by his ex-partner, and sprung by his wife who was, after all, still your sister.

Ruth had not been pleased, even though charges hadn't been pressed in the end. The judge could've stuck Max with 'interfering with police work', since it had turned out to be a murder scene, but he hadn't and Max had touched nothing and interfered as little as possible. He'd gotten his first lead when he'd walked in, and since the trace he'd been after was dead, it was probably moot anyway.

He'd solved that case, too, before the cops did, but then the cops had so much else to occupy their time. Max only had this, and 'this' came down to the face in the mirror and the blunted ambition that kept it moving. Max knew the military and some of its equipment, and he knew investigating, and that was it. The military didn't feed him anymore, so investigation had to, and he'd long since learned it wouldn't make him rich. These days, he felt lucky to eat.

Apparently, Ruth felt the same way. He was due there for dinner in an hour. Eddy would be dressed up in his best casuals, drinking slowly but steadily because he hated dinner parties and precinct politics expected them. Ruth would be wearing some pretty thing she'd made up herself because she scorned the styles that were supposedly in fashion, chatting with the other officer's wives in low, cool voices about the latest political event, and what somebody's wife had gotten up to at the last party (somebody's wife being absent from the present gathering). Eddy would be spreading drinks around to oil the social wheels, talking stiffly to the men he worked with every day, but who all seemed to become strangers as soon as the badges came off and the civilian clothes went on.

Max would stand in a corner, occasionally exchanging a word or two with whoever had been drafted to be his dinner partner, usually some low-rank cop who tried bravely to keep the outsider amused while the others played at social interchange and the ice cubes in Max's drink rattled against the side of the low-ball every time he took a sip, sending iron-cold bourbon and bitters down his throat in little mercury rushes that failed to spread any of that lovely artificial heat higher than his stomach, leaving his heart cold and alone.

And Ruth couldn't understand why he was cynical and bitter, when the parties were no longer fun, when he couldn't play at facades anymore, having peered under one too many in the constant search for the truth, and the liquor didn't warm him any longer, didn't fill the gaps between him and the other poor bastards flailing around in the darkness trying to be popular, trying to be liked, trying to fit in.

He'd have to shave, though. There was no reason to go pissing off Ruth by showing up looking like a bum, insulting her hospitality and making her say, "You all remember my brother Max," and then having to scramble for a polite lie to explain why he looked so shabby. Ruth would expect him to be clean-shaven if he came crawling to her front door bleeding from multiple gunshot wounds. He'd have to shave.

By the time he found a shirt that was fairly clean and draped on the silk noose and jacket, and polished the tops of his wing tips on the end of the bed spread, it was time to get moving. He grabbed his hat, pocketed the unbroken pair of optic filter glasses, strapped on the gun—in case he wanted to go downtown later—and dug out a fresh notebook that still had empty memory. He added a hard copy notepad just in case the batteries were too low like last time, and spent five minutes looking for a stylus. Finally equipped, he spared a last glance in the mirror. It told him he still looked like a bum, but at least he was a well-dressed bum.

II.

Friar

The sun never seemed to shine. Daylight illuminated an ugly gray sprawl of techno-glazed, failing metropolis, frosting faces with unforgiving gray light and ruthlessly exposing every flaw and glitch in the whole rotten machine.

My city. Lucky me.

It's probably better than I deserve.

My partner and I took seven at the same boring bland-food café we always ended up eating at, and I sat over the second cup of coffee and watched the kid play with his badge and stir the godawful adulterated concoction he always made out of coffee, no matter it was good or not to begin with.

"Ya wanna talk about it, or just brood all night?" I asked, getting fed up finally.

He looked up like he was surprised and gave me kid eyes wide.

"S'nothing, Friar. Just...s'nothing."

"It's Randall, isn't it." I didn't even try to make it sound like a question, because it wasn't.

He dropped his eyes, surprised for sure this time, and clanked the spoon around four more times.

"I guess it is."

"So what's bugging you? I read the report. You did everything right and nothing wrong and you couldn't've helped him. Sometimes it just goes down like that. Quit kicking yerself about it and move on already."

I saw anger pull down his dark eyebrows, and the coffee got a scowl that would've curdled it if it hadn't been that way already.

"I'm not kicking myself. I know I did the right thing. Book says put down the perp, protect the civis first."

"So? While you were busy doin' that, a second unknown, well-hidden perp caught up behind Randall and did him good. You weren't even in line of sight. You couldn't have prevented it or saved him and I know you've been over all this ad nauseum with the Battalion counselor. What are you thinking you could've done better?"

Sherrow looked at me with the frown slashing his eyebrows into satanic triangles.

"If I'd been more experienced, or a little less by the book, I would've been in line of sight. That guy was fully exposed for at least 5 seconds before he opened fire. Ten inches to the left, and I'd a seen him before he did for Randall. All I had to do was put the perp down on the ground instead of against the squad."

"That would've been police brutality and you know it. The rate you guys were traveling when you caught up with him, you would've broken things, puttin' him down on the concrete."

"Serve the lousy bastard right if I did."

"Sure it would've and it'd serve you right off the force, that kinda shit one month into your active. You can get creative all you want when you're full blue, but until yer off probationary status, you gotta keep it clean or not at all. Why're you all up about this again? Seemed to me you were over the replay last month."

Sherrow shrugged, his gun making a dull clunk against the wooden side of the booth.

"Yeah. 'S just something Hollingate said this morning."

I gave a snort and tried on a scowl of my own.

"He lyin' again about how he almost won the Medal by saving old Trammel during that drug factory bust?"

"I guess. Assuming he's lying." Sherrow's tone suggested that I was the one lying.

"He's lying. I was there. Trammel was already dead when Hollingate got there. All Holl did was get himself buckshot scars and louse up my collar by racing through my line of fire. Idiot. He loves to get you kids all up and fired about being heroes. The only kind of hero we got on the force is the guy who does his job to the best of his ability and God knows you never hear about him. That's the kind of hero you should try to be."

Sherrow didn't like that, but I had nearly eleven years on him and I'd been through it myself. Romance is great for fiction, but it gets you dead fast in action. He took the spoon out of his cup and tasted the coffee. Made a face. Put it down and looked at me.

"Huh," was all he said.

"You'll believe it someday," I told him, waving Sara over for the tab.

She gave Sherrow a smile that would've made his heart roll over if he hadn't already had a girlfriend, and gave me the tab. I got a smile, too, but it had more friend and less interest in it, which made me cynically aware again of the difference in years between me and my partner. I could warn him about the future a career cop could look forward to in this town, but why ruin his day completely?

Canon

Ruth had worn some grey shirt-waisted thing with touches of red to match her lipstick, and Eddy had worn a suit and a tie so bland it wouldn't clash with a 70-piece orchestra. Many of the East precinct officers had been in attendance, including the captain and his disgraced wife, a lovely blonde with a wandering eye. For a brief moment at the wet-bar, she and Max had hit it off well beyond proper social parameters, but Max tried to stay away from Trouble with powerful husbands, and Ruth had eyes like a tabloid reporter for possible scandalous behavior under her own roof, and had sailed up in time to repair the damage to Max's drink and ruin the tenuous net of flirtation that had been building over the ice-bucket.

The rest of the evening had proceeded just like every other dinner party Max had attended at his sister's, and he'd made his excuses as soon after dinner as he could. He'd escaped into a muggy urban twilight, to walk down to the cheap bright neon lights and along the stained sidewalks to listen to the blue-collar music and the blue-collar brawling, and the constant desperate, shrill hustling of the forgotten classes, the grifters, the small time sharks, and the unlicensed whores, little people clawing to get out of the gutter and go Somewhere Else and do Something Better.

Max wasn't so sure about the existence of Something Better, but he wasn't going to tell any of these poor luckless bastards that. As long as they were trying, they were alive, and there was that slim chance they'd get somewhere that meant something to them. Of course, it hadn't worked for Max, but maybe he was a hopeless case: He couldn't come up with too many things that meant 'something' to him. The truth, maybe. Really good bourbon. Ice cubes. He'd been places where ice cubes weren't to be had and had realized that ice cubes were a mark of civilization. Where they weren't, Max didn't want to be either.

He turned into the next doorway, weaving through the spillover of humanity painted all colors in the garish lights. Layers of perfume, sweat and alcohol hung in the air with banners of blue synthetic tobacco smoke, defeating the archaic electric fan Max could hear over the choppy roar of the crowd as a high, vibrating whine. He left his filter glasses on to block out the worst of the holographic and vaporous visual pollution and followed the sound in a shoulder-heavy walk that cleared enough space for his passage and left little outbursts of grumbling in his wake, but no one called him on it, and he could feel the current of bodies shifting back as he passed, as if he'd never been there.

The bartender read him for a low-ball man at a glance, and had a glass on the bar and an eyebrow raised, waiting for Max to lay the name of the poison on the heavy air, while the fan whipped the eddying smoke into spirals, clearing the space around the bartender and little else.

Max put money on the bar and laid his hand next to it, palm down. Through the filters, the 'tender's face was a flat dun monochrome.

"Ice." he said, "And put a little bourbon in it."

"Funny man," said the bartender, and Max grinned for him, to give him something to think about while he built the drink. The man thought he was joking: Some people didn't understand the important things in life.

The drink and the money changed places like a hostage exchange, and Max stepped back from the bar-rail and let the crowd close around him. A surge of people attached themselves to the place he'd been like iron filings to a magnet, voices raised in the litanies of the working class;

"Three beers here, three beers here!"

"Same again, more whisky, hey, same again, hey!", and the various bartender-attracting calls and flashing of money.

Max let the undertow of the crowd nudge him slowly towards the door. By the time he reached it, the drink was gone and he left the glass on the nearest table and walked out through the veil of lights, with an ice cube in his cheek like a chaw of tobacco, all set and ready to go to work, bar to bar, listening, collecting, making notes.

Friar

The traffic lanes were ribbons of energy set up to keep people in controlled areas instead of crashing into each other in stacks of six. Only emergency vehicles had passage through mid-lane sections and these were equipped with a function called cut-out which automatically stopped other vehicles whether they wanted to or not.

It could be a lot of fun to set off a blast of siren and watch everybody lock down in decelerating rows to the grids while you dodged through like a movie stunt driver racking up the cones on the test range, but the department took a dim view of gratuitous use of the cut-out and punished severely any perceived infractions. If you flipped the on switch you better have a damn good reason to be doing it and it was a good idea to have tape to confirm your good reason.

Which was why I didn't rag Sherrow for improper radio procedure when he spotted the runaway and swore in two languages.

"Got him," I marked the racing vehicle with a laser tag and got on his tail with a flicker of cut out and full sirens. The errant looked like the driver was hyped on Independence Day the way he slued all over like there was nobody else on the road. "Looks all jazzed. Run the plates."

Sherrow said bad things to me and did as he was told.

"That was Spanish," I said to him. "You speak Spanish?"

"Dad's a vet. Half his battalion spoke Spanish."

"So you speak it too."

"Nah, man, just the swearing. S'all dad ever learned."

"Like father like son."

Sherrow's face shut down in some untranslatable expression that might've been anger. He deployed the cruiser's stun-cannon and lined up the cross hairs as the runaway vehicle cleared level 6 traffic and spread-eagled neatly over the river, high above us.

"What else do you need to know?" he asked and punched the fire button. The electrified barbs arced across black night like fireflies to ground out on the runaway's bumper in one brief flare. The runaway went dead-in-flight and started to flat-spin, parachutes mushrooming out in spirals, probably too late.

"Call EMS. I think we'll need an ambulance for this one." Below, a patrol boat headed up the river, flashing blue-red-blue to be there for the impact. Sherrow showed me some more Spanish and called Emergency Services.

Canon

There was sharp, sour light and uneven wood at his back, pressing creases into his skin and making muscles cramp while it destroyed the line of his suit coat. When he opened his eyes and tried to sit up, there was pain and nausea and movement, voices sweeping up and down the volume scale, and the light fading out.

By clutching the edge of the bench, Max managed to not pass out again. He'd been hit, hard, he could tell that without thinking too much, and he didn't need to raise a hand to know there was a lump the size of the Taj Grand Hotel on the back of his skull. A bottle would do that when it broke across a man's head. Max brought up his right hand to rub at blurry eyes and felt a sharp pain across the back when he tried to bend his fingers. He turned it over and looked without surprise at the cracked and swollen knuckles. He'd started the bleeding again. Must've been one Hell of a fight.

Somebody laid a heavy hand on his shoulder.

"How're ya feeling, pal? Feelin' better?"

Max looked up into the tired, pale face of a police medic. The medic didn't give a tinker's damn how Max felt, but it was his job to ask, even if he couldn't force himself to look interested. Max smiled for him.

"I don't feel like I'm going to die. Am I likely to later?"

"I don't predict the future, pal, but I think you're safe for tonight. Gimme yer wrist."

Max let the man check his pulse against a steel-cased watch while he looked over the blue-black clad shoulder at the room and tried to piece the evening back together. There was a balding man in an apron who Max remembered as the bartender/owner, arguing with a police lieutenant. The apron was dirty and the hands argued in Italian while the words were English, and the cross-looking LT took notes into a palm notebook. Two uniforms walked around the room waving scanners and asking questions of the cocktail waitress, a distressed blonde who didn't look old enough to drink. Off to the side waited three civilians in party clothes, two women and one man. The rest of the bar was empty and the double-doors to the street were closed and barred. The harsh overhead lights glared mercilessly down on the stained bar, overturned tables and chairs, and a pool of blood that was already dark around the edges. Max wondered idly whether the blood was his or not, squinting in an effort to keep the light from burning out his retinas or making his head explode. One of the uniforms gave him a harsh scowl as he passed on his way to the parking lot, muttering into his self-contained remote headset. It reminded Max of the SCR units he'd used in the war and he shook his aching head to dislodge the sudden memory and turned his attention back to the medic.

"What happened?" he asked, hoping for a few more clues, and that the broken-knuckled hand he could just see behind one of the overturned tables wasn't one of his victims. There didn't seem to be any life in that hand, and the man sitting in the shadows against the back wall was the coroner. Max had met him before.

"What happened?" the medic asked, like he'd heard that punch line before, "What happened, he asks me. Why're ya askin' me, man? I got here after the party."

Max tried to sit up straighter as the lieutenant came over, trailing contempt and an Italian bartender in his wake.

"Okay, then, let's get this finished so I can go home and see my wife before she divorces me. You." He pointed at Max with his notebook. "Let's hear your version."

Max focused with difficulty on the man, trying to remember if they'd met before. He couldn't even recall which part of town he was in, but he didn't think it was East precinct. He kept hearing bells.

"Well," he began, taking a breath. The motion told him his ribs weren't in the best shape either and he had to stop on a sharp breath and wait for the pain to clear with his vision. It took longer than it should have, and when he could see again, he was looking at the ceiling, and the medic was looking dispassionately into his eyes with a little light and saying,

"...Mild concussion. I doubt if he remembers much."

"Well, George, I need to hear it from him, if you don't mind. Is he conscious, or what?"

"Yeah, he's conscious. "

"What's his name again?"

"Canon."

"Canon, Canon, sounds familiar. Jerry, run it through channels, see if there's anything on him," and closer, louder, " Mr. Canon? I'm Lieutenant Mitchell, APD. I need a statement from you. Do you think you can do that for me?"

Max blinked twice at the man and smiled gently.

"I don't remember a goddamn thing, officer," he said, sitting up again, much more slowly and with the medic's help this time. He put a hand to the goose egg on the back of his head and winced, careful, careful, catching the eye of one of the civilian women. He let her have the wider smile with the raised eyebrow. It hurt. Her expression, one of rigid anxiety, didn't change. Max vaguely remembered her, a brunette in a red chase-light dress and projection makeup with a loudmouthed redheaded man. Her projection unit was off and without the enhancing light show flashing across her features she looked pale and scared. The other woman, a big-league blonde in a clinging white floor length that looked like real live silk, was sans date, sipping a low-ball and smoking a long cigarette that put off purple smoke. The drink had one of those terrible hologram mermaids in it. The flicker of the tiny tail caught in Max's eyes and made them water. The blonde's expression was one of weary patience, but Max could see the secret shadows around her eyes. He nodded at her and told the lieutenant,

"Whyncha ask her? She looks like a lady who knows a thing or two."

He wondered if the body on the floor was her date, since a woman like that went nowhere without a man to pay her way, and what kind of selfish she was, to sit like that sipping her drink while there was a dead man in the room who'd probably bought that drink, and another man still bleeding...

Skip that. Women like that didn't notice shabby nobodies like Max Canon, bleeding or not. Still, there was the dead man, and Max couldn't help but wonder why she didn't even pretend to give a damn, whether he had been her date or not. It was possible that her date had killed the man, then skipped, and that could be the truth, to judge by the look on the brunette's face, and the grey-faced, tense silence of the loud red-head, who sat with his big square hands knotted together between his knees while the uniform asked him questions. Those two looked exactly like people in a lot of trouble, people who never saw trouble by the long ton, and wouldn't have recognized it beyond a traffic ticket or a bar brawl, until today. Today, trouble had a new look, and they weren't even sure how they'd ended up here, trading calling cards with the cops, and hip-deep in homicide.

Max wasn't sure either, but a chronological description of the evening's events would be a help, and aspirin would speed up the thought-processes. He needed all his faculties working. Already, the medic was over on the other side of the room, peering over the coroner's shoulder, and the lieutenant was scowling at Max while the beat cop he'd called Jerry muttered official business into his left ear from the radio glued to the right.

"Canon, Winston M. A private detective, huh? I didn't think they made those anymore."

Max nodded carefully, moving his aching carcass to a chair.

"They make 'em. We just don't come with the warranty."

"What were you doing here tonight?

Max pulled out a handkerchief, dunked it in a half-empty glass of water, and wiped down his face from a crumpled slouch in the hard chair, his talking-to-cops posture.

"Business."

"What kinda business?"

"I'm doing a skip-trace for a pal back East. The little bird likes to drink in places like this."

"Did you find your little bird, Mr. Canon?"

"I don't think so, unless that stiff over there is him, which would explain why I hung around after somebody kacked him." There was a heavy silence, and Max raised his eyes from the blood-marks on his handkerchief to look around at the still faces. "Well, I didn't do it, did I?"

Lieutenant Mitchell looked like he'd like to laugh, and the brunette shook her head with a tight nervous little motion and a side-glance at the blonde.

"No, you didn't kill anybody, Mr. Winston Canon." There was an ironic edge to the man's words.

Max let out his breath.

"Well, then. Am I free to go?"

"I still need a statement."

"Only if you promise to forget my first name. My friends call me Max. People like you call me all sorts of things, but it's usually 'Canon.'"

"I suppose I can restrain myself to 'Canon,' Mr. Canon. Can I get your statement, please?"

"I thought I already gave it. I told you I didn't remember a thing. I wasn't lying."

"Okay, then. You don't remember--what was it? Oh, yeah--a godamn thing. You're free to go, then. Good luck on the trace and stay outta the brawls. You could end up like that poor asshole over there."

Max stood up with a creak and a groan, and tried to find balance around the pounding in his head.

"Sure thing, Lieutenant. Mind if I ask your witnesses what happened?"

The officer gave him a long, narrow look, as if trying to decide if he was worth trusting. After a moment, he shrugged.

"I don't care. But you might want to get your head looked at by a doctor. George isn't very nice, but for a medic, he's pretty smart."

"Oh, that's right. I got a concussion with my last drink. I'll think about it, officer. Thanks for a great evening."

Max moved over to where the blonde was idly chasing the ice-cubes around her drink with a cocktail straw, and ignored the lieutenant's sub-vocce imprecations upon detectives without badges.

"Mind if I sit?" Max asked with one hand on the back of a chair to steady his still-erratic balance.

Gray eyes turned up to give him a level look under gold brows.

"Are you going to ask me questions about Barry?"

Max sat, pulling the tangled knot of his double-Windsor away from his throat and freeing the top button.

"Would it upset you to talk about it?"

The blonde dropped her eyes to her drink and toyed with the straw with long, crimson-lacquered claws that looked to be about the right length to tear out men's hearts. When her eyes came back up, they were crystal with unshed tears, and her perfect mouth trembled at one corner.

"I didn't know him very well, and now he's dead. It's pointless to ask me what he was into, because I don't know." A few tears spilled over and rolled down ivory silk cheeks, past the most kissable mouth Max had seen since he was sixteen and Samantha Thomas was ready, willing, able and in the back seat.

"Is that so?" he asked, idly wondering how much time it took her daily to keep such beauty flawless. He would've given a substantial chunk of money to see her in the morning, all mussed up, without make-up, but he knew gut-deep that even if he could tempt her, she'd be gone before midnight, trailing an expensive brand of mystery, and leaving her perfume all over his pillows. She'd never be caught without her lipstick or more than three miles from a hairdresser. Her kind of mystery was more dangerous than the kind he could buy off the Captain's wife, because all the cops would do was beat the shit outta him and send the wife away to relatives back East again. This one looked like property, and property with a view that nice cost a lot of upkeep. Maf-upkeep, usually.

Max raised an eyebrow as another tear rolled down, and leaned his head forward just enough to press the abused handkerchief to his aching head. He watched the woman from under that raised eyebrow and a stray lock of hair that had needed combing back sometime before the brawl, but after the second bourbon.

The blonde's eyes got huge and, finally, tears tumbled over like spring thaw. Her shoulders shook, but her nose stayed well powdered, and her mouth stayed kissable.

"It's a good routine, but you don't need to waste it on me," Max told her, "I'm nobody."

She stopped sobbing and flashed her eyes up, a pair of drowned gray summer skies, and Max winked with a crooked grin and added, "I'd rather you tried to side-track me with sex. I'm easily side-tracked."

That got her mad, and she stood in one smooth movement that set Max's heart all aflutter, and sashayed over to the other two.

"I'll be in the car," she announced in a shaky tone that seemed just a touch more real than all that had gone before. With one final glare at Max, she locomoted out the steel door that the coroner held for her with a deferential,

"G'night, Mrs. March."

Max waited until the view going was gone, and pressed a hand to his heart.

"Oh, my. Who forgot to install her safety rails?"

"Some very dangerous curves," Lieutenant Mitchell agreed, coming up behind Max. His eyes had been tracking the same sights Max's had. He came around the table into Max's line of sight, and there was a twisted grin on his face.

"Mrs. March, the supposed 'widow' March, is not, unfortunately for you, the sort of woman you want to piss off, Canon. She's got very powerful friends."

Max nodded.

"I guessed as much. The name confirmed it. She's Daily Caulder's showpiece, innit she? The widow without the dead husband."

Mitchell nodded, eyes sharp, and gestured towards the other civis, who were listening to something the trooper felt like telling them.

"Those two, we're not sure about. The way they tell it, they're Mrs. March's friends from way back, before the 'widowhood', outta towners. The woman certainly has no idea what goes on in Caulder's house behind closed doors, and the man is too scared right now to know much more than his own name."

"And the stiff?"

Mitchell sneered delicately.

"I don't gotta tell you anything, wise guy. You're a Private License, you figure it out."

"He's a Caulder bag-boy, caught drinking in the wrong bar at the wrong time."

"Very good, Mr. Canon. He wasn't the only one caught in the wrong bar, was he?"

"Why are you sharing all this with me, if it's not ungrateful of me to ask?" Max tried to correct his posture a little.

Mitchell's grin was wry.

"I talked to Frank Skills and he told me I better tell you enough to keep you outta trouble, or I'd be scraping you off my shoes until the case is solved."

"Frank speaks from experience," Max said, checking the handkerchief and adding some ice to it from the Mrs. March's drink. "Do I get to talk to the hayseeds, then?"

"If it'll get you outta my crime scene and keep you outta my face, sure. Be my guest."

Max smiled at him and nodded.

"Thank you kindly, Lieutenant. I don't suppose you'd do me one more favor and ask 'em to come over here. You ask me to walk too far, I might cry."

The police officer grinned sourly and said,

"Sure thing, Canon. Oh, and don't let 'em confuse you: No matter what they say? You're no hero." He patted Max's shoulder once on the way past.

The brunette came first, looking a lot less anxious and a touch angry. She had a fine pair of sparking brown eyes, and the name Jolie Laide, if Mitchell was to be believed. The redhead wasn't far behind, though he looked a lot less excited about making Max's acquaintance. The other uniformed cop went outside to join his partner in the parking lot, to do whatever it was they were supposed to do once the detectives got working. Direct traffic, maybe.

The brunette beat him to first launch. Her brown eyes glittered in the overheads.

"What did you say to upset Stephanie like that? Who the Hell are you anyway?"

"Max Canon."

"That's what he said," a thumb-jerk at Mitchell, who stood grinning in the background. "Which tells me nothing."

Max cast a look of mild resentment at Mitchell, who grinned wickedly and bowed with an 'all yours' gesture, sarcastic as a gasoline cocktail.

With a sigh that made his ribs ache two tones louder, Max flipped an eyebrow and turned to the brunette.

"I'm a private detective on a job. I got caught in something here, and I'm not real sure what. Would you mind fillin' me in?"

A frown marred the woman's rather pretty countenance. Put next to the blonde, she'd fall into shadow, but on her own, she was very nice to look at, with a sort of glow. Max could see up close that she had been celebrating with something possibly-illegal earlier, which might account for the glow.

"You don't remember?"

"Not a thing, ma'am."

"Oh." She sat down, all the wind gone out of her battle-sail.

"In that case, there was a fight, and Barry was stabbed."

Max dragged himself up to go over and look at the corpse, executed a brief once over from a stand so he wouldn't lose his balance, and navigated back to the table on sea legs.

"OK. He's certainly dead. So how do I fit in? Someone hit me, and I don't figure I'd be dumb enough to hit on Mrs. March and give her an excuse to do a thing like that." A bad thought crossed Max's mind. "I didn't leap to anybody's defense, did I?" The last thing in the world he needed was to make enemies of the Caulder-clan or anybody they thought were big enough to be a threat.

Ms. Laide shook her head. The redhead was standing behind her chair, listening sullenly. His name was supposedly Steve Albrecht, but he looked like he'd have trouble recognizing even that. He probably hadn't been all too bright before the evening plunged straight into Hell.

"You tried to break it up." The brown eyes softened a fraction.

Mitchell was right: That wasn't heroic, that was stupid.

"I didn't. I couldn't possibly have been that drunk."

The brunette recoiled slightly.

"It was very brave."

Max let that go.

"So who hit me?"

The redhead spoke up for the first time.

"Barry. He thought you were on the other side."

"The other side being?"

"Some man in a white sports coat. Tall, thirtyish... Lt. Mitchell has the description. I don't know who he was."

Max had to raise an eyebrow.

"He picked a fight while wearing a white sports coat?"

"I guess you weren't the only one who drank more than he should've."

Max was trying to recapture the angle he'd seen that had sent him into the brawl in the first place. He kept the alcohol consumption down while working, and if there was any form of alcohol on the face of the earth that could souse him on three drinks he would've found it long ago in his youth. He hadn't been drunk, nowhere near, but it didn't do to let the civilians know your secrets. Max got up and went back over to where the corpse of Bartholomew Capelli was being tucked into the black rubber bag. He stood looking down at the staring black eyes, a bruised and blank heavy face over multiple stab wounds from a knife the man in the white coat still apparently owned and both Max and Mitchell knew would be in a foundry by now, melting down into bullet-blanks, a perfect set of fingerprints burning away as the handle disintegrated, evidence floating away with the rest of the dross.

"What did I want you to tell me?" Max muttered to the dead man. "Why get all excited over a guy like you?"

He crouched down, knees protesting, to get a closer look. The M.E. voiced his opinion of that loud and clear, but Mitchell made the man wait with a single quelling glance, and turned his eye on Max as if he could watch the wheels go around and around.

Max didn't see anything unusual about Barry, certainly nothing that connected with the skip trace. He flipped down the man's collar to get a better look at the facial lines, trying to remember past a headache the size of a small moon. A little collar pin nestled up under the dead man's chin, a collar pin Max recognized with a jolt: 101st Fast Launch Infantry.

He sat back on his heels suddenly, the breath gone from his lungs like he'd been kicked by an all-star. Barry? Bartholomew? It couldn't be the same man.

"What was the name again?" He asked Mitchell crisply, one hand on the side that'd been kicked the most: His ribs hurt like Hell and his head hurt, and he couldn't believe his luck to get so clear a clue as a Honest-to-God Unit pin.

"Bartholomew B. Capelli. Don't know what the "b" stands for yet."

Same man, then.

"Bertram. I served with this guy. In the 101, back in the earlies." Max stood with difficulty, creaking like a clipper before the wind, and staggered. Mitchell caught him and pushed him into a chair.

"Yeah? You changing your statement then, Canon?"

"I guess I gotta. Shit. Bart Capelli. I'll be damned. What a small goddamn universe."

"Isn't it, though? Did you have any contact with Mr. Capelli after you left the service, Mr. Canon?"

"Hell, no, we weren't that close. In fact, we didn't much like each other." Max had to bite down on his tongue to keep from blabbing out a remark anent the barracks'-room argument that nearly got them both cashiered, the yelling, swinging, gun-pulling homicidal argument when Capelli had accused Max of slacking off to see his honey and Max had decided to put a bullet in the man for calling Anne a flash. The sergeant had broken it up, being bigger and meaner and backed up by three huge MPs. 'Course, neither Max nor Capelli had been much better than animals at that point, battle-trauma, scars and emotional attrition taken together. Max sometimes thought Anne was the only reason he'd survived those months at all, providing him with a point of focus that wasn't insane, incomprehensible or violent.

"He's changed. I never woulda recognized him."

"You must have, or are you saying you dove to the rescue of one of Caulder's bag-boys with no real reason?"

"Bag boys?" Ms. Laide asked. "Who's Caulder?"

"Local big-wig, ma'am. Ms. March's 'friend'."

"She never mentioned him."

Mitchell shrugged. "Everyone's entitled to their secrets, ma'am." He turned back to Max. "Any other news flashes, Canon?"

"Not that I can think of, Lt. Mitchell. Guess you can go home to your wife."

"I wish. I gotta wrap this scene before I go anywhere. Right after you civilians clear out. Ms. Laide? Mr. Albrecht? You're free to go, thank you for your time. Go home, Canon. I'm tired of looking at you. And stay in town for awhile, huh?"

"Sure. G'night, Lt." Max got all the way to the parking lot before he had to sit down. The curb was nice and close to the ground, and he was so sick he could hardly keep his eyes focused, so he sat for a little while, watching the civis come out and get into a silver sedan and pull out of the parking lot, the big engine's rumble shaking him down to the bone, but skipping the ears. The sedan passed, moved on, and Max lost interest in it, trying to find the energy to get up and walk across the street to the taxi stand. If God loved him, there'd even be a taxi there.

He made a slow grab for the curb when he caught himself nodding off, and refused to decide whether he was falling asleep or unconscious. The smothering silence of the parking lot was briefly interrupted by the slamming of the metal bar door and the voices of cops while they deployed police-line markers. Then they got into their cruisers and left. The Medical Examiner's van started up and pulled away. Max's head was clearing, slowly, slowly.

A low rumble vibrated him down to the ground and he raised his heavy head to look into brown eyes framed by a silver sedan window. Ms. Laide had turned her projection unit on again. Sultry purple shadowed her lids and pale gold flickered in her irises, trapped fireflies. Her lips glistened with hologram moisture, like a fresh harvest apple.

"You need a ride, Mr. Private License?"

Max wasn't in the mood.

"No, thank you. I'll take a cab."

"Do you expect it to appear by magic or would you like me to call you one?" Jolie Laide asked with delicate sarcasm.

"I've summoned one already, telepathically. Didn't you feel the energy, or aren't you a sensitive?"

"Please be serious, Mr. Canon. I don't have to be nice." Impatience smothered her sarcasm.

Max smiled gently.

"Then don't be, Miss Laide. People will take advantage of you. Good night, now."

The car pulled away rather abruptly as Albrecht responded to something Ms. Laide said in a sharp and unladylike voice as she rolled her window up angrily. Max smiled a minute longer, knowing he was being an asshole, and not really able to feel bad about it. Oh, well, it had been a long night, and he wasn't in a social mood. He climbed to his feet, which was a slightly easier climb than, say, Everest, and tottered his way to the taxi stand so many torturous feet away.

God did love him.

Friar

Witnesses are iffy. The two bystander civis were upset, horrified white to the lips by what they'd witnessed, according to Sherrow who had the questioning of them while I ran around outside keeping the scene closed off and herding non-witnesses out of the area. By the time I got inside all I had time for was a quick glance that showed me Caulder's woman March standing between a redheaded man and a dark brunette, both jittering with adrenalin and fear, while March literally threw her shadow over both. She'd be the one with the best reason for hysterics, but was in fact professional calm, real calm right down to the eyes which told me there was no love lost there for the dead guy. Go figure. Sherrow wanted to question her with bright lights real bad, but the Lt. Detective had already done what he figured was enough, so mere uniforms couldn't buck the decision to let her ride. Mitchell wasn't a bad cop, maybe over-cautious. Daily Caulder was a rough customer. And maybe Mitchell was gonna do a little side-snooping later on his own. You couldn't tell with detectives.

Which went for the Canon guy. The whole affair— otherwise classifiable as a standard brawl-killing—got a little sticky with one of those self-styled detective/private license types around, though this one looked like he'd rather be attached to thumbscrews than try to remember what happened after he'd been koshed on the head. Mitchell had even let him question the witnesses, which was not SOP. Detectives. I don't know.

Sherrow was having kittens about letting Mitchell take over and fuck it up, when we'd been on the scene first, but there was the book again, saying we had to let him have it. I had to sit on the kid until the coroner pronounced and Mitchell's missing partner showed up to clean up. After that, they cut us loose and we called in off 6 and hit the street again, and I got to listen to Sherrow ruin his teeth for three blocks before I felt compelled to help out his dentist and try to talk him down.

"It's SOP, partner. Let it go."

"It was our collar."

"What collar? We haven't found the guy yet, have we? You keep your eyes open, maybe it can still be our collar. Mitchell's stuck there another thirty minutes on wrap up, gives us a head start. You remember the description?"

"Tall, dark, thirties, white coat."

"You can forget the white coat. That's the decoy, and it's gone by now."

"So what do we look for?" There was definite impatience in his voice.

"Tall, dark, thirties, slouching along trying to look casual. We can hit the usual suspects and the dives," here I pulled over next to Melba's All Night and parked the cruiser, "and look for somebody who looks like he just killed a guy or like he gets paid to kill guys."

"Huh." Sherrow wasn't mollified, but he turned his headset and remote on and followed me into the diner to check out the clientele for tell-tales, still complaining. We did the area on foot for awhile, backtracking to the road house, but there wasn't much open that time of night so close to the county line. I was guessing that the perp had skipped over to the next county to ditch the weapon and lay low until whoever he was working for called him. It'd looked like that kind of killing. It was too bad the PL had gotten his ass in the middle of it, coz I could feel the call coming on to go pick him up for more questions. We knew he hadn't done it, but the department might decide to make things hot for him just on principal. You never knew, and so many of them turned out to be dirty in the end, probably why there weren't many of 'em left anymore. Nobody likes a cop without a badge, 'specially the ones with badges. He might be involved. That March woman might be involved. Had to be. Sherrow gritted his teeth some more, guaranteed to pick up on the dispatch audiotapes.

It was a long two hours til the end of shift.

III.

Canon

The night was a failure as far as a good night's sleep went. After a quick ER checkout to be sure he'd live the night, he'd had battle dreams all night long, waking up every two hours or so with cold sweat, adrenaline, a locked throat and a death grip on the bedclothes. Around dawn he finally surrendered and sat up at the kitchen table to watch the sun come up in the windows of the apartment stack across the alley. It was a sight he hadn't seen for awhile with his night-hour work.

When the sun had fully risen, Max found that he could sleep after all, and went back to bed where he had more war dreams to torture him until the buzzer woke him up at half past ten.

He came awake with muscle-spasms starting in his arms and a terrifying shortness of breath.

By the time he got his feet on the floor and his eyes fully open, he had identified the sound of the buzzer, and shambled over to take names.

Eddy wanted in, and Max wasn't in any shape to fabricate a decent excuse, so he fumbled a finger over the button and buzzed him up.

Max met him at the door while still hoping for a full return to reality. The double take and the look on Eddy's face let Max know how far from it he appeared.

"Jesus Christ, Max, sit down already. What the Hell happened?"

He'd arm-locked Max into a chair by the time the question-mark rolled around, and Max tried to get his eyes to calm down and quit flickering madly at shadows. He lit a shaky cigarette to make time and waved a hand at Eddy.

"Bad dream. What's up?"

"No, man, you look bad. I mean beat up, like."

Max sat back. Oh.

"That was last night. What's up today?"

Eddy stopped short, stared a second and sat down abruptly on the sofa with a stunned look.

"You are some piece of work, Max," he said finally. He didn't look happy about it.

"One of a kind," Max mouthed the tired old response and got up to make coffee in the percolator that always sounded like a freight train falling off a cliff.

Eddy followed, though Max couldn't've said why with three clues and dental records until he had trouble opening the coffee jar, and Eddy took it away from him. Eddy's face said it all.

"Why don't you sit back down and tell me about it, Max? Before I hear it from the precinct." He found the grounds-basket, scowled into it and took the whole pot to the sink to rinse, looking exasperated. "You know I'd rather hear your version first." The pot was filling with cool clear water and he was watching Max steadily, waiting for the response.

Max shrugged irritably, not wanting to discuss so trivial a thing.

"Bar-brawl. I was working leads on a skip-trace and got caught in the melee. I didn't start it, and I didn't make it over the finish line."

Eddy looked relieved that Max hadn't been involved in anything that might get him arrested. He filled the basket, capped the pot and plugged it in before he turned his intense brother-in-law eyes back on Max's new beauty marks.

"Anybody I know?" Eddy asked, helping himself to one of Max's cigarettes.

"The brawl or the skip-trace?" Max asked, stubbing his own out and trying to decide whether he should shave before coffee and save time, or after coffee and avoid the risk of self-mutilation.

"Either one, I 'spose," Eddy had those bright eyes fixed on the end of his cigarette as he tapped, watching live ash kamikaze into the butt tray. Max knew he was only being cop-casual and realized he wouldn't get away without explaining his wild-eyed wake up. Eddy didn't much care about bar-brawls, but he was brother-in-law enough to care if Max was on the short road to Hell, and he'd use all the tricks he'd learned on the force to get the story out of Max. Eddy was also cop enough to know that Max didn't care about bar-brawls either.

Max breathed a hard sigh out through his nose, and decided to risk the shave. He started in on the expository on the way to the bathroom, leaving the door open so Eddy could hear, raising his voice over the sonics of the razor, twisting words past the faces he was making to get the razor to go where it didn't want to, and even managed to slide a few toneless curses in when he nicked his chin, all the while delivering only basic facts. It was a short time in the telling, though, and he only had half the shave done when he capped the tale with the morning's wake-up:

"Had some nasty nightmares going, too, when you rang and woke me up out of the Stalag. Don't know if I should be happy about that or not."

The echoing silence from the kitchen told Max that his sarcastic dig at Eddy would go unchallenged. They didn't talk about Max's POW time. It was years ago and far away in another world. Everybody seemed afraid to ask, and Max wasn't too keen on giving out details, so it was ignored pretty much, until something brought the subject up in which case they all got out the 10 foot poles.

Max met his own gaze in the mirror, picturing Eddy at the counter, elbows propped up, eyes down, cigarette forgotten while he wondered what the Hell had happened in that damned prison and felt vaguely guilty because Max had been trapped there while Eddy was flying missions back home, racking up test-pilot glory.

Small change. There was no pay-off in regrets. Dabbing blood from the tiny nick, Max took pity on his brother-in-law and called out,

"Eddy? You asleep or playing dead?"

There was a screech as the counter stool went back and Max heard the coffee pot come off the counter with its distinctive clank.

"Just thinking, buddy," Eddy said, a classic non-answer. Max let it drift, throwing water on his face and turning away from the mirror so he wouldn't have to meet his own eyes and the same old tired paranoia.

"If you say so," Max said, coming out of the bathroom and joining Eddy at the counter. "What did Ruth send you over for this time?"

"She didn't." Eddy gave him a full stare and half a smile. "She doesn't know I'm here. I caught your name on the stat-net this morning on that road house thing, only they didn't say you'd lost." He tipped his head sideways, almost like an apology. "You might wanna be prepared to be called in for more questioning."

"You boys turned nothing up yet, then?"

"Mitchell's got the duty now, but he's not the only one looking your way. I heard Friar and Sherrow from the West beat were looking into your records this morning."

"I don't know those names. They the two uniforms were there when I woke up?"

"They were first on the scene, yeah. You were unconscious, then?"

"You read the report."

"Yeah, well, sometimes reports are exercises in creative writing, too. You out long?"

Max grinned without humor at the casual nagging.

"I don't know. Nobody told me. I didn't die in my sleep, though, so I must be okay."

"You're not as funny as you think you are, pal."

Max took another look at Eddy Archer's face and swallowed the smart-ass reply.

"Sorry."

Eddy drank coffee and looked at his watch.

"Yeah." He looked around at Max's grim little apartment and it seemed to depress him. "Max, if you remember anything or you need anything—"

"Like legal counsel?"

"Or a friendly face, call me. My pager's on all the time."

"Like I want my face hologrammed up in the precinct house."

"Send it damped, then. Just call me, okay?" Eddy got up and straightened his coat. As a rider, he added, "You know Ruth'd kill me if I let anything happen to you." He said it like it was the only reason and Max chose to believe him rather than dabble in emotions he'd buried 100 years ago.

"Sure. Women. Have a nice day, Ed. Thanks for the warning."

"Sure. Anytime."

Eddy let himself out while Max watched from the kitchen counter. The man made pretty good coffee for a cop. Must be a defense mechanism. Max shut his eyes and tried to remember anything useful about last night, about Capelli, about Caulder and his woman. Couldn't. He got up and got his shoes and coat to go to the office so he'd be handy for the cops to find.

The day looked like it was going to be hot and long.

Friar

I never wake up well, and having the phone ring off the hook didn't make it any better. Phones during sleep time usually mean bad things. Double shift, for example. Or dead guys who might also be friends. Here I was four months out with a new partner, a rookie no less, and the phone was ringing at 8 am, the dead of night for me. Sometimes swing shift sucks.

"Yeah." My voice sounded like a cement mixer on slow speed.

"S' Sherrow. Listen, man, can you meet me?"

"It's—It's the middle of the fucking night, man!"

"I know. I'm sorry. I just..."

His voice got through to me. Something was wrong with the kid and he didn't know who else to call, so he called his partner, even if the guy wasn't very nice to him. Even if it would put him in debt to him. Even if it was middle of the subjective night and he'd pay, pay for the next three weeks, buying coffee, doing the dirty work, kissing butt. He was in that kind of trouble.

"I'll be right there. Where are you?"

"Um. Lemme..."

There was a pause while all sorts of ugly things went through my head and I started to get worried I'd be finding his body in the river by afternoon. Then he came back, sounding even more blurry and anxious.

"Twelfth and Oak. Some dive. Friar, could ya kinda hurry?"

"I'm there, kid, keep yer pants on."

I was out the door and moving before I remembered I wasn't supposed to be worrying about him yet. You gotta break partners in. Looked like he'd already started on me.

Sherrow was in some dive, all right. A lot of things weren't illegal anymore depending on where in town you did 'em. Money, politics, convenience and time had decided which laws applied to which area, laws about things like drugs, prostitution and mugging. Civic beauty was unfortunately not covered by law, and the part of town I went to was a sad example. The bar I found Sherrow in looked condemned and smelled the same, and he wasn't making it any better, bleeding on the upholstery in a dim corner booth. I slid in and eyeballed his cuts and bruises with a sour expression.

"This better be good, Sherrow. But it don't look good. It looks like drunken brawling. Convince me otherwise."

Sherrow tried to fumble more ice from a lowball into his handkerchief to apply to one of the more lurid bruises on his jaw. He looked like hell on a biscuit and I felt a pang of sympathy because I'd been there too often myself, with Stephen Kay, senior partner, scowling at me while I hurt and tried to explain.

"I went for a drink after shift at this place I know." It even started the same.

"Go on."

"So, I wasn't in a very good mood and this guy tried to get smart." He looked at my expression and got defensive. "I ignored him, I swear. That wasn't it. He got bored calling names and wandered away. Then some chick comes up and wants to get cozy. She's cute so I'm not really saying no, y'know, and just when I begin to think my drink tastes funny, smart boy comes back and starts in. The cute chick put me in an arm lock and laughed the whole time." Sherrow looked abashed and transferred his gaze to the cup of ice. "Serves me right: If Shelly ever found out..." The thought of his girlfriend seemed to make it all seem even worse and he looked up at me again, angry and sick. "They knew I was a cop, man, and I wasn't even in uniform. They wanted to fuck with me the minute I walked in, I know it, and I made it easy."

"Criminal types make a living spotting cops in and out of uniform, kid. Don't feel bad."

"Quit calling me kid already, wouldja, Friar? You aren't ten years older than me."

"Well, eleven." I couldn't help it, he was so young to me. It seemed so long ago that I'd been in his shoes. "I'll try not to call you kid." I took a look at his collection of wounds and thought maybe the cut across his cheek could use some stitches.

"Maybe I should get you to the emergency room, ki—Sherrow. You look well-done."

He looked angry and embarrassed at the same time.

"You think I didn't know that? This fucker's gonna scar, man! I can't go to the hospital, that's what I'm trying to tell you. The bitch put something in my drink; I'm so stoned I could hardly work the phone to call you. What that'll do to my record…"

I could see his point. Accident or no, illegal chemicals in the system would be reported and go on his record, and if he went to the hospital for any reason, they'd cross and type him for blood match, standard op, and they'd find whatever he was on. It must be something major, too, from the look on his face. He looked a little scared, and that probably meant he was feeling the symptoms of Warp or Galaxy, both street drugs that gave maximum possible punch per dose of anything going today. Both drugs carried the added excitement of high risk in that overdose was easy and usually fatal. They were extremely illegal and supposedly near-impossible to obtain. Obviously the reports had been overrated or Sherrow had gotten a Maf god on his tail. The mobs always had access to the biggest and the best.

"You come with me. I'll get you fixed up. Off record, even. Don't worry." I stood and gestured for him to join me. A waitress hovered nearby, looking worried.

"He gonna be okay?" she asked. "He came in all screwed up, but he wouldn't let me call anybody."

Sherrow was handsome in a bruiser way. The waitresses all seemed to love him anyway.

"He'll be fine." I assured her. "Come on, champ. Let's get you patched. Thanks for looking after him," I told the woman, and she followed us to the door anxiously, while I tried to steady Sherrow's wandering steps. He was fucked up but good, poor kid.

I took him to a doctor I know who used to work for the underground, but claims to be straight anymore. I don't believe him, but I don't care either. He's one of my wandering sets of eyes and random information producers, and if I let him operate his little clinic, he drops me the hint every now and then about bigger things than unreported gunshot wounds.

Sherrow was too sick and scared to notice anything beyond his current physical state, so no questions came from either side of the transaction and I got stitches, counter-agent and antibiotics into him before I took him home with me and parked him for the night. I took the sofa and let him have the bed so he could actually get some sleep. He'd be making up stories fast and furious anyway as soon as he walked into the precinct house with a face like that, so he'd need to be on his toes. And I'd have to back him up, whatever he said, 'coz that's what partners do, sorta.

I hoped he told a good story, 'coz I sure didn't want to nod to a dumb one and look like an idiot when the captain shot it full of holes.

I didn't sleep so well after all. Sherrow crashed hard from the drug and its counter-agent, and it took him all day to do it.

IV.

Canon

Walking eased some of the strains and aggravated most of the bruises, and, anyway, Max really didn't feel up to driving his clunker-car down multi-level streets narrow enough and crowded enough to create a new little adventure with every corner you turned. Max normally used it like coffee, to wake up on his way to the office, but in his present state, he figured the adrenaline would probably cause a fatal heart attack.

The office wasn't anything to bring a smile to his face, but it was familiar territory.

The chair slumped under his weight, tilting back at roughly the same angle as his hat, which he hadn't removed yet, tilted forward over his eyes. He felt well over a hundred years old, figured he probably looked it, and acknowledged with a twist of irony how well he was coming to fit the mold. He'd never read, seen, heard about or met a detective, city-owned or private sector, who looked clean, rested and shaved more than 10% of the time.

Curiosity was a great motivator in a job that usually treated the curious in the time honored tie-cat-in-bag-and-toss-in-river fashion. Max often wondered with some vague part of his mind what he thought it would get him besides his next meal and maybe dead.

He flipped the chair down and shot his hat in the general direction of the coat rack. He missed it, but he also missed putting it in the garbage can, a good omen. Maybe he'd find that skip-out after all. Besides, Bart Capelli was the police's problem now. Max would know soon enough if it was going to be his problem, too.

Helen, his receptionist/bookkeeper, came in around lunch to sort the files and mail and stare at him through the door like a mother with a wayward child.

"Looking good, boss," she told him, an obvious lie.

Max looked at her fresh, well-rested, pretty face and sighed.

"I know. Archer already screamed high C for me. Anything interesting for me?"

Helen leaned against the door jam and paged through the mail interface with long fingered hands.

"Bill, bill, traffic ticket, ooh, payment!"

"Who?"

"That Yeltsin character with the wandering wife."

"'Bout time. There's tonights dinner."

"Oh, yes, and your answering service called. Marie left a Dear John."

"Again?"

"Sounds pretty serious this time, Max. She flew out on this morning's shuttle to Century Callistas."

"The colony?"

"I'm sure she wouldn't just threaten to go to the beach hotel of the same name. I checked the records. She did leave. With some guy by the name of Roshford."

"Great." Max ran a hand through black hair shot with silver from war scars, and got up to check if coffee had spontaneously happened in the monstrous contraption of a coffee maker. Helen made an exasperated sound through her teeth and got in front of him to make it. Max watched her dully.

"Look." She flipped the switch on and turned to study him for a moment. Her mouth softened out of its thin line. "Oh, Max. You're hopeless. Of course Marie left you. You never called, you forgot dinner engagements. When you're working you forget everything else. And your hours are weird. I'm surprised she stayed as long as she did."

Max nodded, still blank-faced.

"How broken is your heart?" Helen asked, a note of concern creeping in.

Max looked at her for a long moment before answering.

"Sorry. I knew she was going to leave someday, I guess. Right now, I'm sorry to say that coffee means more to me than the Dear John. Is that terrible?"

Helen nodded.

"Yes, Max. It is."

She poured him a cup of coffee and left the inner office, closing the door behind her. Max looked after her for a long moment before nosing down in the coffee and paging up the mail. He hoped vaguely that it had more payments in it.

Friar

The morning was a chore. From the minute Sherrow showed his bruised and hung-over face in the front door of the precinct, he was evading questions and funny remarks. He told the captain he'd been involved in an off-duty donnybrook, so sorry, and that seemed to do it, being the truth for the most part. Sherrow looked like he'd lost, too. He must've felt like it, and I didn't have the heart to be mean to him.

The unusual deference must've relaxed him, because once we were rolling, he turned a long look on me and said,

"Tell me about your first partner, Vic."

Vic. He was feeling informal. I spared him a glance. He just hurt to look at.

"He got shot." I offered.

"Yeah?"

"Not like that," I could hear Randall in his tone, so I corrected him. "Mine was dirty. Got found out, went all rogue, and got shot. He shot me, and Frank Skills shot him."

"Huh." Sherrow subsided into his corner, a thoughtful look on his face.

"What's that mean?" I wondered aloud, slightly irritated.

"Nuthin'. Just wondering what makes a cop go dirty."

"Money usually." That was easy, but if he didn't know that yet, he was in for a long and painful education. There were plenty of bent cops around, they just hadn't been sussed yet. Maybe when they did they'd crack like my first partner had, or maybe they'd just vanish into the underworld, becoming Capellis like last night's stiff or skipping over into the private sector and become W. M. Canons. You never knew.

But with persistence, maybe you could find out. It helped to have access to the archives, a carrot I threw to Sherrow to make him feel better.

"I'll show you the archives files on Canon if you want."

He seemed to like the offer, but he didn't do any handsprings. I couldn't tell if he was losing interest in the case or just feeling too crappy to care. By the time I called us in for seven, he was half asleep against his door, and I was doing all the vigilance. I cut him some slack and felt pretty noble about it all the way to dinner, where he started to mouth off about the detectives again and I had to shut him down. We were eating in a diner some of the detectives frequented and I didn't want them hearing me let the rookie badmouth senior officers. Wouldn't help either of us, career-wise. That made him mad and we didn't say much for the balance of the meal. Second half of shift was full of domestics and suspecteds and one honest to God 211 were we actually caught the perp, but not before he waxed some poor storeowner, so even victory was tainted with the feeling of a job half-done.

We were both miserable by the time we rolled into the precinct. More bullshit jokes came at us in the men's locker-room while we changed as fast as we could and pretended we didn't know each other. Chip Wells was bugging Sherrow something merciless and I could see by the back of his neck that it was getting to him. For one moment, I could've derailed it, but I wasn't quick enough or inclined enough, thinking the kid had to learn to work it out for himself. By the time I looked up again from tying a shoe, it was too late and Sherrow was swinging a white knuckled fist at Wells, who was so much shorter than Sherrow it didn't look like a fair fight. Hollingate, to his credit, jumped between and caught Sherrow before he could assault a fellow officer in reality, and I leapt to help, Wells' admonishments to call off my partner ringing in my ears off-key. He sounded so smug that I found myself holding Sherrow's red-faced lunges back out of anger more than concern that he might try to nail Wells again, and it wasn't until Wells spoke to me directly, that I realized how angry I was getting myself.

"Can't you keep your probie in line, Friar?"

I dropped Sherrow's arms abruptly, my head down, back to Wells. Hollingate saw my face and looked like he wanted to shift his grip from Sherrow to me but didn't dare. He said,

"Shut up, Wells, already. You're not funny." His sandy brows were pulled down tight in anticipation of violence.

"I'm not joking," Wells said in a voice that told us he thought he was. "Friar's slipping, letting his probie get all beat up like that. Some partner."

I heard a growl escape my throat and got a look at Sherrow's eyes going from slitted anger to surprise before I shoved away, whirling to ruin Wells. I managed to keep my hands down and not stuff his nose down his throat, but there was a nasty second or two where we stood chest to chest while I breathed fire and failed to get the anger down. Just looking at him made my day seem worse, right down to his lousy haircut that made his yellow-blonde hair look like it was thinning, and I wanted nothing more than to tear him limb from limb personally and with great prejudice.

Sherrow's turn came and his were some of the hands that pulled me away from Wells, who decided it was time to leave the locker room and go home while the getting was good. Someone else had also noticed the bad hair cut and threw a 'nice haircut, Wells,' after him. I could see him flush on his way out, but there wasn't much satisfaction in it.

"You sure don't know how to lead by example, Friar, do you?" Hollingate drawled once I'd seated myself on a bench to hyperventilate.

"You back off, mister," Sherrow started in.

"Everybody just shut up and go home or we'll have a brawl of the like to put Sherrow's to shame." Dally was the voice of wisdom and wonder of wonders everybody listened for once and did as he said. Sherrow walked with me to the door, looking hot under the collar still, but he sounded calm when he spoke.

"Hey, Friar, wanna go for a beer?" I knew he meant skip the promised archive hunt.

"Sure," I said, "But I pick the bar."

Sherrow looked like he wanted to yell at me, decided I wasn't giving him hell about last night and nodded.

"Right. Your pick."

"Good. I got the first round. You got the second."

He looked surprised. Guess he thought I was gonna make him start paying for the favor I'd done him right off. I knew enough to wait and spring it on him later.

Experience and all.

Canon

The fans were pushing hot wet air around from corner to corner and not helping much. Max loosened his wet tie and tugged at his collar, wishing he were some place where either the weather was cooler or the clothing requirements were less rigid. The newsfax archives would let you in if you were stark naked and painted polka dot. Only the police document morgue required that you looked official. Law said they had to open it to the public, but other laws said it was private property so they could limit who got in. The information was public domain: where it was stored was privately owned.

The morgue was deep in the dungeon of the headquarters basement, well below street level, windowless and stifling as a sauna. A limp uniformed officer looked sourly at Max and Eddy and waved them through.

"Hiya, Ed."

"Hey, there, Paul."

Max nodded to be polite and followed his brother-in-law through gray steel doors. Eddy set him up among rooms of filing cabinets and viewers that were state of the art decades back and left him to it. He didn't look happy about it, but Max had leaned heavily on the kin angle to get in, and he suspected Eddy felt sorry for him because of the bad dreams. Whatever worked: Max wasn't too proud to play an angle for what he wanted.

He started the slow process of hunting blind through ten years of local minor infractions, scanning for the important names: Caulder, March, Capelli.

He checked vice, homicide and drug enforcement and took an hour or so to check Eddy's early arrest records to see if his sister had married a man with any ambition whatsoever, maybe to make up for having a little brother with none, but Eddy seemed to be a good, consistent cop. There was nothing spectacular in his paperwork, but Max did find a name: Capelli, caught in an unlicensed prostitution bust at a place called The Emerald City.

Max knew it. It was six blocks from his office and still doing booming business as a dance club with other options in the cellar. There were plenty of records of routine busts on the Emerald City and Max took a few notes: you never knew when a little random data might come in handy. More names, more places. Capelli wasn't alone, either. Max found a few more names to list; Sandy March, possibly Stephanie, pre-Caulder; Melody Miller, dancer and hostess and linked to Capelli; Georgia Grau, unspecified report, but listed in the same corral as the others.

He shut off the scanner, refiled the disks—disks, in this day and age--and nodded at the cop at the desk on his way to the elevator.

A day more or less wasted. Capelli had racked up a few pick ups for extortion and petty theft in the earlies, but after Caulder picked him up, he never took time for any of it. Caulder was as clean as a choirboy's Sunday hands, by the records, but that was bunk and everybody knew it. He just paid the right people to keep him free, and he had the money to do it and spread it on thick.

The elevator door opened on the lobby and the noise hit Max like a doublejack sledge after the silent tomb of a basement. Shrill hustlers and loud pimps competed for volume over red-faced cops in ceramic armor mesh, and unlicensed prostitutes and pickups waited to be booked behind the rail, hard voiced women who were still a tiny bit soft underneath and trying to hide it for safety, and soft voiced women who had whoring down to a science and didn't give a Tinker's damn for anything but the money and a good night's sleep.

One of 'em looked like a man in drag and the hard-jawed face reminded Max so forcibly of one of the more sadistic Stalalg guards that he had to look twice. The relief was that it was not the same person. The creepy bit was that the memory it had brought up lingered, and followed him into the darkening twilight.

He could still hear screaming sometimes, way back in his head. It was called a mental scar or some thing like that, but to Max it was just screaming, just leftover horror that wouldn't go away. Alcohol didn't work, designer drugs didn't work, even full holographic VR psychotherapeutic vids hadn't worked, though he hadn't been able to give that the full shake because of the cost. After the war, anything was available, drugs, new identities, new lives could be bought. The war-years technology had made such advancement, anything was possible with enough money.

Of course, Max hadn't had any money. He'd gone home, a place that didn't exist anymore, populated with people he didn't know anymore, and tried to hold down a job as an environmental controls mechanic, popping painkillers like they were breath mints so he could keep getting up every morning and using the shoulder that'd never quite healed properly from the time that asshole guard had pulled it out of the socket and twisted it around like Max was a wind-up tin soldier and he wanted to see him march.

It still hurt when it got cold out, but that wasn't something Max had to worry about for a few weeks yet. He flapped his hat at his face in an attempt to generate a cooling breeze.

He was overdue at Eddy's, having promised to show up for dinner again, family only this time, in exchange for getting into the archives.

At least it would take his mind off that damn camp. Much more of this and he'd start seeing Anne again, and Ruth would want to put him back in the VA cage for observation and drug therapy, which meant long stuperous days wasted while people looked at him and wrote things down and didn't help at all.

And Anne. He always saw Anne when they put him on drugs. Anne had died in the Stalag, the nearly-war bride Max had nearly brought home, but the drug lords running the war had gotten 'em both first. It took half the home fleet to liberate that planet, and twenty of the Stalags had been bombed before the allies had realized what they were.

Max, in his blackest depressions, sometimes wished wistfully that they hadn't figured it out so quickly.

But all that was ancient history, the battles of a little set of planets a long way away from the civilized center of the galaxy. The only reason it was still talked about was because it was the most recent major military event, and because of the massive scale of destruction it had encompassed; three planets wasted completely, drifting armadas of dead ships endlessly orbiting a wide-spread selection of moons, and fucking up traffic in major parts of two sectors.

Max smiled. A monument to Man's achievements, certainly. Made the triple-domed Galactica Center on Remos look rinky-dink by comparison. Destruction always seemed to beat out engineering marvels. Another testimony, maybe, this one to entropy.

Max headed towards the Archer household, well ready for that dinner and, hopefully, a drink, though Ruth frowned upon it.

Let her. It was too late for him to stop now, and it wouldn't be any fun if he did.

Street lights flashed red, green, red, green, and a hover car nearly gave him a haircut, cornering on the edge of its air-cushion in a fast, tight turn. Max grinned a little and hunched his shoulders and the city thundered around him.

There was life in the old gal yet.

Friar

The captain called us into his office after shift next day to give us an ass chewing about off-duty brawling and on-duty near brawling. Sounded like Wells squawked loud enough for the brass to hear, the pitiful weasel. Sherrow swallowed it, red-faced and I did the solemn nod trick like a dashboard dog over cobblestone. Cap let us off the carpet finally and we trailed into the locker room to change into civis and ignore the rest of p.m. watch as they tried to bait both of us into snapping. Wells nearly got Sherrow going, but my old academy pal Strindberg got into it and beat Wells like a yellow hound dog at verbal combat.

It didn't make Sherrow any happier to see Wells slink off with his mouth for once in neutral because it wasn't his victory: I, however, loved every golden moment and gave Strindberg a grateful hand salute. He tipped one back with a crooked dark eyebrow raised over a tilted smile and bailed, leaving me to deal with Sherrow's mounting frustration with his chosen profession.

"Relax," I told him. "Wells only jerks yer chain to see if he can make you bark."

"Works on you," he snarled at me, all lurid bruises and puffy face. "You bark louder than anybody."

Guess he was feeling like everyone was the enemy today. It certainly hadn't been the best shift I'd ever pulled, with three domestic violence calls, always dreadful and they made you feel worse than useless, a potential riot over at the VR banks, and a slew of other mundane bullshit that kept us running from the get-go and got us nothing but report work.

'Course, looking at Sherrow, I couldn't blame him for hating the world. I'd bet his face hurt less than the rest of him, and his face had to hurt every time he spoke. He'd been pretty quiet all shift and after asking one careful question about my little ratty doctor pal in the Speakeasy, he'd left off asking details about the other night. Probably wondering if I was dirty or not. There was a lot of dirty on the force if you looked right, but it was so hard to pin down. I figured it for a lot of little guys on the small-time take, but there was always the chance that it was the top brass taking water for the big town heavies we had coming out the ears since the drug wars scattered the conglomerates all over the map into little crime boroughs and not so little Mafias.

Like the detectives, it was hard to tell. I just tried to be happy keeping my own corner swept clean, and making it inconvenient for the Maf gods to do much business as usual. We couldn't stop it, but we could put a big kink in the air hose and maybe suffocate it down to stompable size.

What a job. Fighting the impossible to enforce the questionable. Too bad I hadn't been smarter, or I coulda gone to school to be a plastic surgeon or a cybertechnician. Noel might not have divorced me, then, but I don't know if that'd be a good thing or not. She wasn't a bad woman, I hope, but she couldn't seem to share me with what she referred to as "the other woman", the Department. She'd known she was marrying a cop, but she hadn't known it. The uniform was just a really cool-looking suit I wore to work. That parts of it were bullet-proof didn't ever quite sink in til old Croner, the asshole first partner of mine, got nailed. Then the battle was big enough to wake the neighbors and end in divorce.

"He's dead! It could've been you!" Noel at top volume and piercing pitch.

"He was crooked, honey." Me, trying to be reasonable.

"But he's dead!" Noel, final words, end of discussion.

There was more at the divorce hearing, but the upshot was that she didn't want to worry about a suddenly dead husband that might mean financial, legal, bed-partner difficulties. Maybe she didn't want her heart broken either, I wouldn't know about that. The hearing was, in the fashion of the time, devoid of any reference to the marriage as anything other than a legal business arrangement, but that didn't keep the screaming accusation and finger pointing out of it either. Noel's play-acting of the wounded little victim hadn't been easy to swallow, and I hadn't tried. We came out of it hating each other, and it made it all easier for awhile, until the packing and moving part came up, but that's the way it goes.

I secured my rig, trained like a spaniel by years of practice and academy drills, and buttoned my shirt on crooked. Sherrow almost laughed, a change from the long-jawed dull anger of the day, but I wasn't feeling sorry for him then, so I ignored him until he suggested beer. We went to a place where the waitress knew him by his first name, odd for a cop, and had a beer or two. Then I started thinking about the dead guy at the roadhouse and the Canon character with private cop license and the split knuckles, the faceless civis I wished I'd gotten a better look at and Caulder's blonde hood ornament. It was all reminding me of the past a little, and I was trying not to think about the past, mine or anybody else's, and Sherrow hadn't quite noticed or said anything as I got quieter and quieter over the beer. He started out talking like he was trying to make up for less than ten words over a whole shift, and he kept the noise level up for me, which was no skin off my nose, he wanna talk that much about nothing.

But I didn't want him talkin' at me in the archives, which was where I was going, soon as we got done here and he was safe homebound. I wanted a look at the old records by myself, wanted to see if the stiff or the woman or the beat up P.L. had anything interesting in their past that might give a clue or two to who waxed the delivery boy, assuming he had enemies who would kill him in a white sport coat and wasn't just inconvenient for someone who hired assassins in white sports coats.

It had to be Maf. I wondered if it tied to Sherrow's Mickey Finn girl, and the Maf drugs he had been juiced with. Street shit was no way that badass, and the little doc had assured me it was badass in one long low whistle that Sherrow hadn't heard.

But no one targeted a beat cop on something like that. Never that fast, anyway. Me and Sherrow were nothing to this case, and if a cop was targeted, it would be Mitchell as detective in charge of investigation. No way Sherrow was drugged in connection with the killing, but there was a slight chance that the killing and the drug used on him were connected in another way.

It made my head ache, but then that might be why I wasn't in the Detectives Department. Beat cop was much more my level.

"Vic?"

It took me a minute to realize Sherrow had stopped talking and was waiting for my attention. I had no idea how many times he said my name before I recognized it. Nobody called me that now that Kay had retired.

"Yeah." I tried to put a casual, I-was-just-thinking-about-nothing look on, but he wasn't buying by his face.

He tried to stare me down, but I was better at it than him by eleven years, so he had to finally ask his question or let it go. He surprised me and let it go.

Sorta.

"Why didn't you tell me about the truck?"

Oh, Hollingate had payback comin' for this one. He'd given up glorifying his own bullshit exploits and started in on mine. I could hear him now: 'You mean nobody told you? Your partner's a true-blue, dyed-in-wool hero, Purple Heart and honor role quality. They really shoulda told you.'

"What truck?" I asked meanly, embarrassed.

"Come on, asshole, Hollingate and Yarrow were talkin' and Hollingate says, 'That Friar,' and Yarrow says, 'Friar?' and Hollingate says, 'Yeah, the guy that pulled the truck off his own leg and ran after the perp in the Warp-ring case.'" Sherrow took an arrogant, challenging swig off his beer. "Said you got the guy, too, when I asked. Leg broken, cut to ribbons. It sure's shit explains those mother scars you told me you got in a skiing accident."

"I can't even ski. Never could afford to learn."

"I know that too."

"Coz you asked?"

"Only way, I guess. I'm askin' now, about the truck: That more'a Hollingate's bullshit?"

He was learning, I guess. I gave him credit and an answer.

"No." Pause. " It was a long time ago. I was angry. That's it."

"That's fuckin' amazing, man."

"Yeah, well, I was a lot younger, too. Maybe you can do it someday, be a hero like the old man, huh?" I said it nastily, because the truck incident was, naturally, part of the whole rotten deal with Croner. Already I could tell I was in for a bad night.

"Huh." Sherrow gave me a cynical eyebrow back. "I think Hollingate was tellin' lies again."

"Yeah." I wasn't sure if I was happy he let it go or upset that he didn't think I was the hero type. I'm not the hero type, but no one wants to be told they aren't. "Yeah, he likes to exaggerate."

Sherrow cackled wildly and pointed rudely at my face. I tried not to snap at his finger.

"Your face, man. You look like you swallowed something foul." He laughed until tears rolled down his cheeks, slightly hysterical. I felt better when I realized what a state he was in.

"Well, I did." I said gruffly. "Punk kid tellin' me I can't be a hero like some lyin' sack a shit thinks he is."

"You aren't makin' sense, Friar. Maybe we better call it a night." He wiped his face with the back of a hand and waved for the waitress to bring the final tally. She came over with the bill, called him Jerry and looked like she was gonna give him a kiss. I looked away, feeling two hundred years old and lonely.

On the way back to the station where we'd left our cars, we exchanged a sentence or two about the weather and work, which made it all the more surprising when Sherrow turned to me at his car and said,

"Crystal kinda liked you, man. You shoulda smiled at her, get outta the apartment sometimes, take her dancing."

"Who the hell is Crystal?" I asked to hide total surprise. Sherrow as matchmaker? Sherrow trying to set me up?

"The waitress, man. She's a nice girl, really sweet. I think you should look her up."

I had to look away and scowl because I really didn't want to talk about my love life or lack with this guy.

"Give me a chance to look her over first before you marry us off, okay?"

"You are gettin' old, you didn't notice her, man. Maybe I should put in for a younger partner."

"Very funny. Go home, kid. I'll see you tomorrow."

"Whatever. Bye."

"Goodbye."

I watched him drive away, turning up at the corner and merging with the lateral traffic lane on the hover vehicle level. Even drove flashy cars, these kids. I felt even older as I turned around and went back into the precinct house. The clock struck three. There was this statue used to stand in the lobby, a life-sized bronze of a cop in the old uniform, staring sternly so he was the first thing you saw when you walked in. The title was something like "Diligence" but to me it looked more like "Accusation." It was that kind of look, like he was blaming me because the force was riddled with corruption. But I knew how he felt: I took it personally, too.

V.

Canon

Ruth let Max into the apartment without the critical once-over. Max was relieved, though he was sure Eddy had been telling Stalag stories, or she wouldn't be cutting him so much slack.

She wasn't cutting much, though, because after he was seated, one of her eyebrows cranked down.

"You look pretty bad today, baby brother," was her lead in.

"Marie left me." Max shrugged, one arm along the back of the chair.

"I told you she would one day." Ruth didn't produce a smug older-sister look, but Max saw it anyway. It was in the eyes.

"Yeah, well, it was today." Everybody sees it coming, nobody says anything.

"I hate to encourage you, but what do you want to drink?"

That was a surprise, but Max didn't hesitate.

"Whiskey. Thank you."

Eddy came in from the kitchen with a towel in his hands.

"Hey, Max. How'd it go?"

"I got nothing. There's not much for me to work from on this one. I think the guy skipped town again. I'm thinking of looking for him over in Deltavee. Maybe he's got a trail there, coz this one's sure cold."

"Good idea," Eddy looked like he thought it was a good idea. He also looked like he thought it would keep Max out of police business.

"Sis, you handed me an empty glass." Max displayed the article.

"I didn—How silly of me." She swallowed the denial and reached for the glass. "Let me fix you a drink, Max dear."

"Thank you, Ruth dear."

She built him another drink and Eddy announced dinner. Ruth proceeded to tell Max that she thought he was too thin, working himself too hard, taking too many risks.

He knew she meant well, but it didn't help much and he gave Eddy a look. Eddy leapt to defend him.

"Leave him alone, honey. He's old enough to look after himself."

"You think so?" Ruth looked surprised, and Max gave a little brother snarl.

"Okay, already. Eddy already told you about the nightmares and the roadhouse. It's nothing worse than that, so you can lay off. I honestly don't remember mother ever picking at me like you do."

Max immediately felt badly, because sadness flashed through Ruth's eyes before she could fix her expression. She still missed their mother even after all these years.

"I'm sorry." Max said in subdued tones. " But I'm thirty seven. You gotta let me look after myself. You gotta trust me."

Ruth looked down at her dinner and was silent for a few seconds while Eddy looked uncomfortable.

"Okay." She gave a little shrug and had her hard eyes back when she turned them on Max. " But you still have to come to dinner sometimes. I'll try to trust you to be careful, but I know I can't trust you to eat properly."

Max was touched that she'd actually admit she cared out loud. They were not a demonstrative family, and ever since he'd gotten back from the war, nobody knew how to treat him, so they stayed a little aloof, either with too much casual cheer or, like Ruth, with harsh criticism that masked other things.

Max smiled for her.

"Okay. That's a deal."

They relocated to the living room for one more (carefully measured) after-dinner drink, and chatted about things that didn't matter for the balance of the evening. By the time Max left, status quo had been reestablished, and Ruth was telling him to retire his hat for a new one and Eddy was bidding him a hearty good night.

Max went to the office to think about things and avoid going to sleep. He was doomed to failure.

Friar

The duty guard was half asleep, poor bastard, and he checked me through with half a smile, his eyes never rising above the badge I was flashing him.

I pulled files on Caulder, Canon and March, going back a few years, but not too many, careful, careful.

Nothing yielded beyond basic reports of run-ins, charges that didn't stick or were dropped or the easy bail made hot and fast to the tune of some high-pay, low-moral attorney screaming "unlawful arrest, unlawful arrest!" at least

on the part of March and Caulder. Canon didn't cross-file
very well, and I only turned up a few things on cases he'd
been involved in as witness, tip-off man, or interfering semi-
legal civilian.

I didn't even bother pulling the Caulder file for real,
because I was working on a case, not digging up the past. So
I kept saying to myself. It wasn't honest or objective, but it
seemed like a better idea right then, so I lied to myself and
liked it.

Two days later, what with more riots in the VR mall,
and a rash of breaking and enterings along the river and
down into the Speakeasy, the section of town where most of
the criminal types ended up and where most of the truly
questionable and definitely illegal operations existed, I'd
managed to forget all about the roadhouse and Canon and
Caulder and, with it, the bits from the past I didn't like to
think about.

Happy ignorance will always get you ambushed if you
aren't paranoid enough, and sometimes I can be dumber
then three clay bricks in a downpour.

Sherrow told me so later, damn him.

I managed to keep the past completely forgotten for
about three days before it caught me. Suddenly, everywhere I
turned, something was there to remind me again of Croner
and Caulder. I saw the Canon guy coming out of the
document morgue one night with Eddy Archer from over in
East Division, which made me think of the great big file I'd
avoided opening. The newsfaxes ran a series of articles on
street drugs, which only reminded me of the penthouse
variety of the same and Sherrow's brush with them. It shook
me up pretty bad, and I guess it showed in my work attitude.

I didn't know how bad it'd gotten till I noticed the kid
walking on eggs. He bought the coffee for three days
running and didn't say anything. He didn't complain about
the taste, the car, the beat or my driving. They teach you in
academy that sudden behavioral changes can mean all sorts
of things, up to and including drug-use, illegal pursuits and
suicide potential, so when I caught him watching me with
cop eyes, like I was a perp and he was two boots about to

meet my ass, I knew he was wondering why my behavior had changed so abruptly.

Which unnerved me more, and I took to going straight to the bar after each shift of gung-hoeing full bore so I'd feel more like a real cop again, not one who had to measure every action for dirt, make sure you don't turn out crooked like the guy who trained you, make sure the other cops know yer straight and narrow.

It must've been hilarious, the two of us sitting in the cruiser, side-glancing each other and wondering if the other was sticking to the oath or looking for the payoff. Too bad nobody was laughing.

The shift began normally, with role call before deployment and patrols handed out. Sherrow and I drew duty near the Speakeasy, which didn't make him any too happy, and only made me cross when I realized he was going to be looking at me suspicious all day again, wondering what was going on with me these days and was it illegal to make me so jumpy. I made a point to buy the coffee before he could get to the machine, and that put an odd look on his face that I took to be chagrin and made me smile.

The patrol car wouldn't start right off, and when it did, it gave a great lurch and died, because the asshole on the other shift had left it in gear and I didn't have the clutch in when I hit the starter. The sergeant saw it and sent us a black scowl. Sherrow gave me one for good measure when he thought I wasn't looking.

The first three calls were bunk or domestic, so by the time the mobile roll call came around on the three-hour mark, we were already tense. The old boys liked to say they were just checking on the expensive hover cruisers to be sure they were okay, even though mobile roll usually only followed an incomplete, unconfirmed broadcast. Whichever way, it was nice of 'em to include our old land cruisers in the list. The smoke-spewing, gut-churning suspensionless pigs weren't pretty or, in executive eyes, important, but you could beat hell out of 'em and they still ran, and ran fast. Certain civis had paid top dollar for illegal chop-downs of the same vehicles.

Mobile roll rang off the radio with its monotonous cadence, like a dispatcher's lullaby. Unit one, respond. Unit two, respond. Oddly enough in such crime-ridden times, it wasn't often when a unit failed to respond. It wasn't often at all, actually, so there was always a sinking feeling when somebody didn't hop on the net with a quick 'unit whatever, aye.' This time the sinking was followed by a heavy silence in the squad.

After a moment, I said,

"Delente and Crow."

There was more silence and I tried to read Sherrow's expression in the rear view.

"You know 'em?" I prompted.

"Yeah. You?" He was looking at me with stony eyes, hiding behind them.

"Crow's the godfather to my nephew." I had a pair of stony eyes, too, but I don't think I was using them then. Sherrow looked away, out the windscreen at the dark street, lights flashing over his face like raster lines on a faulty antique monitor.

We didn't talk about it any more, and the missing unit didn't show up til late the next day. Crow was supposed to recover, but Delente was already dead by the time mobile role even started. ' Course, we didn't know that at the time and the tension factor in the car went up five clicks, as every civilian became a cop-hating enemy and we remembered to trust no one because you'd get shot if you did.

It was about that time that I started to get the little tick under my eye back for the first time in years and Sherrow started sitting more sideways in the car, so he could watch me easier in between watching the street for perps. At the time, I hardly noticed: Crow was a good friend. I still owed him a beer from a sports bet.

My hands started to ache on the wheel from pressure.

Canon

Max took a sip of coffee. He'd fallen asleep at the office and woken an hour later, stiff and aching and clutching a page of notes he'd taken on Mrs. March.

Taking the hint from his subconscious, he bought coffee at an all night place and was now staking out Mrs. March's fancy uptown penthouse, hoping to see something useful so he wouldn't have to figure out an excuse to go up and get her to let him in.

So far, he didn't have any ideas, and he was going to fall asleep again if the coffee got any colder.

A man in a new style full cut raincoat over charcoal stripes walked past with a spring and a bounce, whistling Cotton-Eyed Joe between his teeth like he was on parade. Far above the street, the Penthouse lights went off. Max perked up and waited. After a moment, Mrs. March appeared in bright red apocalypse fur, one of the new fashions that looked more like she'd been attacked by animal rightists with paint cans than haute couture. A cab swept up just in the nick of time and she never missed a step from door to curb. The cab sucked her in and whisked her away, banking sharply to climb towards the high lights and clearer air.

Max got out of the car and went over to ride an easily duped security elevator up to the penthouse level.

He couldn't fool the lock here as easily as he could the elevator, but he could dodge the cameras if he was careful. A rush and wait trip got him to Mrs. March's door where he examined to door at leisure, long enough to realize he couldn't jimmy it without a computer hack in his pocket. He personally didn't know enough about the high-end of computer-controlled products any more to do it. He was outdated, really. Hackers did the work he did via computer these days, days where twenty bucks and a full name could get you a twenty page dossier on any citizen with credit, car, apartment, property or machine-generated pay check. If you dealt in money, money could find you.

But Max dealt in finding people who fell through the system or learned to fool it. He specialized in the people who didn't deal in money so much as in other specialized goods: The true criminals. He had the lost art of hardcopy search down pat. He could hunt the watering holes and grill barflies for information never committed to computer. He was ex-government, the kings of cover up and evade. The military didn't mess around with computers when everybody else already had it figured. You had to go one better.

Or one back. Besides paperwork, Max went out and pried into people's memories for the information he was looking for, a sort of detective of oral tradition. If you talked to enough people, you could learn anything you wanted, provided you had the time to find the right people and convince them to talk to you.

But it still left him without means to get into Mrs. March's apartment. He took a good look at it instead, and was rewarded for his efforts.

There were scratches on the strike plate of the door and one good deep dent in the wood, like a screwdriver or a mounting pin for an electronic jimmy might've made. The door hadn't been forced, but somebody had tried.

Max looked his fill and went away, pulling the elevator's heavily decorative cage across like a prison door closing and musing on possibles who would want to get into March's place bad enough to trot around an uptown high rise with a fifteen pound piece of illegal and eye-catching equipment under his arm.

The coffee was stone cold when he got in his car. He drank it anyway and didn't notice. Then he fell asleep.

VI.

Friar

After all my preaching and lecturing and wise-older-partner bullshit, I blew it. Between the mobile role, the newsfaxes, the smog level and Sherrow's eyeballs scanning me like I was a set of prints on an arrest report, I didn't have much left to work with, and when he opened his mouth to ask about my nephew, I gave away more than I thought.

I told him about my brother's kid, how proud we were when he'd graduated elementary school with math honors, about my sister in law and her interior decorating business on the Antares out-colony, and how well they'd done, how happy they had been.

"Had been?" Sherrow had been smiling a little, caught up in the fantasy of a gentle, pleasant world, same as I had always been when I got mail from my brother and his family. The past tense made the smile fade.

"Yeah." My throat closed. I'd finished all this two years ago, but every now and then, when I was real tired, or depressed, it got me all over again. I cleared the frog and went on. "The United Liberation Radicals were bombing colonies that year to get interconglomerate attention."

I didn't finish the story, but I didn't have to. Sherrow looked down at his hands, at the shotgun in his lap and said in a quiet voice,

"I'm sorry, Vic."

I didn't remember making him free with my first name, but since he was getting used to it and it meant he was sincere, I let it go and changed the subject to something work-related, to get death and loss off my mind. It seemed to work, but the next call we got was a 211 in flight, and we were off on a wild street chase that ended with Sherrow and I in foot pursuit across the docks, while the air borne cruisers hovered around and flashed hard white light all over us. It was like a scene from an action vid, and the smell of rotten timber, old fish, salt and machinery went through my head like a hallucinogen. By the time I got the perp cornered against a lonely warehouse, both of us running full tilt and out of sight of the hovers, I was remembering childhood fishing trips to the coast with granddad, and hearing him say in his gravel-voice, "Ya gotta pull 'em in slow, Victor, or you'll lose 'em."

I put the perp down on the concrete anyway. Full run to full stop in 0.1 seconds. And I'd been right when I told Sherrow you break things that way: The perp was on the bottom and he squashed like a deer hit by a fully loaded rig. Broke all sorts of things.

Sherrow testified two days later at the inquiry that it was an accident, but he wasn't sure what to believe. He'd felt sorry for me about my brother and his family, and I was really afraid he was lying for me, 'specially when he'd made a little comment earlier in the week about me seeming kinda badge-heavy on a couple of the calls, maybe thinking I was overdoing the routine. Strange that he'd forget about that when I really was overdoing it.

Croner was in the back of my mind all the time now, echoes of the past that woke me up nights feeling bullets tear through my sweating body, all sorts of nasty shit. I couldn't ditch it before shift no matter what I tried, and Sherrow had been seeing it. Poor kid didn't know whether to shit or go blind, and it upset me most when I thought he'd chosen blind.

But he'd only put it off for a little while, keeping counsel until he could get me alone and wring the truth out of me.

He didn't wait long, either. The night after the hearing, he took me, mildly resisting, out for a beer at the place Crystal worked, ostentatiously so I could give her the look over again. It was really an attempt to get me drunk so I'd spill my guts for him.

It's a primitive method, but it works. Between the little smiles of the brunette, obvious but flattering anyway, and Sherrow's liberal application of alcohol, I loosened up pretty quick. A hearing's always a nasty process, because even if you're innocent, way back in your head you're afraid you might really be guilty of something they'll find out about, and even though the car cameras weren't involved, audio could still be a field day if the prosecuting Internal Affairs guys played it right and wanted you out. I hate hearings, and this one sucked special 'coz I was guilty: I never shoulda put the guy down on the ground. There were handy walls all over, and I coulda chosen any one of 'em, but I hated that guy with a personal passion after a day so full of shit, and I wanted to hurt somebody. Maybe. I'm not sure my mind was clear enough at the time to attribute that much intention to the event, but I still put him down with a full flight body check, slammed my two hundred into his onto concrete and heard bones break when he sandwiched on the bottom.

I can still hear Sherrow's voice screaming my name over the snap, and the snick of him putting the hammer back on his weapon. I was lucky the car cameras weren't anywhere nearby. God only knows why the audio came out so wonderfully fuzzy, lucky me.

Beer is a wonderful thing. It's a beverage and a recreation and sometimes a meal. It can be your friend or your enemy, depending on who's had the most, and it can be effectively used as truth serum if applied liberally enough to a damaged conscience.

I was pretty damaged and Sherrow knew it. The kid had done well at the academy. Maybe he'd make detective someday, leave me behind.

He started sometime after beer four.

"What's up with you lately, Friar?"

I turned tired eyes up to see him hunched forward around his beer like he was afraid someone would try to take it away. His face was all earnestness, but his eyes were wary.

I opted for partial honesty to derail him.

"Just some old memories catching me up. And I'm worried about Crow, if ya gotta know."

He moved his beer in a circle on the table, leaving a slick gloss of moisture behind like a slug trail.

"They say he'll make it fine."

"They say that, yeah." Like I didn't have a right to worry anyway? "People sometimes die anyway. The doctors aren't 100% all the time, y'know. I'm worried."

"What about that guy down in the Speakeasy? He 100%?"

I snorted a laugh, sending more beer to join its pals in my stomach, feeling looser, more relaxed, and consequently more depressed.

"He's a weasel. A rat actually, but he can be a good tip sometimes, and he's off the record. Don't you go ruining it, kid, coz he's one of the best tip-men I got running for me."

"I won't spoil it. You did me a favor there. I remember. I was just wondering."

"Just wondering what." My voice was too flat to really make it a question.

"What are you into, man?"

"I'm not into anything." I denied it more hotly than I should've if I wanted him to believe me, but the question, not unexpected, pissed me off. Like it was any of his business what went on with me.

Well, it was. I was his partner. I got my ass in a sling, his ended up there, too.

I put my head down over my beer and squeezed my eyes shut on suddenly fuzzy focus. How many had I had?

"Why don't you tell me about it, Friar?" Sherrow's voice was almost kind. If I hadn't been in the grip of guilt it would've made me mad again.

I realized I was slobbering drunk. The table in front of me was covered in empty glasses, and I got the impression that far more of them were mine than his.

I didn't want to talk about Caulder and Croner and everybody getting shot. It wasn't a good memory, though the shot part wasn't what gave me nightmares. The crooked cop part did that. I dreamt I was the crooked one. I dreamt I was so crooked I had to screw my hat on, into the illegal whorehouses and the drug rings and taking for the Mafs and their bloated bosses, up to my ass in a river of blood and carnage.

But if it was bothering me so much it was affecting my job, then maybe Sherrow oughta know about it. Most of it was on record anyway. The facts, at least.

I started slow, because I was addressing my empty beer glass and I thought maybe annunciation might make it easier for the kid to hear and less likely that I'd be asked to repeat myself.

"Croner was in with Caulder. That dead bag boy in the roadhouse reminded me of it. Then yer little Mickey Finn chick reminded me of what they were into, selling Warp street side, and snagging in little kids for the Playhouse." I glanced up, then away. "You wouldn't know about that, that was before your time."

"An illegal prostitution ring?"

"Yer quick. Yeah. With little kids, like ten and twelve. Croner and I were workin' the streets on that one, the detectives were so backed up on the serial killer with the tar and feathers, so I spend all this time going nuts trying to

lock onto something solid, and every time I get close, Croner
vanishes it. I didn't realize what was going on at first. He
thought I was too dumb to get it, and I guess I was. But
Frank wasn't so dumb. He was a captain back then and
kinda had a thought or two about how much evidence was
slipping through our hands, and since I was a stupid probie
with about two months on active, it had to be Croner with
his fingers in the mud."

"Frank Skills."

"The same. He's not so dumb for a chief. The break
on that case got him enough publicity to get him elected all
those years later to chief against his will, right out from
under the assistant chief at the time, forgethisname Smith-
something, but he took it anyway. Felt it was his duty.
Caulder slid free, of course, his kind always do, but plenty of
his allies went down squealing, and Croner was among
them."

I remembered it in a blur of outraged honor, stunned
by the betrayal and corruption of all I'd still thought holy.
Stunned on the sidelines with my partner's bullet in me while
eight other cops took the bastard down amid babbling,
gloating confession. He'd sorta snapped at the end, talking
like he thought he was in a vid and it was time to spill the
plot to anybody who hadn't caught on yet. The bit with the
truck had come earlier when one of his accomplices tried to
run me down during foot pursuit. Hollingate only had it half
right when he'd told Sherrow I got the perp, because while
the accomplice killed himself running me over, I never got a
shot off at Croner. Until I got out from under the truck and
he turned around and shot me, I never even knew who I was
chasing. I thought Croner was still with the cruiser,
organizing backup. I thought maybe he'd been shot, and
was in a hurry to get back and make sure he was all right. I'd
thought a lot of things, but the truth never even crossed my
mind, until the muzzle flame burped at me and the gods
knocked me down with thunder and extreme prejudice, and
I was looking right at him, my mentor, my partner, the first
man to work with me as a real live cop and listen to me like I
might have a good idea or two of my own, not just academy
shit being regurgitated by rote.

I came out of the memory with a shudder that went from the top of my head all the way down to my sore feet, chilled to the bone and light-headed. That shit always made me feel sick, why I hated talking about it. I took a sip, wondering if Sherrow'd heard enough for me to skip the details, and looked over at him to realize I'd been talking aloud the whole time. I must've been, because his face looked sorta grayish, too, in sympathy, and I could see him wondering what it would've been like if Randall had gone down like that. He pushed another beer in front of me. My hand locked around it, autopilot.

Somebody came up then, and bullied Sherrow into introductions, and I was suddenly standing shaking hands with a stranger, my fingers icy from the beer, probably looking dazed as a triage trauma case. Sherrow did some talking, false cheery, and got the guy away while I sat back down and turned my face to the wall, trying to find composure and finding only utter exhaustion and a feeling that I never should've told the kid anything.

I fumbled with my wallet to pay for the rounds, spilling ID and miscellaneous wallet junk onto the table. Sherrow snaked out an old photo of Noel that I'd forgotten I was carrying and looked at it.

"That's the ex?" He asked.

"Yeah."

"Cute. Looks familiar."

As far as I knew they'd never met. I shrugged. I didn't want to think about Sherrow or Noel or anything else for a little while. Thinking got me memories I didn't want and grief I didn't need. Fuck it.

I sat staring at the wall for a long time, dunno how long, long enough to find little patterns in the knotted pine finish, and to animate them in my head: This one is a junkie robbing a liquor store. Bet the kid doesn't remember when liquor stores were closed on Sundays. I'm old. That one is part of a D.B. in a bag, the rest missing or in the river, no I.D., no one can ID him, he's John Doe and he's buried on the city dime and no one will miss him.

I'm walking. Sherrow had my arm and was moving me out to the car like only a cop can move a drunk, steering for two with just a little extra force. I tried to shake him off, irritated, but he only took a better grip on me and grunted, "Stop it." I stopped it. I was put in the car and we started driving.

After a long time, with lots of city going by, Sherrow spoke again.

"You're fucked up, man."

"You surprised? Everybody in the department is. It's not a job that attracts normal, well-adjusted individuals."

"Thanks." His tone was dry and I stared sullenly out the window, feeling stupid again. I wanted to go home and sleep and forget this was happening.

"You're awful sure the force is full of corrupt officers." Sherrow observed, a sort of question.

"It is." Obvious, idiot, look around.

"How can you be sure?" An offer to convince him.

"Croner was not an unusual case. There are plenty 'a dirty officers, all rotten behind the badge when you poke 'em. Think about it next time you walk into the precinct. Everybody looks like he's hiding something."

"So according to you, half the force is employed by the Mafia gods or are on the take. That right?"

He sounded too sarcastic by far to me.

"Don't sass me, kid. There are plenty of bad eggs, but only a few of 'em are hard-boiled. I just haven't figured out which, yet."

"I need proof, Friar."

"Caulder never goes down. Ever."

"That could be the fault of the judicial system. Or the judge. It doesn't mean the cops are crooked."

"Somebody is. Not only does he stay free, all of his little minions do, too. Croner had more'n one guy in his pocket, and only two people went down, the dead guy in the truck and a clerk for paymaster." I fell silent, feeling like a rubber bag full of sour beer and realizing I couldn't convince Sherrow the sky was blue in summer right now. He saw me as a drunk old man, old at thirty six, and I never shoulda told him anything. Shoulda let him think I was dirty, dirty, but tough. Now he thought I was soft. Damn him anyway.

Canon

There was a tremendous thundering on the top of the metal cage. Max came awake with a nasty jolt, wondering if it was the fever that made him unable to focus through the bars, and cursing in Spanish.

A dry voice said,

"A vet. How nice."

The pounding came again, but this time Max identified an east side accent and the rain slicked windscreen.

He was not only in Alaman, he was in his own car, being told to get out by a human shape in a wet hat.

The shape flashed a badge. Max checked all the mirrors and the curb feelers—he'd forgotten to turn off the perimeter screen when he'd parked—and figured he could cooperate long enough to get a look at the car parked behind him. It was too hard to tell if it was a cop from inside.

He opened the door, and the man stepped back just like a man with a gun and a dislike for point-blank.

"Nice coat," Max said, getting out of the car and straightening a stiff back. Maybe the guy didn't want to have to shoot Max and mess it up with splashed blood and gunpowder. Wool was expensive to dry clean.

""W.M. Canon? Captain has some questions for you if you'd like to come down to the station."

Like anyone ever actually wanted to go to the police station. Like Max had a choice.

"Certainly. If I can just get another look at that badge…"

The detective obliged sourly, used to suspicious civilians. When Max was satisfied with the man's credentials, they joined his partner for the ride downtown, where Max answered questions and told his story all over again to Lt. Mitchell and his captain. He told it three times, three different ways, but they still didn't like it.

Nothing new came up and Max didn't give out anything they didn't already know. He got a ride back to his car by a bored and silent trooper in a land cruiser—they weren't wasting any hover-fuel on him—who dropped him off and sped away without so much as a good evening.

Max saw the taillights fade into the darkness and turned to his car. Three shadows detached from the shrubbery and tree border, and moved around him like three sides of a box, rapidly. He didn't have time to get into his car or run. He smiled and said good evening instead.

"You're hanging out in the wrong part of town, Mr. Canon." One of the shadows said in a voice as dry as the cop's had been, but in a dark and gravely whisper. The three were faceless shapes in expensive suits, shadowed by broad-brimmed hats and an instinctual avoidance of direct light. They were tall. Two were also very wide.

"Looks like it, with all the attention I'm getting."

"You should move on. Attention isn't always a good thing."

Max eyed the betraying bulges of guns on them and spared a thought for his weapon, safe in the glove box and completely useless from where he was right now.

"You don't say. Here I spent my whole life trying to get attention."

"I'll give you some attention," The left hand shadow growled in a voice like a bass drum. The spokesman, slightly taller, slashed a hand at him for silence.

"You should move on." The spokesman spread his hands before him, palm up in a gesture meant to suggest he was being reasonable. The lines in his palms were deep, more like cracks than lines, a fortune-teller's dream: He carried the histories of entire empires in the lines on his palms. It was the only part of him the light had fallen directly on.

"I will, don't get nervous." Max was feeling too smart-ass for his own good, and knew it. He was being warned away from Mrs. March's place, and they didn't have to ask so nicely. He weighed the risk of defying Caulder's people against the value of anything he could learn from the cab when it returned with Mrs. March.

He really wanted to know where she'd gone in such a hurry. His companions stood around like a cromlech and said nothing, waiting for him to leave.

After a moment, the spokesman took a step closer, emphasizing the height difference between Max and himself. Max didn't bother to crane his neck. He looked off between two sets of shoulders.

"Now." the Spokesman suggested to the top of Max's hat.

Max was saved from answering by the arrival of Mrs. March's cab. He took an impetuous step sideways to skirt the car and go after the cabby, but a hand like a sirloin stopped him. In the silence, Mrs. March's heels tapped to the door and Bass Drum growled. The hitherto silent figure gave a ladylike laugh and suggested in a voice like a silver stream,

"I could convince him."

"No. He's smart. He won't need convincing."

Silver Stream looked disappointed, if the shoulder-line was anything to go by. Max wasn't precisely surprised that three was a woman, but the hat and suit had thrown him. The light was very poor, but body language meant a lot.

Maybe he was too old for this line of work.

"Sure. But my car's broke down. Lemme catch the cab and I'm outta here," he suggested.

"No deal. Walk or be carried."

Max didn't say anything, not sure how much slack he had.

"Maybe the vet's got a bad leg," Silver Stream suggested. "Let's give him a ride."

The Spokesman didn't say anything, so Max had no warning. A huge hand shot out and grabbed him around the tie at the same moment Bass Drum and Silver Stream crowded in to catch his wrists. They only had to get lucky and hit him once in the same place the bottle had and he went down like a dropped bag of loose change.

Consciousness flickered like streetlights past car windows, then for a long while there were hard lights and voices and the smell of old wood, and questions from invisible people with eager needles full of interesting pharmaceuticals.

After another immeasurable interval that felt like the passing of eons, and more travel, there was the smell of the river, the creak of wooden piers and metal hulls, then the cold, wicked shock of black water as it closed over his head.

Max wondered hazily if he could still swim. All he had to do was figure out which way was up.

There was no air in his lungs.

Friar

"Take it easy, man."

Strindberg was trying to keep me from getting into more trouble. Sherrow and I had tiptoed around last night all day and it was hard work, so I was tired and consequently the perfect target for Wells' taunts.

"I don't have to take it at all!" I growled, smart-ass remarks about hearings and police brutality still burning my ears red.

"Of course you don't," Strindberg was perfectly reasonable, dark brows level over blue eyes. "It's an exercise in control: you only lose if you club the bastard. Relax, already."

"He ain't worth it, Friar." That was Sherrow, being helpful. The look of contempt he cast on Wells was beautiful. If I hadn't been so hung, I'd've been impressed. Strindberg gave me a pat on the shoulder.

"Kid's right. Fuck Wells, it's quitting time."

"It's not. We still got reports left to write." Sherrow turned a grimace my way and cocked an eyebrow at my face. I was calming down, so I imagine I was less red. Wells was long gone.

"Canon and Warp," I agreed.

"Huh? Who-what?" Strindberg looked mildly curious, eyes already on his watch.

"Had a Warp bust early on. The other one's a guy we pulled outta the river on some phone tip. Somebody tenderized him and dumped him. Bad luck for whoever dumped him."

"Why bad luck?"

"He's still alive." Sherrow looked at his own watch and made an impatient noise. "If it was a hit, they fucked it up."

"He was pretty noisy, too, or we woulda never gotten a drowning call. Let's get it done, Sherrow, so we can go home."

"Yeah." We went to the report station to write, leaving Strindberg to harass Hollingate about his truly ugly civi shirt.

I wrote my part on autopilot, thinking about Canon, who I'd managed to forget along with all the bullshit'd been eatin' me.

The hospital had cleaned him up a little, but he was too groggy to let back out on the streets, so we decanted him into the tank where he looked just like all the other drunks. We'd called Eddy Archer to come get him, the brother in law. Skills had gone down to take a long look at him through the bars, but he never said anything, and Canon only focused on him once, then closed his eyes like it was time to die.

He was beyond beat-up, and again I was reminded of Sherrow's Mickey Finette, which put me in mind of a guy Croner used to tap for info before he got dead, a little guy with a chem set and lots of time on his hands. I bet he could turn out pentathol and he wasn't picky who he worked for. Looked like the past was gonna bite me on the ass, I didn't bite first.

Shit. It was already biting. It had to be my turn soon.

I had a list of tenuous nothing's in my pocket from my archives visit, places that might turn up a little dirt with the worms still in 'em. Then I could really go fishing, maybe catch me some Caulder allies, end up a chief like Frank. Maybe end up on a slab like the Capelli guy.

Nothing like a little adventure.

I went back to the roadhouse to question the 'tender and the barmaid again. They weren't very happy about it.

Canon

They came to get Max and put him in Frank Skills' office, which was maybe a mixed blessing, the way Skills was looking at him. They forgot to tell him what he was there for.

"What're you up to, the maf's got a line on you?" Skills asked at length.

Max considered ignoring the question, but he felt far too lousy to even attempt true verbal combat with Frank. He felt up to lying, though.

"Checking out a friends' place."

"Huh." Skills laughed. "Mrs. March has befriended you? Why don't I believe that?"

"Mrs. March?" Max asked, doing a poor imitation of ignorance.

"Big league blond that pouts."

"She pouts? I hadn't noticed. Guess I wasn't looking at her face."

Skills' smile showed up for real, then was gone.

"Hmp. I'm married, so I'm not gonna comment on that. Whyncha tell me what you were doin' staking out her place?"

"Why should I." Max could hardly work up enough energy to care.

"Maybe I lean on Archer if you don't." A hollow threat, but it made Skills' position clear.

"Is this where I say go to Hell?" Max wanted to know.

"No. That's after we hit you a few dozen times with the rubber hose and deny you cigarettes."

"Oh, no," Max looked shocked, in a tired way. "Not the cigarettes."

Skills grinned dryly.

"You tough guys. Always break around the bad habits. It's yer weak point."

They shared the joke by sitting in companionable silence for a minute, then Skills offered Max a cigarette from the box on his desk and said,

"I'll find out eventually. I'd better not find out you're dabbling in the Capelli case. It's gonna get messy, I get my way and I'd hate to have to go to your funereal just to keep Archer company. Speak of the devil."

Eddy stood uncertainly in the doorway.

"Chief."

"Hi, Eddy."

"What kinda wreck am I collecting?"

"See for yourself."

Max had been listening to Skills without attention and trying to decide whether or not to be sick. Eddy's voice came as a surprise.

He started up, head bobbing a bit on the upswing.

"Ed, shit, what're you, the prison guard?"

Eddy took his arm with no sign of favor and waved goodbye to Skills, leading Max out.

"I'm the death watch. Y'know, just in case you wanna finish what you started."

"You here to stop me?"

"Just record for posterity: ' P.L. beats self to death on gangland fists.' I got a deal with the Post for page one, screamer headline and everything." There was a pause. "So. They break anything?"

Max stumbled a little on a foot not well lifted.

"Nah. Just hurt me a lot."

"And drug you. You sing pretty like they wanted?"

Max snorted.

"Hell, I was yodeling Handel's Messiah."

"But you didn't tell 'em anything."

"I didn't know anything, pal. I'm runnin' blind here."

"Nothing new there, then."

"No joke, Eddy."

Eddy cast him a long, considering side look.

"No," he said at last, "It's not a joke."

Eddy dropped him off at his place. Max knew without asking that Ruth wouldn't hear about any of it from Eddy. He went to sleep mildly grateful.

"Yer little chicky doin' alright? You need a hand with her or anything, you just gimme a call, right?"

Vaguely aware that he was in a flashback dream, Max tried to ignore the leering taunts, telling himself all Capelli wanted was a reaction, telling himself he didn't care—he really didn't—what a man like that thought, but for some reason, logic couldn't keep the high tide of blood from filling his face with angry red pressure.

"Shut up now, or I make you," he told Capelli, without turning his head. Canned air whistled ice cold through the vents at the top of the APC. His visor was open at half-mast and he turned it into the breeze and closed his eyes, Zen, man, let it go. He could feel the others' eyes on him, Marty, Peterson, Linguilli, Rocko, Rose, all waiting with various levels of curiosity and blood thirst to see if he would actually make Capelli shut up. Rose and Linguilli at least hoped he would. Women didn't suffer Capelli's leering innuendo happily. Those two wouldn't even suffer willingly, but Rose was already on probation for brawling and didn't need to count more brig time, and Linguilli had a berserker problem and couldn't even start a mild debate with anybody she didn't want to end up killing.

Capelli shifted on the cramped seat, jarring his arm pack into Max's spare canisters, and drew breath to speak again, too enamored of his own voice and toughness to think twice about starting a brawl in a crowded, moving, monitored APC on its way to a battle.

Max heard the intake of breath and snapped his head around so that his visor smacked Capelli across the nose. While Capelli was yelping, Max gathered his windpipe up like a bunch of carnations and gave a little squeeze.

"Shut up now. Now." Max told him. His voice was oddly flat and didn't match his face.

Capelli had no choice, but he elbowed Max—they were too closely packed for real blows—hard enough to bruise. Max held on a moment longer to let him know it hadn't counted, and then let him go.

Capelli cussed him out fluently in four languages, growing more coherent as his breath returned. His voice had the hoarse sound of a bruised throat.

"Yeah," Max responded to the cursing idly. He couldn't control a grin, but turned it away as the loud speaker blared ready ready. He knuckled his visor closed with a sharp 'snack' on a slightly feral chuckle, the tinted plastic a blank mirror that reflected the machinery from across the aisle and, just off the peripherals, Capelli's evil glare. Capelli put on his own helmet and slammed his visor violently, raging, but out of time.

On the barked, tinny 'ready, commence!' Max hurled himself running out the door of the APC with all the other soldiers, and Capelli was right behind him, covering the rear guard and putting aside everything not job related. At least he was a professional. Max still didn't like him, though. Never had, never would.

VII.

Friar

Next morning was bad: I was really getting too old to booze up to the gun'ls on work nights and after getting not much outta the roadhouse people, I'd gone bar hopping across the border, asking after the white sports coat. Of course I hadn't found the guy. The face in the shaving mirror was that of a zombie. Maybe I could get in a run to clear the shit outta my system. I'd certainly lay off the booze for awhile. I hurt.

I managed to be nearly late, which would've saved me the usual locker-room bullshit, but I wasn't accurate enough, and just about everyone was still there when I blundered in. Hollingate had Sherrow cornered between his locker and Wells.

"Did your partner tell you what a hero he is? He tell you about the truck finally?"

Sherrow was keeping his mouth shut for the most part.

"Yeah."

"So? Aren't you proud to be teamed with a man who can pull a truck off his own leg and still get his man?"

"I guess." Sherrow snapped down the strap on his sidearm and reached for his hat. He saw me come in from under his arm. "I was more impressed that he has a record as good as his after a start like that. He stuck with it and became a good officer. That's better than trucks, ya ask me."

"Really? Huh." Hollingate lost interest in hearing other people praised. Unless it was his story, he couldn't give two shits. "Go figger."

"Yeah." Sherrow tucked the hat under his arm. "Whyncha go do that? Heya, Friar, how y' doin'?"

Not Vic, Friar. My Christian name must be for private use. I appreciated the restraint while grunting a squint eyed good morning. It came out as 'argh.' I cleared my throat and started again.

"Okay, Sherrow, m'okay. You?"

"Just fine, boss," He gave me the senior officer nod. "Anything special for today?"

Like fuckin' Laurel and Hardy, man, the partner game. But it was bulletproof, and no one could touch us while we played it. It was like body armor only better. It deflected insult, interference, mockery and bad jokes because partners are a team and there's a gravity that just spins bullshit off like water off ducks.

No wonder Noel left me: she was competing with Kay as well as the Department.

When we were out of earshot of the others, I told Sherrow,

"Look, kid. The other night? It never happened."

He swallowed the 'kid' and nodded, an old man look in his eyes.

"Sure Friar, whatever you say."

"I say it never happened."

"What never happened?" Hollingate came up behind and pretended he was using the water fountain instead of eaves dropping.

"Trade War II," I smiled. "It was all a hoax to mobilize the people against Rator. You see how much power Rator got later, well the government could see that would happen, so they tried to exterminate them."

"Damn straight." Sherrow put in, a grin hovering behind his intent look. "You see how their hovers always break down and the only people can fix 'em are Ratorese, so they control the market. And the colony electronics trade…"

I agreed heartily and Hollingate looked at us funny.

"I never figured you guys for anti-Rator."

"Oh," I said airily, "We're not. I don't really care one way or the other. S'just something to talk about."

"Like the weather," Sherrow agreed easily

"Yeah. Great rain we've been having lately."

"Yeah, yeah, keeps the city clean..." a questionable statement, at best, but we'd left Hollingate behind by that time and were in better charity all around.

The good vibes lasted until I opened my locker. Sherrow'd put himself between me and Wells, who'd been getting ready to open his mouth, probably about how not like a hero I looked this particular morning, so he was right behind me, and all I could think of when the locker opened and I saw what was sitting on the shelf in plain view was to step in front of it and close it again.

There was a long pause while I tried to think how that'd gotten there and what to do about it and Sherrow asked himself if he'd really seen what he just thought he saw.

I looked at him. He was looking at me already, his eyes flat. He was trying hard to have no expression on his face. The room was emptying out.

I opened the locker again more slowly this time, feeling like I might be hallucinating—this was <u>not</u> happening—and looked again.

Still there. I pushed it to the back with my folded jacket and started unbuttoning my shirt, turning casually to Sherrow just like nothing had happened. He was glancing around to see if anybody else had noticed anything. Nope. Safe so far.

I hadn't even thought to do that. I took a scan around, too, and watched a pack of black shirts leaving for roll-call. Sherrow looked me straight in the eye and said,

"We're gonna be late."

"So we're late." I sat down on the bench, trying to think. The image of the little glass powder-filled vial had burned itself onto my retinas. "You tell anybody about yesterday's bust?"

"No."

"Did you take the evidence to the lock-up personally?"

"Yes."

"And saw it checked in."

"Sure."

I looked up to see if I could read his expression. He was still reserving judgment, so we spoke in low tones and watched peripherally for anybody walking close enough to hear.

"Who checked it in?"

"Myers. I watched him log it and turn the key."

"So you, me, Myers, the Captain and about half the shift know we pulled down a major Warp bust. Shit. Well, that narrows it." I tried to rub some sensation back into my face. "I can't think, dammit. Why do this?"

"You tell me, man. Why do that?"

I looked up again at his tone.

"You don't think I'm that stupid, do you? If I was gonna nick a piece of evidence, I wouldn't store it in my locker, and I sure as shit on a shovel wouldn't leave it perched on the fuckin' edge so any yahoo could stroll along and see it."

Sherrow sat down next to me.

"You callin' me a yahoo?"

"No. Yes. Goddamn, I can't think. Help me out, man."

"Okay." Sherrow gave me a side-glance that had half a smile at his own joke behind the grim expression. "You're not that stupid. Just leaves the question of who and why, since it'd be pretty easy if you wandered in off shift with a sonic key and nobody knew it wasn't your locker you were screwing with. You could just say you lost your keycard."

"Unless your partner or somebody saw you using the card earlier. And you wouldn't use a sonic key for a legit open. You'd get the quartermaster to open it for you or get the code from records, bribe someone. You'd have to wait till the place was empty for a sonic key. The whole building. Those things are noisy."

"So use it when the bell goes off. Wait till the rail goes by. There's plenty of noise around here at the right time."

"Yeah, yeah. It wouldn't be hard either." I rubbed my face again with both palms. "Shit. Go to roll, kid, no sense in us both getting on the late list. I gotta ditch this and change."

"I'll ditch it. You change."

My turn to look at him with flat eyes.

"Why're ya doin' this? It's worse than illegal. We're cops."

"And I should be busting you? I'll think about it. If you're this stupid, you'll fuck up again real soon and give me another chance. So change already and meet me at roll."

"Okay." I had a fleeting image of Sherrow wearing Kay's face. "Okay. Thanks."

"Call it an even trade for the other night."

"Yeah."

He reached behind my jacket and pulled out a fist, which went into his pocket.

"Gotta piss like a race-horse, Friar. Meet ya there."

"Right." Our voices carried the last two sentences across the deserted locker room. I had the feeling that someone was listening out of sight. I had the feeling that they were waiting for us to leave so they could see if their plant was still in my locker or if the frame had gone screwy because Sherrow wasn't quite as by the book as they'd thought. As I'd thought.

I changed rapidly. We got a dirty look and a black mark each for being late, but between us we looked like half a cop, even in crisp clean uniforms, so we got by okay, with only rumor following.

It said I was so hung over Sherrow had to button my shirt for me.

It was funny enough to be a joke from Wells.

Canon

Max had known he was on to something the minute the three thugs had melted out of the shadows. That he'd handled them improperly was also a given, since he'd ended up in the river, which may or may not have been a predestined event.

It was a warning though. He knew enough about people to know that if they'd been told to kill him, he'd be chatting up St. Peter right now, trying to get a press pass through the pearly gates.

Definitely a clear warning with the reminder that whoever was in charge didn't have to be nice. They'd asked politely that he leave Mrs. March alone and now he was expected to comply or the next time he went into the river he'd certainly be dead before he smelled water.

Too bad he'd been too groggy to get a look at the unknown behind the bright lights and the needle, but the odds were overwhelming for Caulder's people. Max had a sudden urge to try to see Mrs. March again, maybe to find out why she was such hot property.

It made him very very curious.

Friar

The morning contained nothing more than a quick run at a speeder in daddy's car, a caddy the color they were calling vanilla at the dealerships these days, with pale holographic "ghost" tracing around the windows. The kid had even run the tell-tale down and left flicker of eyes that happened when those with cop-sensors glanced to see why their toy hadn't reported our presence before we spotted 'em breaking whatever law we'd caught 'em breaking. It was such an easy bust it felt like being cheated. He didn't even whine when Sherrow asked him if he knew the device was illegal. No fun at all. There were no other calls that came to anything and we couldn't dredge up a crime anywhere in our area. Our criminal element seemed to be visiting someone else's beat that morning.

By lunchtime, we were back at the station in the break room with its beat to death decor.

Strindberg and Wells were by the coffee urns. I sent Sherrow for a coupla mugs, giving him money for them to take the sting out of the order, and went to stare down a vending machine to see which plastic pot had my name on it.

The three came back to the table as a unit and sat, Sherrow and Strindberg with pre-bought sandwiches and Wells with the type of lunch your wife cooks up for you.

Sherrow put a mug of coffee between me and Wells like a barrier.

Coffee was the opposite of Beer. It was a social glue, the kind of thing that allows enemies to stand around and talk shop with impunity, like pals, holding steaming cups like little white flags in hands that aren't fists. The cup is something to hold onto to keep it that way, something to gaze into like a crystal ball, to sip from so you won't open your mouth and say something really dumb.

I took up my white flag and had a sip.

And spit it back into the cup. Oh, man. Coffee so bad it was painful.

"Told ya." Strindberg said it to Sherrow, but he was looking at me. I glared, hyper aware of appearances since this morning's little find, and hoping I was reacting normally: I couldn't really tell.

"How 'bout that." The kid nodded like I was some sort of marvel. I clicked on it, finally.

"Decaf. I oughta pulp you, Strindberg. You too, Sherrow."

"Scientists say it's undetectable from real coffee." Strindberg explained reasonably, knowing full well I couldn't stand it. He'd just won money off Sherrow because of it.

"Scientists don't know dick," I proclaimed and got up for real coffee.

"Or they don't drink enough coffee," Sherrow added, still looking at me like I was a sideshow.

"More likely," I said, to remind them I was part of the conversation instead of the subject. It always made me feel like a lab animal when people talked about me like that, and Sherrow had a way of looking at the people he was thinking about like they were on a glass slide. From my side of the table, it looked like he'd picked it up from Wells.

Wells opened his mouth and saved me by saying something so utterly stupid that conversation faltered into a different topic and both my partner and his looked his way in blank surprise while he went on to explain what he meant. I'd once asked Strindberg how he could tolerate Wells: He'd said the man made him laugh, though I'm sure it wasn't in the way Wells thought.

More power to 'em, s'long as I didn't have to serve with the man. One of us would die in the second day. I sometimes wished he'd get assigned to Hollingate and some bored cop-hater would cap 'em both and get shot in the process, thus ridding the world of three people I could do without.

But I only wished that on bad days. We won't go into how often I had bad days.

Only something like a week, week and a half had passed since the roadhouse when I talked to Mitchell next. He still didn't have clue one about the roadhouse kill. Sherrow seemed to have forgotten all about it in the rounds of dailies, corpses in the river, corpses in the streets, corpses in the making. There weren't so many as it sounds, but the car wrecks and flotsam were nasty enough to make a simple stabbing seem kinda boring.

But Mitchell was starting to look white around the edges by the time I got around to asking his thoughts on the simple stabbing. When I asked him why he was so pulled out he only snarled.

"Caulder?" I guessed.

He turned his back on me so I figured I guessed right. He was chewing over a link with Caulder and the case—the blonde, I'd bet—and wasn't sure yet how to approach it without getting into trouble or danger. No telling who in the uppers was protecting Caulder. Could even be off-world heavies, with more pull and more might than a little back-water thug like Daily Caulder.

I wondered if Mitchell'd been warned off. When he presented a report to the higher ups some days later, sourly plonking a copy on my desk so I'd quit bothering him in the coffee room, he looked kinda relieved, like he was glad it was done.

He wouldn't be glad for long.

Canon

Max threw his coat on the sofa and poured a drink before he bothered to lock his gun away or check the answering service.

He pulled a package of self-heat food out of a cupboard and zipped the activator, fleshing out his drink with soda to mitigate the cardboard taste dinner was going to have. There were ones that didn't taste so bad, but he could never get 'em open without spilling them, so he'd gotten into the habit of buying these. They cost less, anyway.

The answering service flashed messages. Marie had left another Dear John long distance on his home system as well as at the office, just to grind the point home and see if he was listening. It was just like her to rub it in. High drama was her favorite game. It was another thing he felt too old for, but he'd never be able to explain that to Helen. He didn't miss Marie.

He'd thought he would.

After he'd eaten, he decided the place was too empty after all and went out again. The office might have a distraction or two. Certainly he could find busy work there and it was too early to hit the clubs.

Not much later, with a few illegally obtained police reports in hand, he became distracted rather thoroughly, all while sitting behind the desk is his office.

He saw her through the door, like a misty shadow, before he heard her heels tapping on the hard floor of the outer office. Helen wasn't in.

"Hello?" A soft female voice, low in camber, like velvet.

"Come in."

The door came open and she walked in, gorgeous from glittering blonde hair piled high over a beautiful angel's face to the jewel studded real-kid high heels. The gown was midnight blue and nearly floor length and matched the expensive handbag, and the fur was real, too, a nearly unobtainable silver fox.

Max was frozen in the moment. A vision had just walked through his door after-hours, and she said,

"I need your help, Mr. Canon," just like in a movie. Exactly like a movie.

Max stood with a half bow for her evening clothes and gestured to a chair, bound by plot and feeling a little paralyzed.

"Please have a seat, Mrs. March."

She shook it off with a slight nervous motion of her head, eyes flashing to the window, to the empty outer office, and back to Max.

"I can't stay. The car is waiting." She laughed a little jittery laugh and Max thought she'd maybe had a shot of Irish courage to bring her upstairs.

"How can I help you, then?"

He opened the right hand drawer of his desk, and she started as if it had been a gunshot. Max put a bottle on the desk and dipped in again for glasses. Again, the plot required it. He was just thankful he had whisky at the office.

"May I offer you a drink?"

She hesitated, then nodded.

"Yes, please."

She sipped at the whiskey he handed her and made a slight face, a nose wrinkling that she tried to hide, but told Max she was used to a higher quality than he could offer. The scene was unreal. It had never happened to him in all his years as a PI. It was his only movie moment to date.

She took a paper out of her purse and put it on the desk. Max read it, saw the careful terms of genteel blackmail and handed it back.

"Can't Caulder's people help you with that?" His voice sounded tough by accident.

"He is one of Caulder's people."

"I see. The police?"

The look she gave him was eloquent of the contempt that suggestion deserved.

"Of course," he amended. "What do you want me to do?"

"Find out who's doing it and stop them."

Max contemplated his drink. Hers was already on the desk, tasted only and discarded.

"How exactly?"

"I don't know. That's your job." Her voice was sharp, nearly a snap. Her lips, he noticed, were a deep wine color, and glistened in the neon from the building across the street. He approved of her preference for classic cosmetics: the projectors always made him wonder what was being hidden.

"I need more to go on than that letter. You got a name, an alias, a phone number, a bank account for this guy?"

She shook her head and her eyes flashed again to the window, the office, his face.

"I have to go. I'll contact you again. It's best if you don't try to get in touch with me. Daniel can be...jealous." By which she meant Daniel "Daily" Caulder. Max was faintly surprised to hear anyone use the man's given name, though of course he knew he shouldn't be.

"So I've heard. Thanks for coming by, Mrs. March. Anything I can do..." he left it hanging.

She gave a terse nod and started out, clutching handbag and letter as if she'd forgotten them.

"Mrs. March?" Max called her around. She gave him a half-turn and a head-cock that posed her like a fashion photo and showed off the long, long line of thigh under clinging blue fabric. "You'd better put that letter away, if you don't want anybody else to see it."

She did so without a twitch to show she'd forgotten she held it and proceeded on her way. The echo of her tapping heels rang off the office walls for several minutes after she disappeared from sight and Max grinned faintly as he realized she hadn't asked him what his services would cost and what that said about her cash flow.

Max finished her drink too and spun his chair around to look out the dark window. There was nothing to see, but he didn't want to see anyway. He wanted to think.

It was a night for thinking. This was definitely a situation for thinking. Without thinking, he'd follow her down like a puppy and probably get squashed by the limo. Definitely needed to think. There was plot here, too much to see all at once.

The movie aspect bugged him a lot. There was just too much that could happen that could get him hurt or killed. Worse, he could end up in jail.

He sat looking out the viewless window for a while, being bugged. Then he went back into distraction, because Mrs. March had looked nice enough to merit a second round of admiration. It was enough to let him talk himself into sniffing around a bit for her blackmailer. If he kept a low profile he might get some information without being noticed.

The slow transfer of hot yellow light to muggy gray began around 7:30 and finally made up its mind to go on to neon-spangled black around 9:30. The heavy shroud of night took the heat from the city, leaching sweat out of the bricks and concrete to replace it with a biting wind that meant rain. Max was relieved: Fall at last.

He'd been worried.

He put a jacket over his gun and a tie over his shirt and capped it all with a long coat. The hat was an afterthought he'd end up carrying under his arm for the rest of the evening. He was getting too old to chase a battered felt down the street.

He checked the mirror to make sure he was still human: Pretty as a picture on a precinct wall. A few more bruises, a little more sleep deprivation and he'd be black and blue all the way to his toenails, like the new fashion the kids were wearing in the dance clubs, all tattoos and paint.

Ah, well, he looked well tenderized, so maybe he'd get pity drinks and easy information out of the post work drinkers.

Or he could party crash that elite affair at the Holyrood Towers. Maybe that: Start higher up and filter down, see what sifted out if he shook enough carpets. He'd need to hit the blue collar haunts afterwards, anyway, because the upper classes always left him with a vaguely bad taste in his mouth, maybe because they did so little for so much money. Some of that money certainly went to blackmail. And drunks love to talk. Rich drunks loved to talk about money.

It wasn't Max's lucky night. By the end of the first round, it was two bits to a tin nickel who would pass out first, Tabler, Raymond or Green, all of the city council, drinking in the off hours as they reinforced each other's bigoted, ivory-tower opinions just like the stereotypes they were. Max watched dispassionately as Mr. Raymond tumbled slowly out of his chair and into the lap of his trophy wife. Green, who's trophy wife had left him months back, slid under the table instead, hitting his forehead quite sharply on Max's left wing-tip. Tabler waved for another round, his face already glossy and red. He'd spent the evening eyeing the waitresses and talking loudly about his business prowess to attract a trophy of his own. Max had arrived too late to get anybody talking about blackmail or money, but he did get quite a lot of information about trophy wives and where to find them. And how much they might cost him.

He pulled his foot free of Mr. Green's head, which made the rest of the trip to the floor with a faint 'smack.'

Oops. Max collected his overcoat and hat on his way out, tipping the check-girl too much because her skirt was a little too short and a little too tight. Maybe he should warn her about Tabler.

He took the stairs down, just to walk off some of the alcohol and cigar stink.

All he had out of this evening was a good view of the higher ups and how they were exactly like the lower down's when you looked close. It had been uncommonly like one of Eddy and Ruth's parties. Max wondered if Raymond's trophy wife had come from someplace near Mrs. March's old stomping grounds: They had the same sense of style and the same mannerisms when they were pretending to be born to the rich and influential.

Time to visit the archives again. He still hadn't managed to track down all the names he'd found before, either. Was Sandy March the same as Stephanie? Who was Melody Miller and how did she figure into Capelli's world?

He looked at another evening spent looking at pictures of prostitutes and sighed. What a way to make a living.

VIII.

Friar

I am not, by inclination, a nice person. My motivation to become a cop had more to do with an oblique sense of justice being served than of helping my fellow man. To protect and to serve was less lime-lit than the parts that involved rapists and murderers getting theirs in the end.

Obviously, my main problem with police brutality is an academic one. It's illegal, for one, and you gotta be 110% sure the guy yer hittin' is guilty as all Hell or these black marks go up against you in the cosmic ledger and you get married to people like Noel or partnered with people like Wells. Or, for that matter, Croner, and they shoot you and park trucks on you to even up the balance.

Or somebody plants illegal drugs on you at an iffy junction in your career.

Sometimes the balance goes off even if the guy eating your fist is guilty as Hell. It depends on whether or not somebody else is holding him down or whether he can fight back, I 'spose.

It depends on how fair it all is. I do believe in fairness: it's a lot like justice.

I wondered who I had beat up unfairly while I thought out a plan for getting a search initiated to find out who could've planted the vial in my locker. It had to be done so I could fix anything that implicated me before it got out, which meant no cop I couldn't trust to believe me when I howled my innocence.

There were cameras and recording systems and five billion crosscheck and security measures to keep track of and tally station house traffic and evidence control and every one of 'em was overseen by a human element, a uniform. Not necessarily uniforms who knew my pure white heart and unstained rep.

And humans are by nature fallible, bribable, trickable and therefore open to manipulation.

I only had one sure-fire safe-as-houses course open to me.

I needed to talk to ancient Pete Blocking, the precinct janitor. Janitors are next to God when it comes to traffic control and head count, and they don't usually have prejudices or favorites.

I callously left Sherrow to the reports and got my jacket. Pete would be somewhere in the upper squad rooms about this time of night.

The first one I entered was full of detectives, all talking. The senior lieutenant stood in his glass-walled office yelling at a man that wasn't me, a uniform, blonde with a baby face and a name from the early-turn, when the fad was to give your kids names they couldn't pronounce without ten years of linguistics training. We just called him Bud, like everyone else with an unfortunate name.

The muttering of a squad room is singular. Fragments of phone calls, one-sided, and conversations like bits of shrapnel to the unwary drifted on smoky air, blue tobacco and gray nic-sym clouds twisting together into the stale ventilation grids, studded with casual horror:

"...face tore clean off. M.O. fits the copy cat Gain, but he's been incarcerated for two years, so I don't see how it could be him." "Maybe another copy cat?" "Mebbe." And "Murder-suicide, and there's the kids screaming blue in the face and blood all over, mom's still got the knife in her chest, blood pumping out and Rex takes one look and says 'Ah, shit, man, these are my new shoes.'"

On days I don't feel so cop-like, y'know the days I'm too tired or angry to shrug off all the cruelty and horror and hard-core bullshit people do to other people, it gets me bad and I can't walk through a squad and hear it without feeling sick. Kay used to call me oversensitive. He never could figure how nearly ten years on the force hadn't wiped it out. He never could figure why I'd joined up if it bothered me in the first place. I told him it didn't always bother me.

I never shoulda been a cop. Noel said I shoulda been a carpenter. ' Like Jesus?' I asked. 'Shut the fuck up,' she says. She never liked Jesus much, either. He's got almost as many rules as the APD.

Then a messenger came in and stopped me moving by saying something low-voiced to Bud through the door and there was everybody saying Jesus right and left, either praying or blaspheming or just flat reacting because Mitchell had just been in a car accident bad enough to put him on critical. Nobody thought that was boring enough to make bad jokes about, like Rex and his shoes.

I wasn't surprised, the only one by the look of it, until I caught a look at his partner's face and knew he was thinking the same as me, automatically connecting it with Caulder and the roadhouse kill, dirty suspicious mind that he had.

We met glances and nodded, meaning we'd share any new info if it came around. I tried to remember if his name was Linden or Lander, as I left to find Blocking for my questions.

The janitor was already on his way back to the boiler-room by the time I caught up with him.

Blocking wanted to think about his answer, and he said I could come back in an hour if I wanted.

Sherrow insisted on buying me a beer after shift. Sherrow had a date, but he figured he could spare a half hour to harass me about enemies. I could come up with an even dozen handy people who wouldn't mind seeing me in hot water, but none who also had access to the lockers at a viable time for sabotage or inclination to frame me. I discounted Wells and Hollingate, much as I hated to, because while I'd never spared 'em either a kind word, they weren't the types to ruin a man like that. They'd choose gossip and calumny, not frame-up.

Sherrow encouraged me to think harder, dammit, but I couldn't give him any good names. The more I thought about it, the less reason I could come up with for the whole business to go down on me. The captain or the chief, yeah, maybe, since they both had more to lose, and were notoriously uncooperative when it came to maf payrolls and looking the other way. Me, I was nobody, just like Sherrow. Somebody was trying to make us both wear the Warp noose.

We wandered off the useless conjecture and onto women. Sherrow thought he could help me out.

"Crystal was askin' about you yesterday."

"Good for her. Man, I don't need you messin' with my social calendar. I got enough trouble as it is."

"But no women. I never see you with women."

"I've worked rattle watch for years. Hard to keep up a social life when you're up nights instead of days. Awhile before that, I was married. Anyway, I know a woman or two. Just coz you don't see 'em doesn't mean they aren't there."

"Humph." Sherrow consulted his beer, a slanted look arcing my way for a second. "Your ex-wife doesn't count."

"Why not?" I didn't put much investment in the question, under vows to keep my feelings secret forever after, as if that would help me live down the mess I'd made over Croner's death. And I hadn't been in touch with Noel for years anyway. "What makes you think I talk to her still?"

"Grocery store two weeks back. There's no potential relationship there, that's why not."

I didn't count the grocery store as contact coz it hadn't been my idea. Still.

"Divorced couples get back together all the time, statistically. Not that I'm considering that."

"You expect me to believe that? I could hear you guys from two aisles over."

"Pet food and cleaning products." I guessed. "How did you know it was her?"

"Nobody yells that loud at a mere acquaintance. No, really, man. They don't count."

"I'm not that stupid, kid. One of us would get hurt we have to share space again."

"Sounded like you guys were on pretty good terms, anyway. Minus the shouting, of course."

I laughed at that, it sounded so stupid.

"She's still a woman. I know a few women, Sherrow. Don't worry about me."

"I still say ex-wives don't count. Specially bitch ones."

"She used to be real sweet. Real pretty and real sweet."

Sherrow took a swig, swilling it past his molars like mouthwash. When he swallowed, he said,

"Specially bitch-ones yer still soft on."

I had nothing to say about that.

In fact, the supermarket scene had been a classic. Noel had come around a corner and spotted me. Her cart stopped so fast the wheels squealed with a tortured gasp of compressed air as the brakes locked. I turned my face to present her with a perfect target for slapping, which she promptly did.

When the echoes faded and the sound system was once again louder than the noise she was making in a breathless stream of profanity, which felt like old home week, I put on a smile.

"Hello, Noel. Good to see you, too. What have I done now?"

"Are you stupid?"

"Depends on what I'm being blamed for. How do you define stupid these days?"

She exhaled heavily through her nose and blew a wayward strand of hair out of her eyes. She was wearing it so much shorter these days I hardly recognized her with her new electric blue contact lenses and the high fashion reader tattoo in her shoulder flashing little designs like daisy chains of colored light onto her left cheekbone. She was wearing a head scarf printed to look like an old newspaper.

"I saw the news brief."

I was obscurely pleased.

"You still haven't take my name out of your buffer-filter? Or is it just the police news that's in the buffer now?"

"The provider makes it expensive to change," she'd evaded. "I never got around to it."

"So you saw the trial transcripts and decided to slap me, too? Was the perp one of your new friends?"

"Of course not." Noel had never run with the low-end types. She turned away to yank a box of some sort of processed soy cereal off the shelf and pitch it at her cart, which had to dodge and expand to catch it within its fields. "I think you're making a fool of yourself."

I selected a box of the same stuff and looked at the label unseeing.

"How fool? Right now? Yer winnin' that contest, lovely."

Noel hissed at me, exasperated and came up close so she could lower her voice.

"You're letting that Croner bullshit drag you down. If you don't dump it and get on with things your career will collapse and you'll end up like Farley. You remember him, don't you?"

I nodded. Farley was an old-time perp-beater who beat up one too many and ended up a drunken barfly with no badge, no pension and no job that didn't include pushing a broom around in places the vacuum robots wouldn't go.

"I look that low to you?" I asked.

Noel frowned harder, quite a feat, and shook her head.

"Just watch yourself. And be careful. And quit drinking!"

The last was delivered on an up note. She was angry or worried, and I felt a little touched that she still cared enough to feel either emotion about me.

"I'm being careful."

"You're not. You're being an idiot. Knocking around punks will not make you a better cop or make up for Croner's evil bullshit, and balling up your record will only leave you broke, alone and unemployed." She paused, then added with a sharp edge. "And since you chose career and alone over being with me, I just thought you might need a friendly warning to not let it slip away because of something so long past it doesn't matter anymore."

"This is the friendly warning?" And before she could whap me again, I added, "Okay, truce. I'll think about what you said."

"Don't make me call Kay."

"Jeez, you still talk to him?" I was surprised and it showed on my face, which didn't soften her mood any.

"No, not really. We exchange Christmas cards." She said it crossly and off-hand, but she was angry again for the next line. "But I still have his number, sometimes I say hi when I'm in town. Don't make me use it."

I grinned, suddenly feeling much better.

"Alright."

She glared at me a moment longer, and said,

"God, sometimes I hate you."

"S'why we're divorced, I think," I said.

"Sometimes I really hate you, asshole."

"Thanks for the warning."

"Much good it'll do," and I assured her it would, except that she was already walking away, cart scuttling along in her wake with one signal light on the fritz and flashing maniacally.

I caught movement out of the corner of my eye and hurriedly went back to the label on the box in my hand, hoping suddenly it was no one I knew. Some of Noel's remarks had been loud. Many had been profane. Certainly the slap had been like a gunshot and I could still feel a red flush across that unshaven cheek. Would've been like slapping sandpaper.

Serve her right.

Rolled soy for breakfast, then. I waved my own shopping cart over and headed for dairy, a tune popping up in my head. What a weird day it had been.

Of course weird days had proliferated since that little meeting and I could see no end in sight. At least I couldn't see then what was still coming at me. Small blessings.

Canon

Max spent the day at the archives again, trying to find pieces for his puzzle. He wasn't even sure he was working the right puzzle frame, but if the data seemed remotely useful, he copied it, or printed it out.

When Eddy came looking for him at clock-out time, Max had a few questions for him. He had Eddy watch the arrest video that had gotten his attention, one of twenty report sections from the same bust years back that Eddy had been in on, and asked him to think back.

"This Capelli the same one who ended up a stiff in your bar brawl?" Eddy asked, one eyebrow elevated in official cop sarcasm.

"I'm askin' you to think back so you can tell me that," Max told him.

"The names don't match, but he coulda lied. I don't really remember the johns we hauled in, Max. The Emerald City gets busted six times a year. It's a lot of names to remember."

"How 'bout the ladies? Would you know one if you saw her again?"

Eddy considered the toe of one duotone shoe for a minute.

"Maybe." He looked Max in the eye. "Depends on the girl."

Max wondered if he'd go along to the whorehouse itself if asked. There was a look about him…Max re-cued the video and froze a headshot. The color was bad from age and lighting, but the features were clear enough.

Looking relieved, Eddy confirmed that the woman in the photo had been in one of the busts.

"'Course, she was wearing a whole lot less when I saw her. Black silk."

"Black?" Max grinned. "On a blonde?"

"She was a redhead, then. Who is she?"

Eddy didn't move in the types of circles that would acquaint him with this kind of woman. She was too high on the social ladder in one way, but too deep in the underworld in another, and he wasn't high enough in the department to be messing with bad guys of Caulder's caliber.

Max shrugged.

"She just looked familiar to me. Thought maybe she knew my skip-trace." Max tossed off the casual lie as a herring to keep Eddy from looking at the photo for connections and seeing Daily Caulder's current hood-ornament instead of some nameless prostitute.

"What's up tonight?"

Eddy grimaced.

"Another party. I'm supposed to ask you if you want to come. What lie do you want me to tell Ruth?"

"Tell her you couldn't find me. She's used to that kind of thing." Max grinned. "Thanks for helping me out of it, Ed."

"Sure thing. I expect you to return the favor sometime."

"If I can, you got it."

They shook on it and parted on good terms without Eddy once commenting on Max's flowering bruises.

Friar

Pete Blocking had seen many people in and out of the locker room. I'd had to come up with a limit on the time frame, and as I sat in my echoing apartment, I held the list in my hand, toying with a take-out curry with the other. My beer was flat.

Hollingate. Wells. Eddy Archer. Frank Skills, probably down to yell at somebody. The Captain, probably down to see who had screwed up enough to draw down Frank Skills for a personal chew out. Plus a dozen uniforms, two of which I knew only vaguely from academy days, a hand full of new faces, and the others all old-timers like me and Strindberg and Myers with his evidence-room.

Evidence room. Bells rang and I cursed for being too close to the frame to see the strings. Both Sherrow and I assumed the Warp came from Evidence. Neither one of us had thought to check if it really had.

I called the station, but Myers had gone home and the desk officer was uncooperative and wouldn't go check for me. I could hear her cursing me out in a tired way to somebody else in the room with her, hand over the phone, and they laughed. I was too tired to really get worked up about it. It would have to be my first task in the morning. Right then I was almost too tired to eat my dinner. I fell into bed hoping to sleep like a dead man, and not caring if I woke up or not.

I domesticated easy, Noel said. She used to brag to her friends about how docile I was at home, doing dishes, laundry, skipping another beer if she asked, never aware that I didn't say much 'coz I didn't know what to talk about; Certainly not the work day, and though she'd rattle on about her own interests, they never seemed to matter when put up

against the real world. Retro hem-lines and the latest
celebrity scandal didn't match up much with an aggravated
assault with a meat-cleaver, so I didn't try to keep up, just
listened so she'd know I was following her, nod, participate
in discussions I couldn't give a rat's ass about, but since she
did, I did, coz I loved her. I often wondered if I should care
more, since it all mattered so much to her, but they were
shadow concerns, gone forever five minutes after the
sentence ended and they didn't actually affect my life.

I'd thought. When it came to messy divorce, they'd
affected me pretty severely. I was a cold, disinterested,
battle-scarred half-psycho cop, according to her lawyer.

I woke up on the edge of the bed, leaning away from
the left-hand side, Noel's side. Divorced for years and living
alone, sometimes I still found myself leaving her side open as
if she'd just come in late.

She'd never come in late again. Some other guy was
worrying about her now.

I got up and went for a long walk. I made a wrong
turn on my therapeutic stroll and three indistinct wise guys
jumped me and taught me a few silent new dance steps that
landed me bleeding in a gutter. It was the first time I'd ever
been shot with a police-quality taser, and in the future I
would use them with a whole lot more respect. A passing
cop recognized me on a routine gutter-sweep and took me to
the ER, still dazzled by the squad car's arc light and limp and
tingling from the electric jolt.

IX.

Canon

Max staked out Mrs. March's place again, this time
careful to be well away from the door and in a rented hover.
He watched a water jug delivery van come and unload, and
four red cars and a white pickup truck drove by, several
minutes apart. A souped up sapphire blue Ares VT with
music blasting nearly side-swiped him where he was parked,
but other than that and the driver of the pickup shouting

unintelligible profanity, nothing of note occurred until Mrs. March emerged from the inner sanctum. She came out around six, wearing an orange and black Chrysanthemum-patterned brocade dress that looked like war over Dresden. He followed her taxi to a restaurant that served very expensive food where she acquired an escort with her dinner. From there, she got into a black sedan of the kind commonly driven by assassins and they went to a nightclub on the river—the classy side—and Max lost them because his tie wasn't for evening and they wouldn't let him in at the door.

He took it philosophically because he'd recognized the place as one of Caulder's favorite dens, the one that pulled in the most money. No surprises here. He wondered where the three shadow thugs were this evening and went back downtown to find a guy who always had information for sale, a spacer called the Wanderer. He had no name anybody knew, just a rep for spinning out gossip and info if you coughed up enough drink money.

Max coughed half an evening's worth and the Wanderer gave him a story or three. One of 'em even fit in with what Max was working on.

Not long after, a couple of cops found him and took him downtown for questioning in the hit and run involving Lt. Mitchell. Frank Skills was not happy to see him again.

"Canon."

"Hello, Frank. What's up?"

"We need your alibi for the hit and run on my man. You got one?"

Max looked at the tight line of the man's jaw and felt sorry for him, having the job he had.

Freedom was much better, even if it got you free swimming lessons on occasion.

"What are you messing around in investigation for? Aren't you exempt these days, being a chief and all?"

"I'm taking a personal interest in this one. And helping out. Do you have an alibi?"

"Yeah. That was when, Wednesday? I spent the whole evening in that dive, what's its with the red upholstery, The Coventry over on Eastside."

Skills nodded to the beat officer who'd brought Max in. The man vanished, presumably to check Max's alibi.

"Donnelly tells me you were talking to the Wanderer. Any good stories?"

"You offering to reimburse me for the money I spent to get 'em?"

"I'm offering to let you sleep out of jail tonight."

"You sure lost your sense of humor when they gave you this job."

"I never had a sense of humor, Canon. What'd Wanderer tell you?"

"Something about a maf man having a little hostile take-over office party out on Bimini Ridge—the colony, not the cruise lines—and ending up with a boat load of Warp he had to dump fast before the ICCIA got onto 'em. Story is they dumped it here."

"Humph. I suppose that's a pretty good story. What do you think?"

Max shrugged.

"I haven't seen much Warp around myself, but that doesn't mean it isn't here." He looked sharply at Skills. "What if I ask you the same question?"

"Is this connected with one of your famous cases?" Skills was all protective sarcasm, the man who'd taught Eddy.

"Maybe. I'm still looking into it. Ya wanna share back my way?"

Skills shrugged himself, one hand making a casual gesture Max thought looked real.

"I don't have much, just a couple of my men made a bust the other day and there was Warp along with the usual. Maybe from your maf shipload. I really don't care where it's from, I just want it outta my cage. If you get any solid information, I'd appreciate your input. You can always use my appreciation."

"That's the truth," Max grinned. "Outta yer cage, huh? So yer sweeping."

"Yeah. Wanderer moves smart enough he won't get swept up in it."

"And me?"

"Looks like you got swept by somebody already. Eddy get you home okay the other night?"

"Oh, yeah. He's the best man you've got, Skills."

"He's a friend."

"Yeah, well, like I said. Can I go now? I got a hot date."

"I heard Marie left you."

"You hear everything. I got a hot date with my mail. I've been neglecting it again and you never know what those bills get up to on their own. I think they procreate."

"My mailbox looks like it anyway."

Skills tossed off the joke as if he'd already forgotten it before he was done saying it and took a breath. He held it for a minute while he looked at Max. Then he turned on the lecture voice and started without preamble. It didn't take Max long to realize it was about his impromptu midnight swim.

"Jesus, Max. Why do you have to stick your nose in? I've seen this all before. You think I haven't seen it all? I've seen this, just exactly what's going on with you. Used to be a guy, name of Rocky, Rockford, something stony. Anyway, a guy like you all set up to hunt for the truth for people who'd pay to have it found. One day instead of ending up in my jail, he ends up in a warehouse over on Brixton with his eyes out and his fingernails torn off and a bullet in his stomach. Coroner said they let him bleed awhile before they hung him up in the rafters and let him drip dry. Didn't get found till three days on when a night watchman heard the rats going at him." Skills' face was thunderous.

"How wonderfully graphic. Don't worry about me so much, I'll be fine." Max told him.

"I'm not worried about you. I'm worried about Caulder getting away with another murder. I'm worried about that poor night watchman finding another mangled corpse in my jurisdiction. I'm worried about how that'll look at the next election."

"Bullshit you are."

"Believe what you want. But believe it far far away from Mrs. March. She is dangerous in more ways than one. I'm telling you once, Canon."

"I hear you. Can I go now?" Max stood up.

"I guess. I really have seen it all, Canon. I don't want to see it again.

"I'll see it doesn't." What he heard, though, was 'I don't want to see it happen to you' and he smiled. "I'll see you later, Frank."

"Be careful, Max, or I will really lock you up. You know that."

"I know."

"Go away, Canon, but stay in town, or let me know why not."

"Sure, Chief. Have a nice day." Max put his hat on.

"Humph."

As he walked out, he could hear Skills yelling through the door for some poor unfortunate soul to get the hell in there. Max smiled, glad to get off so easy.

He ended up prowling the bars, and even his promise to Skills didn't keep trouble from taking too long to find him. This time, it wasn't even personal.

Max blew out smoke sideways, camel-lipped, into a sharp plume and shifted his elbow on the bar.

"Sure about that?" He asked, watching the smoke curl away, but keeping the man pegged with his peripheral vision, just in case he fell for the not-looking trick and took a swipe. Never knew, Max could get lucky.

The man backed up instead, gathering cronies around him with his eyes. A wall of antagonism formed up in front of Max.

Jeez, ask a simple question… Two-score and five against him and then the barmaid. The question about Mrs. March's sugar daddy hadn't gone over well. Obviously Max had found the main den for Caulder's work pool.

He shuddered a whiskey inside as fast as a tight throat could swallow and steel-eyed the 'tender for the same again. Might as well have the anesthetic ahead of time. He'd have to run at the end anyway. In the meantime, he could sense plenty-odd people behind him jockeying for position to be the first to scrag him some Private License ass.

Max made a note of the name of the bar and paid the bartender.

"You got a back way out?"

"Not for you, buddy. You picked the wrong bar to get nosy in."

"I can see that. How about you let me use that back way and I don't fry your nostrils from the inside?" Max showed him the gun butt under his arm, a slight lift of the shoulder and a flip of the coat. "We'd have a lot less property damage that way. Maybe fewer corpses to explain to the cops. Heh?"

His raised eyebrow and friendly half-smile were probably less effective than the power-rating stamp on the bottom of the gun clip. Max turned it on so the bartender could hear the hum of the generator. It tickled his armpit like an old friend saying hi.

"You can't use that until it warms up."

"Who told you that?" Max's tone was gentle and chiding. Get your facts right, pal.

The bartender folded.

"Never mind. Go. Before I let you show me you're bluffing."

"Sure." Max tipped and followed the indicated arm. Unhappy muttering and a few angry yells started up behind him, to be waylaid by the bartender. As he went out the back, Max could hear him shouting them down with something about Caulder's orders about police attention.

Fine. Next time, he'd come back as a different person and try again with more discretion.

Or not. When he reached his office, Max could see a long, dark car prowling the street that hugged the corner of his building complex. It screamed money and influence.

Max went up to the office to see if anybody with money and influence wanted to pay him a visit, or maybe if he could generate any new ideas.

Any ideas at all. He waited, looking out the window, trying not to think about Mrs. Stephanie March.

Friar

That night was the first time since academy that I rode in the back of a cruiser. It would've even been a kind of nostalgia-ride if I hadn't felt so lousy and the jackass in the maroon runabout hadn't missed his ramp and dropped back on top of us. Between the impact (minor) and Hobby's braking to avoid (he'd won awards, but that didn't make him a smooth drive—they were cop-driving awards, not chauffeur-driving awards), we were knocked around a lot. They had their restraint harnesses buckled up nice, but I was loose in the back, idiot me, and Hobby had the charge on in the mesh partition. I hit that only once with my elbow and my whole arm went numb, and stars and lights flashed across my vision for two full minutes after we settled at street level. I complained the whole two minutes.

I had to be lifted out of the back when they got me to ER, still twitching.

A few medi-patchwelds later, I was released, but of course it was too late by then: too many cops knew about it and beyond a little unexpected sympathy next morning, the bullshit was predictably ruthless.

And I'd stiffened while I slept. I felt like Swiss steak with rigor mortis. Sherrow told me I looked like it. Coming from his fading bruises, that made me laugh, which hurt.

"Heard you had an interesting night, last night."

Sherrow handed me coffee without even an arch look to point out that he'd bought it twice in a row.

"Been having far too many interesting times these past few months," I told him, taking the cup and burning my fingers right off.

"Any idea what's up?"

I shrugged. I didn't want to discuss my personal problems at work. The last time I had, I'd left my wedding ring at home for the first time since Noel had put it on me— who needed it when she was gone? —and Kay had asked me all day why I kept fiddling with my naked finger. I told him I felt like one of my fingers had been cut off without it, and Wells heard it, and teased me for a week. I didn't want a replay of that one.

I rolled a scowl around to Sherrow when he looked to be opening his mouth for more questions, and he let it go.

Skills had us brought in once he heard from shift-captain what I looked like, and there we were again on the carpet, hearing the news on brawling and stupidity, only now it was from the chief, which meant it was more serious. This time Sherrow did the wise-owl nod as I tried to look ashamed and not move my face at the same time.

"Are you okay for duty, Friar?" Skills shouted loud enough for everyone in the outer office to hear and shook me out of a contemplation of pain and coffee. I straightened like a Prussian with a click of heels and lied blithely,

"100% sir." Sherrow transferred his gaze to the far horizon to avoid meeting the Chief's eyes.

Skills looked like he couldn't believe I could tell a lie that big straight-faced. A long silence hung in the air while he chewed over whether or not he'd let me get away with it. In the end he did, probably because he'd known me when, and we walked, though I did so stiffly and with maximum control.

Outside the squad room, Sherrow had to wait for me to catch my breath.

"Yer crazy, man. What if we gotta run down some perp today?"

"You run. I'll drive," I told the floor between my feet. My knees held up my hands with only a little shaking, so I figured I could make it to the car. I stopped at the water fountain for another painkiller.

Sherrow couldn't watch. He stood hands in pockets, looking away down the hall like he was standing guard and unhappy about it. I almost felt I should apologize he looked so sternly angry.

"S' not my fault, man," I compromised, wiping water from my chin and realizing I'd missed a spot shaving. I must look like a bum. "I can run," I insisted. "I might curse the whole time, but I can still run. I'm well under 50, y'know."

"You look well over 100."

"It's my innate wisdom. Now come on. I'm okay, really."

Sherrow shrugged an offside shoulder and mumbled something that might've been 'okay', but probably wasn't. We made it all the way to the car before he started up again,

more subdued than he would've been before, maybe out of
deference to the way I was limping around. I was hoping
like hell to shake the stiffness out before lunch, or we really
would be in trouble if someone rabbited or we had to move
smartly. I began to feel guilty, so I let him read me a
watered-down lecture on personal safety. Like he could
teach me something I didn't already know.

It was after lunch that Sherrow got a bad phone call.
I'd just dropped off a long ton of reports to the captain,
leaving Sherrow alone in the break room. He was alone at
the phone kiosk when I walked in, back to the door. It took
a second to see that his shoulders were rigid and maybe
shaking. Reflected in the acrylic snot-shield—to keep dirt
and sneezing off the delicate machinery of a phone that got
used as a hammer on a regular basis—I could see his eyes
were shut tight and red-swollen like he was crying. At my
footsteps, he stiffened, but his head went down and he
wiped his eyes-nose in a quick gesture, like comes after a
sneeze.

I walked back out again before he opened his eyes and
saw who caught him crying on work time.

I wouldn't've said anything ever, if I hadn't come out
of a 415 bar and found him—waiting by the computer for
the kick back on a license number we wanted run—slumped
in the shotgun seat, red-eyed and angry. When he saw me, he
got out to see how the call had gone and report no news yet
on the number.

I shrugged off the call, a nothing call anyway, looked
at his red eyes and asked him what was up with him,
pointedly.

He told me flat out that it was nothing. I argued.
People walked by on the street and looked at us, two cops
arguing and angry.

"Step into my office," I told him, holding open the
door so he could get back in.

For a moment, he stood squared off with me, chest
forward. I was aware of the space between us in that same
tingling hot electricity you get right before a lightning strike
or just before the first punch.

Then he slid his eyes sideways with effort, took a single controlled breath and got into the car, hat off in a swipe, still angry.

I went around and got behind the wheel and drove us away from prying eyes.

After a block or three, I said,

"Look. I saw you earlier. On the phone." I stopped, because I couldn't say the word 'crying'. It's a word that never goes away once you say it, so I didn't say it.

There was a silence while he tracked down what I meant, and what I wasn't saying.

"Yeah?" He said finally, and I could tell by his tone that he knew what I meant.

"Ya wanna talk about it?"

"No."

I shrugged at that and looked out the windscreen again for a tricky merge.

"Maybe I'll buy you a beer tonight, get you drunk. Turnabout is fair play and all that."

He grinned, though sourly.

"We'll just fight. You look bad enough already. I don' wanna explain to Cap how I came to be beating up my partner. Police Brutality, y'know." He imitated me perfectly on that last.

"Who says you'd win?"

He really looked at me then.

"You kiddin'?" By which he was calling me old.

I protested.

"I'm still under 40." I heard his muttered 'barely' and talked over it. "I'm gonna go back to calling you 'kid'. Live with it."

There was a pause while he chewed on that, then he said in a rush,

"My old man called just to say he hates me and I ruined his first marriage."

That stopped me in surprise and I let a silence pass before I answered.

"Yeah? Nice of him to keep in touch."

Sherrow gave a snort of bitter laughter.

"I thought so. He doesn't mean it, though, he means somethin' else. He means he hates that I'm a cop. He doesn't think I should be engaged since I'll probably just widow her. He's saying I'm stupid. Makes me so angry I could..." He trailed off.

"My wife said about exactly that—at the divorce proceedings."

It was Sherrow's turn to look surprised.

"Yeah? And you still see her?"

"Not much. But it's nice to keep in touch. 'Course, she doesn't make me as mad as yer old man. Doesn't tell me how to live my life. More like how I should've lived it when I was with her."

"Yeah, dad can't let that go. S'not like his life's such a great example either. Three marriages, four daughters, one son, nobody who still cares what happens to him."

"Well, you do, or he wouldn't piss you off so bad."

There was a very long and deep silence at that. I drove like I didn't notice.

"Maybe," he said finally. "Maybe I get that upset 'cause I hate him, too."

"He doesn't hate you," I said. "Sounds more like he needs to blame somebody else for his fuck-ups. Four sisters, huh? Holy shit."

I caught a bit of sudden grin in my peripheral.

"Yeah. Ya oughta see the get-togethers around Christmas. Y' never saw so many women fussing."

"They all look like you?"

"Nah. They're okay to look at. Most of 'em 'er married."

"And yer next? When do I meet her?"

"When you promise to behave."

"Sure." I grinned. "I promise not to spit on the floor or put my feet on the table."

"Or talk shop. The really graphic stuff bugs her."

"It bugs everybody, kid, except us. Sometimes it even bothers us. Do you still wanna get that beer tonight?"

"Sure. Crystal's been asking after you."

"What are you doing, flirting with women, an engaged guy like you?"

"S'just flirting, man, nothing meant. You oughta try it sometime."

"Hmmph. Yer lady understand that?"

"Yup. She's as bad as me."

"Hmmph."

Canon

When the day had rolled past and twilight folded down, Max went out and bought Warp. He wasn't surprised it was available after the Wanderer's tale, but the ease of the sale was unusual. A spacer had set up shop in the back alley of a restaurant on a lower level, and Max just asked the right vague questions of the right people and there he was in a hour with a little glass vial and a prepackaged shoot-kit in case he liked to mainline, which was slow suicide of another sort.

The story of its origin came unsolicited, and Max had to doubt the veracity of the spacer's tale by the sheer ease with which he told it. It sounded rehearsed. Max, whose mind sometimes worked in impossibly corkscrewed ways, wondered if the man was supposed to be unconvincing to throw off speculation or if the guy had actually staggered into a cache and was selling it off without accomplices, and felt he needed a good cover story to protect his ass. He'd dropped hints of ex-military buddies, probably to reinforce the illusion of protection, but that had seemed as rehearsed as the rest of it.

Max also wondered whether the Warp was pure.

He took it to the Wanderer and asked.

The shaggy towhead peered at the little vial and shrugged.

"I don't know, man. I just told you what I'd heard." He grinned a broken tooth at Max. "I can road test it if ya like. 'S the only way to really tell where it's from."

"Can you tell if it's pure from lab tests?"

"Yeah. But not where it's from. Ya gotta test it yerself for that."

"Yer sick. And crazy."

"That's me. Which do you want?"

"Which is cheaper?"

"Lab test."

Max took the vial back and gestured the way out of the Wanderer's preferred bar.

"Gimme that then. I'm onna budget."

It was pure which meant an off planet source, probably Bimini like Wanderer had said before, and Max went back to his office with a lab report. He left the Warp with the lab just in case the cops felt the need to send officers to search his office for some unrelated reason and started the process of brewing coffee in the Frankenstein Coffee Maker. Helen gave him a hello and a screen full of bills and bid him goodnight.

Max played phone messages. Ruth had another party going and he was invited—read 'expected.' He grimaced at his reflection in the dark window and rooted through his desk for a stack of notes on the Capelli murder. By the time he had them loosely collated into a semblance of order, the phone rang again.

Mrs. March's velvet purr made him sit up straight and listen. She wanted to talk. Her place. Now.

Was it a trap?

Max put his coat back on and blew off the party, wanting to take full advantage of the invitation to ask Mrs. March a few pointed questions while listening politely. He also took back streets to avoid broadcasting his intentions to any interested parties. A covert-ops slide and crawl down the block kept him in shadows all the way to her door, where she buzzed him in promptly. Ah.

This was far more like it. Max got his questions all warmed up.

Friar

The evidence room had nothing to report that might sound like 'missing evidence' and since I needed a higher-up's approval to go through their records and compare them with my own files and Frank Skills had gone home, I left unsatisfied.

I made the mistake of introducing Sherrow and Kay at the bar that evening. If I'd thought about it for two seconds, I'd have known better, but I wasn't thinking about what it would mean to me, I was thinking about what it would mean to Sherrow. Kay had always had a good word for me when I was angry or confused, sort of the dad I hadn't known, never mind dad had been around till I went to college, and here came Sherrow, cruising in saying his girl'd stood him up 'cause she had to write a report or something, and him having family problems. I traded their names to each other.

They started to compare notes immediately.

Kay started right in with a look at my face and said to Sherrow like I wasn't there,

"He freakin' anymore?"

"Not so much anymore. He seems to have gotten that hammered out." He didn't say who I'd hammered on.

"Finally. How about you?"

"Oh, I'm okay. He's got me hammered out, too. Leastways in the crooked dead partner thing. M' not so sure on the training an efficient cop thing though. We seem to spend a lot of time researching cases that aren't ours."

"And yer not complaining."

"Well, no."

"Oh, he complains all the time," I jumped in. "Mostly about solving cases."

Kay shook his head: he'd seen this so many times.

"Ya gotta get used to a lot of your cases moving on unsolved. That's the detectives' job, solving. You want to solve cases and hunt serial killers, you gotta go for detective."

"That's what he said."

"And I was right," I said.

"Yeah, well, I remember tellin' you the same thing," Kay had to point out.

"And you were right."

"But you don't seemed to have learned it very well. Do I have to tell you to let it go?"

"Nah."

"Coz it wouldn't do any good, would it?"

"Nope."

Kay turned to Sherrow and gestured with his beer.

"There you are, Sherrow, your illustrious teacher. You got questions, you better come to me, okay?"

"Sure thing, Kay." Sherrow gave me a smirk and tinked Kay's beer with his own like they'd beat me in something.

I wasn't so sure they hadn't, but I wasn't buying the beer, so I kept my mouth shut.

I let 'em gossip on and cast my eyes around to see who else was drinking that night.

There were lots of young'uns, a couple of them seemed to be caught buying Hobby drinks, but others were being loud and energetic, and it looked a lot like shop talk from the gestures I could see winging through the smoky air.

Strindberg was there, looking like a dad with a pack of preschoolers out on a field trip, and I met his smile over the yapping heads of younger officers laying bets on whether the captain would penalize the next officer to get the shit kicked out of him so much he missed work or not. Strindberg took the acknowledgement as an invite and brought me a new beer, unasked. He took up station on my other side.

I turned, effectively shutting Kay and Sherrow out.

"Vic. Looking like hamburger, man." Strindberg started off, a common remark this evening.

"Feeling a little like it still. Better though. I'll tell ya, a taser is not a toy, they weren't kidding on that much."

"Yeah?" He looked amused. "I've never been shot with one myself. Who do you think was behind it? Taser's not the usual street weapon, is it?"

"Not deadly enough," I agreed, wondering about that myself. Leaving me living was unnecessary unless whoever was responsible still needed me alive for some reason. To pin a Warp dealing charge on, maybe? "I got no idea who hates me that much."

"Yer ex, maybe." He thought he was joking, but Sherrow's lecture hadn't left me yet, so it hit me on the raw.

"Bullshit." I said it with more force than necessary and earned an odd look from Strindberg and a pause while he tried to read me. "Noel wouldn't have me mugged. She'd do it herself, face to face. With a frying pan. Or a club."

"Hum." The scanning eyes turned away to gaze at the bar over the foam of a fresh beer. The bar special was hoppy and sharp, but it had the benefit of being cheap and high in alcohol content. I could smell it from here. My own was untasted on the bar next to me.

"You have been digging into Mitchell's case a lot. Maybe you dug into the wrong guy's garden, pissed somebody off."

I looked at him, and picked up the beer just to be doing something. He looked totally casual and completely candid, innocent even, and not in a fake way. But something made me think 'there's a rat in the department', and I had to be careful with my voice when I answered.

"Sherrow's been frettin' coz it's unsolved and it was our scene before the detectives showed. I'm just trying to get some clues together so he'll shut up about it and Linden can close the damn thing and call it good. It was a brawl, s'far's I can see. Pretty simple." I sipped the beer. It grabbed the back of my throat like a drowning man does the side of the pier.

"I thought so, too, but it's not my case. All the same, Vic, be careful, huh? Somebody out there doesn't seem to like you much."

"I'm still alive," I pointed out, thinking at least providence might like me okay.

"For how long?" He grinned like it was a funny joke, just like the guy who told me about the percentage of rookie gun accidents on our first day at the academy range with live rounds. And that had been…Strindberg.

Add him to the list, I thought. I turned conversation into other channels, and after awhile, he wandered away. I didn't mind too much.

Sherrow gave me a lift home because my car had decided to die in the precinct parking garage and not start again. I thought about Strindberg, trying to prove one way or another where he might stand, but other than kill conversation with Sherrow, it didn't get me anywhere.

The car sank a good six inches when I went to get in, and it took me off balance. I knocked into the doorframe and hit a bruise good and hard. The breath whooshed out of me, and Sherrow's head came around, but all he said was, 'careful, man.'

I got in more carefully. He'd softened the suspension foil like a racer, so he could take corners faster. I should've guessed: it was the kind of hot rod car that begged for that kind of chop. Me, I liked my foil rigid as four-day bread, so I could do illegal bootlegger turns if I had to. I'd probably been driving department cars for too long, but that was my preference. I started to say so, but the back brake squealed just them, leaking compressed air out of the worn spots in the seals. I changed my statement and raised my voice.

"You ever hear of maintenance, Sherrow?"

He laughed, but didn't answer, and that was the last thing said for miles.

It was a crisp night, and as we came over the river, I could see the city spread out below, looking like a million stars reflected in a mud puddle. It was sort of beautiful in its way, with a very rare mist creeping off the black water to slink among the buildings like the ghost of a python god, hiding the really awful bits and showing off the glitter and mystery.

Sherrow put his hotrod into a hover.

"S'pretty," I offered, gesturing out the windscreen with the barrel of my spread-gun.

"Yup." He gave it a quarter of a second, then put the car back in gear. We traveled about three feet, then stopped again.

"Lookit that," Sherrow said.

I followed his gaze, expecting more view.

We weren't very high, and the slanting headlights caught the patch of mist creeping around one of a hundred generic warehouses that butted up to the docks along the river. What Sherrow found so interesting was the clear delineation where the fog touched up against a force screen of some kind, war surplus, by the look of it. The fog crept up and around it like an opal dome, very faint, but unmistakable.

"Who owns that one?" Sherrow wanted to know.

I accessed my street map memory, since there was no cop link on Sherrow's car computer.

"Foghorn Maritime, I think. Shipping company."

"Wanna bet?"

"Not really." I looked down at the mystery warehouse somebody wanted protected bad enough to pay that kind of security money for. "I'd lose for sure."

Sherrow took me home. Not another word was said the whole way.

Canon

She let him in, sultry voice tinny over the intercom, and he followed clicking mechanical locks up to her penthouse, the computer following his course on the elaborate camera system he'd avoided so deftly the first visit.

It even opened the penthouse door for him, leaving Mrs. March to loll on the sofa in a picturesque pose, all spread out in a puddle of silk peignoir, blonde hair tumbling over one white shoulder. She was smoking a scented cigarette that gave off purple smoke and smelled like somebody's boudoir. The carpet was a deep pile pale robin's egg blue that reminded Max of a summer sky right before a storm. The sofa was a custom metal frame job enameled in French blue with chrome highlights. It looked like an antique car, except for the big fluffy white cushions. Max came in at her casual gesture, sidestepping the blue glass coffee table. It was rigged for video, and she switched it off before he could see what she'd been watching. Max seated himself in one of the matching chairs, noticing the chromed mermaids that held up the coffee table with their tails, sculpted hair flowing around the base like soft porn cover art.

Mrs. March's greeting was lackadaisical. He wondered what she was on.

"What are you doing at the office, Mr. Canon, at this time of night?"

"Is it late? Seems early to me."

"I imagine it would, seeing as you just got up. Do you usually sleep in your office?"

Max tipped his cigarette in a salute and smiled at her.
"No. Sometimes I sleep in my car."

"Don't you have a home to go to?"

"And sleep all alone? It depresses me."

"Why are you watching my apartment, Mr. Canon?"
Her light manner faded and stone appeared behind her eyes.

"I wanted to talk to you. See you." He smiled a tiny
bit on the last line and turned it into flattery. She didn't
bother acknowledging it, as if it was automatically due her.

"And what do you want to talk about?" She blew
smoke, turning her head to the side to give him a good view
of her profile. She looked magnificent. She looked bored.

"Capelli. Your boyfriend, Daily Caulder."

She made a face at Max's use of the nickname, but
didn't comment on it.

"So you have no news at all on my case? How
boring." She turned unreadable eyes back to him. "Bart was
boring too." She raised perfect eyebrows, then let them
drop. Her cigarette flared purple smoke in a fragrant cloud.
"Dan assigned him to escort me that night. He couldn't go
and he didn't trust me alone." She made a petulant face.
"Can you imagine that?"

Max looked at her and could. He wouldn't trust her
out of his sight if she were his. She'd never be his. He
found himself grateful.

"No, I can't. I'd go with you for sure."

She rose gracefully and went to the drinks table, a
chrome and glass antique from several hundred years past.
A chromed globe in the center rotated back to reveal an ice
bucket. Cold mist smoked out as she opened it, hiding her
hands.

Max went over to join her so he could keep track of
them.

"Bourbon?" She offered, handing him an empty glass
with a sparkle that told him she knew what he was thinking.

"Please." He stood well within her personal space,
looking down and breathing her perfume. She smelled like
soft money and summer nights. She was intoxicating, like all
the clichés, and he was enjoying it. He'd have to be careful.

"You know, for an ugly man, you're not too hard to look at," she poured straight from the bottle. She was smiling, like she was telling an amusing story, but there was a jarring note somewhere in the act.

"I'm sure I'm flattered," Max told her, trying to pin down the elusive misnote.

She looked up at him with an intelligent eyebrow arched. He knew then that she wasn't on any drug, she was playacting, and she played to the hilt. Like Marie. Only smarter. But not necessarily better.

"You're not. But it's true. You're very attractive, without having a single feature that could be described as handsome. Why is that, I wonder?"

"It's my charming personality. Does Caulder let you out often without his escort?"

"Don't be boring, Mr. Canon. Max."

"Does this mean I can call you Stephanie?"

She turned her back on him in a move that might be called coy, if she'd worn a matching expression. Max dropped his eyes down the long, bare back of the gown. He blew his breath out slowly and had the satisfaction of seeing her shiver.

"What did Frank Skills have to say to you?" she asked the curtained windows.

Max stepped back, putting space between them, and went over to the sofa.

"You know him?"

"A long time ago."

There was a long pause as she waited for him to go on and he tried to decide what he should say.

"Hmm. He wanted to hold my hand and call me sweetheart. He ever do that to you?"

Mrs. March laughed at that, a sudden rippling sound. There was a trace of unhappiness behind it, and Max felt his stomach sink. He could rapidly be in trouble if she kept that up.

He lit another cigarette, turning away to look at one of the obscure objects d'art that were scattered around the room like spilled salt. There was a priceless vase from an empire that might or might not have flourished in the

Precambrian period on Helios I before the colonists got there. He heard her skirts rustle as she crossed to the windows.

Dammit. Max had been prepared to flirt and charm and parry words all evening to find out what he could from her, and he wouldn't've objected if she tried to side-track him with sex after all, though he'd been ready to watch his back at all times. If only she'd been truly the heartless bitch she appeared to be he would run through her barefoot and leave before dawn to exploit the information he got and good riddance to her.

But she was real under the brittle gloss, and she'd given it away in that sad little laugh.

Max tossed off his drink. He was getting maudlin over a cold pet tiger on Caulder's leash. She couldn't fail to know what kind of man her protector was. There were too many killings and torturings and various drugs and thugs around for her to be unaware. She must condone it to some degree.

She was as bad as Caulder, so what if she was sad over some long-dead romance? Max turned back, determination again at full. She spoke first.

"You're very funny, Max. He didn't ask about...me?"

Max put his glass down on an inlaid table from the Chinese, ancient and priceless.

"Should he have? He asked me what I was doing at the roadhouse. He didn't ask about you, but I'm interested if you want to tell somebody."

"What were you doing at the roadhouse?"

"Skip trace. How bout you? Have anything to do with the yokels you had in tow?"

She turned away from the window, and her eyes were suddenly flat.

"Those 'yokels' happen to be very good friends of mine from a long time ago."

"From maybe Frank Skills days?" Max kept his distance and kept his eyes to himself so he wouldn't teeter back into feeling sorry for her. He didn't realize she was angry until she hit him, one fist on his shoulder. She didn't do any damage, couldn't possibly make a decent fist with nails as long as hers, but she got his attention. He turned his head and looked down at her raging face.

"You bastard. What do you know about it? What do you know about anything? You're a classless, ignorant dirt-digger who spends all his time peeking in windows and chasing errant wives. How dare you?"

Max liked her mad. She looked even better, and her hair got a little mussed.

"Yeah, how dare I? But then, I'm nobody, so my opinion doesn't matter, does it?"

Mrs. March backed off suddenly, tracking away from him to a silk-covered chair in the farthest corner. She sat, her posture defeated, but her gloss was back. She turned a cool face towards him.

"I suppose it doesn't. I should've known you'd be just another thug like Dan's favorite pit bulls. I shouldn't be disappointed."

"Don't be. You must've wanted something when you let me up here in the first place. Why not ask and find out what the answer is?"

She trailed one finger down the silk arm of the chair, eyeing him speculatively.

"I wanted someone to look something up for me. Someone who isn't in Dan's pay."

"Look up? Look up where?"

"Police archives. You have an in there, I understand."

Max tilted his head to one side.

"I can pull strings occasionally. What is it you wanna know? Does this have to do with your blackmailer?"

She got up and walked towards him quickly, suddenly too eager to keep up the cool-bitch front. Max felt the cold in his stomach again and only held his ground by concentrated effort.

"Yes. I think there may be records on him there."

"Blackmailers usually don't appear in the archives until they've been caught," Max put in when she didn't go on. Her gaze had wandered off to one side, and a crease appeared between her perfect brows.

"Well, I suppose that's true. I was just hoping…"

"Have you considered paying them off? Surely Caulder gives you run of the bank account."

"That wouldn't do any good." She looked petulant again, turning from him to look towards the windows. "It's not money he wants now."

After a pause, Max put a hand on her bare arm. She was abruptly still, her hair falling over her shoulder to brush across his knuckles, silken, dazzling.

"I can understand that, I guess." He didn't mean to pitch his voice low, but it came out husky. He hadn't intended to try the seduction approach since God knew she had far more practice than he did in such matters and, like she'd said, he wasn't exactly a poster boy for the vids. She probably had enough men in her life between Caulder and friends from the country. And he was just another thug.

He didn't move, though, waiting to see what she'd do, how she'd respond to his clear interest.

She turned inside his arm and gave him the damsel in distress look. He waited for her to speak, feeling his mouth soften and wondering if he was about to make another huge mistake. Falling for Anne in the middle of a war hadn't been enough, he'd had to keep falling for the wrong women at the wrong time. And this one wasn't for him to fall for.

"I'm sorry," he said, opening his arms and stepping back.

For an instant, stark despair flashed across her features, making her look plain and small. Max thought he really would fall in love if she didn't stop with the revealing emotions. He hoped she was acting and looked hard for it, but didn't see it.

"I didn't mean to lean on you," he said, walking over to the table where his hat lay. "I'll look your person up for you if you promise to tell me a few things when I have. We got a deal?"

When she realized he was going to help her, her composure came rushing back and she smiled a cat-smile for him.

"If it's mine to tell, you have a deal, Max." She sashayed over to the drink table. "Would you like another drink?"

"I better not stay," he said, hat in hand. The look he gave her was level.

She saw it and the cat-smile got wider. With swaying, slow steps she rustled over to where he stood and took the hat from him. She tilted her head back, showing him her long smooth throat, and purred,

"What if I decided to side-track you with sex after all?"

"That's what I'm afraid of," Max told her honestly. "Or I'm afraid it might be your form of payment."

She stiffened, terribly insulted. Max could see it was real outrage.

"I never pay before I get the goods," she said through stiff lips.

Max smiled.

"I'm relieved. I was starting to like you and it would've spoiled everything."

She gave him a look of puzzlement, derailed.

"You're an odd man, Max Canon."

Max took his hat from her hands and nodded.

"I'm ugly, too."

She followed the hat and came up into his arms without warning, kissing him full on the mouth and showing him what he was missing. He was missing a lot. He never should've let her get that close.

When she had him good and breathless, she let go and went back to the sofa with a wag.

"You're not really," she told him, sitting down and smoothing silk over a long thigh. "The person is male. Calls himself Fokke when he deals with Dan."

"And with you."

She nodded, looking too young around the eyes for a second.

"Okay," Max put his hat on. "That's all you can give me?"

She gave him a phone number.

"He sometimes uses that."

"Thanks for the drink. I'll be in touch."

"Goodnight, Max."

"I doubt it." He shut the door gently behind him and cursed all the way down to the car.

Friar

Every morning still hurt until the muscles warmed up. The bruises were at least fading, but inevitably, I was a bastard in the first half hour of shift until I got my coffee in my hand and my live-chip for the laser-system in the car slot. I was early this one day, so I got to wait for Sherrow to change and hear all the usual bullshit in the locker room. I threw some myself at an old academy pal graduated about the time 'a Strindberg and me, who had a thing about spotless uniforms. Like it was actually possible to be perfectly spotless at all times, even if we wanted to project that image to the general public.

By the time Sherrow got there, I at least had some practice in social commerce, so I wasn't a total asshole.

I waited for him to change and eyeballed the inside of his locker door with interest.

There were certificates and awards all over it, top of class, track winner, things from high school, and more from Academy. I wondered if they were there to remind him he was worth more than his current job, rookie partner to a drunk has-been. He certainly had enough stuff up there. He even gave me a glare as he caught me looking.

But I wasn't a drunk. I hadn't had a drink-fest in days. I wasn't a has-been and I could solve a case no one wanted to touch, and I would. They could all watch me and weep.

Hopefully not over my coffin.

Sherrow's locker also had a photo in it I had never seen before, and I perused it thoroughly. She was smiling. She was pretty like Noel used to be before she got expensive, country pretty.

"Nice. What's her name?"

"Shelly. Thanks."

"That the girl yer gonna marry?"

"Yeah." He looked like he was going to stop there, but he lowered his voice and rolled his eyes over the rest of the room. "Don't splash it all over."

"Okay. Well, congratulations, man. She's probably better'n you deserve. She know what she's getting?" The words came off my tongue by rote. I was realizing I didn't know anything about his private life beyond his popularity with the city's wait-staff and his first name.

"She knows she's getting a cop."

"Oh, well, that's a good start anyway," I said, lamely, thinking of Noel and what she thought she was getting and what she decided she'd gotten.

Sherrow gave me a funny look, then turned his eyes on the photo. He touched it with one hand, his expression still neutral, but I could see the mask was in place and knew why. Let Hollingate get a hold of a rookie with a pretty fiancé and he'd make the kid's life a hell of bad jokes and grisly stories about past cops with pretty wives who'd died ugly. It was just his style of humor.

I wasn't the only bastard in this battalion.

X.

Friar

Shift was nothing special for once, and I did help Sherrow in a three-block sprint on a rabbit without falling over or having a heart attack. He didn't seem to appreciate the effort, but he joined me in my records-search after shift. I got the feeling he was smarting less about the roadhouse murder then he was wondering what kinda shape I was in. The hit and run on one of our own had taken a bit of precedence.

We looked for recent files on Warp related arrests and mafia ties, trying to find some trace of people who could and would maybe want to be spreading an expensive drug around into cops' drinks and cops' lockers. I had a suspicion to play out that involved Skills' old enemies, since they'd only look better if he started having messy drug problems within his own department.

As usual with that sort of research, we found a good clue almost by accident, and nothing else useful, though I did make more lists, just in case names started matching up. I was throwing old telefax copies into a box that'd been new some years before the last war, and Sherrow was watching with that glaze-eyed boredom you get when you're thinking of nothing much but food and sleep, a block of video-testimony on some maf-house bust running on the monitor behind him. A news photo in my stack caught his eye and his hand shot out to take it from me before his mouth even opened.

"Wait." He turned a lamp towards the photo. "Who's this here?" His finger stabbed down on a fuzzy shot of a woman, half hidden behind a politician now out of office for misbehavior.

"She's a local thug." I told him, flipping back through the write up it had been with. "Beautiful silver blonde, name of Georgia or something, but her trade name/nickname's Silver. She was out of sight for a while, but I think she's back in town. Why?"

"She's that little chick from the bar. The one with the boy friend and the Warp."

I sat up at that and craned closer to the photo like it would tell me more. My mood was improving rapidly.

"You sure?"

"Oh, yeah. I never forget a chick who burns me."

"She did that, alright. She's got a rep for being the other side of sane. I never met her personally, but she ties with Caulder through the Emerald city and that ties the Warp to him, and that, my son, is our first real solid link." I felt myself grinning hugely, far beyond what my bruised face allowed, and Sherrow tried a tentative smile of his own, probably choking over the 'my son'

"Who's that?" He pointed to a hazy figure on the other side of the politician.

"I don't know. I don't recognize him and he's not identified here.

"That could be her boyfriend...that jaw, those big hands."

I couldn't make out what he was seeing in the fuzzy shot, but I nodded.

"Could be."

There wasn't much more to get, so we called in done for the night.

He dropped me off at home where I went in the door feeling like we might have a chance at finding Mitchell's attacker as well as getting the guy who wore white coats to bar brawls. Mrs. Howard, my landlady, was waiting in her doorway. The boiler was on the blink again and she wanted to know if she should call the repair guys. I told her no and went down to pound on it myself and save her a chunk of money and a raise in rent for everybody.

Then I took out her garbage and went to bed.

Alone, I might add.

Canon

Max convinced Eddy to get him into the archives again even though he'd missed the party and was in the doghouse with his sister because of it. Eddy didn't seem upset, but Max thought maybe that was because he was returning the favor for Max's having said nothing about cat-house busts of the past. He wasn't sure, though. Eddy maybe was just being nice.

He found nothing of use at any event. Fokke used another name with the police if the absence of the name in their records was anything to go by, and his search of the phone number both at the phone company and here had come up nil. The number must be a satellite uplink code. Max thought maybe he could find a hint if he could get a peek at the real police computers, but he didn't have access and he couldn't ask Eddy to do it . Maybe Frank Skills could help. He went up to ask.

"Huh. Yer a riot, Canon." Skills was not in the mood for helping.

"A crowd of noisy violent people doing a lot of damage? Thank you, Chief, I'm flattered." Max hadn't told him what he wanted yet, so he felt okay in being a smart ass, since the answer looked like being no, no matter what his request would've been.

"Why are you still messin' with my town, Canon?"

"It's messin' with me. All I'm trying to do is conduct a private investigation for a client. Confidential. I'll try not to step on any of your chalk-lines."

"Like you haven't already? You toe another line on my turf, mister, you better already have your fists up. I'll slap you down so fast you'll think you crossed against the light. Got that?"

"Sure. I had it last time we had this conversation."

"Huh. Somehow I get the feeling it didn't sink in that time either."

"Yeah, well, I wasn't my usual self, was I?"

"Hardly recognized you, Max."

Knowing the rare use of his first name was a sign of kindness and maybe even friendship, Max gave a shrug and waved the statement itself away, avoiding sentimentality, but letting the other man see a flicker of real smile to let him know the soft edge was appreciated.

"No surprise there. Ruth would've screamed high C for me if I'd been stupid enough to show my face."

"Well, I wouldn't make any plans to show my face for the next week or so, you don't wanna hear her scream."

"Thanks for the advice."

"So what was it you wanted, Canon?"

Max weighed the friendly look and the reality of Frank Skills for a moment and made a decision. He'd save the computers for another favor.

"I was wondering if I could talk to the troopers who were first on the scene at that roadhouse kill back when."

Skills' brow darkened a bit, but not at Max's request.

"That one's been bothering me a bit. You heard about Mitchell?"

Max nodded.

"It was on the news. In a greatly expurgated version, I imagine."

"Of course. I'm beginning to suspect the accident has to do with the investigation he was pursuing on that bar brawl. Canon," Skills leaned forward over his desk and the friendly left for the serious. It made him look angry. "Is there anything you can remember about that brawl that might help us in our investigation? Anything at all, however remote it might seem."

Max transferred his gaze to the window and thought hard, more to help Frank Skills than because he thought he might remember anything that would help them.

"Well, you know about the war," Max began and Skills nodded. "Maybe Capelli kept in better touch with some of our old veteran buddies than I did. Could be he was working for one of them. Or made enemies of one of them." Max smiled with a twist. "You'd have access to records in the war department, maybe. Me, they don't trust."

"Why not?" Skills was surprised. A veteran should have full access to any records not considered defense of the realm.

"Seems I didn't debrief fully after DEROS. That could make me a security risk if I saw something like service records and all."

Max got up and put his hat on.

"Anyway, maybe you could get me cleared to take a look? You are the Chief of Police, aren't you? And if I think of anything else, I'll call. I think I somehow owe you one this time."

"You probably do, but I won't try to come up with a reason why. Be careful out there, Canon."

"You too. Seems that its cops getting hit by cars, not PLs."

"I hope you're not trying to be funny, Canon."

"No, Frank. Never about people getting murdered. Anything else, maybe, but not that."

"Glad to hear it."

Max grinned.

"I'll bet you are."

Out on the street, he thought about what he'd just told Skills and wondered if it might be a viable lead. Candy colored air bikes flew in swooping flocks as kids got out of schools and headed downtown to shop and make trouble. Max headed into his own less desirable part of town where fewer good transport ramps, less neon, and more advertising made the rents lower. Seedier, maybe. Home, anyway.

Friar

I beat Sherrow to work again, and for roll-call, he was off on a special assignment—coffee, I think—for Skills, who hadn't apparently bothered to go home after last shift. From the bellowing that could be heard down the hall, I suspected that the rumors that he'd slept in his office were true, but less because he was a diligent, go-getter cop and more because he'd been kept there late for some reason or other and had fallen asleep in the chair. It'd happened before.

I heard he went home to get some sleep right before we hit the streets at sunset, and the tension in the department noticeably lessoned. I wondered what kind of woman his wife was, to put up with it.

Today, Sherrow was bitching again about having to let yet another collar go to the detectives, as if he didn't know his own job description. My coffee tasted viler than usual and the day was shitty gray and pissing rain. I could see he'd have to start casting his sights higher if he wanted to be happy on the force and told him so. He ignored me and kept up the stream of whine.

"It feels incomplete," he was saying in the aggrieved tones of a man whose last quarter just disappeared into the broken coffee machine in the first AM of the day.

It was the first AM of the day, so I was not in the mood to play dad.

"It is incomplete. That's our job. It's about incomplete. You want complete, ya gotta go for detective, like I said and like Kay said too. Pass the creamer."

"Why haven't you? Gone for detective, I mean. I know it bugs you as much as it does me."

"I like the patrol uniform better'n the suit and tie."

"No, really, asshole."

"Never had much time to think about it, I guess." I put the coffee down with a grimace as a lost cause. He didn't seem to notice, which meant he was hot on the topic at hand. "First there was Croner, then Noel divorced me, then I seemed to spend all my time training rookies…"

"Liar."

"That, too. Detectives are required to be truthful."

"Bullshit."

"Well, at least smart."

"Oh. Now I understand."

"Thought you might. Yer driving after seven, okay?" He nodded, then came up with the question,

"So how come you haven't gone up for Sergeant, at least?"

I didn't have a good, short answer for that one, so I ignored it.

We spent the first half of the day chasing shoplifters at the Skyway Mall, then a chunk of time booking a guy from an out colony who didn't understand enough Standard Trade to realize he was under arrest for breaking a few laws he'd never heard of. We were stuck at the station for hours, waiting for an interpreter who spoke whatever it was he kept babbling in, since the computer translation device didn't recognize it either. I just patted him on the shoulder and kept handing him bad coffee that he drank sorta absent-minded. Sherrow spent a lot of time glaring alternately at me, the perp and out the window at the gray sooty rain. I had no pity for him.

When we finally got released and let loose on the streets again, we went straight from the station into the aftermath of a four way crash at Poindexter and Olive. Traffic Cleanup shoulda been on it, but there we were on the scene before the glass even stopped falling, so we got to head off the insurance dogs and wave traffic and try to sort out three confused and injured drivers and one corpse.

That kinda crash, with two levels converging, it was lucky there was only one.

And back at the station to sign out, I had a phone message. Noel had called me at the station for the first time in nearly eight years to talk about doing dinner. I had to sit down I was so surprised.

Sherrow sorta flipped me shit about it, but he was already out the door and gone to Shelly in his mind, so I only had half his attention when I told him about going to visit Mitchell in the hospital.

"Yer a good man, Vic," he said, looking surprised in a distracted sort of way.

"Yeah, Mr. Heart of Gold, that's me. Go away already and see yer fiancé. I got the reports."

"Thanks man. I mean it."

"I bet you do. You gotta be nice tomorrow or you'll owe me big time for it, too. Go."

He flew. I got a great view of shoulders and shoe leather launching out the door like a galaxy class cruiser hitting faster than light.

Ah, to be young again.

"Hey, son, what's on for tonight?"

And here came Hobby to tell me how young I was by a vantage of 10 years older and smooze for a free beer or four to toast his seniority. Cheap as a cardboard match, was Hobby. I had to plead hard day and report writing and I still got stuck listening to ten minutes of regrets. I escaped finally to visit Skills so I could ask permission to visit Mitchell and get him to look in at evidence for me. I just hoped he was in a better mood than he had been lately.

When I finally got to his office, news on Mitchell wasn't much.

"He's doing okay, I guess. He's awake at any rate. You gonna go see him?"

"If it's allowed. Anybody question him yet?"

"I did." Skills didn't sound proud of it. "He's pretty beat up."

"Is he intelligible?"

Skills was quiet for a minute, his eyes all squinted down at me in a hostile way. After a minute, he said,

"I don't want him upset or excited. Or questioned, to be honest. He's still in a lot of shock. That kind of trauma is severe and you don't get over it in a hurry."

"I was just gonna take him flowers, boss, but I'll wait if you think it's best." I made to rise.

"Friar."

I stopped.

"If you think you can shed some light on this by asking Mitchell a few questions, I can okay it."

I considered carefully, sure he wouldn't offer this if he wasn't hoping I could.

"I can try. I'm not sure, though."

"Let me know if you get sure." He was the gruff, mean old bastard again. I decided not to push my luck and turned to take my leave.

"Friar." Something in his manner stopped me, telling me ahead that what was coming behind was bad news. It was. "Linden's been pulled off the case."

I didn't have to ask him what case.

"Why?" was the best I could summon.

"It wasn't my choice, or his." He looked angry.

"Whose, then?"

"It was political, so I'm not sure. When I am, I'll know who wants Caulder left alone, then I'll know who to burn for complicity and racketeering. But it came from higher up. That's all I got."

Higher than the Chief of Police? Wow. I nodded, what else could I say? and left without asking after permission to check evidence room records. I'd have to tell him about the Warp in my locker then, and I didn't want to be asked questions I couldn't answer. Similarly, I didn't need to ask him questions he couldn't answer about Mitchell and Linden. We both knew something bad was going on. Talking about it wasn't going to fix it until we had something to talk about. I walked down creaky linoleum halls and brooded about a lot of things, including Canon and his relationship to Skills.

As far as I could figure, Max Canon was almost a friend to Skills. I don't think he knew it, but I did. I'd found out a few days back when Frank Skills had jumped down somebody's throat for making a derogatory comment about PLs in general and Canon in particular. He'd said at least he knew where Canon stood, even if it was something outside the law. He said it was better than the people who stood with one foot on either side and acted holy holy when they were into maf work and double pay. The back stabbers and the two-faced corrupt ones.

Cops? I'd asked, sidling closer, and Skills looked suddenly like he'd forgotten where he was and shook his head, spat, and walked away, leaving a disgruntled officer, and me with two cups of cooling coffee and a lot to think about. And questions, like who did he suspect in the department of being two-faced backstabbers?

I didn't feel like telling him that spitting was still on the books as littering.

There wasn't any point, and I wanted to be pals so I could ask questions later.

XI.

Canon

Max sat in the semi-darkness of the quiet office and communed with the bourbon. Somewhere in the back of his cluttered mind, he was tracking the skip trace to the bar he should've gone to that fateful night, and wondering if he could still make good on that case.

Another part of his brain was thinking about drugs and their political uses.

Who was selling Warp on the street and why? It couldn't be Caulder, but it had to be. He was the big fish in crime and if anything was going on, it was in his pond. He had to be allowing it, but what would it get him? He couldn't make enough money off it streetwise coz it was so cost-prohibitive that the common junkie preferred cheap highs like Smash or Seven. He could be running it for a friend, playing clearing house to earn favor points, but again, what could he need off planet when he already controlled everything on it, unless he was feeling shaky? Max had heard a faint rumor of shifting loyalties in local maf muscle, but Caulder had always come out on top, always. Was the Warp to keep the cops busy and out of his hair? They'd jump after Warp certain sure, especially after the big trouble coupla years back, Skills' big victory, plus Warp was designer, read unpredictable, read really dangerous and no cop wanted to face that person 'cause you either got shot, or shot and got inquiries.

Warp was a black eye for the cops. Look at what had happened on Jupiter 5. Nice laid back vacation orbiter turned into a battle zone it took 1500 troops and police officers in riot gear to bring back under control, and it turned out the head of security—an ex-cop himself—was the head of manufacturing. That had been another drug of course, but still.

A big black eye. Max thought maybe he should take a look at people who hated cops more than Caulder did. Maybe Caulder hadn't found the perp yet himself, which explained a lot of corpses and maybe explained the thug trio's frequent forays into places Max had never seen them before. His own levels of the street, for example.

The phone rang. It didn't do that too often at half past ten on an ugly Wednesday night. That might've been because his posted hours were 10-6. More likely it was because everybody with a brain not already baked into pudding by the day's hassles were in a proper bar unwinding. Very few would sit in a dark office and nurse the office bottle until the phone rang.

Max picked up the receiver, hoping it wasn't Ruth, and didn't bother to cap the bottle.

Mrs. March was on the line, inviting him over.

Max grabbed his hat, wondering when the other shoe was going to fall, and would it explode when it hit.

The high rise was right by a golf course. Max never much liked golf courses. The big stretches of green always reminded him of cemeteries. The graveyard at Antioch where his folks'd lived had flat grave markers and they mowed it just like a golf course. Too bad Mrs. March had to live right across from one: it always made him think of death when he visited her, not a thought he needed to dwell on, with her boyfriend the man he was.

But Max didn't see any of Caulder's muscle outside and she buzzed him in promptly.

In a dazzling rush, he was allowed glimpses of her pink satin outfit, a lush flash of cleavage, and a waft of soft heady perfume, then he was in a chair clutching an unwanted drink while she gave him business and no more lovely half-promise images to keep him entertained.

"Bart was into something Dan didn't know about." She was saying earnestly. Max tried to gauge her honestly, but she was professionally painted and had her eyes in shadow with a well-placed lamp. "He kept hinting that maybe one day he'd take me away from Dan, be the top dog. I think the man who killed him was one of Dan's out of town connections, though I can't be sure. New people have been coming to town a lot lately."

"Like your friends Albrecht and Miss Laide?"

"Steve and Jolie are from around here. Well, Jolie is. I've known her for a few years now. I think she may have been in some trouble with the law at one time, because she stays pretty much out of the main stream of things with Steve." Mrs. March blew smoke and toyed with the large polished Mars sapphire ring on her right index finger. "I don't get to see them much anymore as it is." She laughed, a little sadly. " And I suppose we don't know each other all that well. Even her name's a dodge. 'Jolie Laide'. It's Cajun, you know Creole, for a beautiful ugly woman, an ugly woman who's still attractive somehow, anyway. Like all of us, I guess."

"Well, you aren't ugly for a start. Either of you." Max put the drink aside and dried his palm on his trousers, feeling like he was hearing more than she meant him to. He was getting to like the candid Mrs. March. He was getting to like her maybe a lot. He was sure now.

"Not on the outside, Mr. Canon." She sent her eyes down just to be sure he couldn't read them.

"Don't go all formal on me, Stephanie. Do Jolie and Steve work for Caulder?" Max shifted in his chair, got up and started to prowl the apartment, looking at everything instead of the intoxicating Mrs. March with her dirty secrets and murdering friends.

"I'm not sure, but I don't think so. If they work the underside, it's for somebody out of town, because they aren't in town enough otherwise. But I called you because I need your help."

"With your blackmailer?"

"Yes. I don't have the money to keep up the payments, and like I said before, he's asking for…other things, too, now."

"You're afraid they'll expose your Oz days?"

Mrs. March looked startled, eyes wide through a sheet of tobacco smoke. Max crossed to the cigarette box and helped himself to expensive real tobacco, too. He'd almost forgotten what it tasted like. He put his back to the nearest unadorned piece of wall so she'd have to turn to look at him and put her face in light.

"Why's that so blackmailable?" he asked, dragging in a lungful of rich smoke. He almost coughed, it was so alien to his synth-trained lungs.

Mrs. March gave him one brief glance before she foiled him by getting up to walk over to the window and gaze out at the night sky.

"It wouldn't look good for Dan." She turned to face him, backlit by neon and spangled light. She looked absurdly like an angel of the more metropolitan sort. "I don't know if you're aware of how important reputation is to a man like Dan Caulder. It doesn't take much for one of the underlings clawing to get on top to push him out of favor and take his place. All the underling needs is the favor of a Mafia god or one of the Borough kings and his people. He builds a base from there, allies against the others, then he starts chipping away at the foundations of the man he wants to replace, stealing his men, corrupting his work force, buying off his dealers and prostitutes…Dan's rep has quite a bit to do with the fact that's he's always seen with the best: best car, best house, best women. A one-time cathouse nobody doesn't quite qualify as a Best. Street trash is more like it."

She looked back out the window, maybe at the lights across the dark stretch of park or the river's dark mirror, or maybe at her own sad, distorted reflection in the glass. "It doesn't take much."

"You are the best," Max went to join her by the window, repeating the word off the street about her to make her feel better, maybe, he wasn't sure. He stayed behind the curtains, just in case, but he stood beside her in a sort of moral support, wondering what the hell he was doing, falling in love? And wouldn't Eddy just kill him.

Mrs. March turned her gorgeous eyes up to his and smiled the sad smile that made him feel like his heart was breaking because it looked real. He wished he hadn't gotten a good look at her eyes.

"How nice of you to say that."

"Just fact." He could smell that damn perfume this close, like a summer evening on an isolated island blooming with flowers of the sort that probably ate small birds and insects during the day.

"Now you're being silly. I'm beautiful right at this moment, maybe, but that doesn't make me the best. It just makes me beautiful at this moment. That doesn't take much to change, either. One good assault and I'm just like any other ex-prostitute without a work permit, out on the street with no money, the clothes on my back."

"You'll never be ordinary. Caulder wouldn't have picked you if you were."

Max looked into her pleased, strangely real smile, the naïve smile of somebody ten years younger and in a different line of work altogether. He should leave soon, very soon, now maybe. Like last time. When he hadn't slept all night. All week.

"Here." Mrs. March took his hand. "I'll fix you another drink." Her eyes said something else, something much more interesting than mere alcohol.

Max followed her to the drinks cabinet, tingling. Idiot, he thought. How have you lived so long? Idiot.

She built him a double. The bedroom decor had mermaids in it, too.

In his own empty apartment, in his too-hard bed with neon striping across his eyes through the blinds, and the faint smell of Mrs. March still clinging to the suit he'd worn, Max dreamt of the APC, skiing the controls, feet and hands in a slow glide to the left towards the LZ, just like a VR Alps run game, minus the recorded shush of snow under the skis. He dreamt of a good landing, but a bad deploy, artillery and flame and black rain on an unnamed planet, puddling in the dusty earth and looking just like human blood. He heard the crash of body armor colliding in testosterone rage, blind rage between himself and another soldier, for no clear reason, and the Stalag walls of rotten wood, no windows or doors, damp stone floors and the smell of mildew and rot everywhere.

Max didn't sleep well, and when he woke up, he went onsat to look up a few names and numbers that might be involved off world with Caulder and would keep his mind busy until he shook the dreams.

He was at the computer for hours.

Friar

I might've been dreaming, it was such a familiar scene, but I felt too crappy for it to be a real dream, so I must be actually at the archives again, late-late and doing useless research that more or less copied Mitchell's research without adding a shred of useful new material to the file. I had a beat cop's inspiration to look into records so old that nobody even knew where they were kept anymore. Mitchell hadn't thought to look, and I only came up with it because I'd tracked a kidnapper—call it a hobby, since it can't be called detecting without the detective's badge, like Mitchell suggested—after Noel left me and I had long dark nights to resent the fact that a kidnapper was stealing women from restaurant bathrooms and keeping them somewhere, and here I was a cop without a woman and no clue where to start looking for the guy's den. I'd started into the property deeds where they crossed over with high crime areas and cases that'd made it to court, and there was this old house down in the Speakeasy that nobody remembered because it'd been surrounded completely by high-rise warehouses and one massive on-ramp for the airway. And there was the name of one of the prime suspects we had on tag for the latest kidnapping. After that, it was a strike and a collar and hero of the hour Friar takes home a 'good job' from his captain and Chinese take-out from the corner.

Of course, it hadn't given me a life or made me feel better. But it had given me something to look at now when I was in the same space and didn't want to go home to the empty bed or out to the bar where I'd see dating cops with their sweethearts or married cops getting away from their spouses. Even Ketchikian from the west precinct, a lovely young woman with the highest marks in sharp-shooting in the department, who I'd had eyes for for months, had a current steady man, and he didn't look anything like me. Then again, he might have actually asked her out, too. Maybe I should call Crystal and see if she still liked me. Sherrow said she did, and she'd smiled real pretty for me the other day …

I couldn't call her at three in the morning, no matter how pretty her smile. I went to the dead records room, down in the ground under the media-morgue. There wasn't even a lock on the door to this one. I think the only person who even knew it was there besides me was Pete Blocking.

Thirty minutes later I was detective of the year and nobody there to congratulate me. A single fold of paper, yellow and crispy, smelling faintly of synthetic cigarette smoke and with the obligatory coffee ring right across the federal seal—no paperwork is official without the coffee ring—was in my hands, saying in bold letters that it was a Bill of Property Sale from Halland Speltzer to Mr. March. The property had been involved in a court case over a murdered bookie, and the bill had been updated on form 3-12 which wasn't included, though the binder mark in the upper left corner indicated that it had once been so. I went back to the box it had come from and dug some more. Form 3-12 materialized shortly, and I got to see that the property actually belonged to Daniel Caulder Holdings.

No surprise there, but I did find it interesting to note that the property involved had burned to the ground a month before the case had come to trial, and that the street address put it in the part of town that held two things of note: lots of park and a brand new barely four years old complex built right over the old foundations, that housed Mrs. Stephanie March. The one and only.

I kept looking, even returning to the upstairs records office to hunt down another hazy lead among the mega K files of digital voice prints, retinal scans and vid testimony. I was there so late that I was still there, red-eyed and patient, in the dead hours of shift change when the coffee machine maintenance woman came to refill the unit. No one drinks more coffee than cops.

I was standing there, waiting for the mysterious chemical mixture to heat up when Skills came in, which told me I'd been there way too long and, if I wasn't careful, would be going on shift soon, wrinkled, unshaven and on no sleep. And aching. I hurt all over. My eyes burned from monitor strain.

"What're you still doing here?" Frank Skills charm all the way.

"Ah, research. Just some things bugging me..." I was too tired to lie.

"Research. That's not beat work, Vic." Frank Skills still ragging my ass. But he didn't ask if it was Mitchell's work.

"Never was." I sounded defensive to my misfortune.

"You're always doin' this kinda thing, but you still won't go for detective. Not even for sergeant. Why?"

It was just like Skills to jump on defense with both feet and grind. I rubbed a gritty eye.

"Psych says I'm afraid of failure." I offered.

"Yeah, you aren't so smart, s'true." He paused. "I was kidding, Friar. You can laugh."

"Huh?" I was too tired to focus for long. "Oh, sure. Yeah, ha ha. Whaddya know about Canon?"

"Max Canon." Skills gave me a funny look, then transferred his gaze to the far wall, his eyes skimming just past my left ear. He recited, "W. Maxwell Canon is the finest private license this end of the colonized center and a real live war hero."

"Oh." I had no answer for that.

"He's also a pain in the ass and always getting in the way of official police investigation. But he's good. He's damn good. Stupid sometimes, but good.

"Stupid, but good."

"Like you, Vic."

"Thanks, I think."

"Don't be flattered. It's not really a compliment. I'd ask what research you were doing, but I don't really want to know, do I?" He waved me off, stomping down the hall towards his office. It was as abrupt a departure as his arrival had been. I shambled home to get some sleep before I had to come back and pretend I had actually left just like everybody else.

I didn't want Sherrow to know I'd spent another shift there. I'd never hear the end of it.

Outside, morning was a foreign country. There was a fine mist in the streets, floating low and gold-shot in the few rays of sun that managed to get down that far. It smelled cool and wet, like dawn, but there was the scent of old dust coming on the edge of day as the new air was burned away and left the old behind. It would haunt my dreams and make me think of wasted opportunity

XII.

Canon

It was yet another party, this time Ruth's society friends. Max was still stiff and sore. He must've looked it. Eddy met him at the door with a drink.

They wandered through the crowd to a window that afforded a form of audio privacy. Eddy started it off by commenting on Max's disreputable state.

"Ruth says you like being a bum. That's why you went Private License instead of cop."

Max raised an eyebrow.

"This just came up in casual conversation?"

"Yeah. After we discussed your drinking."

Max looked out the window.

"I just had my fill of uniforms after Fleet."

"I somehow doubt that or you'd'a picked another profession." It was wryly said, and Max gave Eddy a glance. The honest brown eyes were squinted down to see past the reflection of the two of them in the window. There was nothing to see but rain and a few distant lights from downtown.

"Yeah, I sure see a lot of 'em anyway, don't I?"

"Who's fault do you think that is, Max?"

Max only gave a small chuckle and sampled the drink. Eddy must've mixed it himself, because it was strong, very strong, therapy strong. Or sodium pentathol strong.

"What're you mixed up in this time, Max?"

"Why?"

"Coz it's bad. Ruth noticed. Last party, you didn't flirt with Cappy's wife and you didn't even finish your second drink."

"Oh." Max was silent for a long moment, wondering what to say that wouldn't get either of them in trouble with Frank Skills or Ruth.

"It's a woman, isn't it?" Eddy supplied the answer, unaware of how grateful Max suddenly was for the dodge.

"Probably." He took a sip of the drink.

"And that means?" Eddy gestured with his own glass. "It's not the redhead from the Emerald City, is it, Max? That kind of woman will get you nothing but trouble."

"She's not that kind of woman anymore."

"She's far worse trouble, isn't she." It wasn't a question. "Be careful, please. There are people who care what happens to you. And I'd never hear the end of it."

"Ruth'll be okay."

"It's Frank I'm thinking of. He hinted that I keep you out of trouble. Like I could. Flattering, really."

"To you or me?"

"Oh, me. Definitely flattering to me."

"Thanks. I'll be careful."

"I don't believe you, but thanks for pretending." Eddy was already drifting away.

***

"Shall I use one-syllable words, Mr. Canon?" This cop wasn't one he'd seen before, but Max was always ready to dis authority. He looked around for Eddy, wondering if he could piss this guy off and not hurt the work-politics of his brother in law.

"If you have trouble with the bigger ones, sure, whatever you're most comfortable with."

"I just want to make sure you understand the situation once and for all." The man was ignoring Max's smart-assing, but Max got the distinct impression it was only because he was saving it up for later when he could beat the shit out of the PL and get away with it.

"Oh." Max shrugged. "In that case, use big words. I hate to be lied to in words of less than two syllables."

The man hesitated a moment, anger obviously getting the better of him. When he had it under control, he spoke again.

"All I'm saying is, keep your nose out of business that isn't yours."

"And that business would be?" Max prompted gently, eyes traveling after somebody's red-dressed brunette wife and back to the cop.

"Just stay out of things that don't concern you!" The man wasn't prepared to elaborate, and Max could read a bit of uncertainty in him, new to this, then. Max wondered how crooked the man really was.

Later, when he asked Eddy who he was, he got a shrug.

"He came along with somebody, not sure who. He's out of the west side, I guess. Why?" Again with the Eddy-special sharp eyes.

"He just looked familiar when he was asking me about myself," Max half lied smoothly.

"Yeah. That all he was asking about? He looked a little ticked off."

"I was being coy." Max grinned.

"Huh. You would be, just to piss him off."

"In your house? I was all that was polite."

Eddy grinned.

"Now I know yer lying. You need anything? Drink?"

"No, I'm okay. You guys gonna want a hand cleaning this up after?" He gestured with his empty glass at the mess the party was making, glasses all over, cocktail napkins littering the furniture, the general debris you got with a polite party that included alcohol and finger-foods.

"Sure. That'd be great." Eddy cast a knowledgeable eye over the gathering. "They'll be drifting off in half an hour or so, I think."

"Good. I got an errand to run later."

"I don't wanna know about it," It was a flat statement, like concrete is flat. He was walking away.

"No, you don't," Max told the back of his jacket. "You'd just worry."

The guests were gone and the scrubbers were running, sending the low harmonics of machine-song through the apartment.

"I guess I shouldn't be surprised at your tenacity, Max," Eddy sat on the arm of the sofa and let Ruth's disapproving glance rocket off the back of his clean-cut head. He was referring to Max's unfortunate tendency to get into police work that didn't concern him. "You were one of the military's finest, after all."

"Not really," Max said. "I was never that. I was good, but I was never committed enough to be that."

Eddy evinced surprise and looked over at Ruth.

"Max wasn't a volunteer. He was drafted," Ruth clarified, and there was a tone in her voice Max hadn't heard for years. She'd never wanted him to go. The family arguments had been like a world war all in themselves. Duty, honor, civic pride, peace, right vs wrong, whose war was it, whose job was it, whose son is it, you can't seriously just hand him over like conscription isn't robbery, it's generational murder, it's historically proven, It's His Duty, Be Thankful You Haven't Gotten Your Notice Yet.

Eddy looked surprised, but he didn't have the family history to give it emotional depth, so he just shrugged.

"Oh," he said. "Well, whatever you did, you must've learned your stubbornness somewhere. I tell you, Skills was seriously tired of it today."

"But, Eddy," Max got up to stretch his shoulders, "I learned it from him."

Eddy laughed, but he was uncertain whether Max was kidding or not until Ruth said,

"No, you didn't. You inherited it from Mother."

"So did you, sis. So did you. Help you with anything else?" Max asked.

"No, Max, thanks. Go home and try to get some sleep. You look like you've been sleeping in the car again, like a bum."

"At least I'm clean," Max offered.

Ruth gave him an exasperated look, but she wasn't as upset as usual. She even looked a little worried around the eyes. Max gave her a one-armed hug and surprised the hell out of them both.

"Night," he helped himself to his jacket from the closet and made the escape with one quick handshake for his brother in law and a nod to Ruth, who hadn't come past the kitchen door. She waved one hand, frowning

Max could hear them talking even before the door was fully shut behind him.

He headed downtown, to take a look into one of the clubs a certain group of women danced in a few years back. The few years were significant, and this club had seen her ladyship March and a few other maybe-tie in women kicking up their heels for the general populace to drool over.

Friar

The end of another featureless, dull shift, a stretch of the same old unexciting bar; I'd barely gotten my landing gear down before Strindberg was bellying up to the bar next to me, snuggling a stein of some pale watery shit that might've been called beer. He looked tired, so much so that he was like a black and white sketch with his dark hair and brows against bluish pale shin. I was afraid to ask, so I didn't.

"What did Skills want with you?" He asked it casually, but there was an edge to his words. He was pissed off at somebody.

"Just being my pal and asking after my health." I was still interested in keeping my old 'pal' at arms length. Who knew who was doubling the old paycheck dirty around here?

"He ragging on you for chasing Mitchell's hit and runners?" He took a long, sloppy drink of beer, splashing it over his cuff. He'd had too much already. "Maybe he did it. Maybe one of his enemies did it." He sounded bitter and sarcastic all out of proportion, like something about it all was personal.

"Enemies?" I put the word out to see what might rise to take a bite out of it. Strindberg's eyes darkened and he nodded vigorously.

"Yeah. He pissed off a lot of people with that 'cleaning up the city one borough at a time' speech when he took the Chief's chair. Maybe he pissed off the wrong asshole, got himself an active enemy."

"What speech was this?" Sherrow leaned around me to look at Strindberg, and his eyes weren't friendly, even if his expression was.

"Inaugural. Yeah, I forgot about that one. Heh-heh." I laughed a little like it was funny. "That sure rubbed some people the wrong way. Sounded like he was threatening the mafs and their little gerbils at the same time." I nodded to Sherrow. "It was a good speech. Heartwarming."

Strindberg didn't really agree.

"He was threatening. If he doesn't have enemies, I'd be very surprised."

"Everybody has enemies." I took a sip of my own beer. It wasn't much better than what Strindberg was drinking and I made a face: shoulda stuck with the house brew. Sherrow pushed his whiskey in front of me and waved for the bartender.

"Well, Skills has more than most, I'd bet." Strindberg spoke to his beer. After a blank pause he laughed suddenly as if something struck him as funny.

Sherrow and I exchanged a look and I bought his new shot for him.

"But the mafs have always behaved when it came to high profile authority. Good PR and all. They like to deal with underlings. They get a better cut that way." I tapped Sherrow's new glass and sampled his preferred poison. Not bad for Islay synth-scotch. Good buzz, anyway.

"Skills wouldn't take money," Sherrow objected, looking angry at me.

"Not holy high Skills," Strindberg agreed.

"Pure as driven snow, our chief," I put in just to keep the ball rolling.

Strindberg laughed his not-funny laugh again and nodded. The nod went on a bob or two too long for sobriety, but even working together, Sherrow and I couldn't get anything more interesting out of him.

In the end, we left him on the bar telling war stories to a coupla rookies Hollingate hadn't gotten to yet. I don't think either one of us was ready to ask out loud what had Strindberg so worked up on the whole enemies issue. And I was sure I didn't want to know what he'd been laughing at.

Of course, I was right.

XIII.

Friar

Sherrow wasn't looking so good today, sorta run down and harassed. I thought maybe it might be more of his dad's bullshit, but I didn't have a chance to ask about it 'coz Skills had me sent to his office for a blast of shit soon's we walked in off beat.

"Why are you messing around in homicide?" was the first thing he said, before my ass even touched the seat. I'd been hoping he wouldn't figure out what I'd been doing in my off hours. "Did you wake up one day and think you'd made detective? You haven't. It's not your job. It's not your authority. It's probably illegal."

"Is it?" I settled and tipped my head in question, wondering why this speech was coming now instead of the morning he'd caught me researching.

"I'm not sure. Yer the one digging through the books. Whyncha look it up while yer so busy turning over garbage so old it doesn't even stink anymore."

I looked at him steadily for a minute, then said in a quiet voice,

"It must stink or you wouldn't've smelled it all the way up here. Anyway, you knew I was looking into things and you didn't complain last time we talked."

He grunted.

"If I'd known what it was you were looking at, I would've ordered you to cut it out. Honestly, trying to get any of you guys to do something is like herding cats."

He let me get the image of that in my head, whip and wailing and all, then went on.

"Maybe I don't want more trouble than I already have, Friar. Between you and Canon, I got my plate full. When I told you you could question Mitchell, I didn't tell you you could take over his investigation. Leave it alone, will you? You and Canon are gonna crash head on you keep on the way you've been."

"Canon? That half-life PL we pulled outta the river?" I already knew his opinion of the man, but I wanted to see what bait would rise if I loaded the hook right.

"Watch yer tongue." Anger was suddenly hot in his eyes, even if it didn't reach his face. "He's my old partner's brother-in-law. If one of you's gotta be forking this shit over, I'd rather it was him."

I'd expected him to defend the man, but his reaction was more than I'd anticipated. Guess he liked Canon after all.

"Coz he's your old partner's brother-in-law?" I asked.

"No. Coz he's not my problem. You are. So toe this line I'm laying or you'll be seeing a whole lot more of me, probably in the end with the council behind me, asking all sorts of nasty questions you don't wanna answer, and a wolf ticket in your profile."

"You could always make me detective instead." I said, ignoring the bad fit rep threat. I didn't really want to make detective, but the smart-ass comment came right out.

"I'd have to make you sergeant first. And you haven't solved anything yet."

"And I won't if I listen to your orders."

Skills didn't actually drop his eyes—I'd never seen him do so and no one ever would—but he transferred his gaze from me to some paper or other on his desk and put some wrinkles in the corner of it.

"It's not precisely an order, Friar. It's more of a warning. I don't need this kicked up right now."

"So I can keep doing what I'm doing if I'm more discreet? Should I still visit Mitchell?" I was puzzled. "Are you saying this is an official warning only?"

"Call it that. But I don't wanna hear about you bugging anybody important."

I nodded and got up to go.

"Right."

He suddenly had a sideways grin for me.

"Unless there's a solid conviction to go behind it."

I grinned back.

"I'll see what I can do. Maybe me and the PL should compare notes."

He arched an eyebrow and looked thoughtful. He said maybe he could set up something. He looked at his calendar, not really seeing it, and added a final as I went towards the door.

"Friar."

I gave him my attention over a shoulder.

"Yeah?"

"Be careful." The grin was gone like it had never been. In it's place was a grim seriousness that was just a little scary, because he was acknowledging that the people I might end up bugging didn't want to be bugged and would do something about it.

It was something I'd been avoiding really thinking about, but it was firmly in my mind when I left his office and

went to join my partner for the day's work. It stayed in my mind and tormented me in the wee hours of my sleep time.
***

I went to see Crow and Mitchell just to prove my heart of gold to all who might notice. It never occurred to me that it might put a laser-tag on my ass for the same guy whacked Mitchell to send a torpedo after. I'm not always thinking with the part of my body best suited for it.

Crow was looking okay for a nearly-dead dude, and he cracked all sorts of jokes about how I was looking and who should be on the IV. I told him about our end of the mobile roll and he told me how good it was hear the sirens comin' his way and see the back of the guy shot Delente. There was a dangerous moment where emotion almost showed up, but we blew past it and were out the other side safely without getting mushy, and I promised him the beer I owed and he cursed me good-naturedly for a shirking cheapskate, and off I went to see Mitchell.

Mitchell had been pretty fucked up by the hit and run. Many things had broken and ruptured, and, insult to injury, the back blast of the hover had left luckily fairly minor burns over his face and upper body. Mostly, he had no eyebrows when I saw him, but that was about it. So he looked funny, so what, he was alive and going to be well, if the doctors got their way.

Our conversation was fairly stilted at first.

"Mitchell. How're you feelin'?" .

"Friar. Okay. Thanks for visiting." Pause. "Any news?"

"On who dunnit? Not yet. But the bogeyman was involved. I'd bet my badge on it."

He lowered his already weak voice.

"Caulder? You got a stronger link than I did?"

"I'm not in here with you yet, what do you think?"

"That'd be a no, then, unless you were just smart enough to keep quiet."

"It's a no. I'm still looking, but they pulled Linden off the case, wouldn't say why. He's pissed as hell, but I think he's still spending spare time on it. Like he has much of that. Anyway, he sends hellos and says he'll be by soon, keep y' up to date. The guys all send their best, which isn't much, but they send it. You get the flowers?"

"Yeah, but they gave me allergies."

I laughed then, and he squinted through a smile that looked like laughter would've hurt too much.

"Maybe you need a new job," I suggested. "Get a private card like that license, Canon."

"I'd like to finish the one I started," he said, but I'd caught his attention. "The one from the road house? Has he been involved with your investigations?"

"Not really, but I think he's poking his nose into shit's not his business, if the way he looked at the station the other day 's anything to go by."

Neither of us mentioned what I was doing about shit that was not my business.

"Skills had him picked up again for questions?"

"Didn't have to. He came in all by himself like a drowned rat."

"Voluntarily?"

"Hanging like wet laundry from his noble rescuers." Which had been Sherrow and me. "Somebody tried to drown him, which makes me think he's poking his nose into the right areas. Also tells me he's not our road-house killer, witnesses notwithstanding. I think I'm gonna buy him a drink and see if he talks."

"Will he talk to a cop without the official summons?"

"No, but his sister is married to one, who's Skills old partner, and Skills got me an invite to one of their parties. I got him cornered."

"Poor bastard. I almost feel sorry for him."

"Almost?"

"He's badgeless, isn't he? Never much liked Private Licenses. Snoopers without badges."

"What about snoopers with badges?"

"You talking about the detectives or yourself?"

I shrugged so I wouldn't have to answer a question I hadn't really intended to ask. Mitchell let his eyes drift shut, clearly ready to sleep again, and answered his own question.

"Same-same, pretty much," he said, "Y'know."

I thought I did, since somebody with a badge had to be the one who put him in here. His report fingering Caulder hadn't been made public at any point.

I was just getting swamped in clues pointing me to the door marked "Internal Affairs". Problem was, I didn't trust them either.

"I know." I told him, and left quietly so he could shut out the world some more. It sounded like a great idea to me by that time, and I cabbed back to the station to get my fritzing car. After the cigarette dispenser and the heated foot rail in the cab, my junker looked as inviting as automat food after a year of real cow steak.

It only exacerbated my bad mood, and I brooded about it all the way up fourth street where the car gave out again with a lurch and a cloud of evil smoke.

Canon

Max thought the girl looked dangerous, but the big man bugging her was very, very big, so he kept an eye in that direction.

The very big man made another in his long list of mistakes and grabbed the girl's arm.

He might as well have lit a keg of black powder with a two-second fuse. He probably did things like that on a regular basis. He certainly hadn't paid any attention to her warnings. The fragile misunderstood heroine blew up like ChemBlast and, in three sharp moves, a flash of lightning and two pivots, she had the very big man doubled up and retching on the sticky floor.

Hapkido, Max wondered, or that new one no one could pronounce without practice. It had less keening and more evil-minded pummeling than Karate. Whatever it was, it was effective.

Max gave the lady a nod.

"Blast," she said, one eyebrow going up. "I spilled my drink." Her voice was like silver.

She was Silver. He'd know that rippling voice anywhere. She was one of the trio who'd worked over and nearly drowned him.

"Buy you another?" he offered, trading calculating looks with her.

She declined, maybe because she'd seen his look of sudden recognition. She didn't look nervous exactly, but she looked like she wished to be elsewhere, and Max let her get away on a flimsy excuse and an eyebrow that said they both knew she was lying.

He didn't bother to follow her. He knew she worked for the Caulder crew, and he thought he could find out her name without even leaving the bar. He worked his way into the space vacated by the woman and waited until the owner and 'tender spotted him in the mad swirl. The very big man had been collected by friends and hauled off like a dead 10-point buck. The space cleared by the brief altercation had already filled.

"Ya look good, Max. Never looked better."

Paul Grace shoved a glass across to Max without ceremony. He was constitutionally unable to speak without sarcasm. As long as Max had been coming to his bar, he'd never heard him speak otherwise. Paul made the time of day sound like a bitter joke.

"Thanks, you too."

"Right, 'License. What're you diggin' for in my bar tonight?"

"Not trouble. Who was that little slip with the voice like silver and the fast feet?"

"Dunno, really. They call her Silver. She beating you up?"

"Some Joe too stupid to deserve better. She come here often? With company maybe?"

"You scoping for some dangerous fun, Max? She's not safe, that one. Not...sane."

"Yeah, I thought so too. She come with company ever?"

"Sometimes she has an escort. Usually a tall guy, big shoulders, hands like road maps and eyes like jungle midnight. He's crazy too. You stay away from 'em if you know what is, Max, or just don't do it in my bar."

"You bet, Paul. Maybe I'll take 'em outside, let 'em kill me there."

"If that's what you're looking for, pal, I can set you up much sooner than that."

Somebody yelled for service down at the other end of the bar and Max waved him goodbye and shot the drink down.

Interesting. Silver. Interesting that his mental name for her had been accurate. Wonder if it had to do with the silver wrapped knife handle Max had spotted under her coat or her silver blonde hair.

He really didn't want to find out, but he was pretty sure he'd have to, or it'd find him.

*

Max dreamt. There was a bar and a beautiful woman, Mrs. March? No, it was Anne, Anne in an evening gown, the same gown Mrs. March had been wearing, only there was blood on it. Anne was dancing with a large man in a brimmed hat and the two looked very intimate. The man had handcuffs hanging from one wrist and Anne had an issue rifle in her hands behind his back, locking them together. She was grinning.

Before Max could figure out what that all meant, a familiar face hove into view blocking the dancing couple.

"Talked to Anne lately?" Bart Capelli sneered. When he looked, Anne and the large man were gone, and Mrs. March stood by Capelli, looking arch. Capelli was wearing a uniform with a bloodstained flower in his buttonhole, grinning with broken teeth at Max over a spilled drink and a bar stool. "Still missing your little Annie?" The grin became a leer. "I don't miss her, Max. I get to see her every day. Every day. We live in the same house." The hint was as clear as it was lewd.

Max put his fist through the leer. Capelli's face collapsed around it like a rotten pumpkin, jaws and teeth shattering like shrapnel and perforating Max's forearm. Damn. He'd wanted him alive to answer questions about Anne. Was she still alive? He must be dreaming this. Hadn't Capelli joked like this back in the war, hinting about Anne and some maybe not-so-legal activities going on in the

squad? Max swung to his feet, trading blows with the
headless corpse over the honor of a woman many years
dead.

There was a spectacular blow to the back of his head
and he went down.

He woke sweating, with his right fist clenched, the arm
asleep.

He shook it out, getting up to pace, shake off the
dream.

Then he remembered; Swinging at Capelli in the bar,
for real, and missing in the sudden melee. Somebody else
jumping him from behind, a flurry of strikes and blows and
the whirlpool of fighters coughing up Capelli again, with
hatred flashing in adrenaline-bright eyes. The bottle in
Capelli's hand, someone else with a knife behind, women
screaming. Sudden light like bright mercury on the raised
blade, dodging away and incidentally under Capelli's bottle.

That was more like it. That's what had happened in
the bar.

Max sat down, looking towards the moonlight
splashing palely onto the bare floor under the window. So
Anne hadn't been there. There was no Anne. But there was
Jolie Laide and Mrs. Stephanie Lovely March and the
random dancer Melody Miller from Mrs. March's dancer
days. And that bastard Capelli had been in a fight that Max
had to get him out of, had to make him answer questions
about...Anne. Had he really said something about Anne?

Max's head whirled. It was as unpleasant a sensation as
it was unfamiliar and unwelcome. He was so tired. He lay
back down and tried to concentrate on the dream, to sort the
truth from the fiction. He laid one arm across his eyes and
fell back asleep.

When Max woke again, it was close to dawn. The
room was in shadows, starkly offset by the slashes of blue-
white neon stamped across the walls from the blinds.
Movement in the living room brought him up, rubbing
uselessly at gritty eyes. A black silhouette hove into view

suddenly around the doorframe and paused, head turning towards the bed.

Eddy. Max fell back on the bed and rubbed his eyes again. Only Eddy.

"You dreaming about Anne again?" Eddy's voice sounded tired. He turned on the overhead, a pale yellow flood, not quite strong enough to hurt Max's burning eyes.

"Was I?" Max rubbed again, hopelessly and sat himself up like the body belonged to someone else. He tried rubbing his head instead, but hit bruises and stopped. "Ah."

Eddy leaned in the doorway in his shirtsleeves, tie at half-mast.

"Yeah. You were calling her name like you do."

That was more than Max wanted to believe was common knowledge. He swung his legs off the bed and contemplated the floor. He wondered if he shouldn't ask Eddy how he'd gotten in, then didn't want to know.

"I do that, do I?"

"Yeah." Eddy came around in a careful slouch to lean on the wall in Max's line of sight. "Max. What are you into? It's got you bugged, if you're dreaming about those days. I know that much." His posture said 'interrogation stance' but his face said worried.

"I don't know." Max got to his feet and avoided his brother-in-law into the living room. He went to the window and pried the blinds open a tiny crack to look out on the street. "I really don't know. But I think it's big." He grinned at that and flashed it around to Eddy. "That sounds stupid, doesn't it?" He looked back out the window. Light touched off his left eye and showed him colorless gray in the slice of window that showed between the slats. "But there's something."

Eddy didn't say anything. Max let the blinds close, and turned to look at the policeman. The silence stretched for a long, fragile moment, then Eddy picked up his jacket from the back of the sofa and started towards the door.

"I won't say anything to Ruth."

"Thanks."

"Don't mention it."

Eddy left without the lecture Max knew he was dying to give, or asking any of the burning questions that had obviously brought him here uninvited. Grateful, Max watched him go in silence, wondering how much longer Eddy would be so polite. It couldn't be easy, and Max knew Frank Skills enough to know that he'd start leaning on them both if things didn't start resolving soon.

Max began to feel like a target standing in the window, blinds or not, and he moved back into the room again, unhappily reminded of his army days and wondering if he'd ever get past it. At least it was a change from worrying about Capelli and dreaming about Anne.

Wasn't it? He tried to concentrate on something innocuous, but it didn't work this time. He kept seeing dead men and elegant, cool women. And guns. Always guns.

Friar

I left the smoking car in the hands of the tow guy and went to the nearest bar to wait for the cab. It turned out to be a Caulder-owned nightclub and, with Mitchell so clearly on my mind in all his near-dead glory, I lost what temper I had left and beat the shit outta the doorman when he tried to give me trouble. I avoided getting scragged in return, retreating in good order and muttering something inane like, 'that was for Mitchell, scum sucker,' as I fled the scene, but it wasn't my finest moment. My head hurt and what I really needed was a good workout to clear my system, but this was not the part of town for the kind of workout I was needing, and I ended up waiting for the cab in the well-lit strip where the prostitutes jobbed. One of the ladies asked me to stand further away because I reeked of cop and it was spoiling business.

The whole thing didn't get me into trouble surprisingly, but it didn't earn me any points with superiors, either. I certainly wasn't proud of it myself. But I did find out by rumor and facial expressions the next day that it earned me plenty with my fellow officers when it was seen as defending the side from cop-killers and their bosses. It was seen as turnabout being fair play, with the wounded doorman written off as a football casualty, the coach dogging along after the players, slapping asses and bellowing good-boy. Coach here was Strindberg, who was unnecessarily gleeful about the whole thing. I hadn't been wearing anything on-dutyish while I brutally satisfied my need to pummel something, but Cop is stamped on my forehead, and it was a rumor that swept three precincts and the Speakeasy before I'd even made it home with my bruises and three loose teeth.

Ballistic was sometimes ignored by superiors, too, especially when it looked like retribution. I'm not proud of that either, but it's sometimes true. I was reprimanded, but not punished, and no one actually had the nerve to ask me if it had really been me. Caulder didn't say a thing, and the press-dogs were left twisting in the wind of rumor, with nothing solid to print.

All my captain had to say was loud, disapproving and largely unprintable. Crocker was not a condoning superior, and the only part that stuck with me, and stuck with me good, was the accusatory, disgusted bit that went,

"Who told you that was appropriate behavior, Friar? Where'd you learn that shit? Cause you sure as Hell didn't learn it in Academy and you didn't learn it from Kay or your other partners. I hope to God you can unlearn it, and quick, or yer no better than Caulder's thugs. I don't want thugs in my department. I won't have thugs in my department."

Thug. Was that me? Maybe I was 'cause I'd been acting like it. The captain obviously thought so.

I was thankful in retrospect that it wouldn't go on my record along with the police brutality charge, because it had been stupid in the first place, and the guy hadn't deserved it. He'd done okay for himself, but strained a wrist or something which cost him work, so I'd actually taken bread out of his mouth. It left me feeling shittier than I already did.

There was so much for me to feel shitty about these days that I wondered if I should just give up my job and retire to a nice production job where the only temper problems I had could be taken out on a machine with a hammer.

But there were still bad guys who were getting away with it. That had to be finished first.

I was doomed to an eternity of cop-hood. And I'd always be right on the edge of bad-cop unless I learned to control my temper.

Which was what counseling was for, so I called Kay and we went out for drinks that very night.

XIV.

Canon

Max wore a new suit, gray with a slight silver weave, black tie and hat to the rendezvous with Mrs. March at the shopping mall on ninth level of Meeker Plaza.

Her smile was wide when she saw him. They way it lit her eyes was distracting.

"Fancy rig," she said.

Max grinned, acknowledging that she was aware it was new.

"This is nothing," he told her, "You oughta see me in church."

"Unlikely," she said.

"Lapsed?" he inquired, turning to look at the bodyguard she had with her. The man gave him a considering look.

"Lazy." She gave the bodyguard a small nod and turned her back on him as if he had ceased to exist. "You?"

"I was never much for religion." Max eyed her outfit. She was in Nazi Chic. Tall black boots over second-skin black trousers, tailored black jacket with red ornaments and—the French underground touch—a beret over hair braided into a thick flaxen coil around her neat head. Ah, retro couture.

Max nodded approvingly and fell into step with her. Around them the shopping mall bustled with activity. Mrs. March's bodyguard trailed them unhappily, eyeing Max with an expression that told of an inner conflict. Max knew he had about five minutes before the bodyguard decided to act.

Mrs. March got her first good look at his face. She controlled a smile and said,

"When you're working the johns you learn to use makeup to cover the bruises," she said, "It keeps the rest of 'em from getting the same idea. Plus it improves commerce." She tilted her lovely head and slanted a cat smile at him. "I could teach you."

"No thanks." Max looked around, gauging the crowd, the venue and the general mood. Bodyguard was looking like thoughts were crossing his mind and causing him pain. "Bruises make a man look tougher. Opposite effect, I guess."

"That's a common misconception," Mrs. March turned to look in a store window, her smile more pronounced. "It makes a man look like he lost." She turned it back on Max. "Offer's still open."

"For makeup lessons? No thanks. Why don't you tell me why you're allowed to see me these days? Most of these bruises came from a friendly warning to stay away from you."

"The terrible trio, right? Dan has them busy elsewhere. They won't follow you for a few more days at least." Despite her casual air, Max could see she had no appreciation for the so-called trio. There might even be an edge he could call fear in her voice.

"So, what's up?" he asked, directing her attention to another window display as if either of them actually cared about the latest trend in shoes.

"Fokke sent another letter. I have two days to come up with the installment."

"So he'll take money even if he can't have you. Do you have it?"

She turned her head to look at him, eyes huge and glossy in a perfect, matte-finish face.

"Yes. Are you telling me to pay him?"

"You have been, haven't you? Or do you prefer the alternative?"

She dropped her eyes, then put them back on the Chinese stilt shoes. She made a gesture that implied interest in the lime and yellow patterned pair. Max looked at black butterflies on lemon-lime and winced. The bodyguard hovered just out of earshot, or maybe not quite.

Max cast him a look and smiled for the man, who was glaring blackly. Two minutes to decision.

"Go ahead and do the trade. How do you meet him?"

"I drop the money at a deposit box, at a link-café on the west side. Murphy's."

"Irish." Max gave her a look. "You Irish, Stephanie?"

"No. You?"

"No. I'm a mutt. We're a bit of everything in my family."

They started walking again and the bodyguard fell into step again. Max caught a look at him in an angled window and decided he had maybe a minute more.

"Let me know when the drop is. I'll figure something out."

"Okay, Max. I will." She stopped walking again and took his hand. Max felt the bodyguard move up close enough behind to make him feel crowded. "Thank you, Mr. Canon."

"My pleasure, Ma'am," Max let her cue for formality lead him and he shook her hand, tipped his hat and walked off.

As they separated in the crowd, Max heard her telling the bodyguard in a sharp voice that something was none of his business, and something about old friends.

Whatever. Maybe they'd have a lead to go on soon. That was what mattered.

That and that no one had beat Max up yet today.

Thank heaven for small things.

Friar

I called Noel back. She said she was going to be in town again for a few days, and would I like to go out to dinner? I thought, hey, would I ever, but I said, sure I think I can fit that into my busy social schedule. She said, oh, is the Department Picnic so soon?

Ha ha, I said.

Sherrow told me not to go, then he told me okay, but be careful, and I wasn't sure why. He'd wanted to eat at the automat on 49th, which I didn't, but it wasn't my turn to choose the place. I hated the place coz it was done in Road Warrior, and looked like a junkyard, with old-fashioned cars gutted and set with vending units and dinettes, and tribal-apocalypse decor all over the damn place.

But I had zero desire to court indigestion by eating anywhere Wells could get at me with his latest joke-fest about rogue cops who went after innocent doormen, so I didn't kick too hard, and there we were in an old Mercury hulk with a ring mount .50--belt-fed, no less, it belonged in a museum—eating prepackaged irradiated-heat food under a threatening ceiling ornament made out of a junked truck radiator fan and a hover exhaust sleeve.

We didn't look as out of place as I woulda thought.

I took a bite of lasagna and couldn't control a grimace.

"At least I'll eat real food tomorrow night," I said, without much energy.

Sherrow was poking at his meal like it had moved and he couldn't decide if it had to be killed again before he ate it.

"Not eating at home, then, I guess."

"Everybody being funny today. Noel's in town. She's meeting me at the Pearl Harbor for dinner."

"Noel. Oh."

" And that means?"

Sherrow wasn't looking at me, a sure sign he didn't really want to answer my question. When he looked up, he was very serious and uncomfortable, eyes flat across the bottom.

"I don't like it, Vic. There's something not healthy about your relationship with that woman."

That set me back and I'm sure my face changed, not in anger, though it may have looked like it.

"I don't mean it like that," he started in a rush, then paused, "Well, I do, but, look. That chick in the roadhouse…Does Noel have a sister?"

Another set back for me but this one brought blank astonishment.

"No. You think she looks like the civi from the roadhouse? Wassername, Laide? The Laide woman?"

"Sorta. Maybe. I dunno. There's just something…not right about it all." His eyes were down again, on the fork doing major damage to his meal but not actually carrying any food to his mouth. "Could she be in town more often than you're aware of?"

"You do think it was her." I sat back and pushed the terrible food across into the disposal hatch, not hungry anymore. I was getting angry at his insistence and what I wanted to believe was stupidity and rookie faith in a chance resemblance—I hadn't gotten much of a look at the Laide women myself—but there are really things like hunches and the people drawn to be cops and detectives and priests sometimes have 'em in quality and in quantity. I didn't want to think about his maybe-hunch.

"I don't," he insisted, lying in the face of my upset. I wasn't hiding my reactions all that well, not unusual for a guy like me. Reactions were usually linked to emotion, something I never got good training in handling.

"You do. So maybe she's in town often and doesn't call me, so? We're divorced, and it's not like we're friends anymore."

"So maybe she's into stuff incompatible with yer job and that's why she avoids you. Maf stuff."

"Nicely put. Bullshit, but nicely put."

"Why bullshit? It wouldn't be too hard, and it wouldn't be the first time a cop's ex went to the other side."

"Nah. I'd hear about it. Jees, you think she could be into illegal activities without some smart ass or other on the force rubbing it in? No way. Noel might go for illegal games, I can see that, but no way a cop can keep his mouth shut when he can flip another cop shit."

"She wouldn't come to police notice if she was never caught."

"Depends on who she fraternizes with. I think she's not in town. Not often." But I was remembering her in the store, how new her look was now, how different from then.

Sherrow sent his meal, largely untasted, after mine.

"I'm sorry, Vic. But I have to tell you I think she's with Caulder's crew. I'm sure it was her in the roadhouse. Her voice on the phone message… and the photo you forgot to take out of your wallet and the one in the back of your locker…"

"That's still there?" I'd forgotten it was even there: It was usually buried behind body armor.

"Contact lenses, hair dye, drugs, you didn't recognize her, but you hardly saw her and you never heard her speak And she was scared white before you left the room. Really scared, I mean."

"I already said it coulda been her, lay off me." I was getting mad again, because he was convincing me it could be so and the photo in the locker thing was truly a shock to me. Did I still love her deep down? I still cared, sure, but maybe Sherrow was the kind of partner who made you look at yourself in a new way, exactly the kind of partner I didn't want at this stage of my life. Every time he opened his mouth, I got to see myself in a new way, and these new angles weren't flattering.

"I'm just saying."

"So stop already. It's bullshit, okay?" I stood up, but he saw my eyes before I managed to turn them away, and I saw his expression. His tone said it all.

"Whatever, man. Just…when you do go, be careful, huh?"

"Sure, yeah." I kept my back to him, looking at the street through the window behind me in the reflection of a chromed truck grill. The hood ornament was a bulldog. It looked a little like the reflection of me right now, all jaw and low brow ridge. Yeah, the kid had really upset me. "Yeah, I'll be careful."

I actually thought he meant to watch my back, but he meant be careful with my heart.

Some kid, huh.

XV.

Canon

Eddy visited Max at his office for the maybe second time ever. He looked around at everything like he was memorizing, then looked at Max's current state of disrepair, like it surprised him after the kind of night Max had had. He shook his head.

"Didn't get a good look at you earlier. What'd they do this time?"

Max waved him to the sofa and started to the back room to get coffee.

"Nothing. It's a war of attrition."

Eddy shook his head again.

"Yer gonna lose, man."

Max offered him coffee.

'Sure, long's I don't have to make it."

Eddy was referring to the coffee maker Max had inherited from him. Ruth had bought it for him one Birthday as the cutting edge coffee-making contraption of the year, and Eddy hated it. It was a mess of fancy glass globes and chrome tubing that made noise like an unmuffled distillery, which it also resembled. It had ended up in Max's office, replaced in the Archer home with a discreet black and white plastic cube that belched out reasonable coffee in polite near-silence.

Max flipped the switch on Coffee Frankenstein and a low rumble began. Glassware trembled and smoked. Eddy came to the door to watch, at a careful distance.

"Damn," was all he said.

Max shrugged.

"Coffee in five."

"That in minutes or hours?" Eddy asked, eyes following the mad rush of liquid through various tubes and receptacles. "Only I'm on my lunch break."

"Very funny." Max led him back into the office proper. "So why another visit so soon? They finally decide I'm guilty of something worth dragging me in over?"

"They wouldn't've sent me if that was it, Max. You know that. I'm hiding from my partner. He's all hot on this latest case and I can't bear it anymore. We've been over it so many times my brain is swiss-cheesing. I needed a break."

Max nodded, recognizing the feeling.

"I know that one. You only go so far on logic. I thought you guys were trained in abstract philosophical assembly."

Eddy grinned ear to ear at the term. It was a complicated logic-grid system that the department had toyed with for a year or so before discarding it as a waste of time. For a little while, the man who had developed it had been very famous, and a large number of police officers had been encouraged to think non-linearly in an objective and de-constructive fashion. It hadn't done much but frustrate the same large number of officers and make the creator briefly rich.

"Out of fashion," Eddy said to Max's back. Glassware tinked and rattled and Max returned, bearing coffee in two thankfully normal mugs.

"Here." Max handed one over.

"So tell me what's going on in your work." Eddy urged. He sounded hearty and cheerful, which meant he had little hope Max would tell him anything at all.

"Well," Max sat down behind his desk, "I haven't actually tied anything up yet, but I have some names to play with." He looked at Eddy, weighing choices. "Caulder was one of 'em."

Eddy sat up straight and spilled coffee over his hand.

"Ow." He wasn't referring to the spill. "Max..."

"I know." Max didn't make him scavenge for a response. "I know. I told you it was big. There's something about that roadhouse kill that's got me bugged. The guy was in my unit in the war, and something keeps bringing me back to that." He looked out the office window as if the city would cough up answers for him if he looked long enough. Gray daylight showed him the ugly buildings hunching together like they were trying to keep him out, like linemen on the opposing team.

Eddy waited, but Max didn't go on.

"You think this has to do with the war?" he prompted after a pause.

"I don't know. Possibly." Max turned his eyes back inside the office. "There were rumors of drug runners in the military, I'm sure you heard about that way back when. You always get opportunists during a conflict, and there were so many drugs around after we'd capture territory. Maybe Capelli was one of 'em. It sure fit his character."

Eddy shifted in his chair, his turn to weigh Max.

"You've heard about the flush of illegal drugs in town, then?"

Max grinned and sipped coffee.

"Oh, yeah. The Speakeasy's rotten with Warp right now. Rumor has it that it's home-source, but I have proof it's off-world."

"And you think it ties in with Caulder?"

"Maybe. I just don't know. If Capelli was working for Caulder--he was escorting Daily's woman, wasn't he?—and he was streaming Warp into the area for an off-world supplier, wouldn't one of the Mafs be upset enough to scrub him? Even Caulder himself?"

"Sure. But you have no proof of any of this, do you?"

"Nope. I have Capelli with Caulder's lady, I have off-world Warp in town, and I have a pack of memories that keep getting in the way of clear thinking. Maybe I need a break, too."

Eddy drank off his coffee, and stood up, eyes on the clock.

"I gotta go, Max. Whyncha take that break? It sometimes helps."

"Did it help you any?"

"Nah, but I got away from my work for awhile, anyway."

"Bullshit. You're just as curious about what I'm doing. And I don't believe for one minute you turned off the cop when you came in here. You think of any nice connections, let me know? It is Caulder I'm dealing with here."

Eddy Archer put the mug down on the desk, eyes dark and grave.

"I know. If I could warn you off and make it stick, I would, too. Promise to trade nice connections with me and it's a deal."

"You're not working the case, are you?"

"No, but the guy who was got a warning that nearly killed him, so I'd appreciate it if you could give us anything that could help."

"Cop solidarity." Max stood up to shake Eddy's hand across the blotter. "Deal. I understand that kind of network."

"It could work for you, too, if you were more cooperative more often with the department."

"And ruin my rep? Don't be funny, Eddy. Give my love to Ruth."

"Do it yourself. The royal presence has demanded your attendance tonight at a party over on the east side. Cappy's throwing a shindig."

"And Ruth just wants me along for why?"

"Hell if I know, Max. You don't exactly enhance my reputation with the department. But Ruth wants you there, so please do this one for me? You owe me a favor after all."

Max sighed and looked towards the glare-filled window.

"I do. I'll be there. Meet at your place?"

"Sure. And Max…" For a second Eddy paused, then he shook his head. "Skip it. Have a nice day."

"Sure. You too."

Eddy left on the tail of that unfinished sentence to Max to be careful, but just like the night before, the warning hung in the air long after he left, imprinted by worry.

It made Max feel like a lousy brother-in-law.

Friar

I met Kay for lunch, something unusual, but Sherrow's girl had shown up at the place we went to eat at, and I thought maybe Kay was there for a reason, like maybe Sherrow called him in to run interference by being my date. Whatever reason, he'd been told about my dinner plans that night with Noel, and he seemed to think I needed advice about her.

"It's good you two are still friends," he was saying around bites of roast beef sandwich.

I nodded, encouraging him to rattle so I could eat my meal in time to get back on shift without penalty. I figured it'd take me ten minutes to pry Sherrow away from his fiancé.

"Still, you need to let it go, Vic." He was looking fatherly, something I'd come to dread over the years. "The divorce, I mean. It wasn't your fault. Do you see Noel married now?"

"No." I had to answer, but I didn't have to say much.

"Right." He nodded firmly. "She tried once more and dropped him within a year. She's not the marrying kind, Vic."

"She sure looked that way at the judge's office."

"All women look that way at the judge's office. It's at divorce court that they look different. And yer FNG told me you were screaming at each other in the cereal aisle at Brisby's."

"Asshole. You got him spyin' now?"

"We ran into each other at the water fountain and he introduced himself."

"You mean you bought him a beer at the watering hole, the other day. He ask you to marry him over a nice cool drink?"

Kay got up and gave me a pitying look as he tossed off his coffee and threw money on the table.

"Don't be stupid, Vic," he said, glancing around the restaurant. He turned his eyes back to me. "He's married to you."

He left me alone to gaze across to where Sherrow sat with his fiancé. He glanced up at Kay's movement through his peripheral vision, then looked over at me. His lady said something more to him, and it took a second for her to get his attention back. After that, she patted his hand and rose. I was seeing, I thought, a woman who might actually understand about partners. Maybe she had brothers. Maybe she was a cop herself.

Maybe I was the only one who picked women who didn't understand and didn't want to try. I ate the last of my BLT and checked my gun while standing, wiping my mouth and greeting Sherrow with,

"We set?"

"Sure thing, Vic. Thanks for the time out."

"You bet, kid. Just don't sic Kay on me anymore, okay?"

"Not my idea, man. Hey, is that the radio I hear?" Like he didn't have the mobile rig hanging off his collar.

"Let's go see," I said, like I didn't have one of my own.

We went back to the car, pretending.

My little brother came to my wedding in a T-shirt and ostrich jeans and told me how weird it was to see me in a tailored suit and how it made me look bigger, big, like, like a great big guy. Intimidating.

That was before he fell in love himself and married and went away to a colony doomed to get wasted by tetchy terrorists.

Sometime I hate my life.

Sherrow drove me home again, damn my broken-down car, and he'd changed into a tailored suit to meet his lady.

We went by the warehouse, you know the one, and the rain fell through whatever force field was there and made it look like there wasn't one.

"High res," he said, guessing.

"Electro magnetic. Fog beads off coz of the repulsor-effect," I guessed.

Sherrow and I looked at it a while longer, then he shrugged and drove on fast and loose enough to scare the old man.

I bid him goodnight then went to stare into my closet and see if I had anything to wear to this party Skills had gotten me invited to. I would rather have danced naked through the Speakeasy with 'cop' painted on my ass, but if I wanted to talk to this Canon, I'd have to start on neutral ground.

My wardrobe was Noel-old and I had nothing to wear. I ended up at an all night shop where the sales girl giggled and dressed me in the latest fashion like I was an AstroTrooper doll, i.e. stupid, but capable of looking okay, if somebody else did all the work. When she was done, I was inclined to think she was right, but it would do and it didn't quite bankrupt me.

Hell, and now I had something to wear when I saw Noel for dinner that she wouldn't recognize. I would look a touch less pathetic. That thought vaguely cheered me, and I hailed a cab and set off in a fairly good mood.

Canon

Max did his duty by his family by being there, but after the fruitless stake out of Murphy's with a no-show Mrs. March, he wasn't really in a party mood. The party was exactly like one of Ruth and Eddy's, except that there was a library at this house where Max could hide when he wanted to stop feeling like a pariah. Then he'd cruise out again so Ruth could see his face and know he hadn't run away yet, get a fresh drink and slink back to his lair.

The third time he executed this maneuver, he found somebody else had the same idea. He got a good look at the back of the man's head as he examined the painting of a quasar field that hung over the fireplace. The painting reminded Max of an armada burning, and the man's haircut made him look like a cop, even if he was wearing a cutting-edge full length flanged bronze leather coat and black microfiber paramilitary trousers of the latest cut. When Max saw the multifunction watch, he knew.

"Good evening, officer." Max announced his arrival, but he got the impression the man had already known he was there.

The officer turned. He was a cop Max had seen once or twice before in the precinct halls. His eyes were the same color as his coat in a rough face. Rugged might almost describe him if it could also be stretched to describe a climb up K2. He held a bottle of local brew in a blunt-fingered hand.

"Hi." He barely managed to pause before adding, "You're Max Canon, aren't you. I'm Friar. Victor Friar."

There was no question in his statement, and Max shook his hand warily, nodding.

"Pleasure to meet you, Mr. Friar."

"Don't even." Friar's face stretched in a grimace that might've been meant to be a grin. "Call me Friar or Vic or something. 'S too late for formality."

"Too late?" Max took a seat in one of the painfully traditional leather armchairs, putting the fire on his left and his drink on an end table of cypress knee.

"Skills sicced me on you. Well, actually, I asked about you and he arranged this." Friar sat down while he cataloged this confession then gave Max a real grin. "You've been set up."

Max let a smile tug up one side of his face, but he was still wary.

"Set up for what? You two seem to have the better of me in this."

Friar put his bottle on the hearthstone and wiped the moisture off on one immaculate pant leg. Max could smell the leather of his coat it was so new.

"I'm not sure how to broach this. Skills said we were gonna run into each other, we kept on looking into this same case, and I've reached a point where I'd like to maybe compare notes with another interested professional."

His expression was open and honest and maybe a little bit angry. Max tried to decide if he was for real.

"The Capelli murder."

Friar nodded.

"Are you working this one for Skills?"

"No. I'm beat cop. I'm pursuing this without authorization or authority." It was baldly said and definitely angry.

"Well, that makes two of us then." Max picked up his drink and gave Friar his first genuine smile of the evening.

He sat back in the chair and tasted the latest mix. Too weak. He put it back on the table and looked across at the beat cop. "You initiated this, you go first."

Friar looked uncomfortable.

"I'm not sure how to go about this. My usual informants, I can squeeze. Yer a free agent." He looked into the fire for a moment, lighting his eyes red and gold. "You heard Mitchell, the officer originally on the case, had an unfortunate accident? And now his partner's been pulled off the case by persons unknown. You see why I'm talking to you."

Max nodded. He did see.

"I'm not department. But is this the best place to be talking about this?"

Friar shrugged.

"Ya gotta use the chances you get. If I cornered you on the street you'd think I was official or something."

"And that would be illegal. What's that called, fraud, intimidation?"

Friar reclaimed the sweating bottle and took a long pull.

"Dunno. Don't care. I want your help, not your antagonism. So I'm trying to play fair. You willing to compare notes or what?"

Max thought about what he had and what he might be able to get from a cop who didn't seem as picky about cases that weren't his as Eddy, and then he thought about swimming in the river and crooked officers. He squinted over at Friar and asked point blank,

"Why do you care?"

Friar turned his head away from the fire to look across the room and his bronze eyes went black in the shadow cast. One thumb slicked through the film of moisture on the bottle like it was thinking of other things that might or might not include throwing the drink against a wall. There was tension in the line of the man's shoulders that looked like bottled rage, or undiluted hydrochloric cynicism.

When he turned his eyes back to Max, the shadows didn't leave them, but Max couldn't be sure what they meant. He'd rarely seen eyes so hard to read.

"It's a favor for a pal."

Max didn't believe him, but he was willing to risk it for a chance at information. He nodded and rose.

"Let's go get a real drink, away from your compatriots."

"These?" Friar grinned at that, but it didn't reach the eyes. "These are detectives, mostly. I'm street."

"So you don't mind leaving them behind."

"I was thinking I'd have to suggest it myself."

They traded grins and left in wary charity with each other to retire to a nearby bar that served anybody at all who could pay hard cash and wasn't too choosy about what they did while they were there.

Friar

The PL turned out to be an okay guy, even if I still didn't put as much trust in him as Skills did. I was maybe biased by his profession. I'm sure he was biased by mine. We drank a few drinks in a dive off Kilder Avenue in a corner booth where nobody could see or hear us, the place was so dark and noisy. We ended up head to head over the table just trying to hear each other without shouting.

I started it, since I'd started it by asking Skills for the intro, and gave him the run on the warehouse and the March woman belonging to Caulder. He knew that last one, I could tell by his eyes, close in as we were, but the warehouse was new to him, and not of immediate interest, though he did write it down. I told him about Mitchell having a lead that tied Caulder into the murder before the hit and run, and the woman Georgia Grau, aka 'Silver' and her penchant for giving out free samples of illegal drugs. I didn't say who she gave them to.

In return, Canon told me about the March woman and a Melody Miller working at the Emerald City together, and we agreed that there was evidence that tied them both to Capelli. He had data on Caulder's trio of enforcers that included Grau and he really surprised me when he mentioned serving with Capelli in the 101 Fast Launch. I hadn't figured him for a vet, though looking at him with the faint scars that marred his temples and streaked his hair with white it really wasn't much of a surprise.

After that, we discussed the sudden appearance of Warp in our fair city and speculated on Caulder's participation in it. He talked about rumors of import from Bimini Ridge Colony and I mentioned how much property Caulder owned in this city and how easy it could be to set up a distribution center, as long as it didn't stay in any one place for too long. Everybody knew exactly how long it took us to find patterns and track 'em. Sometimes undercover is the way to go. He looked interested when I mentioned Caulder owning Mrs. March's building, but neither of us could come up with a way to tie it into the Warp ring, unless there was a storage facility in the basement being used for contraband, but with no way to check it out, we had to shelve that interesting idea for a later date or a court order.

By the time we'd gotten that far, it was so late it was early and while I knew we weren't done, neither was I going to be able to function if I didn't get some sleep. My greatest concern was that Canon would regret the collaboration and dodge me if I tried to tap him again, but it finally reached the point where I couldn't control my yawns anymore and when I resplit my lip, Canon called it.

"Yer bleeding into your drink. It's time to go home, Friar." He threw money on the table, but I waved it away.

"I got it. At least I got a steady job, and yer good to come out and talk with me. I don't know what good we've done, but maybe there's a new lead in there somewhere." I fed money into the table box and got a receipt back. "You let me know if you come up with anything else?"

"Sure. And you."

"Sure. You got my number?" I unearthed my card case from the depths of unfamiliar pockets and handed a business card over to Canon. It was a fumbly process: The new coat looked comic-book cool, but it would take awhile getting used to it. I wasn't sure I liked it enough to wear it off duty. I felt like I was dressed ten years too young. Canon didn't seem to notice anything unusual.

"Right. Nice meeting you, Friar. Good night."

"Yeah. You, too, Canon." I watched him leave, seeing how he blended into the room around him like camouflage. It was a skill that took years to learn, and I heard the word 'vet' run through my mind again. Maybe I should look into his past a little more. You never knew what could come up.

I checked to make sure my notepad was off and stored safely and fished around for the filters that had come with the coat. They were antique bronze-framed with mirrored lenses, and while I hated wearing filters, they were compulsory for fashionable street wear, and I was trying to look less like a cop.

As I slid them on, I thought I saw a familiar face across the bar. When I tilted the filters down to look over the top, the face was gone in the crowd. Nobody I knew was in sight. With an uneasy feeling of being watched, I left in Canon's wake, far less good at the urban blend. I couldn't tell who it had been if it had been anybody, but I wasn't easy until I was home and locked behind my own armored door.

I only hoped it wasn't the same guy who liked to hit and run detectives. I didn't have a chance if it was.

XVI.

Canon

It was raining. If it kept up, it might eventually cool down the city from the residual heat of a surprisingly hot day. Max spent the afternoon in the telefax records morgue listening to it drum on the roof and by nightfall, all it had done was fill the city with twisting wraiths as water steamed off the hot streets and cooked off bank after bank of neon and colored marquis, shrouding even the dirtiest change bar in smoky mystery.

Max thought it was the biggest steam bath he'd ever been in clothed. Indian summer was only good if you had countryside. With concrete and a city so hugely vertical there were parts where you could see the stars at noon it wasn't so lovely or welcome.

It was steamy. Sweaty. Sort of like this day had been. And weird. Sort of like this night would be.

Max took a look around the place while the owner's wife went to find the owner. She had danced there, too, according to the photos along the wall. There was a Technicolor movie shot of her doing some complicated wiggling in an abbreviated costume maybe 20 years ago. She'd been gawky then, but she'd certainly grown into her looks. Max cast an appreciative glance her way as she came back up the narrow aisle between bar and tables and milling patrons: she had a gyration like oiled pistons, and it made Max pleasantly aware of the more enjoyable sins. Too bad she was married.

"He'll be right out. He's doing the books, so I can't guarantee his mood."

"I'll risk it," Max had to smile at that, thoughts of his own bills looming into a rare moment of focus, then fading thankfully back into the unimportant recesses of memory. He'd have to deal with them soon, though, soon.

Harold "Hank" Browden had owned the Lucky Lucy Lounge for the past thirty years. He was on the shady side of 55, and the graying fox sort, though the beef in his shoulders was turning soft from too much bookwork and not enough bouncer work. Max knew he'd been divorced from a cute young thing about 6 years back but she was not so cute now after three kids and a string of lovers, so maybe he'd lucked out in the end.

There was nothing remarkable about the man, really, until he spoke.

Max listened to the deep bronze tones greet him hello and grinned.

"I'd love to hear you sing," he said, extending a hand.

"Can't carry a tune in a bucket," Browden grinned back, and shook. "What can I do for you, Mr. Canon, was it?" Lights from the dance floor colored his eyes green-gold.

"Yeah. I'm a privately licensed detective looking for leads on a dancer who worked this strip about 5-7 years back, name of Melody Miller." Max pulled out a promo shot from his archives search on the Emerald City. Somebody down at one bar or another had identified this girl as Miller and decided she'd worked at the Lucy before she graduated to the Emerald City as a cage dancer on the top floor and maybe a hostess in the basement levels. She'd been in the business at the same time as Mrs. March. She'd been one of Caulder's hangers on and she'd been linked in the arrest reports to Bart Capelli's crowd.

Browden took the print and turned to the bar light to squint over it.

"Yeah, I remember her. She used to come in here sometimes even after she quit the circuit."

"She quit? I heard she'd moved on to the Emerald City." Max leaned closer in an effort to defeat the noise of the crowd and secure at least a modicum of privacy.

Browden waved the 'tender over and made a loose gesture asking Max what he wanted to drink.

"She tried to hire in, but they wouldn't take her. She worked volunteer for a few months, y'know, working for tips, that sorta thing, with house approval, but she got arrested one time too many with the wrong sorts and they gave her the heave ho."

Max accepted a whisky and sipped. Browden slid a wet beer across the polished marble bar-top in a collision course with his mouth. Foam spilled like bubble bath down the side as he hoisted.

"Thanks." Max acknowledged the free drink and went on, "I didn't know the Emerald City knew what a wrong sort was. Half of Daily's crew came from there originally, didn't they?"

"Well, if we're talkin' about Caulder, I'll have to ask you to leave. Not good for business."

Max nodded.

"Okay, we won't then." He smiled. "I hate to waste a free drink. You have no idea how few people will even talk to me once the initials come out."

"PL? I had a cousin was a license." Browden grinned back and shrugged. "I got no fight against 'em."

"Great. So, Melody Miller."

"Melody Miller." Browden sighed. "Pretty little thing, she was, but she couldn't really dance. Not good enough for this place anyway. I have standards, believe it or not. But she served tables for a few months, good waitress, friendly, or a good actress about it anyway."

"You said she used to come in. Was that recently? Why'd she stop?"

Browden shrugged again.

"Dunno. About a month or two back she just stopped coming in." He squinted in an effort to remember. "The last time I saw her she was with someone. Hey, Margot!" He yelled for his wife who was at the other end of the bar entertaining what looked like a very good friend.

She came over with that patented walk. Browden watched Max watch her progress and his grin grew to stretch his face in wicked amusement.

"I can see you're a man who appreciates the classic style."

"They don't make 'em like that anymore." Max agreed wistfully.

Browden laughed and punched Max's arm in what might've been a friendly slug or a casual warning.

"More's the pity. At least for men like you."

"Undeserving men like me," Max sipped his drink and turned his eyes away, breathing fire at the bar mirror. Browden had another hit off his beer.

"You're bitter, Canon. Hey, Margot, do you remember anything about that guy was in with Melody that last time? The one she was arguing with?" He turned to Max. "Big guy."

Margot shook her head, eyes distant with memory. Her black hair swayed in seaside ripples. Max could smell her perfume. He drank more whisky and the fumes cancelled out any other smell. Damn. She reminded him of Stephanie March.

She had one hand on her hip and she inhaled deeply before she spoke. Max kept his eyes on Browden.

"I don't remember him much. Just a big guy, like Hank said. I remember the guy she left with, though. A redhead. A loud redhead. He looked maybe Irish. Maybe. Wore a dark gold suit with an electronic-reader tie in orange to look like flame, you've seen 'em, they're really popular with the painfully fashion conscious right now."

Max nodded. She was describing Steve Albrecht in the same outfit he'd had on in the roadhouse. He must have only the one get up. Max felt a little sorry for the man. Not high up enough on the ladder to have the budget, but high enough to need the look. Poor Albrecht.

"You know what the argument was about?"

Mrs. Browden looked at her husband with a devastating shrug. Browden gave her breasts a fond glance, then his brow creased again in an aid to memory.

"I'm not sure. She was drinking alone, and this big guy came up to her, I mean big, with huge hands, like plates. They started in, and when I came over to see what he wanted to drink, I heard her say something about wasting product on Blue, well, that was his problem and why didn't he just call the media. And he said she better start working or she was out of the program. Something sinister about the way he said it, too, like it was a threat, and then he said the media wasn't reliable and no he didn't want anything to drink." Browden rolled his beefy shoulders and sucked down a mouthful of beer. "I left 'em then, not my business. And it sounded like trouble. I haven't been in business for thirty years courtin' trouble. I cooperate with the law and stay outta maf biz and we all get along."

Max read a warning in the man's words and put up an empty hand.

"And I won't bring you any trouble. I'm just looking for Miller for a client. That's all." He put the empty shot glass on the bar. "Did Miller argue with the redhead?"

Mrs. Browden frowned.

"No. She didn't seem happy to see him, but she seemed sort of relieved. They left pretty much the minute he got here."

"Did it look like she knew him?"

"Oh, yes. They knew each other."

"Anything else either of you can remember? Any other place she hung out, worked, drank at?"

"Maybe over at Carny Freak. I remember her saying she liked the ambiance. Her words, not mine." Mrs. Browden made a face.

Max nodded and got up.

"Well, thank you for the information, and very much for the drink. You've been a great help."

Browden cocked his head at Max, with a sidelong look.

"You sound like a cop."

"Sorry. I'm just an ex-spec op turned PI. You hang out with the wrong sort of people long enough you pick up all sorts of unfortunate speech patterns." He put on his hat. "Thanks again."

"Sure. Just don't make it a habit." Browden waved him off good-naturedly. "And don't get killed like Vinnie."

"Vinnie?"

"That cousin I mentioned, went license."

"Ah. Yeah, I'll try to avoid that."

Max put on his filters and started working his way towards the door. When he hit the street, the fresher air almost made him feel drunk after the smoke and steam of the Lounge. Too bad his next stop was Carny Freak. After the Lucky Lucy, it would be like descending into hell.

Max dialed up the filters to block more neon and the street turned into green-tinged gray. It made lights dull and people ugly, but at least he could see them clearly without interference from beamed data. For the first time in years, Max thought about moving to the Rurals. There was another continent on the other side of the planet that might do if he didn't mind farming.

Max wasn't sure if he could farm. Maybe they could use a crop duster. Or a security chief. Or someone to dig post-holes or latrines.

Somebody screamed obscenities at somebody else and a fight started on the sidewalk. Max shoved through rather than suiciding into the street, got his hat knocked off and left it behind for lost. Post holes. Yeah.

Ahead of him stretched Coney Island Avenue, murky and purple-lit. He was on the edge of the Speakeasy, and this was the hell-gate that led to one of its most famous and lurid showplaces. Max squared his shoulders and dialed the filters over to mirrored. He unsnapped the butt tie on his gun and kept going like the world belonged to him.

As if he'd take this particular part of it if you paid him. Post holes and latrines. He sighed wistfully, wondering idly how Stephanie felt about livestock.

Carny Freak was closed for repairs. Max remembered then that there'd been some sort of brawl or battle there last week. The sign said reopening soon. A crowd of highly colored exotically dressed kids hung around the entrance, trying to decide what second best venue to honor with their presence. Max sidled through their contemptuous glances with a twisted grin. Ah, to be young.

He went down along the street a few blocks. Since he was here he might as well take a look at the Emerald City. He checked his gun at a street locker bank rather than at the door: A man never knew when he might have to leave a place by unusual means, and he wouldn't leave the gun behind. Through a light mist spangled with colored smoke from building generators he went through the high gothic arch entrance of the Emerald City. Max went through the club and down the nearly hidden back stairs to another arch, this one a sullen ruby in the dark corridor, where he stood waiting until the gatekeeper felt like letting him in. When the buzzer went, he passed through the door, which was actually a triple set of gates, each set discreetly with various scanners that led to behind-the-walls security stations and also let the Madame guess ahead of time about the incoming customers. Max grinned crookedly at the impression he must make. And him in his best suit.

He gave his true name, to see if anybody recognized it from some of his previous underworld dealings. He was satisfied that somebody did and wasn't happy about it when he was made to wait in the outer vestibule for twenty minutes before he was let into a interview-selection chamber decorated in British Raj. A tiger clawed chair took his weight without creaking and the glazed eyes of taxidermed animals, crossed with the weapons that supposedly killed them, watched menacingly from the walls. His guide, a rubber-clad girl with reader-tattoos left him alone with a bottle of some multi-colored multileveled liquor that promised hallucinations the like of which he hadn't known for years and had never seen outside of the medical ward.

After another twenty minutes, a woman Max's age came in and sat behind the teak desk, fixing a pair of emerald green eyes on him from under gilt eyebrows that matched her lips. Her gown was slinky gold brocade and Max watched her all the way down into the chair with an admiring look she didn't bother to pretend to miss.

"Max Canon. You'd better tell me you're here for pleasure. If you say you're here for business, I will take the price of that drink out of your account and have Helen and Marco throw you out the back where we put the garbage."

"It's nice to finally meet you, Madame Ebony. Or are you no longer going by that name?"

"I never did. It was a press-tag. The media hates normal names. Why is a trouble-making Private License in my whorehouse?"

"Looking for love, ma'am," Max showed her the empty, unused glass and a friendly smile. "What kind of special does a person have to be to merit your personal attention?"

"You are not a good liar, Mr. Canon. But I will take you at face value until I see otherwise, and let you shop. I, however, am not on the menu."

She turned to take up a projector, modeled to look like an eight hundred year old hunting rifle of the great game variety, and handed it to him, ignoring his sincere, "That's really too bad."

"Point it at the elephant and select with the trigger."

Max followed her instructions, paging through projected holograms of women, men and a few outlanders, any of which could be had for the right price. He was maybe ten faces in and wondering how he could open the subject he really wanted to talk about in the face of her iron-willed rejection of him and his job, when he flashed up a familiar face.

His breath stopped in his throat and he flashed a look at the Madame.

"You like that one, do you? Just got her in, so she's fresh and untainted. She runs eleven hundred per hour and she can't be damaged. You want that kind of thing you need to see Macy. Do you need to see Macy?"

"No. I like this one." Max took another long look, careful with the expression, and then handed the projector back to her. Her fingernails flashed verdigris'd copper in the light of the fake-flame wall scones.

"Very well, then." She rose in a cascade and shush of gold and moved panther-like to the wall, teasing Max every step of the way, a faintly smug smile on her face. "If you'd be so kind as to follow Keri…" She moved a death mask sideways, triggering a hidden door. It whooshed open on a moodily lit corridor decorated like a cross between Cocteau and the Wizard of Oz. Max stepped out under the green crystal shaded lights and looked along the corridor. A six-foot silver-leather clad woman was slinking down the hall, straight jet hair swinging counter time to her hips. Max grinned again at the selection that had been made for him and took a good look at the spots the criss-crossed bondage style outfit left open for viewing.

"Nice," he said.

She nodded as if it was her due and beckoned him to follow. He did so, noting the high gloss of the leather and the way the green lights hit sparks off each curve. It was distracting, of course; it was meant to be. Max didn't have anything to think about for the moment but he couldn't let himself be distracted in this place. He didn't know it and he didn't trust it any more than they trusted him. It was an uneasy relationship being facilitated for money only. He missed his gun.

The corridor led to another anteroom set with unmarked doors on one side and one way glass on the other. Part of the dance floor could be seen through the glass which was vibrating slightly from the music behind it. A version of the same music was being piped at a lesser volume into the corridor.

Max's guide turned silver-lensed eyes on him and smiled. He smiled back, trying not to be unnerved by the lenses, and they went through a door and up stairs to a hall of much more business-like doors. This part of the complex looked more like a hotel and less like a club. Keri let Max into a door on the right, shutting it behind him.

Max went across the burgundy carpeting to the bedside lamp and turned it up. He was alone.

He looked around at the windowless space, saw where the cameras were, wondered about the bugs, then another hidden door slide open and Jolie Laide came stumbling out as if she had been pushed from behind.

"Mr. Canon! Oh, thank God!"

Max caught her as she tripped and veered her towards the edge of the bed. Another movie moment. Something bad was going to happen to him for sure.

"Ms. Laide. I'm surprised to see you here." He was a little surprised to see her outfit, too. Green silk in the creative torn lace style—a retrospective look, actually—that barely held her in. Most of her was on display in accordance with the place they were in, but Max didn't goggle at this one: The look in her eyes made him think of the word 'victim.'

"Why are you here, Ms. Laide?"

"The cops were bothering us about that horrible thing with Bart on the county line, so Stephanie's friend said he had a place we'd be safe from that."

"And that safe place is here?"

"I didn't know!" It was a wail. "Now I'm trapped! In a Brothel! And I haven't seen Steve for days!"

"She got you trickin' yet?"

"What?"

"Am I your first customer?" Max pulled the bed throw over her shoulders and paced around the room, glaring down cameras and looking again for audio bugs, knowing full well they'd be too small to see.

"Yes." There was a damp nod to accompany this admission.

"And you've been here what did you say two days?"

"Three."

"Well, somebody loves you, coz there's no way she'd wait before putting the goods out unless somebody's paying to keep you safe."

"They obviously aren't paying enough!" It was a return of the spirit she'd shown at the roadhouse, and Max smiled at her involuntarily. With the tears still glistening on her cheeks and the lamps setting up a glow in her big brown eyes, she looked terribly lovely.

"Maybe you're being taught a lesson," Max guessed, putting his hands behind his back and wandering around to the sliding door she'd entered by. "Where's that lead too?"

"Access corridor." She sniffed, looking a little less watery.

Max took her hand.

"Let's go, then. We're not getting any younger."

She pulled her hand back,

"Don't you think they'd be waiting?"

"Maybe. Only one way to find out." He let her be, though, while he went to run his hands over the paneling, looking for the switch. It made no sense to only have one trigger. There had to be one on this side, too.

When he found it, the panel opened without warning, scaring a small scream from Jolie, and making Max flinch back despite his brave words. He didn't really want to engage in a fist/knife/gun fight right now with a half-naked woman who certainly couldn't defend herself if her cowering was anything to go by and he wasn't armed with so much as a sock full of sand.

No one was in the corridor. God still loved him. Max gestured the girl to follow along behind. She came quickly enough now, the bed spread trailing behind like a badly patterned cloak. Max moved quickly ahead to each crossing, checking for cover, for ambush spots, for other people. There were none of the above, and the naked, smooth-walled halls made him nervous. He was holding his breath at each stretch, expecting to get caught, then surprised when they weren't.

They made it all the way to the kitchens without meeting anybody, and Max peered around the corner to see an area of seething activity as wait staff and cooking staff rushed to fill trays for rooms and replenish the snack trays in the waiting areas. One counter was entirely given over to a Dr. Frankenstein set up of tubes and glass ware the was producing, not coffee, but good old-fashioned moonshine and a few of the simpler recreational drugs, by the smell and the color of the smoke. Max grinned, and turned back to explain his plan in a hurried whisper to Jolie. She nodded, wide-eyed but with the start of a grin in her eyes, and without giving either of them time to think too long, Max jerked his tie askew, ruffled his hair and staggered loudly and tilted into the kitchen, bellowing for drink, food and women.

Jolie Laide came hurrying after when he had made it halfway across the kitchen, skirted by wait staff who dodged and darted at him in nervous attempts to shoo him back the way he'd come. Somebody was reaching for the intercom when Jolie skittered around the corner, looking wildly about, then focusing on Max.

"Thank God!" she exclaimed, only slightly more melodramatic than necessary. "Sir, please, come back. Room service can have all that sent to us."

Max teetered around in a circle and a large waiter made a grab for his arm. Max let him have it for a moment, and owl-eyed the man, who had fifty pounds on him and six inches, easy.

"No need to get personal," Max said with stuffy dignity, pulling his arm free and pulling his tie further off center in an "effort" to straighten it. "I told you I'd fetch it, lovely lady, and so I will." He bowed a sweeping bow to Jolie and staggered back a few more steps towards the unguarded back door. The large waiter did not touch him again, but followed along like a tug ready to nudge a lolling tanker into place. Jolie clattered clumsily up to Max in her feathered heels, shoes she'd made no noise in at all in the back halls, something Max would marvel at later, and fluttered her hands about, throwing big brown eyes to the watching staff and making soothing noises to Max.

"It's ok, it's ok. Come on, maybe you need some fresh air. Does that sound good?" She sounded just like a mother with a fussy child and Max saw hidden grins flash by on various faces. Jolie nodded to the large man, who stepped to open the door. Already the head cook was herding people back to work and the alert tension was going out of the others.

Max knew they were far luckier than they should be and could only be grateful his pathetic plan seemed to be working. He stumbled over the threshold, managing to capture and hold Jolie's wrist and drag her with him.

"Only if you walk with me, lovely," he slurred and winked horridly at the large waiter, who stepped up with a frown to free the lady.

Jolie hurriedly set a hand on the waiter's arm.

"It's okay. I'll just see him down the alley."

"Madame will want to know," the waiter said, still frowning. He obviously didn't know the working girls by sight or he'd be trying to stop them and howling for security with stunners and gas. Max swayed, made a gagging noise, gulping and jerked on Jolie's hand. <u>Hurry</u>.

"I'll only be a minute," she said , casting a frantic, nervous look at Max. She was standing as far from him as his hold on her wrist would allow, and she looked like she truly didn't want to go with him. Max applauded mentally. "You want him to puke in here?"

"Okay, but hurry back. And yell if you need help."

The last was called after them as Max lurched out the door into the alley, dragging Jolie along. She nearly lost a shoe on the threshold, but she nodded over her shoulder to the waiter and mouthed thank you. Then the door was swinging to half shut and Max had her ten feet away. Fifteen and the waiter's shoulder could be seen propping the door open so he could hear, but his attention was inside the kitchen again. Twenty, and the cook's voice was at top volume cursing drunks and harlots who invaded his sanctuary.

Then they were at the corner and running. Max felt a moment's regret that he'd never be allowed inside the place again after abducting one of the working girls, particularly this one, but it wasn't like he had a habit for places like that. And maybe he could throw enough cash at the Madame that he'd get back in if he needed to that badly. Street talk cost, but it was priceless as far as rumor went, and rumor went very close to the truth in places like this. You just had to sort it well.

Jolie had had to leave her bedspread in the hall outside the kitchen, so she stood out more than Max would've like, but he hustled her into the car and gave her his coat. He put her in back so she could put her feet on the heated foot rail if she got cold and could duck down if she needed to hide, and jumped the car from nothing to forty in the slow lane, making for the quick getaway. He was beginning to regret the whole evening, and realizing he'd gotten nothing from it, no news, no leads, only a few burned bridges, and his name splashed all over the underworld where people could look at it and go hmmm, Canon, seems I heard of him once: Is he worth killing?

Max slewed into the high lanes for speed and distance and hammered on the wheel in a brief, hot moment of anger and disgust. He saw Jolie's eyes in the rear-view, watching him, frightened, and he shuttered it down. Dammit anyway.

He turned for home. He could pick up the gun tomorrow.

"So. Is that what you had in mind?" he asked her conversationally.

She surprised him by producing a ragged grin.

"Not exactly, but it's better than being there. Where are we going?"

"Home. My home. I don't know what else to do with you right now. If they really want you they'll look at the overnight places first. Tomorrow, I'll start looking for a safer place for you to go."

"Safer?"

"My place is the second place they'll look, if they can find it. I'm unlisted, but…"

"You didn't give your real name." She sounded like she didn't want to hear the answer.

"I did. They'd have it by now, even if I hadn't. Relax. My apartment isn't registered under my real name anyway." He paused for a moment. "I wonder why they let me get away with you?"

Jolie snapped her mouth shut on that, and Max couldn't spare the attention from driving to find out if it was surprise that he'd noticed or surprise because she hadn't thought of it that way.

"Maybe they'll take it out of your credit. You know, one prostitute, 20,000, one bed spread, 21.50."

"Ha ha." Max considered her for the split second they were in a straightaway, and tried to decide if she was for real or a plant to spy on him. And why would they spy on him? It was too elaborate, but then many people liked elaborate. Especially rich crime people with too much time on their hands. Maybe Madame wanted him to steal Ms. Laide and get her off her hands. Maybe Ms. Laide had been planted there for him to steal.

Maybe he was going to die sooner than he thought.

"I gave them a dummy account. Number comes up okay and feeds out about 5,000, then it goes pop like a soap bubble in a hurricane. Whoosh. Nothing left."

Jolie gave him an admiring glance.

"You're pretty good."

"Not good enough, I'm afraid. We only have maybe three days safety margin on this. I gotta think what I'm gonna do with you. I gotta think now."

The fierce tone in his voice made her fall silent again, and they didn't speak for the rest of the ride.

Max stopped over at Helen's to get some clothes for Jolie. Helen gave him one long look and produced a complete outfit. She didn't ask him who it was for or why he needed it, and he didn't offer.

"Add it to my paycheck, Boss," was all she said.

Max nodded.

XVII.

Friar

Nothing is new in this work. I can't tell you anything you haven't already heard, 'coz there's nothing new. People will always do what people do, and that's what this job is about: What people do.

So the next riot, Sherrow and I were on hover duty, sitting in the cruiser with the 360 degree screens popping off images to the Ranch and the dispatcher and the recording units that piped straight into the Internal Affairs computers and toggling the little targeting stick to shoot stunners and marking paint into the rioting crowd outside the thick reflecting glass of the windscreen. We were a coupla big kids playing a video game. It was a far cry from the one-on-one copping you got down on the street, but I didn't mind so much that day, since we were both shadows of men, and not really up to the shield-to-club combat going on down below.

Still, it wasn't the same, even though it reminded me of how not alone we were most of the time. Unless we left the cruiser and went on foot, in which case our only contact with the guardian angels at the Ranch were the radio units we wore, we were surrounded by tech at all times. There were cameras and radios and we rode around like bionic extensions of the sergeants back at the precinct house as they paced up and down the monitor banks with headsets of their own, listening in on half a dozen pursuits at once. IA listened in, too, especially on the juicy action. I was just lucky that the cruiser vids hadn't been POV when I muscled my perp into multiple fractures that time.

By the end of the day, I was looking forward to return to street duty, where we could key off the mikes now and then and talk without eavesdroppers. There were too many cruisers to keep the radio's on all the time, so job priority allowed us to create our moments of privacy.

When I went to the bar that night with Sherrow as my shadow and Kay as my drinking buddy, I found that I wanted to be alone more than I wanted company, and I made lame excuses and left for another bar where the smoke was thick and varied and nobody knew me. There were dancing girls there and that reminded me of something I'd copied from the archives, which got me paging through screens in my notebook and trying to read the dim screen in the crappy light. My batteries were low.

Mrs. March had been a dancing girl back in the day, Canon had said. I looked with new respect at the latest crop and started hunting for older ones who might've know the March woman before she became arm candy for Daily Caulder.

Nobody in my little dive fit the description so I ended up on a bar hop tour that landed me down Coney Island Ave at the Helloween Danceteria, choking on chemical fumes I hadn't smelled since the last big Seven bust I'd been on and talking to women I wouldn't touch with rubber gloves. What surprised me the most was that Canon's name came up under the topic of dancers from back when. He'd been busy looking, too, it looked like. Anyway, nobody could tell me anything other than the name Melody Miller, and when I started to feel watched, I bugged out for home.

I couldn't tell if I was being followed, even when I ditched the damn filters for a better view, fuck the street cred. I had an unhappy thought that it was Kay or Sherrow. Like I wanted to hear about my choice of company tomorrow. Like I wanted to hear any more criticism whatsoever about my life from either of them. Home looked like a bolt-hole and I bolted, fizzing from the inhale I'd gotten in Helloween and jumpy from bad booze, bad sleep and bad company.

I made it safe and secured my perimeter, locking locks and engaging alarms. I was too keyed up to shower, so I took a bath where I could have my gun handy and hear the hum of the empty apartment around me, and think about the people I was meddling with and the odds against me finding anything that would make it worthwhile before somebody took a swipe at me and put me in the bed next to Mitchell, or into the morgue.

Of course, I didn't dream happy that night, but then, that wasn't anything new. Some of those nightmares were just like old friends.

Canon

Jolie stood uncertainly in the entry of Max's place, peering around the dim room with a doubtful look on her face.

"It's nothing special, but it's safe for now," Max told her. He decided not to try and excuse the mess. He was a bachelor; it shouldn't be a surprise.

"It's fine," she said before he got the lamp on.

Still, she didn't revise her statement, only going to the sofa and sitting down as if she couldn't stand any longer. "Thank you." She added.

Max waved it away and looked around, trying to marshal the long-dead host circuits into kicking on line. Coffee?

"You want something? Coffee? Tea?"

"Coffee, sure." She looked around at the Spartan furnishings and undusted surfaces. "No wife, then. No girlfriend either?" She seemed to be relaxing.

Max was in the kitchen, and ignored the question.

"How do you take your coffee? Not with cream, I hope. My refrigerator is where food goes to die."

"With sugar is fine." She pulled his coat tighter and got up to look at the one photograph in the room, one of Ruth and Eddy on vacation on Kantars Port North.

Max came back into the living room to see her pick it up.

"Family," he said to her questioning look.

She put it down and circled away to look at the drawings on the other walls, a pair of ink sketches, one such a mass of black violent lines that it took staring to figure out that it was a portrait of a man in a military style cap, and the other a hazy rendering of a ship in star light with a nebula just tipping over the horizon.

"These are lovely," Jolie said, with enough animation that Max wondered where all her nervous tension had vanished to so suddenly. "Did you do them?"

"No. Guy I used to know."

She nodded and moved on to look out the window. Max dodged after her and drew her back.

"Not a good idea," he said, putting her back on the sofa. "It's better if no one knows you're here."

She nodded again, eyes wide. In the dim light, Max couldn't be sure what the expression in them was. He would assume it was fear, but he didn't feel certain enough about anything these days to start making assumptions.

"If you're cold, there's an afghan on the back of the couch you can use." She nodded once more and he went to check the frig for survivors to offer his guest.

It looked like he'd have to go out for supplies. He could pick up his gun at the same time.

"Are you hungry?" he called through the door, hoping the answer was no.

"I ate earlier. Madame fed us well, anyway. Coffee will be fine." She shifted to tuck her legs up under her, pulling the afghan over her shoulders. She didn't take off Max's jacket. Max went to the thermostat and bumped the heat up for her.

"You have clothes with you, in town?"

"At the hotel." She turned her eyes towards the window as she spoke and started chewing on a fingernail. This time Max was sure it was fear.

"Gimme the key. I'll go get 'em."

"It might be dangerous." Big brown eyes, luminous in the throw of the kitchen light.

"You can't live in an afghan and the suit Helen lent you. And I can't exactly take you shopping." He took another jacket from the closet and put it on. "It's early yet. They may not have it staked." He picked up his keys. "I'll be right back."

She didn't say anything, but he felt her eyes on him, burning a hole in his back even after he shut the door behind him. It was going to be a tough in that tiny apartment. She needed to have more clothes or he couldn't do it.

Hell, he might not make it anyway.

Friar

There wasn't much going on onshift so we were doing busy work that helped to pass the time of an otherwise totally useless waste of civic money. Sherrow was at the wheel, and I'd pick out a likely-looking vehicle and have him skooch up real close behind to let the laser read the plates— a sort of vehicle laser-tag system that sometimes even worked—then I'd download to the hot sheet and the computer would spit back info. We struck out 99% of the time, and only hit one vehicle with warrants, and those were for the previous owner as it turned out.

So we were sitting at a stop light, trading rookie-training stories. Every rookie goes through a sort of orientation month where they plug you into various department jobs to see what you seem best suited for.

Sherrow sounded like he'd had half a chance at something flashy like upper level homicide, but he'd opted to start at street level, and I was giving him shit about it. He was flipping it right back because I had slid into the street-cop job like I was greased and jet-propelled. There was no fancy promotion on my horizon.

We made it through the next light and had to stop for the one after. Conversation had come down to the mature adult equivalent of 'anything you can do, I can do better,' and we'd given it up as lost in the time it took to go one city block.

I was staring idly at the six-deck light on the corner, waiting for it to change and thinking about not much. I mentally rostered it off in that ridiculous way you do sometimes to pass the time, though I should've been scoping the neighborhood. Two yellow, two red, two green lights in banks NSEW bottom, mid one, mid two, top and the on and off lanes, a camera at each corner wide-angling the scene to a video recorder so the traffic boys could make the adjustments and squeeze that extra micro-second out of the slow lane and slap it into the busy lane to hopefully and a prayer prevent jams.

I wondered if Linden had checked the vid logs for the day of Mitchell's accident. It was commonly done, but not SOP. Not every detective used 'em since the pictures weren't great, but there were no leads right now, what could it hurt? I made a mental note to check 'em out.

So later I was sitting in the traffic department, scrolling through lousily filed data tapes from the day of Mitchell's accident, trying to find the one from the right camera.

And there it was. The picture had shit-resolution and the angle was lousy, but you could just make out the accident. There was Mitchell, who kindly looked directly into one of the other cameras to verify his identity, and then (switch to another camera) here came the car that swatted him, a big black car, moving fast fast, two maybe three riders and one bonafied angle that, properly enhanced, might yield a photo of the driver if I wheedled enough.

Or if I could get Linden to front the enterprise, even if he was off the case. They could make him stop working on it but they couldn't make him stop caring, and I'd seen his easy acceptance of the leash every day in the white, tight jawed tenseness that marked a very unhappy man. I went upstairs and found him and did a few handsprings for him, and he came back down to Traffic Research and threw his gold badge-heavy chest around with what I'd have to say was great pleasure. They even got in an expert to mess with it for him, and I was pleasantly surprised to find out it was an old flame of mine recently transferred to the traffic analysis section.

Suzanne was all tea and oranges and at the end we had ourselves a grainy, possibly useful shot of a guy in a hat. His eyes were covered by brim and shadow, but the end of the nose and jaw were clear.

I didn't recognize him, yet, but I would: I'd keep looking until I did. Linden said much the same thing, but we both knew he was being watched to make sure he kept his fingers out of it, partner and all to the victim, and I said I'd let him know. Suzanne said was I busy later and how about coffee?

I got all excited before I remembered why we hadn't bothered to find each other after graduation. But hell, let her remember at her own pace. Dinner once or twice couldn't hurt either of us, and it might get Sherrow off my back. No one else had come through yet.

I crept off after shift and did another round of bar-hopping, looking for more Melody Miller/Mrs. March/Caulder gossip, and this time I wore the hat the little sales girl had sold me that I hadn't had the guts to wear yet; filter lenses were more than enough for a guy like me, farm raised and uniform-trained. But the hat seemed to give me a little of that Max Canon patented urban blend, and I got fewer bug-eyed looks than the night before. Guess I stank less of cop.

I kept my eyes open for that nose and jaw from the photo, but I didn't see anybody except a skulker who might've been Sherrow pretending not to be there. It irked me to have him hanging around, did he think I was going rotten he had to follow me all over? But when I looked directly, it wasn't him, and by the time I was so tired I could hardly stand, I got a confirmation on Melody Miller as a Caulder lackey and a trail that said she may or may not be of this earth yet.

But it'd have to wait. I went home and tried to find sleep, laying eyes open to the dark ceiling and smelling the smoke on the clothes I'd worn to the bars, thinking of women and colored lights and dead guys.

More happy thoughts to sleep on.

XVIII.

Canon

"I'm terribly worried about Steve. He never came back."

Max was sitting on the sofa next to Jolie Laide with a box dinner in front of him and the fork halfway to his mouth. Jolie had changed into some sort of robe that didn't help him concentrate, even if it was better than a dinner jacket and green lace. He emptied the fork and chewed for a minute.

"When did he leave?" and asked again, "Sure you're not hungry?"

"Four days ago." She waved dismissingly at his dinner in answer to his second question and put her head on his arm. Max looked down into brown eyes full of innocent trust and anxiety. It almost made him suspicious. It almost made him feel old. It certainly made him feel uncomfortable. "Please find him, Mr. Canon. I'm so worried."

The Mr. Canon did make him feel old.

"But yer not worried about Mrs. March."

The brown eyes hardened.

"You have to ask after she sold me to that, that...whorehouse?"

"You said her friend did that." Jolie didn't seem mollified. Max had another bite of food and added, "Okay, I guess I don't blame you. I'll find him. Would he go back to the hotel? Did you leave anything important?"

Not that he'd seen any sign of Albrecht there when he'd hastily jammed clothes into Laide's bag and done a quick once-over for clues. Who knew if Laide was telling the truth? Certainly Albrecht looked like the kind of boy to get himself mixed up with Caulder's sort.

Jolie frowned in abstraction.

"He might have. I don't know. He seemed very concerned about some letter or other. It was why we came here anyway. He had some letter or other that got sent along with one of Stephanie's, by accident. He thought we should return it personally, which I never did understand." Again with the big brown eyes.

Max hesitated over the word 'blackmail,' and swallowed it and the question mark along with the last tasteless bite from the self-heat.

He gave a non-committal 'huh,' and got up to dispose of his dinner garbage. On the way back into the living room, he stopped at his overcoat to collect his notebook and a handful of scraps. Ms. Laide was definitely scared of something, he ceded, but she was lying, too.

He seated himself on the floor by the coffee table and started to sort the even dozen data files and pieces of paper into some sort of order. His reluctant houseguest watched silently, nursing yet another cup of coffee.

Max stared at the notes. He got up, fixed himself a drink, offered Jolie one, was declined, gave it a stir and sat back down in front of his notes. He stared some more.

"Line up, ducks," he told the notes, trying for a blank mind so the ideas could organize themselves in his head. He sipped his drink and tried to just let it happen.

After a minute or two of nothing, he rattled his ice cubes over the table in a circle like a voodoo rattle and chanted 'ohm,' long and low.

Jolie laughed and told him he was nuts, and got up to take her coffee cup to the kitchen and start another pot, like the kitchen belonged to her. Like a wife.

Max sat back and sipped reflectively. Miss Innocence had been married before. He'd lay money on it.

But what else was she hiding? Was it important?

It had to be. Max stared at the papers some more and tried to reach the zen-detective stage. Maybe if he punched it into the console it would look more inviting...

It was going to be a long evening, either way.

Friar

I found Sherrow standing in the break room doorway, watching two of the maid units corner Hollingate who had yet again spilled coffee and creamer all down the counter and tried to walk away. The units were little multi-armed boxes on half-tracks, kinda cute really, but they had a hell of a pinch when you pissed 'em off and they musta gotten tired of following old Holl around years ago. Lately they'd started reprimanding. The new programming roughly coincided with the new influx of the latest batch of rookies in the station. I think Sherrow knew who was responsible, but I wasn't asking: It was worth the price of admission as it was.

Sherrow was laughing silently to the tune of Hollingate's yelps and curses and badly aimed kicks, and I joined him for a few bliss-filled moments of watching true justice be served immediately upon perpetration of the crime.

Then Hollingate spotted us and his bellows took on a more personal hue. Rather than get involved, I waved at him with a grin and ran, Sherrow at my heels, wiping away tears of laughter. We'd hear about it later, loud and profane, but Hollingate cruised for it. It was good to see a little payback, no matter how petty.

It was the only justice we'd see that day, but that wasn't necessarily new.

I was on my way out through the parking lot heading home when I passed Strindberg talking to one of the she-cops, an old drinking buddy of mine from the academy, Amistad Evans, Amy E.

She gave me a long time no see and said,

"Looking good, Friar," obviously lying and smiling all over her freckled face. "Aren't you on swing shift?"

"Yeah," I jerked my head at Strindberg. "And him."

"He's escort duty today, for foreign office, poor baby." She was highly amused by it. He didn't look like he was.

"I get to walk around two paces behind the Orion delegates and get shot for them if anybody wants to have a go."

"Lucky boy," Evans said, a chortle in her voice.

"Ah, politics," I said, grinning myself. "Don't they have their own bodyguards?"

"Don't trust 'em. Might as well hire assassins as Orion bodyguards," he looked like he thought that was even funnier than Evans thought his recent assignment was. "Drive around in black cars that cost too much and shoot people one shot one kill or hide for 'em and garrote...much better bodyguards than Orionese, those assassins."

"You sure got a thing for assassins, Strindy," Evans said, turning away. She was already getting bored.

"Nah." He laughed a little. "Just did some reading on the trip back from vacationland last week. Interesting job. Easier than ours, at any rate."

"No gray area," I nodded. "Whyncha get a career change then, you so hot to kill people for money?"

"Don't be stupid. I'm doing what I'm doing to help people, not get rich."

"Ya got that right," I said at the same time Evans said, "That's no shit, pal."

I asked him about his two days off, the place he'd gone to and the flight back, and we parted without really exchanging any new information, but I still found myself trying him on in the bad guy slots in my profile. He didn't actually fit for most of it and I'd never seen him around suspects that fit Sherrow's description of Warp chick, but you never knew.

Man, you just never knew, and I keep finding that out even after all this time.

XIX.

Friar

The call came in the dead of night again, just like before. On the other end of the line was an officer, off-duty and screwed up, hurting and scared.

When I realized who it was, I was suddenly wide-awake with all the danger alarms ringing like Christmas Day. Wells. Wells was calling me to haul his ass outta a bottomless pit of danger. He'd been in a bar. Somebody had drugged his drink. Beat him almost as bad as I had been. Dumped him in a gutter. Told him to stay away from some girl. It sounded like a Warp high, too. Surprise, surprise.

When I got to him, he was so cross-eyed I was amazed he'd been able to operate the phone.

"I dunno if I want you helpin' me," was the first thing outta his mouth when I white-knighted up to his place with my patch kit in hand.

It pissed me off, here I was out in the middle of my sleep time helping a man I couldn't stand get out of a drug-charge—God help us all if they did a random drug-test anytime soon, the lot of us with unsolicited drugs in our fat cells still—so I wasn't very friendly.

"Fine. Cure yourself. The crash is a nightmare, though." I turned around like I was on a pivot and went back out the door.

"Wait, wait, wait," He looked bad, just like Sherrow had. "I mean, I was thinkin' about the rumors goin' around, oh man I'm fucked up."

"Rumors." I stopped, spun again and prompted, flat voiced.

"Oh, man, oh, man, oh man, help me, man."

"Rumors. What rumors. Wells. What rumors."

"Y'know, where yer selling on the side. S'why I thought you might've set 'em on me."

I stopped breathing at that, speechless, breathless, red rage and disbelief blossoming up like a firebomb in my stomach.

"What."

"It's only rumors, I guess, I mean you wouldn't do this to me, would you? Ruin my career?"

"I hate you, pal, but not that much. This I wouldn't do to anyone. Nothing worse than an involuntary Warp high. Where did you pick it up? You got any idea? Tell me, man. Help me find these sonsabitches."

But he couldn't do much more than repeat the oh, man litany like he was reciting prayers.

"The bar, maybe, the chick and the guy. The chick and the guy, oh, man, Friar help me."

I took him back to the blue print sofa must've been picked out by his mother-in-law the pattern was torture, and sat him down.

"I'll help you, Wells. Relax. Why'd you call me, Wells? Huh?" I had to catch his wandering eye: he was much further gone than Sherrow had been. "Wells? Wasyer first name, Chip? Chip? Why call me? Why not somebody else, like, like," I scrambled for someone who Wells might actually consider a friend, "Why not Strindberg?"

"Oh, man." He focused on me with difficulty and looked so scared and lost I almost felt sorry for him: I could feel sorry for this strange lost kid looking out of the eyes of an asshole. He didn't really look like Wells right then, and he sure didn't sound like him. "Oh, Friar, I'm fucked up. Strindberg he'd...he'd maybe say something. I don't trust him and I heard you got a line on private clean-up..."

He trailed off, desperate-hopeful in a sort of fatalistic way that told me he didn't really think I'd help, no matter what I said. So he knew I didn't like him, fine. But a cop was a cop and even asshole Wells could be a good cop more often than not. The job didn't really require saints and heroes. Neither of us was anything even close.

"Oh, Friar, oh, Friar. Oh, man, you can't tell anybody about this. Oh, man."

"Yeah, sure. Come on and I'll get you squared away, Chip. Chip, is that right? How 'bout I just stick to Wells? That okay?"

I unassembled the rescue pack I had from the rat doc—foresight I'd hoped not to use—and started in on him with the emetic and the antidote. It had to be in a form— liquid, in this case—that would leave no marks, another thing they looked for in the random drug testing. The antidote might show on a test, but it looked a lot like over the counter cold remedy or too many sugary drinks, so we were okay if they stayed away from the intensive tests. He wasn't particularly coherent, and I began to get worried that maybe he'd gotten more than Sherrow had. Maybe whoever was doping cops in my House was trying to get more air- time, make it public. Nothing like a cop dead on highly illegal highly unobtainable (supposedly) recreational drugs to make a precinct look bad.

Disaster, inquiry, rolling heads, closure, lost jobs.

I ended up taking Wells to my little rat doctor, just to make sure he'd make it through the night. I didn't want a dead cop in my part of town, and I needed to think, really think this time.

Sherrow and Wells, the plant in my locker, the easy Warp bust, it all combined to look like a setup or preliminaries to a setup. No one had tried very hard to make sure I got caught with the vial, and so far, no cop had been caught actually under the influence, but things were looking to be getting worse.

Wells complied with everything required of him, defeated, like a tortured prisoner of war, and I asked him questions the whole time and got an impression of Sherrow's Mickey Finn chick and a tall man who might've been wearing a white sport coat sometime in the past somewhere in a road house. But I couldn't be sure. He did have a square jaw, but, Hell, so do I.

When I left him back on that awful sofa, Wells was a limp rag and would live. He'd have to crash alone, 'coz the wife was outta town visiting her mother and like I'd told him, I hated him. I'd help him out, but I'd be damned if I'd stay and hold his hand while he had the nightmares.

And it left me wondering who would frame me by drugging up the guys around me. Sherrow was my partner, Wells was my enemy, and hadn't Strindberg looked nasty today, like maybe he was crashing on something he was afraid to report? Or was it me they were out to frame? I wasn't really all that important. It wasn't even like I was really a hero cop like Hollingate tried to tell Sherrow. I just had an interesting soap opera past. Who was setting up who and why this way?

A man could wonder about stuff like that all night and never get an answer, but that doesn't stop him thinking.

The next morning became one of my favorite memories of my days on the force. I got to watch Wells suffer the bullshit that had so far been reserved this year for me and Sherrow with all our battle scars and hangovers. Our track record hadn't been much for health and beauty so it was something extra special to see the main shit-thrower getting rained on by everybody else. I got to be all noble and nice and say things like "give him a break, guys, can't you see he feels awful?" and other straight lines designed to engender such responses as "I can see he couldn't look more awful without being dead, Friar."

I didn't earn any good-cop points with Wells, but then I wasn't trying for any. He owed me, big-time, and let him sweat it. It was such a relief to have him off my back that I accidentally gave him an honest smile at one point. He didn't recognize me at first, and there were three seconds of utter confusion before we settled back into bridled hostility. It was a good day until we got the call out on more riots. City going to Hell all around me, it looked like.

This time the riots were all about some damn toy that was too high in demand and too low in stock. Protesters had come along with hysterical shoppers to protest the off-world manufacture of the toys, while professional agitators showed up just for the fun and the looting.

Ah, yes, my least favorite part of the job next to report writing. Report work I hated only slightly more, that and court. The courtroom benches looked just like church pews. People sat along them in their good clothes, quiet, hands folded. Uncomfortable. Being told they weren't good enough. I hated court. But riots were a close second.

The crowds were too dense to pick off the real trouble makers from the squad cars, so we had to take our tasers and our tranqs and march 'em in hand to hand. It was a dry night, pre-storm clear and windy and the street static snapped off our armor and the ends of the batons, reflecting blue in mirrored face plates, and we must've looked like robots advancing through the swirling whirl of paper kicked up by the wind, the charges on the tasers flickering like tongues from snakes made of fire and free plasma. I could find it in me to almost feel sorry for anyone dumb enough to be there to see us coming, but good, well-behaved citizens do not hit each other over the head over a stuffed fluffy pink elephant—reputed to fly spacecraft against alien races if the cartoon is anything to go by (try to find good programming when you're an insomniac who works swing)—and good citizens did not take the advent of social disorder to find opportunities for robbery and vandalism. I could only almost feel sorry for them, but not quite.

The easy part of the work was that most people suddenly became good citizens when they saw us coming in a long double-skirmish line, and those that tried to commit crimes and get away by hiding in the retreating crowd got tagged by the hover-squads or called out to us so we could bag 'em from the street or the catwalks. The hard part was climbing ladders in 60 pounds of riot gear or running shoulder to shoulder with a left-handed guy and his tranq rifle, getting the stock under the chest plate every third step and trying to keep order instead of just driving the mob into another possibly undamaged part of town. Riot control pretty much has always sucked. I'm sure it always will.

Whatever, it makes for a hell of a long day, whether in the hovers or on the street.

By the time I got home, I felt like a well-used shop rag, right down to the oil stains. I sat down to take off my boots and instead fell asleep in the armchair, looking, I bet, like a dictionary picture of exhaustion. I certainly didn't feel any better when the phone rang, and there was Crystal and did I want a date and sorry to wake you, I was going to leave a message, didn't know you'd be home yet, with all the trouble on the streets, Friday? After shift, then, you get off when? Great, see ya then.

The phone went back in the cradle and I looked at it dully. Suzanne, then Crystal. Two for two, not counting Noel. The crowd goes wild. I stared at the wall opposite and wondered what that said about my luck.

Canon

Max took Jolie out for dinner. She walked beside him, face hidden by a holographic makeup projection, looking up at the lights and around as if she'd never seen the city before. Max wondered who the performance was to benefit.

"Where are we going?" she asked, turning her head to look at him, brown eyes tiger striped under the holo screen, bright as jewelry.

"Irish bar serves great food. You'll like it." He looked down at her, amused.

"I've never been to an Irish bar. I've never been to this part of town, either."

Max looked at her sharply, but her eyes were elsewhere. Surely if she was such good friends with Mrs. March, she'd have been in this locale, in a vehicle at the very least. It was too upscale and fancy to be ignored by March's set. Caulder certainly had several venues next street over, which was why Max was walking Jolie down the smaller back streets, holo screen or no.

Max watched her body language as they moved along, noting the false notes in the innocent act, but also aware that some of her interest in their surroundings seemed genuine. Her head turned constantly as she absorbed the scenes along their way, and her hair floated in the static that collected like litter along the streets, pushed down by down drafts and kept down by the suspension fields of a million hover vehicles racing by on four levels of traffic. She looked like a child at an amusement park.

He smiled and led her along to one of the smaller alleys, not wanting to spend too much time in the view of people who might recognize one or the other of them and wonder what they were doing together.

He wanted her relaxed so he could see what information he could get out of her and a good meal was step one. Next to the Irish bar was a little pub that specialized in 'snugs,' those enclosed booths that grant absolute privacy, a throwback to the true Ireland. This particular pub also served other recreations besides liquor, and Max bet Jolie might appreciate the variety. He had a feeling it wouldn't be new to her either.

They ate more than they should and wandered over to the pub, where Max had to bribe the wait staff for a snug this late in the evening. Once they were settled, she started immediately to bug him about Albrecht. He promised once more to look around. Another highly dangerous visit to their hotel had showed him only an angry manager and no clues to Albrecht's current whereabouts. Jolie had no constructive ideas on where he might be, and Max was wondering if it was time to contact Mrs. March again. He hadn't come up with anything on her blackmailer, but he thought she might talk to him anyway and he could ask her why she hadn't shown up at the drop off rendezvous. Whether she gave him any helpful data was still in question.

Jolie certainly wasn't providing any. Max's idea to mellow her up a little was ill-founded. She turned out to be fond of Bliss, which, unfortunately, the pub carried. The first hit of purple, rose-scented gas made her relaxed and happy. Max even joined her for one. The second made her flirtatious and the third made her change seats so she could sit next to him and show him how short her skirt was by sliding her thigh up against his and *smiling.*

Max sighed and rang for the bill. He wasn't adverse to her kind of games, but he had so much work to do, and she wasn't helping. He'd have to go to the office after all.

He still had to find someplace else to stash her and he couldn't bribe Helen, because he was linked to her professionally. He couldn't impose on Ruth, either. He shuddered at the thought of asking, and Eddy was a cop after all, and also linked to Max publicly, so that was out. One more night, then he'd have to find a hotel for Jolie.

Jolie made absolutely sure he got to the office much later than he'd planned, and reminded him again how uncomfortable the office sofa really was, and how cold.

XX.

Friar

Had Crystal just called me for a date? I closed my eyes and sat like 200lbs of sandbags, thinking about it. The TV screen on the far wall was a neutral blank, the way I usually left it. After a long day at work, punctuated by shouting, accusation and rage, both street side and in-house at the precinct, I like heavy silence at home. The only sound tonight came from the ubiquitous creaking water system and the wooden clock on the kitchen pass-through that had belonged to my great great great something grandfather, having been made from German oak by his father and carted across three home-world oceans and a coupla star systems to end up here with me. The thing had to be wound once every three days or so, but the spring was nearly good as new even if the case was scarred by years of use and blackened by generations of winding hands. It was the only really precious thing I ever owned besides friendships, and they tended to shift as the department thinned and changed. Everyone moved on except me, sad lonely me.

But I'd gotten three dates in one week, the entire sum-total of the previous three years.

Sad lonely man. I fell asleep in the armchair and woke up late with Sherrow on the phone, demanding of me and the neighbors if I'd died during the night and it was my turn to buy breakfast.

At the station, Ketchikian came out of the women's locker room so fast she nearly ran me down, but she stopped when she saw who it was.

"Friar! Long time, no see."

I'd heard she'd broken up with her current, and I was glad to see she remembered who I was.

"Heya, Gail. S'up?" Turning into a hick as usual.

"Oh, I'm switch-hitting for Jenkowitz on a case'd got too personal. Guy she knew got beat to death with an office chair."

"Ugly," I nodded, looking at her blue eyes and thinking the opposite.

"Really. So I'm on your shift for awhile. Maybe we should have a drink and you can tell me how you manage to work when everybody else isn't and sleeping when everybody else is."

"Sure, you bet." I couldn't believe this. Sherrow complains about my lack of women and look at 'em coming at me.

I was almost scared.

"Great. See ya," Ketchikian tucked her helmet under her arm and headed off to wherever she had been headed before we nearly swapped paint.

I avoided Sherrow's eyes and hurried to change.

He cornered me at my locker.

"I was talking to Ketchikian," he started in immediately, "and she had all sorts of stories about you, you lying dog." He'd talked to Gail. When was this?

"Dog? How dog?" I was sure this was shit I didn't need aired.

"Seems like you got around quite a bit once upon a time, man." There was something slightly mean in his tone, and I wondered who it was for.

I'd forgotten how old lovers talked. Sherrow seemed pleased to catch me out as a once-tomcat, and I had to wonder if it was because it made me seem less of an old deadbeat or because he was mad about something and wanted to pick on me.

I grinned weakly.

"Women exaggerate."

"Nah," he said around a mouthful of energy bar. "Too many corroborating stories."

I absolutely didn't want to know who'd corroborated, so I didn't say anything and he left it after a few more jabs.

We had one of those not-pals days where neither one talked much. I couldn't read his mind, so I ignored him for the most part. If he was mad at me, he'd have to tell me so. He certainly had a mood on.

I didn't bother to tell him I was seeing Crystal that night, and went to our usual bar for a quick shot of courage before I met her.

Sherrow and Kay were ganging up on me about her and had we gone out yet, when Strindberg wandered over with beer.

"Vic always went for the silly women, the idiot. Sounds like he finally found one with sense?"

"I found her," Sherrow defended.

"Good eyes, boy. What, you give her away then, she eyeballing Vic like he's dessert?"

"Sure. He needs someone, she's lookin' for a dependable guy, there he is." Sherrow's approach was so simple, it took my breath away.

"How do you know he's dependable?" Strindberg wanted to know while Kay laughed.

"You told me. Kay told me. His records told me. The perps tell me. Everywhere I look I see he's dependable. Not well-adjusted, maybe, but dependable." I'da been surprised at the praise, but the last bit fixed it, and he had a sneer to go with it.

"The lady doesn't deserve a well-adjusted guy?"

"Bet yer ass she does, but I'm already spoken for and I never met another," Sherrow swigged beer back and flashed Strindberg that cocky asshole kid smile he sometimes got after a few drinks.

"Huh." Strindberg gave it the consideration it deserved.

"That's yer opinion, Strindberg."

"S' right. My older, wiser, dependable opinion."

"I'm not touching that one," Sherrow ceded. "Let's just call it even."

"Ok. Who's paying?"

"Oh, Friar, why not? S'his turn."

That pleased everybody but me, but who was asking what I thought these days?

Luckily, I got away early to meet Crystal off work. We went to a VR show, a restaurant she chose (cheap and good—I admit I was surprised, but of course it was her field, wasn't it) and climbed to the top of the Elworth tower to look at the moon.

All in all, it was a good time and a nice girl. The upside was that I hadn't enjoyed a woman's company so much since before things went bad with Noel. The downside was that it reminded me of Noel, which kinda put me off my stride. If Crystal noticed, she didn't say anything and we parted on tentative plans for another round.

I even remembered to send her flowers next day. It sorta scared me.

Canon

It was small and it would've been harmless in any other place but the middle of his desk blotter in an office he'd personally locked the evening before.

Max looked at it for a long moment, shutting the door with his foot and locking it behind himself, flipped his eyes around the room to be certain all the shadows were familiar and untenanted, and took two steps forward, tucking his second best hat under his arm.

A matchbook from Dixie's DownHome, a restaurant who specialized in antique atmosphere. White, with red ink cracking along the fold lines, five matches left, like the teeth the dentist missed, charring along the striker strip and an address in blue pen scrawled on the inside cover. An address in the Speakeasy. Seemed like maybe his search for Miller had been heard. Or Albrecht. He'd put out a feeler on him.

He'd be a fool to go there. It was a clear invitation to be killed, and it was dark already. Who would bother to break into his office and leave an invite? Something about the whole thing meant trouble deep and he'd have to go there alone, cause the cop wasn't his pal yet and PLs didn't really do the buddy system anyway.

He'd be killed for sure. He'd be a fool to go.

Max put his hat back on.

The address was a bar and the barkeep had a letter from Albrecht. The handwriting matched that on the matchbook. Apparently, Albrecht had heard Max was looking for him. The letter was an invitation from a scared man to a stranger he thought he could buy help from. Clearly Albrecht was desperate enough to take the risk that Max was looking for him to kill him. Probably, he was less afraid of Max than he was of whoever was really after him. Max started to get more worried about Jolie Laide all alone in the empty apartment. He had to find a better place for her to hide.

The hotel Albrecht was hiding in was across the street from the bar. Max went to the room number given in the letter and shoved on the door, which was ajar.

The room was a shambles. Two chairs and a table had been knocked over, scattering cushions and glassware all over the map. A roll-top desk looked like a hurricane had happened in it, hotel stationery in drifts, and several of its drawers hung out like tongues. The roll-shutter had jammed half way up, crooked on its track, and all it's electronics were smashed. The screen was a web of crazed laminate.

Max stepped further into the chaos, sweeping his eyes over the scene, but careful not to step on anything scattered on the floor.

Which was just as well, since he nearly planted a size 10 ½ narrow on the pale upturned palm.

They didn't come much deader than this one: Dental records would be a plus when the cops arrived. Max thought he knew who it was anyway, but he called the cops from the lobby phone.

He was already rethinking his plan to relocate Jolie to a hotel before the police arrived.

XXI.

Friar

It was a Saturday, and my fingers ached from flipping through files of photo-CDs and my eyes hurt from scanner-burn. The electronic eyepiece that allowed you to scan for finger prints on evidence then transmit to the photo-repro dug into my eye socket like it was never coming off, and I didn't find any new prints, not surprising from evidence so many years old. I was covered in filth and clinging dust from the shelves at the far back in the evidence warehouse and I was coughing up grit.

Might be time to go home after all, and nothing to show for another wasted eternity. The fun time I'd had with Crystal had certainly stirred up memories and I'd discovered I couldn't bear the empty apartment, so I'd slid into the station house with the next shift and started digging half heartedly through data that all looked the same anymore, hoping for a name to The Jaw, who'd 480'd Mitchell, or for a reason why Caulder'd frame cops when he had a good thing going already as it was.

But I didn't go home. I decided to switch back to the records archives again instead, telling myself, 'only another hour, okay, an hour and a half, then,' then I'd go home and sleep. I took the stairs to get there and shake out some of the stiff.

I came out of the stairwell by the labs, breathing the odd mix of chemicals, the plastic smell of hot computers and that weird electricity you get when too many lab machines are crammed into the same room and running from the minute they're plugged in until they fry. I spared a glance in out of personal curiosity, but there was nothing there to help me past the Capelli autopsy report and I'd read that at least five times. They had somebody on the table, so I didn't linger, and dragged off to the dusty dungeon of hard copy.

It was more like two and a half hours later, despite my plans, when I found something misfiled in a box in the damper section of the stacks that they hadn't gotten around to burning yet. Some items get transferred onto computer log, others rot. This one was left to rot and the only reason I even picked it up was because it looked interesting and also totally unrelated to this stupid chore I'd set myself out to fail at.

It was in a folder of things set aside and lost from the office of an officer killed in the line of duty about the time Caulder came to prominence. The man had graduated from academy about the time Skills had, and he sounded like a run of the mill guy, except that he kept a journal and here it was.

I took it home. It wasn't like I was sleeping much anyway these days, and it might keep me from prowling the streets looking for trouble, or out of archives I'd long since squeezed dry of useful information.

When I started to read it, it nearly did put me to sleep. I skipped ahead a few chapters before Finley, that was his name, started entering only the interesting bits of the day. He looked to be getting very busy as the journal wore on, and only hot events began to appear, with less of the saw-Mary-at-the-market-again-should-I-ask-her-out stuff. By the time five hours had passed with me forgetting to eat and getting no sleep as usual, I was getting a good feeling for the time line he was describing. It was mostly small crime of the street level variety—my level, so familiar—but the density of crime began to pick up markedly and then suddenly, there was Caulder on top of the heap, a little nobody skyrocketing above crime legends like Chatty Baker and Fred Francossi in a matter of months. The whole mess was maybe five years in the running end to end, and it tailed out right around the time that I was assigned to Kay, say six years ago.

Finley listed his suspicions of Caulder in detail, the most wonderful being a discovery of military equipment in a Caulder warehouse. The address given was no longer a warehouse, but a set of laundries, but it set a precedent. Finley hadn't gotten the arrest since the contraband was gone by the time he'd been able to come back with a search warrant and back up. But that counted as big. Caulder had been importing illegal military surplus and that certainly meant he had had off-shore contacts. I seriously doubted he'd have dumped such valuable contacts. He was hooked up-atmosphere with somebody big.

That's when I got really scared. God bless Finley for writing this stuff down, but did I really need this? Here I was being all brave and courting death by Caulder, but what I was really digging around in was off-planet muscle territory. Why wasn't I dead yet? Hadn't we had a war with these people awhile back? Canon was a vet of that same war. These were people who nuked whole planets because it was more convenient than attacking by land.

Oh, I sure didn't need this.

Again, I wondered why I was still alive. It wasn't until later that I found out it was because I was too insignificant to bother with. It wouldn't've made me feel any better, even if I'd known.

Monday was no better. Delente's widow finally came in to pick up his stuff. No one had seen her since the funeral. It was strange and sad and depressing, not the least of which was because we all knew her socially and some of us had even been close friends with her as well as Kevin, and no one could think of a single thing to say to her.

A horrible wake of silence developed as she passed through the precinct. When I heard she was there, I headed that way, coz I knew it would happen just like that. I'd seen it before. I'd also been there myself when I finally got out of the hospital and came back to the place where everybody knew my own partner had shot me. There was nothing you could say to that. There wasn't much more to say to a surviving SO, but you also had to try: Some of 'em had no other social circle outside the Department. They were like family.

I must've been the senior guy there when she arrived, coz none of the vets had shown up to break the silence. She looked scared and she was crying just a little. The kids and rookies watched her with hollow eyes or looked away, excruciatingly uncomfortable as she keyed in Delente's code from a card the clerk had given her. She was coding it in for what must've been the sixth time when I got there. I took the card out of her hand and pegged in the numbers.

"I'm sorry, Sharon. We're all really sorry to lose him."

Of course, she cried then for real—sympathy can be hazardous—and I put an arm around her for comfort. She turned into my armor and cried all over it, then Skills himself arrived behind a passel of reporting-for-duties and took her off to his office. Knowing Skills, he'd called up a wife or two the minute he heard Sharon was on the premises, so she'd have a support net any second, small consolation for the loss of a husband and the wall of strangers she'd met where there should've been an army of grieving friends.

But you can't show stuff like that in front of the FNGs or you scare 'em: tough is a front and a shield and a social parameter that dictates proper procedures in awkward situations. Tough was the part of the job most people signed up for. Even if you were faking it, you were it.

Which was why my drunken confession to Sherrow had been so bad. I'd fucked with the Prime Directive.

I spotted his eyes turned my way as Skills led Sharon off and turned the dry side of my armor on him. Fuck him. Tough was also a handicap. I wasn't going to let a friend be alone just to uphold a ridiculous tradition.

There was a neutral greeting between us when we finally hooked up for sign in. I doubted we'd even discuss widows and orphans. Sherrow was too young and too new. And it made me feel too old.

We weren't talking anyway, coz we apparently weren't friends today. He didn't even ask me about my date, not even to give me Hell about it, which was highly unusual since he'd been pushing the girl at me in the first place.

By lunch I couldn't fail to notice that Sherrow was throwing crappy attitude my way again and I wondered if it was the bad phone calls he'd been getting or the dark circles under his eyes. When he nearly took my head off for reminding him to download the upgrades for the squad car, I figured I'd had just about enough and better do something about it.

"We need to talk. Get in," I said, opening the passenger side door and waiting for him to get in. There was a dicey moment that looked like hang fire, but was indecision. I was ready for the explosion, but instead of going off like triple X, he took a breath and climbed in. I shut the door on him and went around to the driver's side. Rain hit the top of my hat like hail from an angry god.

This oughta be fun. Again.

"I don't know what's up with you and I can't pretend to care unless you wanna share with me. Make up your mind and talk to me, go see a counselor or apply for a new partner, cause I've had enough of it."

His jaw dropped and he stared at me in complete surprise. I could just about read his mind. It went something like, 'After all the shit I go through for him and all the crap I put up with, he pulls this shit on me? Who the hell does he think he is?'

I thought I was his senior partner. I didn't have to take shit. I'd been there and back with stamps in my passport.

"It's not your business." he said finally. He had his jaw clenched tight now, all white edged and nasty.

"Don't play this game with me, kiddo, cause I'll win. I'm older and nastier and uglier than you and my bullshit-storage unit got all filled up with Wells' crap this morning. Do you wanna tell me why you're so pissed off at me, or do I send you to Skills' pet psychiatrist with a little note pinned to your shirt?"

He dropped his eyes and slouched down in his seat, turning that white jaw down and grinding a chorus of teeth before he let it relax a little.

"I just got a lot on my mind these days."

"And what did I do to bring the whole load of it down my way?"

"You didn't." He sighed a little bit and picked at the edge of the dash where the fake leather was peeling away from the scanner mounts. "You're just the easiest target, I guess. All this running around... You must've noticed me trailing you most nights. I'm not very good at that yet."

"I noticed." I let my tone slide back to normal and put the key in the ignition. "Call us in."

He did and I let the clutch out.

"I don't know why yer tailin' me, but you don't need to be. I'm not up to anything very exciting."

"You're trying to trace leads on the Mitchell hit and run. The roadhouse kill's square one on it. We both know that. I've been watching you, see how you do it."

"You should save it for when you get a chance to watch a real detective. We'll both get in trouble if I get caught poking around in this. It's not beat-cop work."

"I know that. But it's still a learning experience. And I have watched a real detective. You're not much different. Whyncha ever go out for the promotion again?"

"Try to imagine me as a Sergeant, huh? Now that is the funniest thing you've said all week."

"Why's it funny?" He was defensive again, and mad at me for some reason I couldn't determine.

I eased us into the traffic lanes, checking the five way for oncoming.

"Ask Frank Skills the next time you see him. And don't let me catch you following me anymore or we'll have words. Lots of bad words."

Sherrow didn't say anything to that, but his expression looked like angry resignation, so I let it go.

XXII.

Canon

It was the night after he'd found Albrecht, and he still hadn't told Jolie. He was sitting in the twilight of the light throw from the outer office overheads, thinking about other career options when the hall elevator squealed open, loud enough, as usual, to be heard through the closed outer office door. He expected the footsteps to go on down the hall to the homeopathic pet clinic (business had been slower in the PL department than in pets lately) but instead a key jangled in the door and he heard hard heels—female heels—on the tile. Helen. He was relieved. Something about Mrs. March, lovely as she was and dangerously, mysteriously tempting, made him feel cold, way down inside where things like bad dreams and premonitions came from, and Laide was supposed to be laying low in his apartment. So it wasn't Mrs. March. Helen. Good. He tried not to be disappointed.

She came to stand in the inner doorway, and look at him for a long moment. He remained silent, watching her.

"Hiding in your cave again, Boss?"

Max stirred and smiled, even though he knew his face was in shadow from the neon in the window behind him. The outer office overheads stopped short halfway across the desk blotter. The computer screen blocked the rest.

"Yeah."

"House too empty for you tonight?"

"Not empty enough. House guests."

"Marie back already?"

"Not Marie."

"Then it's the one you had to borrow clothes for." She turned on the inner office lights, ignoring his squint-eyed wince as the white light attacked night-sensitive retinas, and walked up to the desk. A glance took in his rumpled clothing and the discarded blanket on the faux leather sofa. "A real lady you don't want to compromise."

"I don't think she's a real lady. But I like her."

Helen gave him a look with her head on one side.

"What an odd man you are, Max," was all she said.

He watched her sort through the mail on the message queue, send two to print and turn the lights out again. She pulled the prints from the tray on her way out the door.

"Goodnight, Boss."

"Goodnight, Helen."

Less than half an hour later, the phone rang. The cop was calling, asking for a meeting. Max thought about it for a few seconds, considering, then acquiesced, thinking they might come up with something if they really meant it this time.

Friar showed up in his long leather coat and bronzed filters. Max put on an overcoat, no match for the flair of Friar's but closer than the suit jacket he'd had on when he'd come to the office. His filters were better than the officer's and cutting edge technically, which made him look fashionable, even if the overcoat didn't. Possibly he'd be taken for retro, but he doubted it.

Friar didn't have much to add, and couldn't give Max any data on one Jolie Laide—Max was becoming more and more curious about her and her strange games-- and Max didn't have anything he was ready to share back, so they went directly to the Speakeasy and started in on the circuits.

The first part of the night produced little more than the well-known names of lots of maf gods, dead and otherwise, but all of them out of power. By the time they got to Carny Freak, Friar was looking disappointed and tired, and Max didn't blame him. They strolled into the strangest club on a strip of very strange entertainments and Max thought he saw Friar's eyebrows lift behind the filters. The officer took them off and squinted through the heavy smoke and aerosols that filled the club from basement to beam.

"Interesting lot, huh?" Max yelled into his companion's ear over the deafening music.

Friar nodded.

"I've only been in here on business, and you get a sort of cockroach scatter when that badge comes through the door. Holy shit, are these people for real?"

"Learn something every day, huh? Go talk to the rail talent and I'll prowl the backwoods." Max gave him a heartening slap on the shoulder and sent him towards the bar, turning his own footsteps to the dim and maze-like nether regions where the club became a web of chain link and striped awnings. There were three or four stages in the place, all playing different music and all serving different customers different things. Max didn't have the heart to expose Friar to more than the front room. The man could be so refreshingly naive.

Friar

So the PL left me surrounded by people who took their jobs way too seriously, like I was one to talk. The carnival atmosphere was obviously encouraged and most of the people I was looking at had also taken the 'freak' part to heart. I knew about things like this, but I'd told Canon the truth about the scatter, and there weren't a lot of this kind of workers who actually got busted. There was too much money here, clean money, as well as well-laundered money. We couldn't touch it, if the license was up to date.

I went to the bar as ordered and scoped. A tall stool opened up while I watched and I slid in, acing out a hovering bookie-type who cursed me, but moved on when I towered over him with my best scrag-yer-ass scowl. I sat and took a look at what I had. To my one side was a woman with either black eyes or expensive lenses. She had prosthetic doe ears that looked too real for me and an artificially enhanced nose. She really looked like something I'd last seen through a gun site as a child in the woods behind the farm, and it shook me enough that my early questions sounded stiff and awkward. Not that that mattered, since she read me as Heat from one and lied to me for ten minutes. I gave it up as lost and ordered a drink. When she left, another customer took her seat, and I turned to my drink, feeling like I'd had enough for the night. I was questioning like a cop, which was what I was after all. I was just deciding I should've let Canon go it alone, God knew he'd probably get better results without me, when the woman on my left sent her admirer off and turned to me, displaying three perfect breasts under a blouse without any buttons at all. I looked, then looked again.

"That's nice." I said, curious despite myself. "How'd that happen?"

She leaned in close with a smile that said hiya sailor, then got a look at my haircut, I guess because she started that good old recoil. I sighed and gave up the fight, showing her the badge from a low angle, why spread it around?

She closed the shirt, looking disappointed and pouted with those ripe red lips.

"I saw it in a movie once."

"Everybody here do plastic?" I asked, casting my gaze around at a few movie star clones and a man done up like a porn elephant.

Madame extra-breast shrugged. The hydrokinetics were interesting, definitely. I watched appreciatively the little I could see with the blouse closed, and she let it fall open a little more.

"Some. That one over there—" she pointed to a tiger-stripe woman wearing a lamé evening gown with cut outs down both sides, "has a stripe of fur all down the center of her back, and a tail. They call her Kitty Kitty."

"Yeah? This place just keeps getting more interesting by the minute."

She smiled, "Yeah?" and leaned forward, letting go another inch of blouse. The neckline gaped a little more. "Bachelor cop, huh?"

"Yeah, but still a cop. So I gotta ask some questions."
I knew I looked like I wanted to test-drive number three,
and it warmed her up a bit. It was mostly curiosity anyway.
Mostly. She had a cute smile for a pro. "You ever work
with this gal?" I showed her a file photo of Melody Miller I'd
dug up for Canon.

"I'd like to work with you." She let the top fall open
and leaned close enough that I could smell her. She smelled
like soap, which surprised the holy hell outta me.

"Would you now? But about this chick, first. Y'know
her?"

"Nah." She sniffed at my drink, so I gestured for the
bar tender. She went on, "I saw her, though. Maybe over at
the Iron Lung. Or it coulda been at the Relic. But I didn't
know her. Not well. We weren't drinking buddies, or
anything."

"I see. You seen her lately?"

She shook her blonde curls and the triplets displayed
the usual physics plus one. My eyes followed the action. Not
what Noel would call a nice girl. I grinned.

"May I?"

"Bachelor cop," she purred and skooched closer so I
could. Somewhere in the back rooms, Canon was working
his way back to me, having scanned for and spotted no
dancers of the Miller woman's stamp. He'd unfortunately be
in time to save me from myself.

Canon

Max made the run of surprisingly empty rooms and
came back around the dark maze of mirrors to spot Friar at
the bar doing the sort of research that wasn't going to help
them on this case. He worked his way over through the
press of the dance floor and hailed the bartender, leaning
down to Friar's offside ear.

"Discovering anything helpful, Officer Friar?"
Friar grinned and took his hands back.
"Learning something everyday, Canon. I'd introduce
you but…"

"Is he a cop too?" the blonde said, looking pouty again at the interruption of commerce. Authority generally paid very well, probably out of guilt.

"I'm not. But you can charm me anyway." Max gave her a big smile, and she flounced off, angry.

"How'd you manage to offend her saying that?" Friar wanted to know, his tone purely academic.

"It's the smile. Calculated offence. Don't tell me I haven't used it on you yet?"

"I don't think so. I think I'd remember."

"You would. Excuse me, I think I see someone I know." Max took up his drink, paid, and was off again. Friar took his drink to a corner near the dance floor where no one would try to pick him up.

"Madame Ebony, how wonderful to see you," Max used the real smile for her, and nodded at her companion. The man looked like Friar wasn't the only cop in the place tonight, but he was smaller and thinner than Friar, dark eyed and dark haired with a handsome look that didn't stretch to his eyes. Max remembered him as the hostile at one of Ruth's parties, warning him out of some unspecified business that apparently wasn't his.

Madame Ebony turned and regarded Max with disfavor. Her friend moved off to the end of the bar and she was able to give Max the benefit of her full displeasure.

"I can't say the same."

"What're you up to with him?" Max gestured towards the man, who was ordering a drink with a scowl on his face.

Ebony shrugged elegantly, a beautiful roll of smooth shoulders.

"Delivering his mail. What's it to you, License?"

"Nuthin', only I think I know him and I'm jealous that you like him enough to bring him his mail and I don't even get a friendly smile."

A shapely eyebrow rose in surprise.

"After robbing me of one of my girls and giving me a false account, I'm supposed to be friendly? Anyway, he pays for the service. His usual girl wasn't available and I needed a night out." She looked Max up and down critically. "So. Are you clumsy as well as rude and ugly?"

Max grinned.

"Would you care to dance, Madame Ebony?"

"I thought you'd never ask."

As Max put his arm around her and danced her to the floor, Friar saw them and raised his drink in a small salute. Max nodded back and Madame Ebony followed his gaze.

"Who's your friend?" she asked, eyes lingering in a considering way.

"He's a cop. You don't wanna talk to him."

"He looks like a rocky mountain. A nice rocky mountain. I like hiking."

"He's not nice."

"I don't mind. You aren't nice either and I'm dancing with you."

"Yeah, I wondered about that. Why are you, if I'm rude and ugly?"

"Because you're sexy anyway."

"I'm relieved to hear you say that. After your reception at the Emerald City…"

"That's business, Mr. Canon. Tonight I'm on my own." Her eyes glittered in the multi-lights. Somewhere a projection unit turned, splashing a holographic jungle their way.

"So have you ever heard of a dancer called Melody Miller?" he asked her, off hand.

"You ask about other women while you dance with me? I take back what I said. That's not sexy at all."

"I'll find you another partner. Do you know her?"

"I'll find my own partners, thank you." She really did seem angry and was pulling against his hands.

"No, no, you like hiking, I'll bring you a mountain. Never heard of her at all?"

"I don't keep a list of the thousands of women in the industry, if that's what you're on about."

Max danced slowly backwards towards Friar and neatly turned Ebony into his corner.

"Found you a partner, wallflower," he told a horrified Friar. "Madame Ebony, Officer Friar."

"I can't dance," Friar said, taking the one step back that he had.

"Nonsense," Madame Ebony said, tilting her face up to his with a velvet smile. "Any man can dance with me."

Friar suddenly smiled, changing his whole face. Max thought he'd never seen the man smile so much before. Must be the low company. Which made Max grin, too.

"Now that I believe," Friar responded.

"Go on," Max nudged him with an elbow and handed the lady over. "Real quick, though, you know that man at the end of the bar?"

Friar held his filters up to cut through the haze and squinted for a second.

"Strindberg, now what's he doin' here? He's an old academy buddy. Yeah, I know him."

"He is a cop then."

"Yeah, couldn't you tell? We wear it imprinted on our foreheads, for chrissake. Why?"

"I think he's crooked."

Friar face went blank as a granite cliff.

"I don't wanna hear that."

"So don't listen. You gonna dance or what?" Max looked over to where Strindberg was looking back at them. He looked about as happy as Friar, who looked upset, but Ebony was hauling on his arm and he had no choice but to dance or let her break it.

Strindberg ducked away from the bar, losing himself in the crowd. It was one more thing for Friar to be unhappy about that evening but it wasn't going to be the last, either.

Friar wasted the first part of the dance with Ebony trying to relocate Strindberg with his eyes until she complained. Abruptly recalled to his manners, Friar apologized awkwardly and turned his attention to his partner. She had been right when she said any man could dance with her: All Friar had to do was follow her body and they were dancing. It was more fun than he had attention for and he wondered when he'd gotten so old and crippled that he couldn't put aside work for two minutes together to dance with a very attractive and fascinating woman.

When the music ended, he kissed her hand on impulse, something he'd never done before to anyone. Noel would've laughed at him. Ebony seemed to like it, though, and she gave him a cat-eyed smile, all smolder and heat. He grinned, and led her over to the bar, shouting over the next song,

"Buy you a drink, ma'am?"

"As long as you don't call me ma'am, mister." The smile was still on her face, but he could tell she hadn't liked it. He wondered if it was the formality of the tag or the similarity of the word to her profession: He knew who Madame Ebony was. Every cop did. Some knew even better than others.

And here was one of the latter kind now, disheveled and shouting. Friar heard it before he saw Ebony's eyes travel past him towards the sound, and he looked back over his shoulder. Canon was approaching with an odd sort of smile on his face, but not a happy smile, and Strindberg was shouting after him. The words were unintelligible under the roar and crash of the music.

Friar gave Canon a questioning look, but it was returned with a shrug and a casual remark,

"Says he doesn't know Miller, but he does. Wouldn't make that much noise otherwise. We meet again, Lady Ebony." Canon bobbed a small bow her way while Friar tried to burn a hole through his head with hot angry eyes.

"Whaddid he say?"

Max shrugged again.

"Well, he wouldn't say anything. Oh, here he comes, you can ask him."

Friar gave Ebony an apologetic 'excuse me,' and went to head off Strindberg. He had the uncomfortable feeling that Canon's remarks had been phrased to encourage him to question Strindberg himself, but he didn't have time to worry about it.

Strindberg was very drunk, something Friar hadn't noticed earlier. He was calling Canon names, but not making much sense, and the only things he said that were clear were the types of things that told everybody within earshot that he was a cop and a very stupid one, too, who should be robbed and dumped in the river.

Friar hit him full steam from the front in a traveling body check that pivoted him around and had him walking the other way before he realized he'd been intercepted. Strindberg turned blood red eyes—he'd been sampling other things besides liquor tonight—on Friar, but was momentarily silenced by the impact.

Friar marched him into a corner by the restrooms and shoved him against the wall in a pin, stepping in close.

"What're you doing, Strind? Huh? What's this?"

Strindberg glared impotently at him but didn't speak. His hands clenched and unclenched, but he couldn't out-muscle Friar and he knew it.

"None of your business, Friar, keep out of it."

"Tell me why I'm hearing rumors about you being crooked, man." Strindberg's eyes slid away from Friar's and his head starting wandering, looking side to side, anywhere but at Friar. He looked like the classic guilty drunk. "Hey!" Friar grabbed the back of his neck and forced him into stillness. Mouth close to Strindberg's ear, eyes going past to watch the traffic passing close by, he repeated himself with force, so Strindberg could hear him over the music. "What's this I'm hearing about you being crooked? You tell me now or you tell me in front of the Captain."

It was a hollow threat, because Friar had no proof of wrongdoing, but it was effective because Strindberg was too hyped to think straight.

"S'nothing." Strindberg's eyes dropped to his shoes and he stopped resisting Friar's grip. "Just a lil' heat on a girl owes me."

"You're pressuring someone? Blackmail? What're you saying, man?" Friar gave him a little shake.

"Not blackmail. Like a delivery service. She owes me, man, I helped her out, kept her clear. She takes messages here or there for the...for me."

Friar pulled his head back two inches so he could read Strindberg's expression. Was the man saying he was blackmailing a woman he'd helped out of an arrest? And what had Strindberg really meant to say before he changed his sentence? Friar asked but got a sullen glare for answer.

"You try saying anything, I'm denying it all. You got nothin' on me, Friar, nothing." The blood-marbled eyes held his with dull anger and resentment.

"That's true," Friar looked at him with a solid stare, trying to keep the stomach-twisting disgust off his face. Oh, man, who was this guy? "But that could change."

Strindberg laughed, an unhealthy sound. Friar had never seen him so full of alien chemistry.

"It could. And you could find yourself in more trouble than you can handle, tough guy."

Friar was absolutely still for a moment. That had been a threat. He was sure of it. He had an unpleasant vision of Strindberg wandering around the locker room. His imagination added a code card, possibly sweet-talked out of a clerk—Strindberg was very popular with some of the female clerks—and a vial of illegal drugs.

It was entirely possible that Strindberg was up to more than blackmailing a working girl. Which girl, anyway? And carrying messages for who? To who?

Friar took a wild shot, taking his cue from Canon's remarks.

"S'not Miller you're squeezing, is it? Melody Miller?"

Strindberg started physically, a sort of overall jerk that nearly knocked Friar aside. His eyes clouded and the enraged muttering began again.

"Stupid bitch, sending that Ebony cow to do her work for her, thinks she can get out of it, she'll find out, she's in for it now when they hear how she gave away—" He noticed Friar's intent look and recalled himself a minute too early for Friar's preference. He came to a stop and shook his head, a hard, twisted smile on his face.

"But that'd be telling, wouldn't it?"

"Who you gonna rat her out to, man? Anybody I know?" Anybody wants to get the Department dismantled, wants to cause Frank Skills trouble, wants to string us all out on illegal drugs or luck out and get a fatal overdose?

"No." Strindberg wasn't answering the question: he was refusing to say anything else. He folded his arms tightly across his chest. His hands were shaking with the chemistry he was carrying, and with contained rage.

"Who does Melody Miller work for, help me out."

"You go to hell, Friar, you're gonna get me in trouble."

"You're already in trouble, the way it looks, Strind. She didn't show up, how do you know she hasn't betrayed you? Told her boss maybe, to spike your guns?"

"She wouldn't dare. She told the boss, she'd lose more than just her job, I'm telling you—Damn you, Friar, I said no!"

The last was shouted as Strindberg realized he was still talking. He grabbed at his temples like he was trying to hold in something, and Friar couldn't believe this wreck of a junky was his old academy pal. Was a working officer of the law. It made him sick for more reasons than one.

"When did you see her last?" Friar persisted, knowing he wouldn't get a chance to talk to Strindberg ever again about anything that wasn't work related. They certainly weren't going to be friends after tonight.

"Last week, so shut up already, okay? Just let me go, okay? Okay?"

"I can't, you know that. Who's the boss?"

"I can't tell you, you bastard, just leave me alone!" Strindberg seemed to reach his limit and he was shouting again and striking out at Friar.

Friar avoided the flailing, but he wasn't going to leave the man here, crooked or not, if he could help it. He was trying to figure out how to subdue Strindberg when Kay and a pair of day-shifters showed up to flank him. It was sudden cavalry and Friar looked at them in surprise.

Kay shrugged.

"Bourke got a call that he was down here making a scene. You get anything out of him why he's doing this?"

Strindberg was a slavering red-faced blur in the grip of the two day-shift officers. Friar shook his head and started to speak, but he choked on it.

"He's been…he's upset about something. I'd rather not say."

Kay gave him a long look, but didn't press him. To his companions, he said,

"Let's get him home." As the others hauled Strindberg away towards the door, his feet dragging in a fitful attempt to control his path, Kay looked a moment longer at Friar's profile, considering.

"I won't ask why you're down here." It was an invitation to answer anyway.

"Probably best," Friar said, resisting the invitation with no difficulty whatsoever. What Kay would say if he knew Friar was prowling the underworld with a PL looking for a dancing girl and a bunch of prostitutes, he didn't want to hear.

After another minute, Kay left without saying anything else and Friar rejoined Canon at the bar. It wasn't long before he said goodnight and wended his way out in the wake of the others.

Canon wondered what had been said, but he hadn't wanted to upset Friar even more. Not yet, anyway. He'd ask later, when he wasn't as likely to provoke the man into physical violence. Whatever had gone on had left him black with anger. Canon watched him go thoughtfully, then did his best to soothe Ebony's ruffled feelings. He spent ten minutes apologizing for driving off her dance partner and had to make good by substituting for Friar for the next three dances.

By the time Ebony had replaced him with a younger and more agile dancer, Max had sore feet and her opinion of Melody Miller, who had worked at the Emerald City after all, but not for pay. She hadn't apparently been much at all, and since she'd gotten into some legal trouble, she'd been even less. Ebony said she'd danced at the Iron Lung and had gradually gone from pretty and marginally talented to haggard and listless. And then she'd vanished entirely last week. Friar's crooked cop pal had been one of her regulars. He may've been the last to see her.

There was no hint of concern or care in Ebony's tone as she let Max have this statement, but he didn't expect anything else in the world he was dealing in. Business was business and Miller wasn't good for business. Certainly Ebony hadn't thought much of Strindberg either.

Max left with a lot to think about. Sometime in the next day or so, he'd bug Friar and see what had happened between him and his crooked pal. But for tonight, he just wanted to get someplace quiet where the music didn't make his head ache.

Max walked for a lonely four blocks just to clear his head, then he hailed a taxi and headed home.

XXIII.

Canon

The next day, Max called Mrs. March, and this time he had the computer put up a pip accessing the street cameras that showed traffic flow in the good parts of town. The bad parts of town didn't get cameras anymore after they'd all been stolen in the first week of installation. The camera on Mrs. March's block showed a neat trio of lurkers looking casual around a big black assassin's car.

Mrs. March answered on the first ring.

"It's Max. Meet me?"

"Okay." She didn't ask for more, aware as he that the phone was monitored, probably by the three on the street, and if not by them, then by another Caulder operative.

"Suggestions?" Max typed in a rapid command on the keyboard and initiated the scramble. It would only work for twenty or so seconds before it could be sorted out, but all he wanted was their destination concealed.

"How about barbecue? They've got the new vinegar Asian over at Telasco's."

'No, I can't do that stuff. It smells like chem-gel fried soldiers. How about Greek?"

"Sure, yeah, Greek sounds fine. JJK?"

"Great. See ya around dinnertime? I'll send a taxi"

"Okay. See you there."

Max heard the click over as the scrambler was defeated, but it was too late, so he didn't care. He arranged for her cab from another console and went to get cleaned up. She got points for acting: He could tell what he'd said had been too shocking, but it'd just come out without warning. She'd acted like it hadn't happened, though he could hear the control in her voice that said she was trying not to think too hard about it. Definite points. Dangerous woman.

"You don't seem to see much of Caulder these days."

They were at her apartment, watching the lights of the city burning across the black space of the golf course. They hadn't been followed.

"He's busy." She didn't say much more than that, but Max saw the smallest suggestion of a look in her eyes that could've been hurt or jealousy.

"Is that why you keep calling me up?"

"Don't be silly. You're helping me with a problem, that's all."

"So why'd you sleep with me?"

There was a long pause. Mrs. March opened the sliding door and walked out onto the balcony. Max couldn't follow her without being seen, so he stayed just inside the curtains and watched the wind blow her hair off her smooth shoulders. The dress swung and twisted around her, paper thin fabric outlining those long, long legs. Max grinned at nothing she'd understand.

Her answer surprised him.

"I was afraid of you."

"Afraid of me?"

"When Bart was killed at the roadhouse." She turned, leaning back against the chromed railing and gave him a long considering look. "You fought like a professional killer, very…clean. Quiet. It was quite frightening. And you seemed so unreachable." She turned back to look out at the night across the stretches of green, wide park, across the golf course like a lake of grass. "But you're just a man."

"I coulda told ya that." Max lit one of her real tobacco cigarettes and tried not to sound let down. Nobody wanted to be thought of as just anything.

"Why are you here, Mr. Canon?"

Another surprise question. Her tone changed the subject entirely and he knew she wasn't asking about anything relevant to blackmail.

He shrugged and went back into the room, feeling the night breeze brush the back of his neck as he mixed them both drinks at her fancy bar.

"You either move to a town because you know somebody there, or because nobody there knows you. To set up business, or take up old business, whatever."

"And you are doing which?"

Max laughed, slightly puzzled, but he saw no reason not to answer.

"I'm working on the usual business, I guess. Sometimes it feels like I had old business here before I even arrived." He brought her drink to the door.

She came in for it, pulling the curtains shut behind her but leaving the doors open. The wind belled the curtains into the room in long, green-scented gusts, smelling like autumn and grass.

He handed her the glass and watched her seat herself with her usual floating grace on the sofa.

"I know that feeling," she told him, eyes on something he couldn't see. "It's not a nice feeling."

He shrugged again, feeling the movement pull against various bruises and sore muscles. It reminded him of new business.

"You think your boyfriend will have me beat up again for being here, or just killed this time?"

She exploded off the sofa in a sudden flash of color and sound.

"Don't! It's not funny!" Her drink went flying, barely missing his head. Gin spilled across his right shoulder, adding a scent of pine and turpentine to the faint rose traces she left in every room she inhabited.

Max watched her stalk around the room like a caged, frightened animal and kept very still.

When she wound down to the sofa again, she was flushed from her exertion, but something had gone out of her.

"You should go." she said. She sounded defeated and young.

He only nodded, and she looked up at his silence. She looked into his eyes and he was amazed to see a tear slide down one powdered cheek. It looked like a real one, not one of her play-acting weapons.

"Do you want me to?"

"Rather than see you killed if Dan finds you here? Yes."

"But you're not expecting him tonight, are you? Or you wouldn't've asked me over to consult."

She tucked her lower lip, and looked away, but said nothing.

"I know that's true." He sipped from his drink and realized he'd over mixed it. The alcohol was weak and tasted cheap. He set it aside and went to sit beside her. The sofa was soft and cool under him and her scent came to him on the breeze. Rose and Mrs. March. Who needed bourbon? "It's partly why I agreed to come tonight. I'm not in any hurry to die. Tell me who the three are."

She didn't have to ask which three he meant. Her gaze went to her lap, where her hands twined into each other in a tense and constant cat's cradle.

"I don't know all the names. The lead man is called Krueger. They sometimes do heavy work for Dan." She looked up at Max and her eyes were huge in the dim light. "Sometimes I think even he's afraid of them. Taken separately, they're not so bad, except for the woman. Silver, she's called. She's crazy. Krueger keeps her in line."

Max nodded, then asked,

"What about the wide guy?"

"I don't know his name." She shook her head. "And I don't ask. That's Dan's business and he'd wonder if I started asking questions." She looked down again. "I'm not much help, am I?"

"That's not your job." Max pulled a strand of pale hair back from her ear and watched her profile for a moment. "I may've found your Fokke. He's a cop."

Her head came up at that, startled. Max grinned.

"I told you I could find him. I'm going to check him out. I'll let you know."

She looked at his crooked grin and a smile started at the corner of her own mouth. "Are you on a time-table?" She asked, and her voice was soft and suddenly rich with invitation.

Who was Max to say no?

"Tomorrow would do just as well," he said, eyes hooding slightly with a faint lift of eyebrow.

Her smile grew wider and she leaned in to kiss him with the taste of her drink still on her lips, gin and menthol.

The curtains danced and swelled in the shifting winds.

Friar

I hadn't seen Strindberg at all during shift, and I heard later he was 'out sick.' I wondered only a little about it since tonight I was to have dinner with Noel and it took way more of my attention than it should've. Sherrow even harassed me about it, which put me in a foul mood clear through shift and into the cab to the restaurant that night.

Noel had on a necklace I'd bought her one million years ago on our third anniversary, a silver star. It was a sort of joke: it was a lot like an APD badge, and it was also her decoration of valor for staying with me for those three years.

It didn't seem so funny now, and I felt my stomach tighten. The food wasn't as good here as I'd been led to believe, and I hadn't been led to expect much. The place was the latest in Home Earth historical. I guess the atmosphere was supposed to make up for the lack of good food or service, but I doubted weather a vacation in the real Hawaii would consist of queasy motion murals of erupting volcanoes and implausible blue waves studded with flower-decked natives in canoes.

"I remember that necklace," I said, pointing with my fork. A floppy 'appetizer' drooped in her direction.

Her hand went to her throat, face blank, then she smiled with a twist.

"The cop star. Yeah. My new boss likes it. Thinks it's funny."

Something in the way she said it did not encourage questions why, so I let it go. Strange to feel more comfortable when I knew for sure she didn't want me. I 'spose I was half afraid she did, afraid 'coz I still wanted her. But I wouldn't know what to do with her if I got her back. It'd been too long. I was doomed to suffer love in the form of memories and terror in the form of what-if. I didn't want to know what if: The memories already hurt enough for the next three lives.

"So, any new women in your life?" She went straight for the throat as usual. I gave her a grin and tried more salad.

"One or two." I was thinking of Crystal and Ketchikian. She arched an eyebrow.

"Any decent women?"

Not sure how to take that question, I answered her excluding Ketchikian, since Noel was sure to consider another cop less than decent.

"One. Or so."

"Have you asked her out yet?" There was laughter in her face as she picked up her wine glass, blood red lacquered nails against blood red wine. The old engagement ring I'd nearly bankrupted myself for was on her middle finger, next to a ruby bigger than a hardboiled egg. It made the engagement ring look like a cracker-jack prize.

"You still wearin' that, too?"

She looked at it blank, just like she had the necklace, forgetting it was there.

"Oh. Sure, I always liked that ring." Her voice was indifferent. She didn't thank me for it. "You didn't answer my question. Have you asked her out yet? The decent woman?"

"Working up to it," I tried out my own drink, found it bitter. Why do I do this to myself? "If I wait long enough, my new partner will arrange a date."

Noel laughed at that, long and hard. She loved it: It was hilarious.

"You look good, Noel," It came out of my mouth without conscious volition and I could've bitten my tongue because it sounded pathetic. "Looking like money," I amended.

She heard the barb and grinned cat-like, but her eyes weren't smiling at my pathetic existence any more. She was angry that I'd commented on hers.

"Thank you."

After that, conversation dwindled until the dinner came. I went up to the bar myself to get us drinks, more to get away for a moment than to insure that we got decent liquor, like I'd used as an excuse. Noel knew what it was for and looked vaguely relieved. Some asshole as big as me knocked into me and made me slosh booze over a slender little thing in a full holo rig, and her thuggy date looked like he wanted to scrag both me and the asshole, but the fight was averted by the bar tender's timely intervention, and I collected the drinks again, my cocktail, her wine and navigated back to the table, avoiding asshole's clumsy attempts at apologies and clinging hands. He was wasted, maybe, hard to tell, but I was so distracted I didn't much care as long as he got out of my way. I didn't even notice the clinging hands, all road-map lines and blunt fingers, until much, much later when I had cause to look back over the evening and wonder, after I'd learned to count to three.

Noel was lounging back in her plastic Honolulu deck chair among the terrible vinyl tropic decor. My plate had arrived while I was up getting drinks and the food looked like it'd been slipped out of the kitchen via the garbage heap, dropped on the way and scooped back up. I hoped it didn't taste like it looked.

I plunked Noel's wine down in front of her and sat.

"Why do we always meet in this kind of place?" I sounded like a crabby grizzly, my throat frozen from the over-iced drink. Next one was gonna be whisky neat.

"It's in deference to your paycheck," Noel said on the start of a throaty laugh, eyes inviting me to laugh, too, it wasn't personal.

I couldn't laugh, 'coz even if it wasn't, it felt like it was.

"I can spare enough of my meager pay to meet you in a better place than this, lady. You don't gotta slum for poor little old me."

Her laugh vanished and her eyes sobered.

"Maybe I have other friends I meet here besides you," she said with a brittle edge.

"Pimps and pushers?" I looked around at the clientele and realized that despite my disgusted tone, I fit right in. "And run-down cops."

"Don't be stupid, Victor. You're not run-down."
This in the face of my bruises and the hollow black circles
under my eyes that Sherrow was kindly not mentioning.
"You're just tired. You need a vacation. A proper one."

I took a critical look at her face and saw real emotion.
She looked soft and kind and a little sad and it about killed
me. I took refuge in a punishing slurp of the sugary, sub-
zero concoction in my hand and looked away. God, yes, I
did still love her. Yes, I did still want her. I didn't have a
chance in Hell.

"Yeah. Yer right. Maybe I can go flipside for some
country time."

"Oh, no, that's passé'. You need to visit Majon or
Maria."

"Cops don't go off world for vacation, Noel." I
shook my head. Out of the corner of my eye, I saw a few
heads turn and wondered if my voice had been that loud. I
moderated my tone. I was the only cop here, run down or
otherwise. "Anyways, they're too expensive."

"You can get round-trip fare to Maria for less than a
thousand," Noel objected. "It's lovely there this time of
year."

Again I washed questions down with the bad cocktail,
like how would she know? It nearly choked me.

"Fare is only half the battle. A third. I still gotta have
a place to sleep and food to eat when I get there. Maria is
more expensive than most colonies and they're twice dirt
side prices."

"How about a cruise then? See some stars, a few
lovely women, get out of the department and town for
awhile…"

"I'll get him out of town for awhile," a new voice
offered. I left off reading the ice-cubes in my drink and laid
an eyeball on the owner of such a dissatisfied and petulant
voice. Dark hair, blue eyes, long nose, square jaw—Hell, it
could be Cannon's kin, wonder if Skills knows him too—this
one wore a bad hot pink antique bowling shirt worth
hundreds and what looked like flat-line weaponry by the
bulge at his ankle under the black trousers. Behind him
hovered an anxious bar-owner and three or four angry-

looking compatriots, all ready to help me with my vacation plans.

Noel tried to be nice about it.

"Please. We're not threatening you. Let us have our dinner in peace." She made it sound oddly like a command, and one or two of the bullies looked ready to obey, but Pink Shirt was drunk and wanted a scrap. Me, too, if the odds were better, but they weren't and I was unarmed. Like an idiot.

"Maybe I'll join you then." Pink Shirt pulled up a chair and straddled it backwards, classic bully style. I wondered what movie he'd stolen it from. "I think I recognize yer cop here," 'Cop' being a curse word sobering me up fast as I thought of Sherrow's buddies and the overabundance of illegal street drugs around these days. "And I just need a minute to remember where we met. Could it be," big eyes here, like he was surprised by the sudden memory, "that yer the man who arrested me and my pals last year for loitering? Loitering!" He shared the insult with Noel and turned evil eyes back to me. "Loitering."

Despite myself, I felt my own eyes narrow as I thought back: pages of assholes scrolled past double-time till I came up with a match.

"Yeah, I remember you. Diamond-something, something Diamond, you and your guys were making the locals nervous out by the strato-mall."

"And you threw Mickey over the rail." He turned to share this piece of monstrous police brutality with all the watching faces, the kind who needed an audience. To Noel, he leaned close and confided, "He fell twelve levels before the hover hit him. Splat! All over the Gucci store front."

Noel leaned away and looked at me, one eyebrow lifted.

"He was resisting arrest and during the scuffle he hit the rail and overbalanced. There was nothing I could do."

"You coulda grabbed his hand or something." From back in the crowd.

"I did." My turn to play hard-eyes. "One of you idiots jostled me from behind and I lost grip."

"Yer lying. You deliberately threw him off." Pink Shirt Diamond Something gathered his thugs around him. I recounted heads and got seven. Checked options. Felt the drinks I'd had sitting like a descending fog around my upper lobes, cold lead under my diaphragm. Put my thumbs under the table edge.

"If I was gonna deliberately throw anyone over the rail on the stratosphere level, man, it for sure would've been you."

The effect was a remarkable color-change from drunk-flush to purple anger and he half-stood, arm sliding down towards that itty bitty blazer at his ankle.

I launched the table and all its contents that direction. The ceramic palm-tree condiment set hit Pink Shirt square in the forehead and the knot of thugs scattered. I grabbed Noel by the wrist and ran.

The lower levels aren't much to look at, but at least we weren't on the tarmac. The traffic was a snarl here on the third, and what we needed was freedom of movement, so I headed up.

I never asked Noel where her car was and she didn't offer: We both knew I didn't really want to know who'd dropped her off to meet me. We went up a level or two and traffic thinned out. I ran a zigzag pattern down narrow alleys, not entirely stable on my feet as the fumes from that damn fruity cocktail roiled around with the crappy appetizers. We charged between structures, into the defiles behind, where there were no streets, just bank after bank of pedestrian tunnels leading from one cheap hotel to another, to restaurants that steamed all colors into the dim neon, through stores and emporiums that sold junk to the tourists; glitter-globes with shitty holographics of the fancy downtown part of Alaman—ten miles up-river from where we were—talking key chains that narrated a long list of beauties the city had somewhere if only you knew where to look, computer enhanced postcards that made the city look cleaner and more interesting and like someplace else.

Noel kept up like a track-star but I could feel reluctance as I towed her along. I was looking for a clear path to an upper level street with cops. Cops meant allies, meant free ride, and I had no other way to get Noel out of this since I'd taxied out to meet her.

We finally broke clear of the alleys and rat-ways, thundering along the metal cat-walk between an upper-level pizza place and a bank. I could see traffic ahead against black night sky. The lights were leaving streamers on my retinas, another sign that all was not well. My shoulder blades itched, waiting for that first shot from Pink Shirt's weapon. I had no doubt our pursuers were all armed similarly.

Noel saw the traffic and stopped short.

"Come on, come on, they're right behind us!" I pulled, but she wasn't having any, and shook her head.

"Go, Vic, it's you they're after."

"I'm not leaving you!" An outraged roar.

"But I'm in no danger here, darling."

Her voice was almost too low to hear, but I heard it and it stopped me short and cold, then sank in and took my heart with it.

"You know them."

"Go, Vic, hurry. They're coming."

I knew the look on her face and it felt like being divorced all over again, the court, the yelling, the hard-eyed lying sonofabitch attorney telling everyone I was sociopathic, and Noel with her eyes demurely downcast, play-acting the victim for the courts and the papers and my buddies from the department who knew what I'd just gone through with Croner and weren't sure it wasn't true. I turned and ran.

My heart was hammering again, like it would explode as I pelted down the grid work. I spotted an open-top cab in the anorexic traffic-flow, drifting on a smoke-break, probably.

"Taxi!" I bellowed and hunched a shoulder as a bolt of energy tore the air by my ear into a deafening vacuum drowning out what might've been an angry yell from Noel. We were not in the better part of town for sure, 'coz a cabby there would've stuck his nose up and his foot down and left me in a cloud of ozone. As it was, the cabbie went for the big tip and jinked suddenly to the rail, braking sharply. I cleared the pitted metal in one magnificent leap, a sickening glimpse of ten stories—we'd come so far, so fast I was amazed—flashing below, bolts of expensive energy snapping around me as the bad guys got range with their little pocket guns. Then a lucky shot caught me a split second before I faced on the torn red faux leather.

The cabbie had disabled the safety mechanism designed to prevent a vehicle from pulling away from a dock without the roof screen being engaged, and he was accelerating away from the rail almost before I landed. It was a major misdemeanor to take on a fare without locking onto the rail, but it was a safety oversight I was prepared to ignore under the circumstances.

"Pay now," the cabbie shouted into the hurricane of our passage. So he'd seen me take the bolt. I was pawing at the numb spot and rapidly discovering a shallow but lengthy wound that would hurt like hell later, but wouldn't kill me.

I paid him a lot of extra for coming for me and directed him to a downtown bottom-bar where I could pause for breath and figure out what had just happened. Noel's unhappy face as she turned to meet the thugs pursuing me...It looked very bad.

It looked even worse, when I started to hallucinate a few minutes later. I sat in the bar for an undetermined amount of time before I did a Sherrow and phoned for help. I ended up giving the rest of my paycheck to my little rat doctor to come get me from the bar and patch me up just like he had Sherrow, while I watched people in full-color reverse floating and talking backwards, eyes glowing green and red, the space where they passed shimmering black and silver behind them. It was like a time warp sort of, and I could guess which drug it was, even though, good cop that I am, I never inhale. Of course not. Nobody does.

I bought extra supplies in case I needed them later, like last time.

I still had to get myself home. I almost called Kay, but at the last second, I stopped. I'd have to tell him about Noel and I couldn't take it just then. It'd upset him, too, more then he'd show, but I knew him and I'd feel worse than I already did.

In the end I had rat doc put me in another lousy low-level cab and ferry my sinking, sick ass home.

I slept fitfully in the armchair because every time I started to doze off in the bed, I felt like I was falling through it, and I was afraid I'd wake up with springs coiled all through me like an old-fashioned toaster and they'd have to remove each one surgically.

Warp is not a good crash. Sherrow and me had something to talk about now.

XXIV.

Canon

It was very early when Max let himself out of Mrs. March's complex by the back door, her idea. He wasn't sure it would fool anybody, but if it made her feel better, fine. He lit a cigarette, one kyped from the pearl-inlaid box of Stephanie's—Stephanie, what a name for such a magnificent woman! She should have the name of a movie star, not the same name as the daughter of a sergeant Max had known years and years ago. The smell of real tobacco smoke in the sunshine was a smell Max had almost forgotten. It smelled like young ambition, excitement, that first day for combat, the first day in real uniform, not trainee drab. It reminded him of futures with possibility, not just drudgery and hardship.

For a panicky moment, Max thought he really might be falling in love, and it scared him to a standstill. Then he reasoned like a grown-up and decided it was lust and the excitement of the chase. Possibly the strange hour, sun up and bright after rain, the clean green park stretching out like an Eden on his left, the satisfaction of knowing he would solve this case and get a huge payment from the most beautiful mob-mistress on the planet, maybe this end of the colonized universe...

If he lived long enough. And he had to get his mind off the most beautiful mob-mistress, because she was using him to stop a blackmailer and he knew he was being used.

Still, his job sort of encouraged that, and he was having a great time, for the first time in years.

And that was dangerous too.

Damn.

Max let himself into the flat quietly. Jolie didn't hear him, his silent stalk was still that good, and she spun when he appeared behind her in the mirror.

And again, she looked different. Hair, makeup, expression, everything was different except the eyes, the pansy velvet brown that went with the innocent pose and the loud roadhouse redhead from the brawl that'd gotten him into all this.

"Max, thank God you're back!"

She flew to him and wrapped him in scented arms and cleavage. She was spilling out of one of his shirts and her hair was loose and fell in waves around him. He inhaled deeply, gave her a pat and disengaged.

"It's nearly lunchtime," he said. "You hungry?" It was weak, but what else could he say? He didn't believe her. She wasn't as frightened or frail as she had pretended to be twice before, and that opening line was pure cinema. She <u>was</u> nervous about something, though and Max let her keep the arm she was clinging to and led her around to sit on the bed. It gave under their double weight with a soft ping. Through the connecting door, he could see the sofa. The lonely sofa. His bed tonight. He could still smell a faint hint of Stephanie's perfume on his clothes.

"Have you found Steve?" Jolie asked in a voice of breathless anxiety, but underneath, Max heard that touch of real hysteria again. And the scratches along the back of her shoulder weren't painted on. There were some bruises, too. More than he'd gotten a look at before.

Should he tell her? Did she need to know yet? He turned on the lamp on the end table so he could see her better, read her face. He'd made the lamp out of his helmet when he'd left the military and every woman he'd ever brought here hated it. Jolie's eyes told him she hated it, too. He took her hand.

"Albrecht's dead. Down in the 'Easy. I'm sorry."

She was blank for a long moment, then she turned her head away and down, stiffly, like an automaton.

"Dead," She parroted, not soaking it in yet. Shock? Max wondered. Grief? Or something else: Fear. If Albrecht was expendable, Jolie Laide was too.

Max said again,

"I'm sorry."

She turned the pansy eyes up to him then and the fear in them was real.

"Help me." He had to read her lips, she whispered it so softly.

"I will," Max put an arm around her in what he hoped was a brotherly fashion. He didn't have a lot of practice comforting women. Anne had been a soldier and with a professional's hard streak. After her, there were cops and tough types, and then Marie, who needed comfort on a rather less drastic level. What could he possibly say to this woman when he wasn't even sure he could protect her long enough to find out what was going on?

"I will." He patted her shoulder, careful of the scratches and stared at the far wall, thinking, thinking, and wondering, too.

Beside him, Jolie started weeping quietly. He patted her shoulder and thought fiercely. After awhile, he left her to make some phone calls where she could see him through the connecting door but not hear what he was saying.

Friar

Sherrow's face when he finally got a look at me would've been hilarious if he'd been lookin' at anybody else. Disbelief, consternation and what had to be a hysterical desire to laugh flickered madly with budding concern, which was the most disturbing of the lot; I didn't need a pal, I needed a partner—and he settled on a blank,

"How'd dinner go, Vic?"

I growled at him and let him live. I still had to get into uniform without splitting anything open or squalling like a stuck parrot. I'd need all my energy for that.

In the locker room, there was Hollingate this time, giving me a look that said volumes.

"You feelin' okay, Friar?" he said, all concern, "You look sorta like you haven't been sleeping?"

"I'm sleepin'," I defended.

"Who with?" he split a wide leer and laughed, showing me he was joking, and I laughed even though I didn't think it was funny, because Strindberg had just shown up, looking better than he had at the club, but a little like he couldn't remember it. He was looking my way, and I wasn't ready for him yet, so I retreated into locker room bullshit and got to my locker as soon as I decently could.

I'd put on a uniform blouse before I'd left the apartment to avoid flashing my wounds to public eyes, but I still had to get into the rest of my kit. I was way too stiff with bandages and dried blood to contort enough to wear my preferred, unauthorized body armor, so I pulled out the department issue, knocking the good vest out of the locker in my clumsiness. Hollingate had followed me and was there to pick it up, but he paused in handing it back to whistle, which of course turned heads, and being who he was, felt the need to be more of an asshole, and me without any coffee to steel myself.

"Heavy duty shit, Friar. The chief know yer wearing this?"

"I'm not wearing it today, " I hefted the cheap-ass issue and slid an arm through, clenching my teeth against the ducking-head-and-lifting-arm-to-don-armor move that was gonna hurt like hell. Hollingate took it for an angry teeth-clench and grinned.

"Expensive, too," he said.

Sherrow and some of the younger cops sauntered over to get a look at the non-issue military-strength, beam-dispersing, bullet-stopping, 10 pounds heavier save-your-ass-with-huge-safety-margin armor. It went around the circle of hands as I grit-toothed Hollingate while buckling into the issue and he kept up the witty patter.

"Yer ex-wife buy that for ya as a wedding gift? Protect her investment? In-vest-ment?" and he laughed.

I didn't.

"That is heavy shit," Sherrow handed me back the vest and I stowed it, turning my back on Hollingate like I always had Wells when I couldn't look at him without hitting him.

"Stop department rounds," I said, and all the young cops fell silent while they remembered the stories about my first partner. Some nodded at the value of such heavy shit.

Sherrow just said,

"Nothing wrong with that, man," but he had an odd look on his face.

As soon as we got into the cruiser with Sherrow driving, I tuned the radio to a blank space and told him what kind of night I'd really had. He squinted through the windscreen and nodded. I scanned him for signs of I-told-you-so, but there wasn't a trace. Surprised, I looked closer.

While he had lost the bad attitude after our talk, the dark circles hadn't gone away. They in fact looked worse. I was opening my mouth to comment when he reached over to turn on the radio again and an all-call came blaring out for our area. After that, there never seemed to be time and he dodged me all shift, running away at the end while I was still changing. I didn't have the energy to chase him.

Skills wasn't so lucky though, coz I could take an elevator to corner him, so I evaded Captain Crocker who wanted a piece of me about the vest, and skipped up to bother the Chief.

Skills didn't want to see me, but he let me in anyway.

"What," he said, looking tired already.

"Major Warp import. I want permission to track it."

He paused to stare at me hard.

"What happened to Mitchell's hit and run?"

"I think they're connected."

Another stare, but this one ended in a sigh.

"Well, it'll still have to be on your own time, Friar. I need you on the streets right now." He gave a twisted smile. "There's too many drugs around."

"Yeah, and Warp is out of fashion, I know."

"Out of price range, anyway. Dare I ask who yer going after? I just wanna know if I need to start lookin' for a new pair of shoes for your beat."

"And a psychiatrist for Sherrow. I'm not gonna get killed."

"So you aren't going after Caulder?"

I didn't dare flinch.

"Not directly," I told him.

"So you are going to get killed," was his answer.

"Frank, we're being framed." I risked the informality, appealing to his sense of comradeship: we'd been in this boat together for years. "You, me, all the cops in this precinct, maybe in this town. You haven't noticed the number of out-sicks and beat ups? We're being victimized and I'm telling you we got turncoats and takers all over the damn place, here in our own House. There's Mickey Finns being forced on off-duty officers, muggings and car wrecks. We've got rats, Frank. We gotta clean house."

He looked unimpressed by my outburst, but I could see him thinking.

"I want proof." He said finally. "You know I need proof."

"I don't have it yet."

"Or you don't have clean proof. What're you into, Friar?"

"I'm not sure, but most of it I can't tell you anyway, officially. But I'm hip-deep and I haven't located the shoveller yet."

"When you say frame..."

"Yeah, yeah, but we're dodging so far."

"We."

"Me and a pal."

"Meaning someone you feel responsible for. Meaning Sherrow."

"Me and a pal." I shrugged. No way I was mentioning Wells, too.

"Any names I should keep tabs on?"

I sighed.

"Not without proof." I stood. " Do I have permission?"

"Gimme a name. Even you are suspect right now."

"Strindberg," I said after a moment's hesitation. I felt like a rat, but between Canon's remarks and Strindberg's own confession of blackmail, I was pretty sure I was right in who was at least bringing the Warp into our station.

He looked at me long and hard and finally ceded.

"Okay. But don't make me regret this, Vic."

"I'll try. Thanks. And maybe you can keep IA from declaring any tissue drug-screens for another month or so?" I couldn't help but add hopefully.

His scowl told me all I needed to know about his feeling on that unpleasant piece of half-information, but he nodded, barely.

I left his office feeling like I hadn't actually won anything at all.

Next I had to see Noel again and try to get her to tell me about her pals, but her answering machine was on and she wasn't home. I'd try again later, call until I got her.

I went to get changed. In the hatcheck mirror inside my locker door, I looked like well-tenderized beef before the grill, and I felt like a badly rolled cigarette, half-smoked and left in the gutter on a rainy night.

Shining happy face, as usual, lucky me.

XXV.

Canon

Max went back to the apartment Albrecht had been at to talk to the manager but there wasn't much she could add to what he'd overheard her telling the police.

She didn't seem impressed by his license, and when she forced him almost physically out the door, he acquiesced gracefully, sneaking immediately around back and up the back stairs.

There was a little girl with big blue eyes and a blonde bob playing in the hall. Her fuzzy animatronic headband waved at Max as he came down the worn carpet towards the late Albrecht's apartment, and he smiled. She looked up in time to see this and though she drew back on her heels warily, she didn't run.

Max asked her about Albrecht. She bit her lip in an eight-year old way and looked pensive. She looked like she was copying an adult mannerism and Max smiled again.

"I saw him. He was redheaded. Like orange. And mean. He yelled at me for running in the hall in broad daylight, too, it wasn't like it was late even!"

Max made sympathetic clucking noises to this unjust behavior and asked,

"Did he ever have visitors that you saw?"

A vigorous nod made the blonde bob bounce and she got up and walked over to the door of the apartment as if demonstrating.

"He had a pretty lady with long hair over once, and she smiled at me. She even said I was pretty, too." This compliment had apparently afforded her much happiness, and Max rushed to add his own. She nodded happily at him and went on. "She was blonde, too, very pretty. She wanted to give me a piece of candy, but ma wouldn't let me keep it."

"That is too bad. But it probably is better that you don't take things from strangers. A mean person like the redheaded man could give you something dangerous just to be mean and hurt you. You never know," Max warned, having no qualms at all at blackening the dead man's character to prove a point.

The little girl nodded wisely and pursed her lips.

"Yes, I can see where that might be the case." Once again her tone was a copy of something her mother had probably said many times. It made Max laugh.

"Well, thank you for talking to me, pretty lady," He bowed gallantly. "But perhaps you should be at home with your mother rather than talking to strange men in the hall."

"Oh, ma knows I'm here. She'll hit orbit when she sees you."

As if on cue, Max heard a shrill adult voice calling after 'Katie.' With an impish grin, the girl bounced away down the hall and vanished into an apartment four doors down. The shrill voice rose once and then fell to a placating purr. Max took the opportunity to vanish.

He really needed to talk to the cop again. It sounded like Silver Georgia Killer-for-hire was out and about.

Friar

At lunch, I noticed Sherrow still looking peaky. Some girl in a mimetic camo mini had gone across our path on the way into the automat and reminded me of Noel, so it'd taken me awhile to notice how long he'd been gone to the men's room. I waited another five minutes then decided to go search and rescue, coz we only had two to get back on the street.

When he saw me coming through the door, he tucked a bandaged arm back into his uniform jacket in a hurry. He hadn't had the jacket off all day and now I knew why. He turned a black scowl on me, his eyebrows in their don't-fuck-with-me Satan triangles.

"S' that?" I asked, casual.

"S'nothing." Him, defensive and leery.

"Looks sorta like it started bleedin' again. When'd that happen?"

"Bar brawl." He sneered it, daring me to comment.

I considered his expression. It looked like he wanted me to yell about brawling, which meant it was a decoy. Instead, I said,

"What bar was this?"

He took a little too long to come up with a name, so I knew I had him lying.

"Huh." I said. "Whatever. 'S long as work don't suffer," I added a shrug.

He snorted at that.

"Like your performance has been all that great." There was a pause while he wondered if he shouldn't've said that.

"Sure," I said after a full two heartbeats. "That's why I don't think we both oughta be half-assed."

"You haven't been half-assed exactly."

Man, he looked awful.

"Half-brained, then. You look like Hell. How bad is that? Sprained?"

"Cut." He shrugged. "S'nothing. Forget it."

"If it's nothing why do you look so shitty?"

"And you look so good. Maybe we both need to get some sleep."

His tone was funny and I pretty much knew by it that he was referring to my bar hopping, so now I was sure he was still following me.

"You get that at one of my bars?" I point-blanked.

"S'nothing, man. Forget it."

He looked ready to get mad, and after another jab or two, I let it go. Let him think I was willing to ignore his distress in favor of my own troubles. Noel had left me long ago, no matter how bad the most recent betrayal hurt—if only I could talk to her, ask her what it was about—but no, Sherrow was still here, even if neither of us would use the word friend, and maybe it wasn't the right word anyway. Partner was.

And Kay. I had Kay, who Sherrow sometimes talked to. Time for me to talk to Kay again, too.

So I asked Kay for advice, feeling like a heel, but beyond a look that said 'shame, didn't I teach you better?' he couldn't do much to help. My next step was the station Infirmary. I was thinking Sherrow might've been creative and lied to get treatment there, but they hadn't seen him at all, so I started canvassing the closest drugstores to his apartment. I struck gold on number three. The elderly proprietor knew Jerry Sherrow well, such a nice upstanding boy and yes, he'd been in for medical supplies just the other day. Smelled of smoke and booze? Smoke, yes, like you get on your clothes in a smoky bar. He looked a little mussed, you know how boys get into these little fights.

I got a rough day and time from him and it tallied time-wise with a bar I'd left hurriedly to avoid a brewing brawl. That I'd inadvertently left my rookie partner to get a knife cut in it made me feel guilty and angry at the same time. It wasn't my fault he'd been cut, but it was my responsibility to look after him if he'd been there.

So the next time I went scum-cruising, I kept my eyes out for Sherrow, and sure enough, there he was again, tailing me as usual, looking ready to pass out in the dim illumination of the wretched, stinking hovel of a gas and dust bar. It made me livid, and I cornered him near the bar rail, trapping him between board and mask racks.

He made to step away, to buy some room to move, and I kept him in place by simply tacking his hurt wrist to the bar top. He winced, so I knew it hurt a lot. Must be some cut. It made me feel even shittier.

"Why're'ya still followin' me, kid?" I started in on him without warning, and he swayed back from my sudden attack, but didn't retreat.

"I don't want you to get shot. Look bad on my career jacket, losin' two seniors in one year."

He never quite got rid of that faint guilt over Randall's death, and it echoed in his sarcasm.

"It'll look worse if your second senior beats hell outta you for insubordination," was all I could say without touching a nerve.

"Look, just slow down, Friar and I'll quit. Someone's gonna pop you one, you keep sticking yer nose in all over."

"I thought you were just as anxious as me to hear the answers to a few questions."

"Yeah, I am, but the more I see you get beat up and framed and shot at, and the more I get shit dropped into my drinks by strangers in maf pay, the more I think maybe it is the detectives' job and even if you live, you'll probably get busted down to street sweeper before this is all over."

I let that unwieldy statement lay in the air for a while before answering.

"Street sweeping is an under-valued career." I said, then turned my eyes back to the stage where naked men and women romped in what was supposed to be sexy entertainment, but was closer to art and therefore boring and confusing.

"I was talking to Kay the other day—"

I glared at him, but he went on, undismayed.

"You don't talk to me, and I got no friends in the department yet, not that kinda friend, and he said to call if I had any questions."

"Was this before or after I introduced you guys?"

"Same day I think. Anyhow, it doesn't matter. What does matter was that I had questions."

That made me feel like an asshole again.

"I'm sorry I've been such a bastard you couldn't ask me yer questions."

"Well, you wouldn't have answered these questions anyway. So we were talking and we came up with the idea that maybe we aren't the only cops being set up or fucked with. You ask anybody else if they've got shit going on?"

I gave him a look of pure approval then.

"Not really, but I know for a fact that at least one of our shift mates had a run-in with your Mickey Finnette."

Sherrow thought for a minute, then said,

"Wells."

Again with the approving look.

"Very good. I 'spose it was the unusual restraint he's been showing in regards to the torture and teasing of yours truly?"

"That and he looked like I felt the day after for awhile there. So who would benefit from screwing up cops?"

"The question is, who would suffer? Then we ask who would want them to suffer." I looked at the stage and shook my head. "Let's get out of here. I wanna talk where I don't have to shout."

We spent the next hour in a booth in Crystal's section of the restaurant she worked at, and I managed to even remember vaguely how to flirt. Sherrow took his turn casting approving looks at us like an indulgent uncle, and Crystal showed me a truly winning smile and more of that great sense of humor.

She kissed me after bringing our bill, too, full on the mouth in front of Sherrow, which embarrassed me, but seemed to delight him. It was a territorial kiss and it stopped our useless conjecture about bad guys and brought up how that weekend had gone and more importantly, my date with Crystal.

We never got back to brainstorming. It was late and Sherrow swallowed wrong and ended up coughing up coffee all over, and by the time his coughing fit was over, we were both too distracted and tired to try anymore.

I told him to go home and we parted on nearly friendly terms.

Canon

When Max was 20, he was transferred from his unit—
the unit he'd trained with, graduated with and fought with—
and they put him into a front line unit in the wars, planet
hopping from brush war to brush fire and back. He'd had
some pilot-training in his first unit, a conceit of the
commanding officer since pilots had to have school degrees
so it meant all the soldiers were educated if only a little. In
the second duty-station, it made Max the outsider. Ninety
percent of the front line bush jumpers were from places like
Mexico and Afghanistan where their countries had little
more to do with space faring than sending their citizens out
to work. Mexico produced the finest mercenaries, but not a
lot with educations.

Max learned Spanish along with every other front line
solider in the wars, but he was still the school degree, hence
an automatically higher rank, hence, an outsider. He had no
friends.

He stopped trying after awhile, and when the air drops
and running battles of Baditz became bad enough to make
the news and slice a chunk off history with sheer numbers
lost and tonnage of air craft destroyed, he didn't have time to
care. There was loyalty amongst them, the same color shirt,
same team type but the rest of his platoon treated him like
an officer in the way that lower ranks don't play around
officers and don't really talk to them, not candidly or with
any meaning.

So after six months of being flown to far out zones to
fight then flown back through anti-aircraft fire—geo-specific
space drop took too long and cost too much—when the
numbers of loss were starting, finally, to turn some heads
back in the core planets, Max found himself nominated as
copilot after the real one got shot on deploy.

"You cab-driver now, Canon?" Forgot-his-name
asked, cocky in the fire zone of the LZ where they were
deploying in an organized rush.

"Guess I'm copilot," he'd agreed glumly, not thrilled. "I wonder if they remember I only had basic flight. Maybe get us another copilot before extraction."

"You suck that bad, man?" Another soldier asked, a blonde woman with rock-gray eyes. Gavin. She pegged a few shots left flank and was rewarded by a squawk and a flurry of return fire.

"Nah, just…rusty. Bad guys at three o'clock."

Gunfire, then,

"Nice shot, Canon."

"Yeah." He looked at them both, straight on. "You guys better pray for a new copilot."

"Shit, okay, we'll pray. You just start refreshing yer memory now in case we don't get one."

"Yes'm." Like he'd have time to sit and think about flight procedures two years rusty.

And they hadn't gotten a replacement, so there was Max in the right hand seat, nervously watching every thing the pilot did, keenly aware that the cargo bay was full of people who doubted his flying skill—his own fault, shoulda kept his mouth shut—and remembering procedure rapidly, but not rapidly enough to give him any degree of comfort or confidence.

"What's that?" The pilot pointed out the view screen and asked veteran foot soldier Canon to identify an odd warp in the air ahead of them.

"Oh, shit," Max grabbed automatically for the control yoke, while yelling, "Climb, dammit!"

It was a new trap in the oldest school. The defenders would suspend anti-grav balloons over their cities with thousands of feet of razor wire attached to them and charged with the highest voltage it would carry. It wasn't intended to stop aircraft, only mess them up, and this one couldn't climb up fast enough to get over so the rig worked.

Electricity shot through the ungrounded nose cone while the anitgrav balloons clunked down across the chassis. One got sucked into an engine intake with a terrible ripping whine. Chunking noises followed, and while the panels only flickered before the voltage was cut off from the wires now streaming behind the ship like tinsel, the engine was mortally wounded and blew up.

The shrapnel went largely wide, but enough came screaming shipside to pierce the cockpit bubble and the pilot. Max found himself flying with one engine, no pilot, no place to land, several panels flashing madly as the CPU shook off the spike the buffers couldn't quite deflect and a couple of gauges climbing into the red zones.

Antiaircraft fire came next. One of Max's team staggered up the lurching deck to peer through the hatch and ask what the fuck was up only to stop and gape at the novice pilot riding a bucking ship through a maze of black cloud and fire, ankle deep in rolling blood and a toxic wind whistling through the shattered section of bubble. Max yelled at her to seal the holes—they'd never be space-worthy otherwise, i.e. stuck on this lousy planet with an enemy who'd kill them rather than feed them—and she jumped to it without further comment, spraying emergency foam like New Years Eve. Then she returned to the cargo area to ask around and see if anybody else had even the remotest idea how to fly just in case Max got killed.

Nobody did, but a soldier volunteered to sit up front and pretend, so Max had company all they way back to the mother-ship, plus an extra pair of hands to hunt for the controls needed to seal for vacuum and turn on the auto pilot for docking. He was too busy even to notice who was with him until they docked.

She turned out to be a very pretty brunette with a light-up-the-sky-smile.

"Nice job, pilot," she teased when they touched deck-plate and Max pried his white-knuckled hands from the yoke.

"Ha ha," Max knew it hadn't been, but they'd lived. He followed her out unsteadily through the cargo doors where some of the team were unassing. Others were crowding to the cockpit hatch to see what had happened there and mechanics were clustering to the damaged engine and saying things usually expressed by a long low whistle and a shaking head. Corpsmen came to take away the body of the pilot, who got a wake of respectful silence, even though nobody had actually known him.

Max came to a halt in a puddle of soldiers and looked at the black and partially melted engine cowling amid a welter of animated conversation and the outbursts common to people who have cheated death and have something to look at to remind them.

"Holy shit, that thing still flew? Good job, Canon."

Might as well say welcome to the team. They were all smiling at him. Max felt accepted at last and it upset him because, with the adrenaline wearing off, he now knew he'd been hit in the explosion, too, and he was afraid he wouldn't be able to hide how much it meant to him to be spoken to like a compatriot.

He had shut his jaw down, nodded tightly with a tiny uncontrolled smile, then someone had slapped him on the back and he went over like the classic folding chair, just rolling on down 'til he was one with the deck plates and Anne—beautiful brunette Anne, the volunteer copilot—was yelling for a medic and the team was taking up the cry like a pack of hunting dogs, faces weaving in and out of focus, names he knew but people he didn't, looking like they cared that he was hit, someone even saying a prayer in Spanish over him—God protect, God aid.

Max was unconscious before the medic arrived from across the bay, but Anne told him much later how he'd been the hero of the hour, carried by dozens of willing hands to the infirmary and touted up and down ship.

Max was glad he'd missed that part, which sounded embarrassing, but the new attitude of the people he worked with was just fine. The outsider-reserve was gone, partly because he was a pretty shitty pilot, which meant he was still on their level, and partly because he'd saved their lives. Not bad for a day's work. Too bad most of 'em never made it even as far as the Stalag. Baditz was a hell of an unforgiving planet.

Max remembered it every time he navigated to the office during rush hour. He remembered it when he met the veteran's group for bullshit, bombast, tire kicking and alcohol every six months at the car rallies. He remembered every single face, just very few names.

Like Capelli. And Anne.

He woke up with a clammy, breathless lurch and staggered to the kitchen for the coffee ritual. Time to get up anyway.

Jolie was asleep in the bedroom with the bedclothes rumpled and flashing a long leg, her breath the deep and even cadence of true sleep.

It wasn't until the coffee started that she hit REMs and started the nightmare. Max debated with himself for several minutes before he went in to wake her up. She'd been muttering, and the words 'so sorry' and 'never wanted to hurt you', had peaked his curiosity, but he went to wake her up like a good gentleman, wondering who she was apologizing to.

XXVI.

Friar

We had a call about a suicide and we arrived too late, as usual. There's nothing you can really do if a suicide wants to be truly dead, and there we were again, looking down the shaft at the body far far below in the shadows.

When the buildings started to run into each other during the growth and expansion of our beautiful city, open shafts started to show up where four walls met. It wasn't very long before these airshafts got renamed suicide shafts. They were uninterrupted squares of space that went all the way to street level, where access doors allowed city employees to sweep out any debris that might be blown down them.

There wasn't much more to do than call in and sigh, and start the long walk back down to ground level. The ME didn't even have to be here for these. Just a cleanup crew with a shovel and a bag.

We took statements from the complex neighbors and the apartment manager, all of who said the guy had been depressed lately and who could blame him? One look at the soul-sucking rat-hole he lived in was enough to make anybody feel like ending it right there. I sighed again and led a silent Sherrow down to the bottom to meet the cleanup crew. I didn't really think he needed to see what was left of the body, so I took him back to the cruiser before they got the maintenance doors open and called us on-beat again.

"Why would a guy want to do that? Fall all that way, I mean."

I shrugged.

"Drugs cost too much, guns are hard to get. It's available, kid. Sometimes people get too tired to go on."

"You think there was anything else going on there?"

Something in his tone tipped me.

"Don't even think about it. It wasn't murder. There was no sign of a second party. I'd bet my badge the witnesses weren't lying and the security cameras will back me up. It was his own choice, Sherrow. Leave it be."

"I don't know."

I wasn't having any of this.

"I do." My voice was harsher than it needed to be, but I couldn't help that. He sounded too much like he wanted another big case to happen. Or maybe he sounded like the suicide idea wasn't unfamiliar to him. I didn't like it either way. "I've seen too many just like it, way too many. Sometimes people just give up and jump. It's easy math, but it's the coward's way out. And some poor Joe-blow gets to mop you up at the bottom for minimum wage. You call that fair?"

He shook his head, but looked thoughtful.

"Why are you thinking about this so much? What's buggin' you?"

His dark eyes turned my way and he looked like he wanted to tell me to piss off and mind my own business. But he didn't open his mouth for a long minute, and when he did, it was civil, if distant.

"Nothing. I was just wondering why kill yourself that way. It seems like it would take too long."

"You think about killing yourself often?" I couldn't possibly make it a joke, but I tried.

Those dark, bruised eyes stayed on me for another unending eternity, then he looked away and something in him eased off.

"Not any more. After Randall, I thought…well, not any more. And it did seem like a coward's way out." He sat up straighter. "And I only thought about it once."

"Now that sounds defensive." I was relieved enough that I had trouble keeping it out of my voice.

"It's not," he defended in much the same tone.

I grinned at the heads-up speedometer and changed lanes. The radio chattered about an in-progress assault, not in our area.

"Anyway," he went on, eyes again on the streets around us. "There's too much that needs to be done. The world's a mess."

"And somebody's gotta clean it up," I agreed, feeling much better.

"At least we get more'n minimum wage. S'that all the cleanup guys get?"

"Slightly over, but barely." I executed a nasty three lane merge to put us on the loop back, listening with half an ear to another all-call that we might just make if I went really really fast. "They got better retirement benefits'n us, though."

Sherrow was being pushed slowly sideways in his seat by my turn radius and the speed with which I accomplished it, so all he said was,

"Huh."

I wolf-grinned and turned the radio up a notch. By the time we were halfway to the crime scene, Sherrow had the same grin on his face and the redline on the speedometer looked like a birthday ribbon to us both.

Finally break rolled around and we took it at the station house. Sherrow took a cautious sip of the ever-lousy coffee and made a face. The linoleum in the break room reflected fluorescent light into our eyes and made us both squint, shadowed eyes in pale faces.

"You're a doer," he said. "Even with such a fucked up past, yer a doer. That's why I joined up: to do. I don't want to watch life go by and think about doing something. I wanna be doing it while everybody else watches. And I don't mean that in a glory-seeking way." This last was delivered defensively.

"I know, I understand," I told him. I had to add a laugh. "Guess you were pretty disappointed to get a wreck of a cop like me as your partner."

"Yeah, I was at first." He was honest as the day was long and it still bothered me to hear what I'd already known. "Then I saw how you drive. I've watched you pursue this Mitchell case against regulations and common sense, but it's for the department, for the guys, y'know, and I listened to what you had to say, and I learned, Vic. I'm learning from you." The painful sincerity left to make room for smug sarcasm. "And the other guys from academy are jealous coz I got a hero cop for my partner."

I smiled at that, relieved that the spate of youthful sincere appreciation was done, and said,

"Guess they don't know me like you do, huh?"

"And I don't enlighten 'em." He turned his smile down. The hollows under his eyes were like bruises. "What would be the point?"

Indeed. What would be the point? Let 'em believe in heroes. Sherrow obviously still did, no matter what he was saying to the contrary.

You feelin' okay?" I wanted to know, reflecting that hero-worship and self-sacrifice sometimes went together in a young guy's head. "How's that cut?"

"Healing." He shrugged it off, same as before, supremely casual, but he also got up to go. It looked like retreat to me.

"Yeah, okay, if you say so. You look bad, again, s'all I'm saying."

"And you don't?"

"Man, I looked this bad yesterday."

"Man, you've looked bad for weeks."

"Ha ha. Thanks a bunch."

"I'm okay, Friar."

"Uh huh," I couldn't agree, but I didn't argue. Instead, I suggested, "You might start looking better you got some sleep days, 'stead of following me around. Those bars don't seem to agree with you."

"And they agree with you?" This with an angry glare.

"You don't see me cut up, kid, do you?"

"Only because I was watching your back." He hadn't meant to say it, I could tell by his face and the sudden stop.

But he had said it, and now I knew for sure. He'd taken the cut for oblivious me. His statement rang in the air for a long awful moment while I considered what might've happened if the knifer had been a better fighter. Had gotten lucky and killed him.

It took me a minute to find words.

"If I promise to be more discreet and more careful, will you quit following me?" I had to weigh my tone to the ounce; I didn't want to offend him or alienate him.

"I know your good intentions aren't always possible." The way he said it was matter-of-fact, like it was coming from a much older man.

"Who told you that?" I sounded startled.

"Kay."

Ah.

"Figures. Look, I can promise to try. That way, you won't miss out on any of the fun."

"Following you to sleazy bars when I could be with Shelly is fun? Vic, you are something else sometimes."

"Who asked you to follow me anyway? Are we agreed?"

"Sure. But you keep that promise, or we'll have more than just words."

"I don't mind a fat lip s'long as yer still alive to give it to me, rookie."

That made him so righteously angry that he left me alone for the rest of shift.

XXVII.

Friar

I put my after work hours to use doing neglected research, which didn't quite break my promise to Sherrow.

This time I used my badge in exactly the way I wasn't sposed to, to get into other people's records. I got nose down in messenger receipts, tracing addresses, and waded through the back logs of three cab companies with my pants rolled up. What I got was a whole list of commerce radiating from Mrs. March's address. If I thought I could've gotten away with it, I would've tried to bluff out the satellite company for transmission and phone records, but that was federal and I'd hang for it.

I got the general idea from the records I did get access to, though, and a fairly thorough string of interviews with the messenger kids got me a good round idea of who Mrs. March was dealing with. Caulder was top of the list, along with the usual cronies, laundry services and delivery places, but there were two contacts that I couldn't identity.

Some of the cab drops were in the same general area, but never at a specific address. A range of messages went to post boxes of a wide variety, but to no single individual. I ran the numbers, triangulated till I was about to go mad and came up with about five square miles of search grid. After that, I hadn't really slept for a coupla days, and the comments at work were starting to sound familiar regarding my physical beauty, so I decided sleep might again be necessary.

But I couldn't sleep. I kept thinking about Noel, hearing her voice calling off the dogs as I ran down that damn catwalk, bouncing as the metal flexed under my weight, waiting for that charge to burn through my fancy-ass new leather and melt the micro fiber of my shirt to my death wound. I saw her eyes, naked brown without her fashionable reader-filter lenses, asking me mutely to do things for her she couldn't bring herself to say out loud, asking for help and hearing my own voice call her names, ignoring those silent pleas in favor of button-pushing.

Had I imagined it all? The evening was a largely surreal blur after all the excitement and the dose of recreational chemistry, so I could be putting a sympathetic slant onto Noel that hadn't been there. 'Coz Sherrow was right and I did still love her. It was a doomed sort of distanced love, but it was there.

I called Kay with a lame request that he keep his eyes open in case Noel showed up coz I wanted to talk to her. He knew I wasn't telling him everything, but he said sure and asked if I was alright. I said I was okay and almost told him the lot of it, but managed to keep my mouth shut. He didn't need to hear it. I felt like an idiot for calling him in the first place.

We said goodbye. After he hung up, I tried to rip the vid-phone off the wall.

I bloodied my knuckles and nearly broke a toe from an improperly chambered kick, and it didn't make me feel any better.

I fell off the wagon with a thump so loud it should've broken windows. The half bottle of whiskey, magically appearing in the back of a cupboard, didn't help me sleep any, but it made me numb enough not to care so much.

It almost made me numb enough to consign Noel to Hell and good riddance.

But not quite.

I ended up walking instead of sleeping, prowling the dirty streets with a gun on my hip and not a single happy thought for company. I'd walked off most of the whiskey by the time I had to go home and get respectable for work, and a cold hard shower hosed off most of the stink. Coffee filled the empty hollow that was my sour stomach. I left for the station finally, running on that shaky coffee energy that animates the same way electricity animates a corpse: There's motion, but no real control.

By the time I got to work, I was all ready for a plain, normal workday, but I wasn't gonna get one. It'd been days since anybody had had a good laugh at my expense, and when I came in, I set off the electronics/weapons detector because my ohm-age was too high that day, or too low. We called the thing the drunk detector 'coz too much liquor could set you up for the wrong ohm.

I was laughed at, even when the test came back to report me okay for duty. Suddenly I was getting the rep as Officer Alcoholic, a title I didn't want to share with Hobby. It stung more because I knew it was merited in this case.

I made vague plans with myself to go see the counselor, and to call Canon and to call Noel again, and a million things that would never happen. Sherrow came to work looking better with some real sleep, but not much, and between us, we were the raggiest looking team on shift, and nobody wanted to miss out in pitching us shit.

Even Wells joined in, probably forgetting how scared he'd been when he called me that night. Or maybe remembering and hating me for being the one who knew.

Anyway, it was a shitty start to the day, and the saddest part about it was that it seemed sorta normal after the way the year'd been going.

Canon

Jolie seemed extraordinarily nervous at dinner that night and Max didn't have the heart to tell her what he'd found out about Silver and her last date with Albrecht. He offered to take her out dancing, but she declined and kept casting surreptitious glances at the phone when she thought he wasn't looking. Max finally tried to excuse himself to the office to get some work done, and she became suddenly clingy, coming up with a large number of reasons why he should stay, resorting at last to the big eyes and frightened waif act, telling him she was too afraid to be alone. But Max had too much thinking to do and he couldn't do it here. He remained firm and left her sitting on the sofa with her legs tucked under her in another one of his shirts, pretending to read the book she held in her hands. As he drove away, he wondered who she'd contacted and what it meant.

He got to the office so late that he decided he'd sleep on the sofa again, and dug the blankets out of the bottom drawer of the file cabinet to set up camp. The desk bottle completed the bivouac and he settled in to do his thinking, paging through notes and speculating on the many aspects of this mess he seemed to be mired in neck-deep.

The building was new and had real walls, not like Max's place with it's 100 year old lathe. He couldn't hear the neighbors here at all. Without the reminder that there were other people alive around him, Max couldn't sleep. He lay awake, straining to hear noises that weren't there: Running water, footsteps, voices raised in argument, the damn dog barking.

There was nothing and he began to feel he was alone on the whole planet. The feeling only came upon him occasionally when he was totally exhausted, and it was always nasty. He got up and went to the window with the dread that all he'd see were the blasted-out jags of prefab and crooked, ruined wall, blackened by defoliants and the firestorm. Meta. The prison colony.

The office window showed him neon instead and he felt immeasurably relieved. He searched up the bottle and tossed off a healthy sleep-aiding slug and settled on the sofa where the neon could shine on his face.

That was better. Neon meant commerce, meant life. Neon was sunshine, calling in the customers, the cash, the flow, just like the city was a forest and the people it's blood.

No, no, jungle. The city was a jungle, wasn't it? That'd always been said, for centuries, that cities were like jungles.

Max liked it as a forest better. That way you could see what was coming at you. He liked to see what was coming at him, even if all he could do was guess at what it would mean. He'd built a life on guessing what things meant. Too bad he wasn't doing better guessing these days.

Max closed his eyes on the harsh, neon light and slept finally, thoughts spinning down into dreams.

He awoke to a concussive sound that seemed to make the dawn sky reverberate like a pale yellow drum. He sat up, disoriented by it, and took a minute to sort out the jungle/forest thoughts and the dreams of, happily, women. It wouldn't be until much later in the day that he found out what had exploded.

He got up and went to the desk to spread out his notes again and see if he'd made any connections subconsciously while he slept. Early sun slatted through the blinds and touched the back of his neck like warm, female fingers. He snugged down in his overcoat against the chill of the dawn office and read two pages of conjecture out of his notebook before falling asleep again.

The sirens woke him. His coat was a long mass of wrinkles, and he was sore and as stiff as a five thousand year old man preserved optimistically in resin and sawdust.

He squinted at the holographic clock that hung just to the left of the window. 6:00 in the am. He'd only been asleep an hour. He put his hat over his eyes to shade out the light and tried again.

A key hit the lock around 9:00, the outside door rattling open as Helen opened up shop. She spotted him through the open inner door before he had his gummy eyes properly open.

"Don't you have a home to go to?" She asked, and went to start coffee without waiting for an answer.

"Somebody asked me that before." Max sat up groggily.

"Probably me."

The phone rang. Helen put down the carafe and went to get it. Her cool phone voice purred out Max's name. Max couldn't see the projection from where he was, but he heard a male voice asking for him.

"Are you in, Mr. Canon?'" Helen's head appeared around the jam. "No. You are not, looking like that."

Max smiled at her.

"Who is it?"

"Cops. You wanna talk to cops this early?"

"Which cops?"

"The brother in law."

"Oh, Hell, sure. Just dial off visual."

Eddy's projection was waiting at the kiosk with a frown when Max spoke with the video off. There was an unpleasant pause.

"Max? Turn on the visual. I need to see you."

Max felt his heart lurch at the unmistakable tone of trouble in Eddy's voice, a sensation he hadn't felt for many years, and he did as he was asked, saying abruptly,

"Is Ruth okay?"

"Yes, she's fine. You look okay, too." The last was intoned like a question.

"Yeah, I'm fine. What's this all about, Eddy?"

Eddy sighed and turned his drawn face into profile, looking off to his left.

"Well, I'm glad you're okay, but…Max your apartment was blown up last night."

Eddy turned his eyes back to the transmitter, mouth open to go on. He changed what he was going to say when he saw Max's suddenly white face.

"What?"

"There was a woman." Max began, and had to stop. He took his turn looking away from the transmission, unfocused eyes seeing Jolie Laide asleep in the bedroom. Helen came into the doorway, looking concerned.

Eddy recalled his wandering attention and Max went on reluctantly.

"Staying at my apartment. She was involved in a case I'm working…No place else to go. Wait a minute." Max walked away from phone box, wrestling with various unwelcome emotions, the chiefest of which was guilt for failing to protect a frightened woman in his charge. When he circled back, Eddy looked like he was controlling some very strong emotions.

"There's been no sign of bodies, Max, not yet. I just called in hope." Eddy paused, and shuddered a little. "I didn't want to call Ruth until…It was a very neat job, just your place and the adjoining walls gone. Your neighbors weren't killed, though there were injuries. Max?"

Max dragged his eyes up and Eddy said, abruptly,

"Tell me why this happened, Max."

Max shook his head and dragged a now shaking hand through his hair and shook his head again.

"Something I'm working on, Caulder maybe? But I have no proof, Eddy, no proof! I just don't know!" Max took another turn of the room. "No bodies you say?"

"Not yet. But there's not much left. It was very professional, Max. Very high tech work. Possibly military trained work. But you didn't hear me say that. We haven't got much to go on yet. Who was the woman?"

Max told Eddy her name and gave a general description in a dazed sort of way. Helen put a cup of sudden coffee into his unresisting hand.

"Why was she at your place, Max?"

Max knew he could tell Eddy or he could tell the downtown boys, so he said,

"She was witness to the murder of one of Caulder's runners. I got her out of a tight spot, didn't know where to put her, left her there. Shit, I gotta think."

"Is this the fatality in the roadhouse you got in the middle of?"

"Yeah. She was one of the civilians with Mrs. March."

"Christ, Max." Eddy looked ill. "This isn't gonna do you any favors with the department. Oh, man, Skills is gonna have you brought in. You know that, don't you?"

"Yeah. Probably for the best anyway." Max tried to tidy up his necktie. "I'll just come down, shall I?"

Eddy nodded.

"I'll come get you. Wait for me there."

He rang off, his image dissolving in a hiss of pixels and static, and Max was left staring blankly at the transmission box.

Helen came back into the room.

Max hardly heard her questions, and answered vaguely, collecting his hat and keys.

"I'll call you later." He looked fully at her for the first time and saw her shocked face. "We're not open today. Lock up and go home. I don't want you anywhere near anything associated with me right now. Might not be safe." He put his hat on and left her nodding mechanically in the middle of the empty office, the coffee machine gurgling threateningly in the background like a caged monster.

When Eddie got there, they took Max's car.

Max's apartment was gone, just gone. There was a heap of rubble where number 505 had been, neatly, as Eddy said, almost surgically removed from the building. Max thought of shaped charges, of professional demolitions practices. He thought of the demo guys in the 101st Fast Launch, ex-soldiers who ran contraband and he thought of Capelli. He and Eddy rounded one of the numerous neon fire vehicles lighting up the overcast street with their lurid illuminations, and passed a detective Max didn't recognize scrapping something from a fragment of brick into a bindle. The machine vacuumed the evidence in and beeped confirmation as it processed.

"Got something, Stan?" Eddy asked, not sounding very hopeful.

"Maybe," The officer looked up, pocketing the numbered, sealed packet the bindle spit back out. "Might be trace explosive. Might just be mud." He stood. "Archer. Who's yer friend?"

"Max Canon, Detective Stan Gillespie. Stan, Max is my brother in law. He's also the tenant of 505."

"Oh, yeah. The landlord said you aren't married. Any pets?"

Max shook his head numbly, eyes on the destruction. He could see why Eddy didn't hold out much hope for body recovery: Large portions of the rubble were little more than powder.

"Oh, my God! Oh, My God!"

A female voice shrieking. Running feet. Max's heart lurched for the second time that morning, but it wasn't Jolie Laide.

It was Marie.

He stared at her blankly as she ran up, heels tapping staccato hysteria across the pavement.

"Oh, my God, Max, are you okay? What happened? Were you home?"

As if he could've been and still be intact enough to stand here looking at her like she was three-headed.

"No. Marie, what are you doing here?"

She threw herself at him for one of her passionate embraces, golden hair flying in a cloud of sparkling curls.

Her shopping bag, imprinted with the colony logo of Century Callistas, hit him across the back. It sparked a brain cell, but he couldn't isolate the thought. He transferred his abstracted gaze to the pavement, trying to pin down what it had reminded him of while ignoring her impassioned explanation of how much she'd missed him and how awful her latest boyfriend had been. Marie, on finding her embrace was not returned and that he was not even listening, let him go and settled for bursting into tears and speaking instead about how horrid it would've been were he home at the time of the explosion and what she would've done if she'd returned only to find him dead. This seemed to turn her thoughts to what might've happened had she been staying with him, and she fell silent as the reality of the near miss with death came home to her.

Her enhanced green eyes turned to view the destruction in silence. For a moment longer, Max stood staring at the pavement with an intent look usually associated with hunting dogs on point. When Gillespie attempted to speak to him, Eddy Archer waved him to silence, watching Max.

Max finally made the connection. Callistas was a holiday colony off world, very similar to the Bimini Ridge colony, where Wanderer had said the Warp came from. If he could trace the transport logs from Bimini Ridge, they might provide a clue as to how the Warp was being brought planet side, which might, in turn, point to more likely suspects for such an expensive and risky enterprise.

Max looked at the ruins of his home and thought that, more and more, he doubted Daily Caulder was the one behind the importation. He had nothing to gain and everything to lose. He couldn't make enough money on the drug to turn much profit, and if it was traced to him, the authorities would spend every last man and bullet to bring him down. Contrarily, if it was proven to be not of his doing, then it would become clear to the underlings that Caulder had lost control over his own empire and therefore was ripe for replacement. Either way, he lost. The only way it made sense was if Caulder was doing someone a favor by moving it on–planet. And the only way *that* made sense was if this someone was bigger than Caulder. Which wasn't a pleasant thought.

Another strike against Caulder's involvement was that Max had never heard of him using explosives to remove an impediment. He usually sent an assassin, or arranged for an accident. Bombing was new.

"Max?" Eddy asked after the apparent conclusions he saw in Max's face.

"I don't think it's Caulder. But I don't know who else it could be."

"Why do you think that, Max?" Eddy persisted. Gillespie was leaning in now, cutting Marie out with a wide shoulder.

"Somebody is bringing in Warp from Bimini, and he wouldn't do that. He doesn't need to do that."

Gillespie cast a questioning look at Eddy, but was shaken off.

"Maybe it's a favor for a friend." Eddy suggested. "He probably has connections there."

Max turned uncomfortably intense eyes on his brother in law.

"Can you find out?"

Eddy's head bobbed back under the burning glare, but he stood his ground.

"I'll try. You got a place you can go until we get this stage of the investigation out of the way? And not the office."

"You want me to wait downtown, don't you?"

Eddy just nodded and put a hand on Max's shoulder.

Max turned under his grip and walked ahead of him back to the car, leaving Marie standing deserted on the sidewalk. Later, he'd have to ignore days of impassioned and angry messages, but it wasn't going to bother him much. Her either, probably.

Max drove both Eddie and himself downtown, where he answered questions three different times without adding to the statements he'd made to Gillespie and then sat in Eddy's office and tried to decide if Jolie had been on one of her little trips out. He'd known she'd gone out sometimes because he could smell the smoke or the night air on her clothes when he got home, but he couldn't be sure about last night. She must've wanted to make a call or had been waiting for one, but then why had she tried to keep him home? Had she gotten the call? Been warned about the bomb and gotten out? Or had she been told to wait for a call that never came? And hadn't she tried to keep him there?

Had the bomb been for her or for him? Maybe for both.

Max found he couldn't care much either way. He was still too numb.

It was an hour or so before Eddy came back from some interview or other. Max was sitting across from his desk, considering going over to see if Frank Skills was in yet, but hadn't the initiative to walk that far yet. He had spent the hour going over his notes and comparing them to Friar's to see what they could've missed that might be helpful. Concentrating on that helped him ignore the possibility of Jolie's death.

Max collated the bits of data into a more coherent order, trying to line it up, make it clear, but he wasn't having much luck. Eddy's arrival not only interrupted his train of thought, it was a relief. Max put the notes away, his head aching.

"Nothing. There was nobody home when the place went up." Eddy spoke before he even had his hat off.

Max let out a pent breath he didn't know he'd been holding. Eddy looked closely at his face.

"I called Ruth to let her know you were all right. Max, have you thought of anything that might be useful?"

Before Max could answer, Eddy's phone rang.

"Archer," he answered. Max saw Frank Skills face project up from the box, black and white fuzzy, clearly a public phone, and an older one.

"I got a flat tire." The tone was too casual, too flat. It was followed by a long, strained silence. Skills' face was a neutral blank.

When Eddy was sure he was getting no more information, he prompted.

"Where?"

"Third and Royal. I need a hand." Again that strained tone, that over casual flip of the words. A muscle under his left eye twitched.

"Sure," Eddy tried to match the casual and read under Frank's. "Max is with me. S' okay if he comes along?"

There was a longer pause, then Skills spoke again, as if the words were being dragged out of him.

"Why not? A different perspective might be refreshing. But I need discreet from both of you. Swear."

Eddy was insulted that his old partner would even ask it, but it confirmed his suspicions of 'deadly wrong.' Frank needed more than his tire changed. Eddy checked his gun for loads and said,

"Yeah?"

"It's a really flat tire. You gotta see it to believe it. And the location…it's sensitive. A personal matter."

Again, the words said nothing, the tone said all.

"Okay. Ten minutes."

"I'll be here." Frank rang off almost before the sentence was out of his mouth.

Eddy looked at Max and pointed.

"That thing primed?"

Max patted the butt of his gun and nodded.

"All new batteries and everything. Where we going?"

"Third and Royal. Frank has a problem we gotta help him out of."

Max held the door for Eddy who was walking and putting on his jacket at the same time. He grinned.

"So I'm not your only problem child?"

"Brother-in-laws, old partners, you know how it is."

"It's like family, inn't?" Max led the way to his car, tossing Eddy the keys. "Here's your chance to drive her, so I don't want to hear you askin' anymore."

Eddy caught the keys and grinned back, but they drove in silence to Third and Royal, each thinking thoughts that were better not shared.

Skills walked up to meet them as the car slowed. In person, he really looked like bad news. Eddy parked and shut off the engine. Max let him get out first so they could exchange a few sentences before he joined them and ruined their privacy, but they didn't speak. Frank Skills only waited for them both, gesturing Max to hurry up when he lingered.

With a shrug Max joined them on the pavement, looking up and down the street and up at the balconies and rail-work leaning claustrophobically overhead. There was no one else around.

Skills backed up three steps and turned 90 degrees to pop open the trunk of his old gray Ford.

They looked in silence for a few seconds, then Eddy spoke.

"That's a body, Frank."

Max turned to face the wall and one hand went over his mouth then fell away.

"I'll get a blanket," he muttered and went to his own trunk to fetch one.

Skills didn't say anything.

"How'd that get in your car, Frank?" Eddy asked, the words coming out like recorded video dialogue from an action serial featuring spectacularly bad actors. He could feel the wooden expression of disbelief on his face. The body wasn't anything new, but it's placement in the trunk of the police chief's car was, and very upsetting into the bargain. He knew Frank better than this.

"It's Jolie Laide," Max came up with the blanket, scanning the local area again, this time with more purpose. "The woman staying at my place." He stepped past Skills to spread the blanket in the trunk. He stepped back again and looked at Skills, then at Eddy.

Skills jerked into motion.

"You know her as Laide? The witness from the roadhouse? Mitchell's case?" Interest was sharpening away the dull look of shock in his eyes. Eddy nodded, while looking at Max for confirmation.

"Yeah."

"Why was she at your place?" Eddy asked it.

"Hiding from you guys. Hiding from somebody else, too, but I haven't figured out that part yet."

"She was strangled, Canon, and tortured some." Skills said it harshly, and Max could see anger brewing up finally, behind the man's carefully controlled expression. Get mad, Frank, somebody tried to frame you for murder. Get mad and think about who would benefit.

"It looks personal."

Max flipped back the corner of the blanket to look. Pretty brown eyes, like clouded crystal, face the wrong color, tongue out. She'd been strangled by a professional who'd enjoyed it, it looked like.

"Sure does," He agreed.

"You got dirt on Caulder, I need it, Canon." Skills was adamant.

"I don't have anything yet. I'm thinking he might be the one into framing cops, but I can't quite make it stick. What." Because Skills' face had changed.

"This woman used to be married to a cop."

"You know her."

"Long time ago. Go on."

Max filed the information away along with a snapshot memory of Skills' stiff, white face and went on.

"Wanderer told me about a Warp sale went to a cop to frame a cop. Now I see this girl put in your trunk on inspection day." And when both officers looked at him in surprise, Max went on, "It's my business to know things like that. Today is the departmental over-all. Why did you get into your trunk anyway, Frank?"

"I thought I heard something rolling loose. I'm blind lucky that whoever did this didn't get the latch fully closed. I would've driven straight to work otherwise." He turned away and rubbed his face with both hands, looking very old. "Help me out, guys. You two I trust, though I had to think about you, Max, you get into so much trouble all by yerself, didn't know if I wanted you involved."

"I can help, and I'm already involved. Let me take her and you go to work."

"You know how to dispose of bodies? Do I want to know this?"

"And you thought I was just a bum P.I, didn't you?" Max smiled without humor and leaned over the figure under the blanket. His smile vanished as he touched the cold girl. "I can delay her discovery, s'all. It's obvious the body's already been moved: This is what she was wearing when I left her last night. One more stop won't make any difference."

He transferred the body as quickly as he could and closed the trunk. Skills and Eddy were checking over the Ford for tell-tales.

"You guys got any advice for me on how to clean a corpse of evidence?"

"We scan for fibers, DNA evidence, that kind of thing." Eddy said it like it was something he'd forgotten, one hand gesturing dramatically towards the pile carpet lining the Ford's trunk.

"What if I vacuum her first?" Max thought for a second and shook his head violently. "No, I couldn't do that. The river, maybe?"

Skills shut the trunk and sat on the bumper, thinking furiously. His face was gray.

"Maybe. Eddy? Thoughts?"

"Yeah. The river. It won't carry away all the evidence, but it'll blur the lines, the acidity levels being so high. Might slow the forensics boys down a little." He rubbed at his eyes. "God, Max, thank you for this. Frank, we need to figure out who would do this to you, fast."

"Same person who'd blow up my place hoping for a kill?" Max put in.

"Were they trying to kill you or her?" Skills wanted to know, looking up at Max with uncomfortable intensity. Max felt sorry for him. This was pressure he didn't need right now and the fact that they were messing with evidence had to be eating him alive.

"Both, I think. I was there most of the evening, then I went to the office to get some sleep." The ghost of a smile flitted across his face like a travesty. "Ms. Laide had the bed, and I was trying to be a gentleman."

"Too bad I couldn't tell Ruth," Eddy had an answering shadow of humor for his brother-in-law. "She doesn't believe you could ever be a gentleman."

Skills stood like a tired old man.

"Let's get moving, gentlemen." He put a spin on the last word to acknowledge their pale humor, and walked around to the driver's side of his car. "Give you a ride to work, Archer?"

"Sure, chief." Eddy had one last lingering look of thanks and warning for Max and then he climbed into the Ford and they were gone. Max saw Skills' eyes in the rearview watching him, so he nodded.

When he was alone again, he spent a minute or two lighting a cigarette and watching the street out of the corners of his eyes for tell-tale movement that said fleeing eavesdroppers. He saw none, and lazily got into his own vehicle to set about disposing temporarily of the body of a girl he'd come to like. Later, when he allowed himself to dwell on it, he'd have to deal with the reality, and he knew it would be one of the hardest things he faced, right up there with getting captured and losing Anne.

The saddest part of it would be how little he'd known her and how little time any of them could spare to be sorry for her passing. He couldn't be the only person sorry to see her dead.

Friar

Sherrow wasn't in yet when somebody told me the news: Noel's body had been found in the river. I hadn't seen the brief sheet yet, and it came at me from outta nowhere and stole all the oxygen in the room.

There were faces all around, waiting for my reaction, watching my reaction and here I couldn't even breathe to laugh it off or curse their cold interest—was I so damn unpopular that nobody could even bring himself to fake commiseration?

My face was the wrong color, so I turned my back on the lot to face the locker and find my breath. Noel dead. It had to be a bad joke, listen to 'em go on like nothing had happened, were they watching me too closely? It was April Fool's, me the village idiot for the day. Wells was behind it, sure, no, since I'd helped him out he'd been sullen, but civil at least. Hollingate, then, to see if I'd go over the edge with one really good push. There he was, talking, I could hear him.

"…Strangled purple. Even left a ring mark. Someone hated her special. Makes you wonder about ol' Vic there."

"He's been under a lot of stress lately," someone murmured.

"But that much? He used to be a good cop."
Damning with faint praise.

If I'd gotten my breath back, that' would've taken it away again. As it was, things were roaring in my ears. Someone slapped my shoulder, nearly unseating me from the bench. I turned for a 'sorry, man,' sincerely said under insincere eyes. Cold eyes, watching. They were all watching.

What was I, example boy? I had no idea I made such an irresistible sideshow.

I staggered to my woozy feet on a thank you and made it to the men's room in time to throw up in private.

Damn if Strindberg and Hollingate didn't follow me in.

"You don't look so good," Hollingate oozed with patently false concern, as I swayed by the sink, face newly splashed with water that didn't help.

"You don't leave soon, you'll look even worse, Ted," I grated, turning my eyes to Strindberg to see how much of an asshole he was going to be.

He gave me a look of sympathy that looked real, asshole or not, and it didn't help my composure.

I turned to the sink and tried again to wash away the image of Noel, blue-faced dead with some evil bastard's finger marks around her throat. Finger marks deep enough to leave the impression of a ring. Hadn't I heard someone say she'd been beaten, tortured with cigarettes? Had she been raped? Rage and grief rose up in my throat again, choking me, and I turned on Hollingate, the nearest enemy, and charged.

I didn't notice until later that Strindberg let me, stepping back so I had a clear runway for my mad rush.

There was bellowing and Hollingate's partner came slamming through the door to pull me off. In a movie-frame flicker, I saw a hall full of faces, still, watching, detached interest, 'hey, lookit Friar go bug fuck, whaddaya know? 100 bucks says he waxes old Holl.' Then the door flipped shut on the back swing and Hollingate's partner Yarrow was over my shoulders like a bad overcoat. Strindberg jerked into half-assed motion.

"Lay off, Vic," he said, not very loud.

I didn't, though and we nearly had a riot before Hollingate hit me hard enough to knock me into a sink, which hit my ribs pretty smartly. Everything staggered to a halt and we all stood around panting for the few seconds it took Sherrow to come sliding through the swinging door like he was on skis. Behind him, I got a flash of cleared runway just beginning to fill up again as his wake vanished under curious feet, uniform and plain clothes alike.

I wondered what was taking the LT so long. Or the Captain. Or the Frank Skills.

There was an odd little pause as Sherrow came to a rocking halt between Hollingate and me. Then,

"You're bleeding, Friar," he said.

I knuckled my nose. Sure I was. So were the other two.

"You're bleedin' like you been shot, man."

Ah. The stitches were out, then. I looked down at a black slick of wet uniform blouse and shrugged.

"Noel's dead," I said, intelligent as a punch-drunk bull.

"I heard. Let's go sit down, Vic. Okay?"

I let him take my arm because he was my partner. He got me all the way to the infirmary before the shock wore off completely and I was sick again.

Skills came in in a hurry then, looking a lot like I felt. He stopped next to the cold table they had me sitting on and just looked at me for a moment.

"I wanted to be the one to break it to you," he said finally.

"Thanks for the thought," I said, head ringing with a sort of numb misery.

The docs had drugs, a lecture about unreported gunshot wounds, and a half-day for me and sent me home.

Like that was going to cure everything. Like that would cure anything. Skills and Sherrow just watched me shuffle off, not saying anything.

I went home. I called Kay and hung up before he answered. I took out Crystal's number and didn't call her either. I went to the hospital and shoved my way in to I.D. the corpse that'd already been identified.

It was Noel, and she was dead.

I left the hospital in a daze and walked out into the city like a suicide into the ocean, waiting for it to swallow me and make the pain numb, make it all not be.

I walked till dawn and nothing changed.

I went home and took the drugs they'd handed me and slept without dreams for the first time in weeks.

It didn't help much. I woke towards morning and couldn't sleep again, so I stayed up and went over every bit of information I had about the case, over and over and over again until it was time to go to work.

XXIII.

Canon

Max couldn't get a hold of Mrs. March to ask her about Laide, so he buried himself in the city office archives for a few hours, trying to obscure the vision of the dead girl in one of his shirts lying crooked in the back of Skills' car. He was just going through the motions, but it helped a little to be feeling like he was doing something constructive. He wasn't up to facing people yet, and any minute, he knew Eddy would page him and demand he report his whereabouts and come down to the station for safety purposes or further questioning.

When he started getting into the land sale records, he started finding bits that might actually be useful. Mr. March had been a big landowner in this city: that much was common knowledge. There were warehouses and apartment buildings, lots that sold hovers, buildings that housed restaurants and brothels, and half a dozen other enterprises,

all in the name of Phillip March. Mrs. March was on the
deeds merely as inheritor in most cases, and that it all now
belonged to her seemed less important to Max than that she
currently belonged to Caulder. He couldn't see anything
linking Caulder to the March properties, except the deed to
the land on which the Emerald City sat, which, while it
wasn't a Caulder establishment, did pay rent to him. But it
wouldn't be hard to put a line into a will marking Caulder as
beneficiary to it all, being her close friend and confidant as
he was. Combined with the commerce records, there was a
clear and disturbing pattern that looked like consolidation
moving gently and steadily towards Caulder's In-Box, and
dating back, if Friar's notes were correct, to about the same
time that Caulder had begun to peak in his power climb.
And the beauty of the beneficiary line was that Mrs. March
didn't even need to know about it if the document was
marked correctly and encoded from her equipment. None
of which was difficult, and would be a nice safeguard if she
should become inconvenient.

Max wondered if she knew about the neat set up and
if she had a copy of her will in the house for him to look at.
Maybe he'd ask tonight, depending on whether the trio of
thugs was on guard duty or not.

He dialed the answering service for Mrs. March and
left a cryptic message. With any luck she'd recognize it as
him and call him back on a pay phone—an unbugged phone
preferably, or one too close to ground level for a clear
satellite eavesdrop. Would she think of that? He couldn't be
sure, but he could hope.

He found himself looking forward to seeing her, like
she was a long lost friend. Maybe it was the sudden death of
Laide that made him feel that way or maybe it was what he
got for digging into Mrs. March's past: Delusions of
familiarity. It was the first time it had happened to him in a
long career of digging up the pasts of beautiful women. He
wondered why it should affect him so much with this one.

Maybe he was getting too old for this work.

Maybe he was too close to it all.

He went back to work, this time at a local computer bank that kept records the hall of records considered too unimportant to keep officially.

There, he found several public documents that also helped frame out the picture of Mrs. March that had been developing while not helping him at all.

There were apartment rental records from days past in dumpy parts of town, credit records on half a dozen major department stores, utility bills and a car sale on a car Max had never seen her drive, a big silver full hover.

The crowning touch and the most damaging was the library card.

It wasn't right for the kept woman of a king crime lord to have a library account that, by the use-records, was never let to grow cold. She should have a drug habit, be addicted to clubbing, dancing, buying expensive items, thrill seeking, never never never never a library account.

It was so sad and so eloquent of the life she truly led—crime-luxury set aside—that it made Max want to rescue her. Or drink, drink heavily. She was the little match girl, maybe dressed in silk and fur, but she was going to freeze to death in an uncaring world anyway. Max stopped his research for the day, too depressed to go on.

Maybe the cop had something. He had to do something before he saw Mrs. March again, or he might get all mushy and do something irretrievably stupid.

He called up Friar and invited him to meet at the temporary office Helen had found him two hours after she'd been told his old one was too dangerous. He was actually surprised when the invitation was accepted and two officers arrived at his glass door within ten minutes. Max was still trying to figure out how to ask the questions he wanted to ask.

The officers were talking as they came in.

"I told you, I didn't see it until last night. Maybe there's something--we're not arguing about this." Friar was gray-faced and stony looking as he turned on Max.

"What do you know about Mrs. March's apartment building?" Was the first thing he addressed to Max.

"Same's you, I'm sure. Owned by Daily Daily his ownself under all the fallen leaves of paper trail."

"Those records have been falsified."

Max took the crumpled photofax out of the man's hand and looked at it. He'd seen it before about two hours back, but this time he was undistracted, and spotted the double edge lines that usually meant somebody had messed with the information enough to put a glitch in the program. Funny that they'd leave it like that, but it had been done years ago by the document date, another reason Max had mentally dismissed it. Now he wondered what he'd missed that the cop thought was so critical.

"A lot of the records were jimmied to lean them onto Caulder interests. I figure it was done to make him sole owner if Mrs. March dies. Nothing like a little back up of your holdings."

"I guess," Friar was distracted. He looked about as beat up as Max and a faint, involuntary grin crossed the PL's face. The rookie saw it and gave him a Satan-eyed glare out of dark, young eyes. "But it's not owned by Caulder or March. It belongs to the Bimini Outreach Foundation."

That surprised Max. The building used to be the outer edge of town before many years of expansion and rabid growth had eaten up the flat land for another twenty-forty miles. It was near a city park of lovely green stretches and had a nice view of the river. It was one of the only parts of town where you could see the river but not the Speakeasy. It was very expensive, exclusive and old, dating from the days of the crime lords who specialized in things other than drugs, mostly prostitution and alcohol when Prohibition III was attempted.

It was probably full of hidden rooms, a thought that hadn't entered his head before. And the Warp was coming in from Bimini.

"What." Even the rookie could read the change in Max's expression.

"Nothing, I think."

"Bullshit, License. Give or I rat to Skills." Friar was in no mood to play nice. His eyes were black with fatigue and something else.

"I just remembered the pedigree on that place. There was a hotel on that site for awhile for the Caulders of the Prohib III era. The original building was destroyed, but the foundation was reused. Maybe it's still got some secrets. Why'nch you check the police files for that kind of thing and I'll hit the city planning office, look for architectural plans?"

"Okay," Friar nodded tightly, but Sherrow looked like he wanted to protest.

"And maybe see who owns Bimini Outreach. It isn't Caulder, I'm sure of that."

Again, Friar gave that tight nod. Max went on, trying to put a casual spin on his next sentence.

"Another thing you could look up for me. The road house witness, Jolie Laide."

Friar waited impatiently for the request, one foot starting to tap with tension. His partner seemed to read something in Max's tone and he turned his dark eyes on the senior officer.

"I couldn't find anything in her civilian files and I thought maybe the police records…" Max came to a halt, not knowing how to put it delicately and hating Frank Skills for putting him in this situation. "Well, maybe you could take a look for me?" Max paused again, and couldn't think of a single thing to say to soften it. "Her real name was Noel Parson. I'm sorry."

Friar's face went absolutely blank, eyes shutting involuntarily, and for a moment he clearly wasn't breathing. Max looked away and saw the rookie give a start, then squeeze his eyes shut in recognition and jerk his head sideways in the way a man who's just connected something does when the connection upsets him.

"Fuck." He said it under his breath, but it was ringingly clear in the suddenly silent office. He turned triangle eyes on Friar. "Vic…"

"S'okay." Friar's voice had no volume because he had no air in his lungs, but he was trying to make a recover. "S'okay."

The second statement was clearer, if as false, and Max said helplessly,

"I didn't know. Not until Frank mentioned it."

"Sure." Friar walked to the window, putting his back to the others. When he turned back, he had his face under control again, but it was a fragile control.

"Maybe I'll let Sherrow look that up for you." His voice was distant, numb.

"Sure. I wouldn't've asked if I didn't think it might be important." Max lifted one hand in a useless gesture and let it drop again. "I'm sorry."

"Yeah." Friar put his hat back on like it was armor and said, "We'll be in touch."

Max moved on gratefully, wishing it wasn't important and he could've spared the officer this.

"I'll call you, where? No, better if you call me here. Can I offer you coffee before you go?" Helen had brought the monster machine over for him earlier.

The offer was declined, however, and Friar said again he'd be in touch. His partner followed him out the door, looking unhappy and worried, and already saying how he didn't see why they needed a PL's help in the first place before the door had even shut properly behind them.

Max made himself coffee and gave a twisted smile at the rookie's expense. He remembered being young enough to believe he could do it all himself. He knew better now, but doing it all yourself because you could and doing it because you had to were two different things. Max hit the scissor switch and waited for coffee to appear.

The rumble of the machine drowned out the sound of the police cruiser starting up and growling away. Max contemplated the possibility of finding anything useful at city planning, but he wouldn't let the scant chance of getting lucky depress his vague optimism. Sometimes he could tell he'd find a workable lead before he did.

Right now would be a good time for that, and maybe he could stop by to see if Skills had gotten him that clearance to see the military files in city hall. While he was at that, could he have asked Skills to do the research into Jolie's past? Max felt terrible for the long moment it took for him to think about Frank's opinion of sharing cop files with non-cops. No. Friar was the only cop willing to share with Max on this one. It was such a damn shame the woman had to be his ex-wife.

Max filled a mug with coffee and started out the door, forgetting his hat in his distraction.

Friar

Sherrow's hot argument lasted us out to the squad and three miles along and I let him tell me how untrustworthy Canon's type was and how stupid I was to be sharing information with a suspect. I didn't argue or comment, choosing to stare out the window and wonder which of the assholes I was looking at was Noel's killer. Jolie's killer. Damn. All the time Canon had been talking about the witness, this Laide woman, it had been Noel. Sherrow had suspected it, too, but he wasn't saying I told you so, and he never did.

What else did Canon know? Were there things he wasn't telling? What exactly was she into, posing as another woman, and with whom, and what did Canon think a police records search would turn up?

I couldn't process it, couldn't bear to think about it, so I buried it instead, letting Sherrow's complaining wash over me like a balm, just standard daily-daily work fare. Much later I'd wonder if he was so hot on the topic because he hated Canon for doing that to me, asking me to dig dirt on a woman I hadn't gotten over, handing me that pain. Right then, though, his bitching was a welcome distraction.

After awhile, he wound down and when I was sure he was done, I gave him a look he didn't see because he had his eyes on the traffic, knuckles tight on the wheel.

"You maybe heard of the practical use of civilian informants in police work, huh?" I asked. He gave a terse nod. "Just think of Canon as an informant." I told him.

"Like your ratty little doctor?" He asked bitterly.

"Sorta." I turned to look at his angry profile. I had trouble working up energy to care without tapping into the shit I was repressing, so my voice was flat. "The chief approves of Canon in his own special way."

"Frank Skills condones him?"

"I think they're almost friends." I looked back out the windscreen. "The chief flamed four inches off my six when I made a derogatory comment about Canon once." I laughed, not happily, seeing Noel, always Noel, at the department ball, talking to Frank Skills. Who else had she been talking to? Anybody crooked, that far back? Setting ground work for going over to the other side? Jolie Laide, Jolie Laide, the Cajun parable, the beautiful ugly woman. Noel, one and the same. My throat locked and I fell silent, lucky that Sherrow hadn't heard the gulp.

He'd read the silence, though, and spared me a glance. I pointed my face out the side window and ignored him.

There wasn't much else to say and the rest of the shift was strangely quiet. I was thankful for that, barely able to manage even to respond to Sherrow's shoptalk.

By the time I was changing stiffly in the locker room amid a painful wash of noise—were they always so loud?— I'd faced the fact that I'd have to go see the department head-cracker after all. I wasn't getting over this. It was minute to minute and the hollow, screaming pain wasn't fading.

I dodged Sherrow and reported directly to the Captain without him, dragging it out as long as I could, the sheer dullness of the facts damping down my grief, diluting the ache, providing refuge.

For some reason, Cappy played along, dragging out his side, too, asking detailed questions that didn't need to be asked, and consulting my opinion on several areas he most certainly didn't need my weak knowledge in.

I was grateful and his parting goodnight showed me sympathy. I shuffled off on a long wander of the more deserted areas of our huge building, buzzing with the effort to hold the artificial numb, to not think.

Sherrow jumped me in the parking lot. I'd worked myself into a vicious cycle of strain, sleeplessness and these terrible mental images of Noel, unthinkable things that I couldn't stop seeing, and at first, all I saw was his lips moving and what looked like rage on his face. I stopped walking so I wouldn't trample him. He looked like he was in a real hurry. He was in such a hurry he'd startled me and made me drop my keys.

"Where have you been?" Was the first thing I heard him say that made sense. I got the idea he'd repeated it a coupla times.

"Reporting," I said stupidly. I was flushing hot and cold in exhaustion and my whole body screamed to lay down and die. In my mind, Noel begged somebody not to kill her.

"Susmita said there was blood on your locker handle." Accusing. Into his headset, he said, "I got him. Parking level 4," just like he was calling in a perp apprehension.

"I cut my thumb." I bent like a 100 year old man and scrabbled at the keys. When I stood up, I swayed. Sherrow watched me like he was gauging the swing of the plumb bob on a high-rise, looking for the red circle warning that preceded a cataclysmic over-extension. Any minute, I'd start shedding window-glass and topple like a hundred stories of bad architecture.

Kay arrived and I spared a childish glare to Sherrow for calling Dad. Sherrow's return glare reminded me of my brother's face from a lost-in-the-years-ago argument, some typical stolen toy dispute that required parental guidance to mediate. The hollow in my stomach twisted and grew.

"Desk clerk's right," Kay said to Sherrow, "He does look half dead."

"Oh, for chrissake," was all I had to say about it, and I turned away and started towards my getaway vehicle.

Kay grabbed my arm and I shuddered to a halt at the torque. The damaged bits of me weren't up for the battle.

"Hang on, man, you see how you look, you'd worry, too."

"It's cosmetic," I offered and tried to gently disengage my arm. I didn't want friends right now, especially cop friends, people who reminded me of why I'd lost Noel, maybe why she was dead, why I hadn't seen my brother for two whole years before he was killed. All this loss, all this empty echoing hollow in my chest and I was so damn <u>tired</u>. I didn't have room for any of it.

"Ha, ha, Vic, no wait." Kay, trying to be reasonable.

"I just wanna be alone for awhile, Kay, okay?"

Whatever he saw in my face made him agree however reluctantly. I heard him convincing Sherrow as I shuffled away to the car.

I popped the security net, unlocked, climbed in and turned the engine over. Then I sat there staring at the lights on the dash for a long time, listening to the engine rumble all the way down to the chassis and back up through the top of my head. It brought some of the numbness back, made it almost easy to think of nothing, the little lights flashing pretty colors telling me the window was down, the fuel tanks were full and the brakes were set, things that had nothing to do with death or bad guys or law or the things that had gone away to never be again. The car played me a lullaby.

After awhile, Kay stuck his arm through the window and shut off the engine. I couldn't summon the energy to look around. I wished I'd turned on the AC; it was too hot, I could sleep maybe, sleep finally if it wasn't so hot. Sherrow got in the passenger side, just like work, but he touched the side of my face instead of logging us on duty and said something to Kay that he didn't want to hear. Kay opened my door and shoved me over to get behind the wheel. I let him, but I didn't help much, and Sherrow got in the back like we were all going to the zoo together never mind they weren't invited.

I pawed on the AC full blast and fell asleep shivering.

I dreamt I was floating down a river of water so white it was getting up my nose and drowning me. I dreamt the sun had been relocated into my bedroom and was roasting me alive. I dreamt I was being mugged again, and when I tried to fight back, they stole my restraints and cuffed me.

I woke slowly from the sucking black pit of sleep to hear voices: Sherrow and Kay of course, talking about me like a side of beef on the hook. I was on somebody's sofa, maybe Kay's though I didn't remember it feeling so nasty, and my shirt was off.

"Some of those are old wounds: What kinda shit're they sending you guys into these days?" Kay had a med-kit open next to him and was changing out my dressings, which was nice of him, though I'd fail to say thank you until much, much later.

"Hey, man, s' not the department's fault." Sherrow paused, then added in an all-things-fair voice, "Not the honest parts of the department, anyway. This roadhouse kill and the Mitchell thing, Friar's not all that good at being subtle, if you remember. Somebody heard he was digging where they didn't want dug, I guess."

Kay snorted, a sound I knew all too well that really said, 'that's bullshit, kid, tell me what's really going on.' Sherrow fell for it, just like I always had.

"Did he tell you about the Warp, then?" He paused in the vain hope that I had. Kay must've prompted him, because he went on. I wasn't listening anymore because Kay was working while he listened and while none of my wounds, old or new, were mortal, you couldn't tell that when somebody was mauling them around in what I chose to believe he was calling 'treatment.' My head spun from heat, and cold flashed over me twice before I moved to rise.

"I'm gonna be sick," I warned in the voice of an ice giant at spring thaw.

Kay let me sit, but held me on the sofa while Sherrow thoughtfully provided the handy saucepan.

Nothing like an old cop to know the true tools of first aid.

I wasn't sick, though. I hyperventilated until I passed out and only woke long enough later to see Sherrow in wrinkled rolled up shirt sleeves leaving with a backward glance that said worried and a tired-looking Kay baring my arm for a shot of something or other.

It gave me a start, but I trust him with my life and since he seemed to think it was needed, I went with it after the initial jerk of resistance.

"Stop it, Vic," was all he said and jabbed me.

Whatever it was hit me like a freight train, proverbial, and I fell off the trestle and tumbled three hundred black and lonely feet to the riverbed below.

When I woke in that evening, the fever was gone and I even felt marginally rested.

It wouldn't last, of course. It never does.

The captain wanted to give me time off, like grievance time, but I managed to give the battalion counselor the impression that work would be my savior and idle time would lead to suicide, so I got to keep coming to work. It also meant I had to keep talking to the counselor, but the sessions hadn't done much good yet. He seemed to be living in hope.

I couldn't sleep much 'coz I kept dreaming about Noel, which woke me up all fucked up, so I was spending the time walking a lot and seeing how far I could get before I had to metro back to the station or the apartment, whichever, depending on the time of day.

I went all the way into the archives files on Caulder and Croner, Strindberg and Wells and anybody who had been off shift when Noel was killed or who might have it in for Skills...My work was cut out for me. I barely remembered to look up the records I'd promised Canon I would, but it didn't matter anyway: Bimini turned out to be a locked file I couldn't access, and the architecture link, while it did show Mrs. March's building, didn't have any new information and the rest was history so ancient that it told me nothing new.

So I looked up Noel's files under the alias Canon had given me. There were no cop files, but there were civic files, and right off I knew it was her under the name Laide, because she'd given her mother's address when she'd donated blood to the blood-bank, and her mother still lived in the same house where we'd had family arguments and, towards the end, one truly horrendous Christmas,.

Noel's mother had had the retrograde Hepatitis 45 virus, a question they asked at the bank and they asked how often you had contact with anyone with it, must for records since it was still a thing you never cured once you got. Noel, according to the records, saw her mother often: Noel, according to the records, gave blood often, too. 'Specially when the drives went out asking for help for children or the elderly. Or cops.

It wasn't a side of Noel I'd wanted to really remember. It was easier when she was an ambitious, greedy half-bitch.

She loved her mother. She donated blood often.

Sherrow found me in the furthest dark reaches of the civic hall records maze of computer readouts, blue-white from lack of sleep and crying over Noel again. He was smart enough to leave and come back again with Kay for back up. I was not a gracious friend, and it wasn't until much later that I would thank either of them for bothering. I was reintroduced to Kay's sofa and slept there again, under the portrait of his dead wife, who had never done anything more criminal than share software with friends or forget to return library data on time.

I had worse nightmares than the Warp crash, but at least I was getting more sleep than I did alone at home.

Time to visit Canon in person again. He had his new office going, but it was not made common knowledge, not until things became more clear on the bombing case. Only Skills, Eddy Archer, Sherrow and me knew where it was, and we weren't talking. It helped that nobody could ask without hanging a guilty sign around their own neck. It was only a pity nobody tried.

So Sherrow and I went to look Canon up one morning after shift, godawful early for most people, but he was there just like a night shift man.

The secretary showed up just ahead of us, looking like 1:00 a.m. was normal office hours. She was the only one who looked that good.

Nice view regardless. It was distracting, a pleasant sensation, and one I'd almost forgotten. Which reminded me of Crystal and made me feel like I'd swallowed a pound of lead. Crystal. I didn't think I could face another woman right now, no matter how interesting.

XXIX.

Canon

Friar and his partner arrived at Max's office unannounced. The cop looked half dead. The partner looked two parts concerned and three parts threatening. There was back up written all over him. Helen let them in.

Friar's eyes followed her rear view for an uncontrollable second. Max sympathized.

He offered them coffee again and this time it was accepted.

Friar sat himself down in a hard wooden chair and waited with one leg jack hammering out a rapid, impatient beat. There was prison fever in his red-flecked bronze eyes.

Sherrow was just about to join him when he got back up and came over to examine Max's coffee monster. The younger man followed like a guard dog with a wayward child.

Lights flashed across square feet of glass tubing and chrome. Max punched commence. Sluice gates opened and plumbing engaged. The police stepped back.

The device made a loud hissing bonk as water hit the heating coil and a cloud of steam rose up to briefly obscure Max from the officers. Helen always complained when he did that. She turned the heater on after she loaded the cistern, but it was faster Max's way, zero to coffee in mere seconds.

"It's safe," Max assured them, but he'd never been too sure of that himself and uncertainty could be heard in his voice. They removed to the chairs, a safe distance away.

Under Sherrow's disapproving eye, both Max and Friar laid their notes out on the desk. Shuffling and comparison commenced and they were able to ascertain that while the warehouse in the Speakeasy with the powerful force screens was indeed Caulder's property, they'd be hard put to prove it. They also agreed that Caulder had been amassing properties for some time: Max produced unenlightening blue prints of Mrs. March's building, pointing out a few hopeful areas that might contain hidden rooms, but until someone could get in there, only conjecture was possible. Then Friar admitted to finding no useful record of a Jolie Laide in the police files, and Max nodded, saying in a falsely casual voice,

"Didn't think there would be, but we had to check it out."

Friar nodded stiffly.

"Sure."

Sherrow saw a look pass between his partner and the PL, and tactfully went out to the squad to listen to the radio for a few minutes, both officers pretending they weren't wearing portables. Friar and Canon eyed each other across the desk.

"We need to find Melody Miller. She's the only one who connects with most of the principles here."

"Does she?" Friar was unconvinced.

"She danced with Stephanie March, same profession. She worked for Caulder. She was seen with Albrecht. And she was seen with Krueger."

"Krueger?" Friar hadn't heard this name before.

Max described the man and watched Friar sit up straight and tense. He'd just been handed the name of Mitchell's hit and run; the man with the jaw.

The officer produced a photo and pointed.

"That him?"

Max recognized the jaw of the leader of the three who'd pitched him into the river.

"Sure looks like it," he said.

"And he's a Caulder employee?"

"From what I gather. But Mrs. March seems to think Caulder is scared of the three of them, Krueger, Georgia Grau, called Silver, and one other, a dense guy, tall but wide. I call him Thug, don't know his name."

Friar sat playing with his lower lip in flat-eyed thought. He was so deep in his own head that when Helen came into the office he didn't even look up.

Max went to meet her at the door. She was carrying something.

"Mail," she said. "And Marie called again, the last time, she said."

"Do you think that was a promise?" Max took the thick manila packet from her hands, turning it over curiously. Couriered hard copy was almost non-existent these days. He saw the return address and went very still. When he looked up, Helen met his eyes and nodded.

"That's who I think it is, isn't it? Is that classic, or what?" but her bantering tone didn't reach her eyes, which were serious and concerned.

Max flipped one eyebrow in response and went back to the desk to find something to open the envelope with. Helen picked up her keys as if preparing to leave, but she came over to the desk, watching Max. Once she was in his direct line of sight, Friar seemed to become aware of her.

"Hi, Helen," he said in an abstracted sort of way.

"Hello, Officer Friar," she responded, thinking he looked terrible.

However, he seemed to have whatever was bothering him under control, and turned his eyes to watch Max sorting through the packet of chits and hard copy. There was a dangerous moment when he picked up the discarded envelope and read the return address, but other than a sudden and total stillness and the draining of what color had been left in his face, he did nothing.

Helen considered him watchfully for a moment, then turned to Max.

"I'm off, boss. Call me if you need anything work-related."

Max looked up with an intent expression.

"Okay. But be careful. Whoever blew up my place is still around: Who knows if they consider you leverage or not? You think you're being watched, being followed, you call me."

Friar took a card carrier out of his pocket.

"Or better yet, page me: I'm official, and I have better backup." He coded her name onto the card using the carrier keypad then ejected it with a snick and handed it to Helen. She saw that it was an auto-page card, with a little badge icon as the hot button.

"Thank you, Officer," she said and put it into her purse.

Max nodded, but his mind was already returning to the material on the desk. With one last look at him, Helen departed.

When she had shut the door behind her, Friar said abruptly,

"Well? What is it?"

Max sat down and slotted a chit into the interface. Friar stepped closer as images flew out into a layered holographic representation of information, images, raw numbers. His face was blank. Max took up the envelope again and considered the address and the name, written in a hasty and shaky hand: Noel Parson, 5701 Lamont Lane Rd. The hotel in the Speakeasy: The hotel she'd stayed in with Albrecht.

Friar

What Noel was doing with the stuff in that envelope, I didn't want to think about. It was post-marked the day after her death, and had both her name and that of her attorney's on it, and the return address was a hotel she'd shared with a man I'd never heard of before the roadhouse. Canon told me about Albrecht dead and Noel at the Emerald City and let me guess about where she'd stayed after that. But I knew. His eyes were too full of pity and what might've been guilt. It was much easier to gloss over it all and pretend it didn't have anything to do with me, and I turned my eyes on the stack of stuff from the envelope.

There was data and there were hologram cards. The images were the type that appeared in files marked Vice: Unlicensed Sexual Deviance. It wasn't bulletproof conclusive, but it might be enough to put the label 'blackmailer' on Caulder. We looked at cute little moving holograms of employees at Caulder's main brothel, its sign showing as a still-identifiable sliver in one or two of the shots, occupied with government officials of both genders. They were all participating in scenarios I would have to call torture fantasy. It was hard to tell if they were real or staged. It didn't matter: it was enough to blacken the names of any of the paying participants. There was a police official in there, and a mayoral candidate, along with a few lesser, but currently powerful, personages.

The documents included guest register print outs, dated security camera chits and payment records, proving entrance and culpability: these people were clearly willing participants.

I put the cards I'd been looking through neatly back on Canon's desk.

"'S' a good set up. Once the document guys got a chance at those, and proved 'em true, there'd be a whole lot of unhappy people calling for redress. Or re-election."

Canon nodded.

"But it smells like a frame. Why would she blackmail Caulder by documenting a blackmail scheme he had going? And why would Caulder need to resort to blackmail?"

"Maybe it's insurance," I said, with difficulty. I could see now why Noel had felt the need for insurance. Were we looking at why Caulder had had her killed? But if she suspected she was in danger, why not come to me? Why send the lot to Canon, who was also clearly in danger?

Or hadn't she known that?

Canon was silent a moment, and I avoided his eyes. Where the hell was Sherrow? I thought maybe I should turn my radio up again, so I could hear better if he wanted me, but I didn't. I didn't really want to talk to him; I just wanted the distraction.

Canon said,

"Could be. But I'll bet she wasn't high enough in the organization to get this kind of proof. I think somebody else sent it to her for safe keeping. She said Albrecht had received a letter that brought him haring to town to hand-deliver to Mrs. March. I wondered at the time if it had to do with this blackmailer who's got her handing over her allowance. And that," he pointed to the envelope, "Smells like Mrs. March's perfume."

I took a whiff at the envelope, smelling roses and tropical flowers and happier thinking of Noel as a dilettante in the mafs. That would mean she was new to it, which would mean she hadn't been involved while she was married to me. God, I hoped she hadn't been involved while she was married to me. That would be like having her shoot me in the head, total betrayal.

"So the March woman's being blackmailed?" My thoughts turned to Strindberg like a magnet to due north, thinking of his raw red eyes and fury in the smoky din of the club.

Canon nodded.

"Your cop friend, I think."

"He may also be blackmailing Melody Miller," I added. We had yet to discuss my conversation with Strindberg at the Carny Freak.

Sherrow came in on the last sentence and shook his head, looking grim.

"Not anymore he isn't. Her body was just found north side in a refrigerator car." He came into the room and stood where he could see my face.

"Vic. She was strangled."

XXX.

Canon

It took a few minutes for Friar to start moving again. Max watched him do the now familiar blank shut down and freeze, but after a heartbeat or two he took a long ragged breath and gave his partner a glare that was reassuring in its animation.

"I didn't need to hear that," he said, slightly breathless.

The younger officer apologized, but his eyes were watchful. Max thought of the look Eddy sometimes gave him when he was sure Max was in trouble but knew he didn't have the right to say anything.

"Were there any other…" How to say this? "Similarities? In the disposition?" Max asked Sherrow.

"Don't know. That was the preliminary. But we know where she is now."

"But not where she was. They say how long dead?" Friar stood and walked to the window. It overlooked a storage lot for semi-trucks. One was just leaving with the linkage up, gunning out of the lot overpowered with no load to drag it back. There were an even dozen others parked cab to cab like horses in a high wind. The other buildings that backed up to this had no windows on this side, just blank faces reflecting the dim fluorescent lot lights. The sun hadn't come out yet. It didn't look like it would.

"Over two weeks, but no other clues have come up yet."

"Then she was dead when we saw Strindberg in that club, waiting for her."

Max grunted, his thoughts on another track.

"Had the body been moved or was she killed in the car?" Max asked, his tone measured, thinking.

Sherrow cast a look at his partner, but he answered,

"I dunno. Report wasn't very detailed. I'd bet she was dumped there, though. It was an old car in the trash yard, waiting to be crushed down. It's a good way to dispose of a body."

"But not the only way," Max said, thinking of Laide in the trunk of Skills' car.

"What are you thinking?" Friar wanted to know.

"Jolie—your pardon, Noel—I'm sorry, but Noel's body had been moved. At least once."

"Skills tell you that?" Friar's voice was wooden.

"After a fashion." Max turned away from him. He picked up a holo blackmail card, and watched the little figures move. This one involved a whip and chains. Sherrow's head turned at the flash of light and he came over to flip through the stack and look at the mess of interface imagery still projected above Max's desk.

"What's all this?"

Friar answered him, voice carefully modulated.

"Mr. Canon thinks Mrs. March sent it to Noel for safekeeping."

"Looks like a blackmail plan."

"Yeah, we thought so, too." Friar's bronze eyes were on Max, steady. Max wasn't sure what was behind them, but he met them evenly.

"So let's go see what we can find out about Miller." Sherrow dropped the image onto the desk where it sputtered out and tapped Friar on the shoulder. After a tiny pause, he said to Max, "We'll let you know what we find out."

They moved to the door.

Max considered for a moment, then made a decision he was sure Frank Skills would hate.

"Gentlemen." He waited until both officers were looking at him. "You might want to talk to Chief Skills about the disposition of Ms. Laide's body. It's a piece of the puzzle."

The stripped look that passed across Friar's face was gone before the younger cop saw it, but Max gave him the courtesy of looking away, busying himself with deskwork that didn't need to be done.

They left him alone in his office, his mind blank. All he could think of was the last time he'd seen Friar's wife alive, and compare it to the last time Friar had seen her. There was no contest choosing who had the best deal.

Max closed his eyes and tried to think of something else. It was bugging him almost as much as the fact that he'd failed the woman in the first place. Almost as bad as the fact that he was dreaming about Stephanie March at night and caught himself making excuses to seek her out.

He could safely say he was too close to this case. Ruth would have kittens.

The phone rang, and it was Eddy, telling him there was a gathering and Ruth wanted him to come.

Max couldn't think of an excuse good enough to avoid it, and he hung up with his own affirmative ringing unpleasantly in his ears. He just knew Ruth would take one look at him and know. How was he supposed to tell Ruth he'd fallen in love with a suspect when he hadn't even told the suspect yet?

Poor Friar, poor Jolie, poor stupid Albrecht: They were all in over their heads. And poor Max Canon. Especially poor Max.

Friar

"I wanted to talk to you about some of these…potentially embarrassing incidents that have been popping up in our precinct over the past coupla months." I paused to let him register what I was saying and get on the same page.

Skills' eyes went guarded and I could tell he was wondering what I knew.

"I ran into Canon and I know something not so good's been going on lately. But I've got a story of my own to tell, and I think it all adds up to something bigger than just random persecution."

"Go on." He ran his eyes over the office walls like they were listening.

"Are we okay in here?" I wondered suddenly the same thing.

He nodded.

"I had it checked. We are bug free in here, but I don't expect it to last. How about lunch? You taken your break yet?"

"Sounds good," I said, not wanting to outright lie. "Let me get my partner."

Skills didn't like that, but he didn't complain and got his coat. We went out in the cruiser and took him to a place on the south side that was too junky to attract surveillance.

When we were seated with coffee, I started again.

"Sherrow knows everything I do by this time, so don't worry about that. He's probably more trustworthy than me." I made it a joke, but nobody smiled.

"What have you got?" Skills wanted to know.

So I re-told him about Sherrow's spiked drink, and my spiked drink and the set up with Noel at dinner. I told him about the vial of Warp in my locker and mentioned again the hint Canon had given us. I brought up the recent finding of Miller's corpse. Then I said how it all looked like it was connected when another officer had a spiked drink encounter, too, and how the people involved seemed to be either the same people or working together, and they maybe had at least Strindberg in their pocket, either working with them or working the same side of the street.

There was a silence while Skills sipped coffee, a look on his face like he was debating whether or not to tell us something that may or may not be part of this. Or maybe he just didn't know if we should be told.

Or if I should be told.

"A body was planted in the trunk of my car last inspection day," was what he said after a time.

I took a deep breath and let it out again. It wasn't as steady as I would've liked.

"That's not good," Sherrow put in. "Planted, you say?"

"Yeah. A woman's corpse," here his eyes flickered, and I knew why. I kept my face carefully blank. So this is what Canon meant. "I think I was 'sposed to drive into work with it and get caught in inspection."

"Clumsy," I said woodenly, giving up on my cold and tasteless coffee.

"Too clumsy for a professional." Sherrow agreed, turning his triangled eyes on me when he heard my tone "A warning, maybe?"

"Maybe." Skills sipped more coffee, a glutton for punishment. Even Sherrow wasn't touching his cup, it was that bad. "Maybe a professional warning. I think I was meant to get caught, though. It was put in early coz I was in the trunk the night before, moving stuff."

"It would make you look pretty bad, even if you weren't convicted." Sherrow said.

"How many officers do you figure have been victims of this drink-spiker?" I changed the subject abruptly and they let me.

Skills considered before answering, and Sherrow looked into his coffee and said nothing.

"There's two more that I know about that you haven't mentioned. And yes, I know who your third officer was, and I'm not counting him. So far, no one's been caught, and I've worked my ass off keeping it that way. "

"Maybe the set up happened too early. Shitty organization." Sherrow looked relieved that none of the drug dropping had been against him personally. I felt the same way and could only feel a little sorry for Frank Skills, who couldn't be thinking the same thing. It really looked like someone was beating up his department on purpose.

"Hmmm. Whatever it is, it's definitely aimed at my corner." Skills slammed a hand down on the table in frustrated anger, then looked ashamed for the outburst. "Sorry. I shouldn't even be talking to you two about this. I should be talking to Internal Affairs."

"But they won't let you stay in office while they work. And we both know with you out of the office the nodders and winkers would be letting Caulder and the mafs run barefoot through our fair city."

"Yes." Skills rubbed a hand over his face and looked at the white-faced clock on the wall behind the counter. "I'm in trouble here, and I can only figure Caulder or his kin are out to knock me out of the chief's chair. Get one of their stooges in instead, like you say."

"Who'd be up to take over if you got ousted?"

"I've already made up lists. No one I can prove anything on."

"Maybe they only need the office to be empty for the day or three it'd take to get someone else in there?" Sherrow suggested. "Y'know, something big going down, they want the precinct in chaos while it happens?"

"That kinda chaos is made by more than a temporarily empty chief's desk."

"Like the kind of chaos made by riots, drugged officers and interdepartmental strife?" I couldn't keep the sarcastic edge off my tone, but they both ignored me.

"Big something. Like what." Skills was listening.

Sherrow shrugged. I said,

"Move a huge shipment of Warp, maybe. A cargo of illegal guns to outfit the syndicates."

Sherrow suggested,

"A series of careful murders to clear out some of the maf-god chairs to make way for new blood."

"Some of that's already happened. Lots of empty chairs around when you look," I agreed. "Could be any of that. Or none of it."

Skills rubbed his face again, as if trying to clear his thoughts. It didn't seem to do much good.

"Well, think about it. And I don't have to tell either of you that this conversation didn't happen."

"Right. We'll let you know if we come up with anything solid."

"You do that."

He got up, and we did likewise.

"And be careful. I don't want any more Mitchells on my hands."

Which reminded me.

I told Skills about the traffic cam, and the photo. Then I told him about Canon's identification of Square Jaw. He seemed unsurprised, but glad to get the tag.

I paid the bill, then we walked back out to the cruiser.

"What did Mitchell's report actually say that might've gotten him targeted, anyway?" I asked, tossing the keys to Sherrow.

Skills' face twisted in an angry look.

"He had the beginnings of a case that might lead us to some of Caulder's muscle-boys. Nothing to convict the Man himself, but good leads."

"Maybe we got 'em this time."

"Everybody try and live through the day," was all he had to say to that.

We dropped him off at the station house and went on our way to finish out the day, having eaten two lunches, and not enjoyed either of them, the taco in the cruiser or the coffee in the café.

I had indigestion for days, but I knew it wasn't the food.

Canon

Lucky for Max, Mrs. March was a night person, too. By the time he left Ruth's party, dodging the looks she was pegging him and completely cowarding out on the one question she did land, it was late.

"What's this paragon's name?"

Ruth had known instantly that her brother was enamored of someone. He'd run like a rabbit, leaving Eddy to make his excuses, but he'd have to answer her sometime or she'd never give him peace.

Mrs. March wouldn't let him meet her at her apartment. Max took that to mean that the trio or some other bodyguard or other was watching the place. When he asked point blank if Caulder was there, she said a flat no.

"Did you hear about Jolie Laide?" he asked, checking the scrambler on the phone line. They had about one more minute before it flat-lined.

"Yes." There was a pause. "I received another letter from Fokke."

"How much did he want this time?"

There was a heavy silence and Max got worried. Before he could phrase a question properly, she said,

"It wasn't a demand for money or...anything. It was a threat. A death threat. It said I'm going to die."

Max watched the scrambler tick down.

"I'm coming over."

"They'll kill you. Stay where you are until tomorrow. They have some sort of meeting then. I'll be okay until then."

Max paused, torn, and the scrambler shut off.

"Okay. I'll do as you say. Goodnight, Mrs. March," and he hung up before she could say anything betraying into an unscrambled line.

Friar

The more I thought about it all, the more things looked very much like Strindberg was the nearest available man I could pummel for information. He certainly was crooked, and that made him eligible in my book, whether I had a reason to pummel or not. And there sure seemed to be reason.

I didn't want to find out that an academy pal was rotten, but I also had to know and things were rolling so fast now that I couldn't wait. I thought I knew the answer anyway and it was turning my stomach hard and sour.

I also thought I ditched Sherrow: We'd decided he didn't have to follow me coz I'd tell him anything interesting

I found out, but he had conveniently forgotten all that. Maybe he was reading my face as I said goodnight with half my mind on Strindberg.

I got myself to Strindberg's place after shift without telling anybody where I was going, and rang the bell. There was no answer, not unusual for this time of day. He was either still out, or was entertaining: In either case he wouldn't answer the bell. I would've maybe left then, if I hadn't been so worried about the whole set up stuff that looked to be targeting Skills, the only good chief we'd had in years, if he wasn't actually crooked himself. I didn't know anything anymore.

First thing I noticed as I stood on the stoop and listened to the bell echo inside was that the doormat was askew. There was also a scuff or two in the omnipotent downtown diesel-dust and hover soot that coated every doorstep in the city. A closer look showed me a chip in the door that might've been made by a boot applied to prevent closure. There was a tiny raw spot in the jam that also spoke of forced entry.

And the damn door wasn't locked or even properly latched. It was slightly ajar. I kept my hands off the knob and kneed the door open.

The patterns of blood and scorch suggested automatic gunfire, and not slug fire either, but power fire, like the old sloppy burn lasers with the high-res and low terminus that assassins used to use ten years ago before the racy new Black X came out with its cleaner burn and better looking package. The maf shooters still liked the old boys coz they were light and small and didn't leave slugs behind like our cop guns or zips and didn't have the distinctive Black X signature squiggle in the burn spray. The military had used them for a long time and they could still occasionally be obtained on the black market. And we still had the slug guns. The fucking colonial navy, who never saw combat at all, had newer weapons than the police force.

The shooter or shooters hadn't been shy about hosing it around, either. Blood trails led all over, pale light blood already half dry from minor wounds: The victim had tried to get away. He'd been excited, scared or angry or all of the above, by the high water marks on the papered wall in front of the body, and it took me a minute to identify it as Strindberg. Like I hadn't known the minute I found the door open. Like I hadn't smelled it out there on the stoop, that unmistakable smell drifting under the overall scent of city.

Somebody had gone through his stuff, and a file cabinet in the hall lolled open. No attempt had been made to conceal the fact that disks had been taken. "C" files and "M" files, of course. Caulder, Miller, March? I looked at the corpse again, careful to disturb nothing.

The detectives would sort out the particulars when they got here, but I could take a further look around. Who knew if the killers were still here or not? Telling myself this even though I could look at the body and know it was hours cold.

Either the killer had hated Strindberg with a heat and rage that couldn't be vented by a quick kill, or the person had been having fun before the gunfire had put an end to it. The blood was darker and heavier in the kitchen, obviously the final kill zone. The murderer had hit an artery. The pattern and prints in the blood suggest Strindberg had been on his knees looking up when the fire cut out his throat. Near the door, nearly invisible, was the print of a woman's shoe.

She had small feet.

Sherrow came to the door then to see why I hadn't come back out and why the door hadn't shut, both of us pretending he hadn't been following me without my permission. When he stopped changing color, I asked was he okay. He nodded, but he wasn't. Still, I didn't kid him about it. I remembered my first experience with a laser kill and I didn't want to make it worse for him. When I could tell he'd won and lunch was staying down, I asked him to call the on-dutys and make it official. He went back outside to do it from his car computer. I stood looking down at Strindberg, thinking.

You lucky bastard, this wasn't nearly as slow as it could've been, was all I could think. I knew who had killed Noel. I heard again his admiration for assassins. I could see his face as he talked about style and prestige. I could remember her turning him down at the policemen's ball when he thought I wasn't looking. I could hear his bragging about bedding women who were higher on the social ladder then he was.

And I knew he'd climb that ladder any way he could, but I'd always known that. Too bad I hadn't realized all the ways that might be open to him. It had never occurred to me that this was one way he'd try.

Bet he hadn't counted on becoming a liability so soon.

I didn't tell Sherrow any of this when he came back. I met him at the door.

"Why're you here?" I asked him.

"Just happened by, saw yer car."

"Now that's a lame excuse. I thought we decided you were going to quit with the shadow and start getting sleep instead."

He nodded, eyes completely unguarded as he looked past me into the bloody mess. He took a short breath and rasped back out a cough as his lungs tightened up in objection to the smell and the tension.

"Let's go outside. Just breath easy."

I took his arm and put us both on the other side of the door. We were both a little green. There's a smell you can't get rid of at a crime-scene like that.

"Yargh. Hate the laser ones," I told the traffic lights at the south end of the block. An East-West stream of green starboard and red port lights traded places across the intersection, then the lights changed down the poles for the street level traffic. Another stream of lights marked ground vehicles moving across. Somebody merged out of turn in a sharp dive and horns blared. The sound was distant, cut off from Sherrow and me where we stood on the steps of a dead man's house, waiting for the on-duty badges to take it away from us and hand it to the detectives. It wasn't our call. I sorta hoped it wouldn't be Frank Skills' call, either. I tried to remember if his pal Canon carried a burn gun or not.

"Friar." Sherrow's voice sounded very young and tight.

"Yeah."

"Didn't Strindberg drive a maroon Ares?"

"Yeah. Why?" But I was already following his gaze.

"There's a black Hawker VT Coupe in his parking space. That's his space, innit? Has this apartment number on it."

I looked into the docking cradle marked 671, Strndbg. It wasn't the car he'd driven for the last five years. It looked new. Yesterday new. Status new. Prestige new. Dirty money new.

Did it belong to Strindberg? We wouldn't know until the plates had been run. A squad car with lights but no siren came out of the clog of traffic like a cutter in from a foggy ocean and locked into the cradle right next to the new VT.

I watched a couple of detectives and Frank Skills get out. In the back of my head I re-ran a beer soaked conversation we'd had a while back with Strindberg. He'd been going on about the latest model on the must-have lists.

"...Hawker VT Coupe, top of the line. Retro gearbox, full package engine—the big engine, of course—chromed tailpipes and blast diverter and deluxe security and surveillance system, fully programmable filters with voice lock, and 360 booster swivel. It's a VTOL, man. It'll navigate interstellar."

And Sherrow had said,

"It's space-worthy?"

"Hell, no," was the reply, but his eyes had shown like a man in first love. "But if it was...It's hot, kid, totally hot. Friar here, now, he wouldn't know hot if it bit him on the ass. You still driving that black Chevy, Vic? Black, shit. Assassins drive black cars. I hate black cars." But he didn't, coz he'd always wanted to buy my black Chevy.

"Looks like a mob hit," the detective said at the door. I didn't recognize him, but my eyes were on Frank Skills anyway.

"Yeah."

Skills had a story about recognizing Strindberg's address on the broadcast, and he had a grocery sack in his hand to prove he'd been in the neighborhood, but I wasn't sure. He could've been in the neighborhood killing Strindberg and stopped for a drink with Canon, his accomplice with the burn gun. Or did Canon have a burn gun? I tried to remember what he'd had in the shoulder rig.

But no. I didn't believe Skills had done it, but with all the shit coming down on his department, I wouldn't blame him either, if he was getting rid of the one making it possible. And some gut instinct told me it had been Strindberg harassing the department.. The little connections were all there and he had motive and opportunity for the Warp plant, fingering my dinner date for assault and killing my ex-wife. Noel had worked for Caulder or at least with him. I would bet my pension and five fingers that Strindberg had, too. And he'd never liked Noel. Too bad he hadn't taken longer to die.

"Man, what a way to go," one of the detectives was shifting Strindberg's left hand with a pen, to check under it without destroying evidence. "This had to hurt a lot."

I remembered broken fingers on that hand and agreed it must've hurt. But not enough. The ring mark on Noel's neck would match the ring on Strindberg's broken fingers. I knew, and I was sick with it. Sherrow asked me if I was okay and I told him yes.

"Didn't Mitchell say it was a black car that hit him?" Sherrow still had his eyes on the VT, listening to the detectives and Skills go over the crime scene behind us. The ME arrived and cruised for a parking spot that didn't include climbing two flights of stairs. He found one near the elevators.

"Yeah, he did." I came back to lean on the rail near where Sherrow still stood.

One of the detectives heard the last of that and came out to join us.

"Yeah?" he asked, following our gaze. He swung the mouthpiece of his radio up and read the VT's plates into it for a check.

"That looks personal," he gestured behind us.

I agreed and Sherrow nodded.

"Anybody know him very well?"

I straightened.

"I went to academy with him. Known him for years."

The detective, Seldik, his name was, read my tone.

"But you didn't know him well enough to explain this." He made it a statement.

"Yeah." I nodded. "I might've guessed if I'd thought about it, but...No. Not that well."

He nodded, too, and went back in to join his partner as the ME came up with his bag and his permanently sour expression. He shouldered past us with a nod of faint recognition, and vanished inside to be replaced at my side by Frank Skills.

"You know anything about this?" he asked me point blank.

"I don't know anything. I can guess a lot, though." I looked him square in the eye and asked just as bluntly, " Does the License Canon carry a burn gun?"

Skills jogged his head back at that, but it seemed to be normal surprise.

"Sorta. It's a military special, high end, distinguishable energy traces. And it smells different than this type of burn. So, no, he didn't do it." A faint smile appeared on his face. "And neither did I. Are you suggesting that Officer Strindberg was involved in some of these embarrassing incidents that have befallen the department under my command these last few months?" He put a sarcastic spin on it.

I loved the man's quick mind.

"I wouldn't have phrased it that way," I admitted. "And you would make a great suspect for this if he was responsible. The patterns fit. He fits it too well." I looked out over the rail at the traffic again. "I just wish I knew what he'd done to get on the bad side of whoever he was working for."

"So you have already assumed he was working for someone." It wasn't a question, and Sherrow was now looking at me, too. Skills looked to be regretting the café conversation.

"Canon said a cop was blackmailing Mrs. March. It'd be a whole lot easier to get information suitable to black-mail if you worked for the lady's sugar daddy. Anyway, that," I nodded at the VT, "is what he used to call an assassin's car. With respect in his voice, when he was too drunk to hide it.

Mitchell was hit by a black car. Strindberg was in many places, at many times when it would've been easy to implement some master plan for a maf crew."

"Now there's a master plan." Skills dug out a cigarette.

I gave him a look.

"As if you hadn't had the same thought." We traded looks and he nodded, acknowledging the truth of the statement. He looked like he'd been having plenty of sleepless nights: I'd never seen him look so stressed and worn.

"I'll let you have official access to this case if you want it," he said after a moment, moving back towards the front door. The conversation was finished. Neither of us mentioned how a mere beat cop didn't have training or authority to investigate something like this.

"That'd be good. I'll let you know if we have any wonderful ideas."

"Fine." He vanished inside after the ME, and I could hear the detectives talking between them about the state of the corpse.

Some on duty uniforms showed up and began isolating the scene. Sherrow and I found ourselves on the wrong side of it, and we decided without speaking to get out of the way and let them work.

Then next morning Seldik took our statements, and I remembered the lady's footprint.

I wondered if they had made a note of Mrs. March's shoe size in her early arrest reports.

When the VT proved to be the car involved in Mitchell's 480, we had a tie to the trio, and I figured I knew whose shoe it was.

Sleep didn't happen that night and I spent it eradicating every sign of Noel left in the place I could find. If Kay had seen me staggering around tearing things off the walls and cursing drunkenly he would've hit me with another shot of nighttime drug, but blessedly, nobody came knocking on my door till morning, and then it was the landlady telling me how sorry she was about Noel, which was when I spotted the stasis cube with the single rose from our wedding standing unnoticed on the book shelf.

I couldn't bring myself to destroy that, so I after the landlady left, I hid it in the back of a closet where it burned in my mind like a guilty conscience.

I went to work looking like less of a cop than I had all year, which was saying something.

Canon

Max, after a sleepless night in a cold hotel room, received another visit from the officers, bright and early the next day.

"Tell me everything that's going on with Mrs. Stephanie March." And when Max looked reluctant to share even a cup of coffee after this abrupt treatment, Friar added, "Skills says we have full reign on this case."

"Beat cops are doing full investigations, now?" Max went to do arcane things with the coffee maker.

This time, Sherrow tagged along to see how the monster machine worked. Max looked over his shoulder at Friar, who had a wry smile on his face.

"I'm not exactly functioning within the chain of command on this one," he said.

"Yeah, you seemed pretty cozy with Skills."

Sherrow grinned, but it wasn't nice.

"Sure, we skip the LT and the captain: we're special."

Max was going to make a further comment, but Friar waved it all off impatiently.

"About the March woman…"

Max eyed him for a moment, before speaking. Behind him, the coffee maker shook and steamed and gurgled out coffee.

"Yesterday, she was threatened with murder by her blackmailer, which is new. Before he only asked for money. I think she might be next on the liquidation list."

"You said you thought the blackmailer might be Strindberg, the officer we saw the other night?" Friar didn't mean to loom, but Max could see he was containing some strong emotions.

"Yeah. The upset one."

The two officers exchanged glances.

"But Strindberg's dead," Sherrow said.

"You sure?" Max didn't want to jump to any conclusions.

"Oh, yeah, pretty sure." Friar nodded concurrence and Sherrow went on, "This new threat is how old?"

"Yesterday. Late-ish."

"It's not him, then. "

"We'd better go visit this woman, then," Friar said. Max saw him try to shake off some of the tension, but it looked like more of a shudder.

"Okay, then." Max made it a question.

"Okay." Sherrow answered, eyes on his partner. "We're okay. Let's go."

They were let in without question, and Max wondered where the guards that usually stood outside Mrs. March's building had gone. It made him uncomfortable, and he could also see the cops looking around like they were wondering the same thing.

Three very nervous men passed through the door to the penthouse, and Mrs. March seemed to instantly sense it and become nervous herself. Her manners were impeccable, though and she greeted the two officers cordially as Max introduced them. She didn't seem to recognize either of them from the roadhouse. Friar set himself to be charming. Max could see how rusty he was at it, but he had a sort of clumsy appeal that Stephanie warmed to. She was soon smiling for him, and Max had to grin, too, even though the jealous pang was dismayingly present. Sherrow busied himself by checking out the suite and peering out windows from behind the curtains.

Mrs. March seated Max and Friar and perched on the edge of a chair.

"What can I do for you, officer?"

Friar pulled a photo out of his inside jacket pocket and handed it across the coffee table and its chromed glass clouds.

"Do you recognize this man?"

Mrs. March took the photo and looked at it. Her expression changed, twisting, and the photo dropped to the glass.

"That's him," she told Max, "Fokke."

"Cute." Friar took up the photo and put it away. "So it was Strindberg. What can you tell me about this blackmail scheme he had going? Were there others involved, more victims maybe? Do you know who he was working for?"

"He didn't work for Dan, if that's what you mean."

Friar looked surprised. It was obviously not what he had expecting to hear. Sherrow came over to stand where he could see Mrs. March's face.

"You're sure about that?"

"Yes. When he first came to me, it was at a party Dan was throwing. Dan didn't recognize him, and wanted to throw him out. But by that time, he'd already presented his evidence to me, so I lied and told Dan he was an old friend."

"Like you told the investigating officer about Noel...Ms. Laide...at the roadhouse when Mr. Capelli was killed." Friar barely got the sentence out before grating to a halt. Sherrow looked away. Max took up the question.

"You said Ms. Laide was an old friend, along with Steven Albrecht. Was that a lie also?"

"Only partly." Mrs. March stood to pace, up and down behind the sofa and back to the chair. Sherrow stepped back to let her, keeping her in view, but not interfering. "I'd known Jolie—Noel, you say? I never knew her by that name. I'd known her about two-three years. We had become friends as much as two women in our circumstances can. I...I liked her. I'm sad she's dead."

"Strindberg killed her." Friar said harshly, more of question than a statement.

Mrs. March nodded.

"I think so. He bragged about it to me, how he had been picked to get rid of an inconvenient woman. He never said who, though. And he never threatened the same for me until this latest letter."

Max and Friar were trading looks. Max turned his on Mrs. March and Friar let his fall to the coffee table, his gaze turning inward.

"He didn't send the latest letter. It was somebody else. Can you think of anybody who would benefit from your death?"

The pacing became swifter and more agitated.

"I don't know. Dan? Maybe he found out and thinks the best way to end the threat was to get rid of me? I haven't seen him in days. He keeps putting me off with excuses about business. There's nobody else unless…"

"Unless." Max leaned forward. Sherrow's eyes narrowed, giving the same impression.

"I've often wondered if there wasn't somebody more powerful that Dan, who sometimes used his men, his organization. He never really talked to me about work, but once in a while he'd say something that would make me wonder. It would have to be somebody very powerful, very connected."

"They'd have to be to be bigger than Caulder. He's main fish right now." Sherrow turned to Friar to engage him in the discussion. The senior partner met his eyes and shook off whatever had a hold of him. "You think maybe somebody wants his chair? A coup?"

"Maybe." Friar stood up to look out the window himself, careful to stay in the shadows. "Maybe he balked at the Warp thing."

"Warp thing?" Mrs. March looked confused.

"It's a recreational drug. It's too expensive to make quick street money and too dangerous for true pleasure seekers, but it's been showing up all over town. Caulder couldn't really make enough money on it to make it worth while handling it, but somebody's doing it, or he's doing it for them."

"And somebody's been cleaning up inconvenient people, too. First Capelli, then Albrecht, and a bumper crop of maf biggies, and now Laide." All eyes went to Mrs. March as Max finished the list. "And you, Stephanie. I think you're next."

"Sounds like a coup, definitely. But by who?" Sherrow cast a frustrated glance at Mrs. March. "Think. Think of anyone who might benefit. We have to know who might've targeted you, who to watch for."

"We can trade Christian names in a minute," Friar said, backing away from the window. His gun was in his hand and he keyed on his radio. "Unit 312 requesting back up at 1231 North Palmer Avenue. We have a situation involving firearms. Copy."

Sherrow and Max dodged furniture to have a look themselves and Max drew a breath at what he saw and came over to Mrs. March in three quick strides.

"We need to get you out of here, Steph. They look like Caulder's men. And the trio's here." He took her arm. "Back way best, you think?"

She nodded, eyes suddenly huge in a chalk pale face.

"The cruiser's down in back. It'd be the fastest. Safest, too." Friar tossed over his shoulder as he went to check the corridor.

Sherrow flipped on the security camera screen to monitor progress. It showed four men with big guns, burn guns, stalking up the hallway on the first level.

"The three didn't come inside," he reported.

"They're waiting by the car," Friar said, at the curtain again. "Go, already, it's you they're after." This last to Mrs. March. "We can maybe keep 'em busy here."

"I can't ask you to sacrifice …"

"It's not sacrifice, ma'am. It's holding the perpetrator until back up comes to snag his ass." There was a savage satisfaction in his voice. "If only we could hold those three right where they are…You got a safe place to hole up?"

Mrs. March nodded.

"Take Sherrow. Show him where you'll be." Friar moved to the monitors. "Hurry."

"Run away now, Stephanie. When it's over, you can reach me through Friar or at my new office." Max handed her to Sherrow who didn't look happy about having to go.

"Max, darling, you're so blue collar," she smiled for him, an imitation of her bitch-cat confidence. She kissed him. "I like blue collar." She stopped by Friar and kissed him, too, on the cheek. "I'm beginning to appreciate blue in general. Thank you."

"You gotta go before it's too late to get you clear. Sherrow, go."

Sherrow nodded and gave a brief grunt of acknowledgment, towing on Mrs. March's reluctant arm. She gave Max one last look, then fled, leaving him with the feeling that she'd done more than kiss him goodbye. It felt like farewell, and it didn't make him feel any better about the four thugs coming upstairs.

"They might have guards on the back doors," he told Friar.

Friar panned cameras and had a look while speaking, inwardly cursing the blind spots in the camera coverage.

"Sherrow will think of that. He's smarter than he looks. Okay, better get behind something, here they come. We got maybe a minute."

Both men found spots to wait with weapons ready. It was slightly less than one minute when the automatic fire began to perforate the door. Friar could see the camera monitor from his place behind the door and saw Sherrow whip Mrs. March out the back and into the cruiser a full ten seconds before he had to trade gunshots with the guard they'd sent around. The cruiser jerked to life and rose with her engines blasting and Friar gave Max the thumbs up just as the door crashed inward under one healthy kick.

There was a confused moment of gunfire, then one of the thugs fell over, gun clattering away, while Max grappled with another. Friar pegged a shot at the next man through the door, but he only clipped him, missing the good wound and making the man howl. He ducked another shot that sizzled past his hip, reminding him unpleasantly of the night with Noel when he'd been hit, and he took careful aim again, only to have the weapon shot from his hand the next instant.

He dodged and rolled for the safety of the sofa, trying to find one of the downed weapons on his way. The room spun past him too fast for any such effort to succeed, but he caught up a low-ball glass in his flight past the bar and threw it with long unused muscles to smack the arm of the man aiming at Max's back, spoiling the shot. Another howl made Friar smile and he found another weapon, this time a table lamp, which slammed off the first man's head to great effect. Two down.

Shots were turned on Friar and he ducked again, moving away from the sofa rapidly as the burn fire set it smoldering. Max's victory was self-announced with a single, loud crack that Friar didn't want to think too hard about, oh, yeah, he was a vet in the special forces, and the last man standing swung his fire back towards Max.

Unable to reach the man safely for a disarm, Max leapt out of the path of fire and found himself nearly hitting Friar coming the other way, as the cop rushed the man while the gun was turned away. They did a strange sort of spinning embrace and Friar fell away on the door-side, sweeping out an arm and catching the thug's gun arm more by luck than skill.

The last weapon skittered away and the man leapt after Friar with a snarl of rage. Friar liked to see a man stupid enough to let anger control his fighting, but he wasn't on balance yet, and the onslaught caught him and sent them both over. Friar fell kicking, and caught the other man under the right knee with a happy crunching sound. He received in return a blow to the stomach that took all his air away and made him very aware that this man was stronger and in better shape than he. He disengaged as rapidly as he could, scrambling back as the man tried to gain his own unsteady feet.

Max grabbed the nearest weapon to hand and wound his arm back for the pitch. Blue Lapis flashed in his peripheral vision and he reversed suddenly, unable to bring himself to destroy the priceless vase.

He set it gently back on the table where Friar snatched it up, shouting,

"Are you crazy? Run, dammit!"

The vase made a lofty arc across the intervening space and struck dead center between the enemy's eyes.

Max ran, shaking his head as such sacrilege. Friar was right behind him, wondering how long it would take the three professional killers to reach the penthouse and see what all the commotion was about.

They made it to Max's car with a minute to spare.

Friar

We caught up with the cruiser rapidly. I spotted it before Canon did, and waved him over to follow. Sherrow led us back to his own car and pulled over, leaping out of the squad and triggering off the security and locks as he ran, yelling for us to all get in.

We did, and I knew he wanted a car faster then either the cruiser or Max's older model so I didn't ask any questions. He peeled out at a 45 degree high push take-off that had us smashed into the seats, then off we went in another direction entirely.

When we were all sure we weren't being followed, Sherrow asked Mrs. March where she wanted to go. Canon wasn't happy with her answer, and his frown told me exactly what he thought about the safety of such a move.

"Not good enough. You can be traced to that."

Sherrow changed course abruptly.

"Where you goin'?" I asked after my stomach settled back in place from his classic Sherrow's-in-a-hurry merge. I was blinking away the vision of ten square feet of garbage truck grill from a cool three inch, 60mph near-miss as he hauled us around 360 to a new course and another level of traffic. From the back seat, Mrs. March said in a faint voice, like an apology,

"I get motion sick really easily."

Sherrow smoothed out and trimmed off a whole lot of speed.

"Sorry, ma'am."

"It's alright," she told him, which I didn't believe for a minute.

"Where are we going again?" I repeated with an irritated note in my voice.

"Takin' 'em to my dad's place. No one knows where he lives."

"I do," Canon said.

"Yeah?" Sherrow looked surprised, but let it go. "Well, yer special. I meant no one on the force, since that's where a lot of the bad guys' info seems to have come from. Dad hates the cops."

"I see."

"Yeah, and me, too. But he'll do it coz someone has to and it's the right thing."

"If you say so," I said, doubt in my tones.

Sherrow ignored it and set his jaw, putting all his attention into driving. By the time we arrived, I think he almost had himself resigned to the coming interview.

When he got back in the car, sans the PL and the lady, he looked stormy.

"D' it go well?" I asked, not very hopeful in the face of the evidence.

"Well enough. He'll keep 'em here a night or two. Wasn't happy about it, me dragging trouble to his door. And trouble outside the department, too."

"So he hates you being a cop. Was he a con, he has such a problem with 'em?"

"Nah. Contract engineer. Makes tons. He says being a cop's stupid, all we do it sit around pushing buttons and making reports."

"Ah, he thinks he knows what the modern police force is all about." This amused me highly.

"Yeah. He doesn't know how much good old-fashioned running around and getting shot at we do."

"Maybe he'd be proud if he did."

"He wouldn't believe I could do it. He used to accuse me of slacking in school, not trying hard enough."

"He'd believe it he saw you chasing down one of our fleeter perps. Yer a good runner, kid."

Sherrow snorted.

"Yeah, I'm so good. Like that time we ran so far and hard after that asshole robbed the liquor-store that I puked right after I got him cuffed."

"Well, he wasn't doing much better, Sherrow."

"True. And you weren't far behind."

"Yeah. Having a heart attack."

Sherrow gave me an amused look.

"You seem to have survived it okay."

"It's my virtuous life."

And that got him laughing again. I was beginning to hate his father almost as much as he did.

By the time we had Canon and March all stashed, Frank Skills had heard about the melee from our backup, who'd brought in three slightly scorched bad guys. One apparently woke in time to beat retreat, but the others were inconvenienced by the fire that consumed the sofa. Most of the apartment was miraculously intact, but the fire department came and committed their favorite water damage just in case.

Sherrow and I went back to the station to debrief and hear all of this. After keying in a few hours of reports, we were allowed to go home, but I could tell the Captain was pretty upset that we were not only colluding with the Chief behind his back, or rather, over his head, but we were committing the cardinal sin of including a civilian in our powwows.

Then it was the weekend. Sherrow checked on Mrs. March, who seemed to be getting along with his dad simply because she'd seemed excited at the prospect of spending all day reading through his library and playing chess with the old man. Sherrow rolled his eyes and shrugged, and went to spend time with his own very neglected fiancé. I watched him go with envy, because I had a meeting with Canon. We were going to try and find out who was really behind all this, and all in one weekend.

Like we'd had all that much luck to date.

Canon

Skills called Max to tell him he'd finally arranged clearance for him to search locally held copies of the military records. This was good news, but Max had a dangerously wound-up Friar on his hands and that had to be dealt with first, so he collected the man at the arranged time and off they went to Mr. Sherrow's house. Sherrow Sr. let them in, but it was made abundantly clear that he disapproved of them greatly. Mrs. March, however, seemed to have made another conquest. She was wearing a man's shirt and a pair of what had to be Mr. Sherrow's old work pants, belted tightly and still too big, and her face was clean of makeup. She looked ten years younger and innocent as a schoolgirl, though her sarcastic elevated eyebrow suggested to Max that his expression of astonishment at her lack of glamour was shared by her, and she wasn't particularly happy about it. Mr. Sherrow seemed to think her the most wronged creature in existence. He apparently held Friar and Max responsible for her persecution.

After much labored civility, Mr. Sherrow agreed to leave them alone to 'discuss plans.'

Max began by asking Mrs. March if Caulder was hiding Warp in her basement.

"Maybe, I don't know," she said honestly. "He likes to store certain luxuries there. You know, imported stuff. I'm sure some of it wasn't legal because he never let it be talked about."

"Do you know of any hidden areas in the building where such potentially embarrassing items could be hidden?"

"There are rooms there, yes. But the apartment manager knew about them and so did one of the girls I used to dance with, so they couldn't have been that secret could they?" She looked at Max in question, and he got the full benefit of her lovely eyes.

"The girl wasn't Melody Miller, was it?"

"Yes, why?"

"Just another loose end I'm trying to tie up." Max paced away and back, trying to think. "Can you think of anything Caulder might've said that could give us a clue to why he was letting drugs into his territory that wouldn't profit him?"

There was a pause long enough that Friar turned around to look at Mrs. March. Max paced back and stopped in front of her. She sat with her head down, eyes on her hands, which were folded together in her lap, very tightly.

"Stephanie?" Max asked, something in her posture warning him what was coming.

In a very small voice, she started to speak, sounding much like the schoolgirl she looked like with her ponytail and baggy borrowed clothes.

"I couldn't say anything before because...for a lot of reasons. And I was afraid. But nobody knows where I am, do they? You weren't followed here?"

She looked up at Friar as she asked this and he was taken aback by the stark fear that aged her face. She was clearly in fear for her life, something she hadn't displayed last night at her apartment as she talked about death threats.

"We weren't followed. You're as safe as we can make you right now." He sat down in one of the leather chairs and put his hands on his knees as if to keep them still. "That may change, but hopefully we'll have this figured out before that."

"Okay." She took a steadying breath. "That somebody more powerful than Dan I talked about yesterday?" She addressed this to Max.

He nodded encouragement, his expression inscrutable.

"I know who it is. I work for her."

XXXI.

Friar's breath went out in a rush, and his expression was an amusing cross between amazement and rage. Max spared him a glance only, and kept his own face expressionless.

"Go on."

Mrs. March wrung her hands together and stood to pace, but there wasn't enough room. She sat down again.

"I'm sorry I didn't say anything! I was watched all the time. I've been watched for years!"

"Your apartment's bugged?"

"Yes."

Max thought of some of the things that had been said and done there and wondered about this boss.

"Your boss knew you were being blackmailed and did nothing about it?"

"It amused her to watch him try to be a big shot. When he went too far, I guess she had him eliminated."

"Went too far." It was a question.

Mrs. March waved her hands in the air, a despairing look on her face. She spared a glance at Friar, who had his expression under control, but the anger came off him in waves, and she turned back to Max quickly.

"When he killed Jolie. He wasn't supposed to know that much about the real operations, but he must've found out somehow, because he started to get more demanding. Dan didn't know I wasn't loyal solely to him. That's what Fokke found out and was blackmailing me with. If I'd known he was a cop...But that didn't come till later. By that time, Steve Albrecht and Jolie had come to town with that damn package I'd sent them for safekeeping in the first place, like it even mattered to anybody anyway. Jolie knew about...her...the boss, but Steve thought he was working for Dan."

"What about Capelli?"

"Oh, he came with her. He was one of hers from the start."

"Who's this 'her'?" Friar put in, in a remarkably calm voice.

"I don't know her name." Mrs. March looked over at him nervously. When he didn't attack, she went on, "She came to town about the time Dan started making up to me at the Emerald City. We just call her Boss. She took me and a few other employees from the E.C and gave us jobs with her. Mine was to be Dan's girl. That wasn't so hard at first. Dan can be really sweet when he's not distracted."

Max made an impatient gesture at this. He couldn't help it and he didn't want to hear about her 'work' with Caulder.

"What about Melody Miller? What was her job?"

"She worked as a runner, mostly. Delivering messages and mail to various members of the organization. She did okay until a year or so ago, when she got tangled up in some bust or other. She was just never the same after that. She's the one who used to deliver my blackmail notes to me, until a month or two ago, when Fokke started bringing them himself. Sometimes he'd meet me when I was out, sometimes he'd arrange a place to meet."

She shook herself and got up again, to circle her chair, hands folding over and around each other till the knuckles were white with strain.

"Jolie was pretty new to it all, as far as I could tell. She didn't have the gloss most of us working girls and guys did. I don't know what she did before she came to us, but I know the Boss actively recruited her. She used to call Jolie her little joke. I never knew what that was about."

In a strangled voice, Friar said,

"She used to be married to a cop."

"Oh." Mrs. March considered that for a moment. "Yes, that would make the Boss laugh. She likes to corrupt people, as she's so fond of saying." With a sour twist of a smile, Mrs. March added, "Never could figure out why she'd come to the Emerald City to recruit if she felt that way."

"Maybe she needed an instant work force," Max suggested. "Fresh off the boat and looking to take over a piece of the action."

"Yes, that could sum it up pretty accurately. I take it you've done your research into my past? You know how much property is in my name and in Dan's through me?"

Max nodded.

"It's a front. If it defaults from me, it goes into a holding fund. Guess who controls the company that maintains the holding fund?"

"The Boss."

"Correct. Dan's been taken for a sucker and he doesn't even know it. He's been fencing this fancy drug of yours as a favor to the Boss. He thinks she's part of an offshore syndicate, and he wants to be friends. He's an idiot, and he's weak."

"Which is why she'd keep him," Friar stood up, his hands folding into fists and out again. "What about the plan to mess up the Department?"

Mrs. March cast him a confused look and turned to Max for elucidation. He told her briefly about the drug plants and the body in Skills' trunk, leaving out much of the less important detail.

"Maybe she wants Dan in control of the city?" Mrs. March hazarded. "I really don't know. She doesn't tell me much more than he does. But she likes to talk and sometimes she talks too much."

"Lucky for us," Friar said in a low growl. "Well, Canon?"

"Yup." Max nodded. "Guess we gotta go find this Boss. Know where we could go for that, Stephanie?"

Mrs. March went paper white at this and started shaking her head. She didn't stop.

"Oh, no, she'll kill you! You can't go to her, she'll kill you, then she'll find me and kill me, too! You'll die, you can't go! Officer Friar, don't let him go!"

"Go where?"

But she wasn't that easily caught and she folded her lips shut and sat down again, white to the fingertips, but adamant in her refusal to answer. Friar had just enough compassion left to leave her alone.

Friar

So I had the brilliant idea to see what Noel had been doing with Canon's home phone the night she died. I dragged him to the satellite company and flashed my badge like it would do any good. Strangely, between my badge, his flirting and pressure on the freedom of information rules, we got a look at the records. It probably helped that it was his home phone and that there was an investigation going at the time: The satellite laws are so convoluted; no one really understands all the ins and outs.

Noel had called out on the night of the bombing. We got the number but the sat people wouldn't cough up an address to match, so off we went to the station so I could tap into the department computer system looking for a match. Canon sat in a chair nearby and looked at the computer like it was an active enemy.

"Hate those things," he told me.

I was surprised and said so. Seemed to me a guy in his line of work had no right turning his nose up at anything that helped him gather information.

"Talking to people is more effective," he said. "You can lie to those. And everybody does. It's harder to lie to a guy's in your face."

I shrugged and tapped in a code-line.

"Lot of information isn't considered important enough to lie about. Most of it's as accurate as word of mouth, anyway. Anywhere people go, lies and mistakes happen."

He couldn't argue that, so he didn't.

The reverse directory didn't want to let me in for some reason, since the number was unlisted, but I wasn't in law enforcement for nothing, and this was a computer in the system. It just took a little longer to get the address, but I got it.

Canon and I looked at an address not far from Mrs. March's place, and realized that we had a place to go, but no plan to go there with.

"Whaddya wanna do about this?" I said after we'd sat for a long time, thinking. "You wanna go on over or what?"

Canon took the scrap of paper I'd scrawled the address on and looked at it like it was written in a foreign language.

"We can't just charge in. We will get killed. No way this place isn't guarded."

I turned back to my trusty console and called up city planning files, added the address. It threw up the image of a lovely bunker-like complex, elegant above ground, fortress-like below. We didn't have a hope in hell of sneaking into a place like that.

"Should we just make an appointment?" I joked in an unhappy way. It was too frustrating to have a goal and no way to get there.

Canon shook his head, and got up. He handed me the paper back and stretched his shoulders.

"I got something I wanna look into before we tip off the big guys that we're onto 'em. Krueger and his lot'll be on the prowl for sure now, and there's a few more things I'd like to get done before I run across them."

"What're ya gonna do?"

"Depends on where I start. How 'bout you get me more data on the Miller case? Find out who killed her and why?"

"Like I can just pull that outta my ass." I stood, switching the computer off, without bothering to wipe my tracks. If anybody was that curious about what we'd been looking up, it wouldn't take much to reclaim the data. Could help 'em know where to go to find my body, anyway. "We can look at the initial reports, anyway. C'mon, this way." I led him off to forensics.

Everybody knew by now that I was pursuing investigations I had no right to as a lowly uniform, and I got various degrees of cooperation or antagonism depending on who I was dealing with. Anyway, it took a few minutes of fancy lying to get the duty officer to let me have a look at the coroner's report on Miller. The officer, Ross Taggert, another guy Kay had trained, actually wanted to give me advice on staying out of business not my own, but I could see him fighting with it after I met his first sally with a blank glare. That's when he told me he was sorry about Noel, and I had to spend a minute or two blinking at the folder he handed me like I could actually read it with my eyes out of focus.

Canon, clearly unwelcome, took the folder from my hands and started flipping. Taggert growled, but I told him Skills approved of Canon—I was getting a lot of mileage out of that assumption—and he subsided.

Miller had been strangled. She had not, it looked like, been killed by the same person who had killed Noel, which meant that Strindberg hadn't done it. I think I was disappointed, but the sensation in my stomach was as unidentifiable as it was acidic, so I ignored it. It looked like she'd been killed merely to get her out of the way, since there were no signs of torture or fun-loving sociopathic game playing in the condition of the body. Canon pointed this out to me and I only nodded, looking at the photos and finding that I could do so without superimposing Noel's face over Miller's. It was a relief, since I'd been beginning to wonder if I could work in the business anymore, when everything I'd seen or heard in the last week or so had reminded me of Noel.

Taggert seemed to become accustomed to the fact of Canon's presence and my dabbling, and he produced Strindberg's autopsy report without being asked.

"You might be interested in this," he suggested, handing it to me with an odd look on his face.

As I opened the folder, he went on,

"Strindberg had high levels of Warp in his system."

So he'd heard that rumor. I put folder down on the desk with a slap and Canon picked it up.

"I'm not dealing Warp," I said flatly. Canon looked up at that, apparently the only living being in the whole city who hadn't heard that particular lie about me.

Taggert shrugged, but he seemed convinced by the expression on my face.

"Didn't say you were: just thought you might be interested, since whoever is, is following you around."

"Following me around?"

Taggert picked up his coffee mug and took a sip, looking at me over the rim with a considering expression in his pale eyes.

"Well, everybody knows your rookie got dosed. And someone was saying you were the man to call if anybody had a problem with that particular drug. There was even a rumor about you doping the water coolers."

Wells had obviously been the progenitor of the second statement, and while I didn't have a clue how people found out about Sherrow, I also just didn't want to know right now. Maybe rat-doc informed for some cop on another shift. It was commonly done. The last rumor had me, though.

"How or why would I dose the water?"

Canon put down Strindberg's file like he hadn't been listening to all of this, picked up Miller's again and said,

"I think that's how they've been smuggling it on-world: water barrel delivery to several high end areas in this town have coincided directly with what looks like Warp arrival." He smiled faintly at my expression and added, "At least, that's what the patterns look like. There's pretty frequent deliveries of imported water to 1231 North Palmer Avenue, anyway, Bimini water. "

"Which is where this Warp is coming from?"

"So I've been told." His expression told me he considered that moot. He flapped Miller's folder in the air once.

"A big man did this."

I was diverted despite my interest in the Warp trace. I thought about big men with big hands.

"Krueger?"

"Who's this Krueger?" Taggert wanted to know, hearing new things all over the conversation. He looked to be waking up, which I wasn't sure was a good thing. Who knew who he was working for? I'd become too suspicious for my own good, but I decided if he was working for the other side, he knew it all already.

"Same guy hit Mitchell, I think." I told him, knowing Skills wouldn't like my flashing that around, but unable to resist lobbing that particular grenade, just to see if it surprised Taggert.

It did. He went through all the right emotions in the right order for an angry cop at a cop killer. I was relieved.

"Does the Chief know this?"

"I don't think so. I haven't had a chance to talk to him. You're about the only one working on a Sunday, Taggert, you lucky bastard."

"Yeah, I'm so lucky." Reminded of how lucky he was, he fell silent, looking sulky.

Canon indicated he was ready to leave, then, and we took off, thanking Taggert for his cooperation, and leaving him unhappily bored again.

By the time we hit the street, Canon was ready to ditch me. He didn't phrase it that way, but it was the same effect.

"Why?" I wanted to know.

"Got some things I'd like to check out before we decide how to storm the fortress." He put his hat on, slanting it down. "And I'd like to check on Stephanie."

I nodded, shifted my feet.

"What kind of things?" I asked, ignoring the second part of the statement.

"Military things. I'm seeing more military here than I'd like. Capelli; the firearm used on Strindberg; the Bimini cruise lines that import the water are war-year leftovers."

"I didn't know that."

"Coz no one does. I just recognized the owner's name from a long time ago. Was big brass on the flight line. It needs to be looked at, anyway. He could be behind this, or friends. We really want to know if we're dealing with vets here. Trust me on that."

I did, but he was talking about going alone and I wasn't sure he was making sense. What he was saying was valid, but I wanted to hear that he was going to be smart about how he did it.

I didn't know how to ask without sounding critical of his intelligence, so I didn't say anything.

I'd wonder later if things would've been different if I had.

It was Monday, and the early part of it went fine. Canon was off looking up war records as far as I knew and Sherrow and I were back at work. Mitchell visited the precinct on crutches and we all promised to buy him beer he wasn't 'sposed to have after shift. Linden was in conference with Skills to get caught up with all the new data and was back on the case. Skills' name was all over the media for blocking drug screens in the department and IA was all over the locker room with scanners, checking lock-logs and looking for evidence that may or may not point to Strindberg's nefarious activities between shifts. It might also just firm up those nasty rumors about me, but I hoped not.

I was ready to ignore the lot of it. Too many things were coming to a head at once to sort properly and still keep my mind on the job, so I didn't try, concentrating on what was going on on the street. Sherrow seemed to have reached the same conclusion, and he was all professional as we ran from pillar to post on little shit that wouldn't get us medals, but wouldn't get us dead, either.

It wasn't until after break that we spotted a likely looking vehicle, all assassin's glossy black, loitering near the edges of another unit's crime scene. The other squad on the job was tied up in the mess, so when the black car started to pull away, doors slamming, I hit the lights for a flash to let 'em know not to try it. The car had cut-out blockers and screamed away from us, sparking reflections off its perfect, multi-coat custom roof. Sherrow ran the plates and got a vehicle not owned by Caulder, but licensed to one of his companies. Neither one of us needed the confirmation: we'd both seen Sherrow's Mickey Finette, Georgia "Silver" Grau, get in and the others looked to match the descriptions of Canon's other lifeguards at the river, Thug and Krueger. I'd know that jaw anywhere. Sherrow chuckled low in his throat like a guard dog and I felt a grin flit across my own five o'clock shadow at the thought of an actual capture of actual felons we could hold. And levers. These were levers we could use to pry at Caulder, maybe see who was behind him, if we could pry him loose.

But we had to catch 'em first. I laid on more speed while Sherrow called it in and maybe corralled some back up.

Of course, busy night in the big city, there was no such critter to be had. We were on our own.

The black car was gorgeous, long and sleek and worth as much as an atmosphere shuttle, easy. It slid and dodged and fishtailed through the streets, unable to take off because of the overhead rails from the ped-movers and the ancient el-systems.

We were good to follow for another twelve blocks, then we'd lose 'em when they took off for the upper traffic levels. We could see he was heading for the 45th street cut-over to the ramps, so I took a reckless and against-policy detour through a construction site while he rocketed on ahead. After Indy 500 in the mud puddles, we came slewing around a far corner at an abrupt angle to cut him off perfectly, only he wasn't quite there yet. I had to slam on the brakes to stop him and he nearly hit us, going into a full broadside slide, smoking his brakes. At the last second, he powered out, heading east again, back into the old part of town and its overhead restrictions, going for the ramps on the other side of the crumbling slums.

Treasuring the wild-eyes looks I'd glimpsed through the tinted clear-kev windscreen, I followed, the old squad lumbering up to quite a decent speed before the black car found his perfect opportunity to ditch us. Backup was still nowhere to be had and Sherrow had been too busy holding on to report our position.

I followed the black car around another hairpin, this time on slightly less than two wheels—I heard Sherrow's knuckles pop as they tightened on his safety webbing—and saw the asshole engage lift just to get him over a six foot stack of bar and plate blocking the road.

Sherrow said,

"Uh, Friar?"

I saw the 'not a through street' sign flashing past. But it used to be one, my mental map told me, and I vented a string of curses that paralleled Sherrow's, though he might've been praying.

Well, the squad used to have an emergency lift cushion, a prototype of the modern full-lift models. She couldn't fly, but she didn't need to. We only needed six or seven feet. I fumbled for controls unfamiliar since I was a rookie. They didn't even teach this maneuver anymore. I prayed the field still worked. Sherrow, in the dark, just cursed continuously in his preferred Spanish, not even sparing the breath to ask me if I was going to brake or kill us both.

I found the switches, and flipped 'em all with my fingers crossed and a prayer in my heart. The old bitch wallowed up onto a lift cushion so old it screamed and listed on a half dozen leaks that popped and burbled little bubbles of vacuum into the lift field. It wasn't reliable, it wouldn't last, but all I needed was six or seven feet and we were free and clear and still in pursuit.

The obstruction came at us at speeds well beyond the recommended limit. I think Sherrow closed his eyes, though he'd deny that. At the last second, I jammed the lift ratio control all the way into the corner. The squad lurched higher on an explosive moaning hurricane of wind that sounded like all the souls in hell howling and smelled like coolant and fossil fuel, then we were over the barrier and accelerating.

We scraped bottom going over, and I had to slow her down and ground her again on the other side or we'd break down completely. The idiot lights on the dash looked like a riot in a dance club.

Sherrow creaked his neck over stiffly to look at me. His eyes were wide and shot with adrenaline. The smile could've been excitement or it could've been terror.

"Friar, you are one crazy sonuvabitch."

I took it as a compliment and nodded a bow of acknowledgement. We had the bastards.

We had 'em. There was a 6% downgrade that let gravity help my old ground car but didn't do anything to speed up his high-tech hover, and he'd just turned at Field Street, which was a mess of warehouses and run down dumps, and I knew like the back of my hand.

That's when I saw the face that looked a whole lot like Canon's, only more beat up, peering like a hostage through a streetlight-flashed rear window.

A hostage. Oh, man.

I told Sherrow to call it in again, hoping backup would miraculously become available to us.

"Did this just get ugly?" he asked as he keyed his headset.

"Yeah. It did." There wasn't much else I could say.

Shortly, I was saying plenty, all of it unprintable: I lost them. After all my inspired driving and the dodge and weave, I lost the damn car. Somewhere along the road, he turned and I didn't catch him. It made me so mad, I almost didn't fix the situation, but old habits drilled in die hard and the next thing outta my mouth after blasphemy was to tell Sherrow to start hacking into the ad neon along the side streets while I circled the block. The bounce-back they got from the reader systems manufactured into every new car could be scanned. While he did that, I called in the car again and this time had them tell me its ping-rate. There was still no back up available, but they knew where we were and what we were up to, at least.

Sherrow fed the ping-rate into the car comp and started running the numbers.

And there it was, a Chinese restaurant neon in pink, gold and red, the dragon's mouth opening and shutting on stylized smoke and flame, pinging the black car's signature to us along with the send-ad; "Eat Drink Dance Sing Best Food Best Wine Best Entertainment Come Now!"

We were only a few blocks off, and the next sign, an ad for car insurance, that told us we needed more coverage and that we were going in the right direction. Mere seconds passed before I spotted the black car squirreling along behind a warehouse. Sherrow reported the warehouse sign's confirmation of their passage at the same time I spun the wheel to chase in behind them.

They ran to the end of the block and turned suddenly east. Our speed was too great and I couldn't trim enough to make a proper turn, so I stabbed the brakes, the gas, the brakes, the gas, whipping the wheel through a classic bootlegger that upset Sherrow's equilibrium again. It was another move that hadn't survived the transition to hover vehicle training. I think they still mentioned it in classes, but it wasn't taught in practical. A great loss, I thought, and so did Sherrow, to hear him talk later.

The long black beast came to an abrupt stop at the far side of a large parking lot, brick building on one side, empty streets on the other three. Krueger came skipping out of the car to the trunk as we rolled over the curb across the lot and he hauled out a big, two-handed gadget I didn't recognize, pointing it at our cruiser. It flashed green, and Sherrow and I were already diving out the doors, dunno his thoughts, but mine were screaming 'grenade launcher.' The cruiser lit up briefly and everything died, except the battery-powered bubble gum lights and Sherrow's SCR radio. He'd made it out a split second before I did, and got his radio out of range of what I assumed was some sort of electro-magnetic pulse projector. Nothing exploded, anyway, and we both came up into firing position as the car sat down heavily like a big dog performing for a biscuit as the anti-gravs pooped out. Hot, ozone-scented air washed past my legs, and then there was nothing for a second but the creaking of the chassis settling before the shooting started.

Out of the corner of my eye, I could just make out Canon in the back of the black car, struggling. Somebody in the front seat turned around and clipped him one across the head before going back to firing at us, and Canon slumped. I'd been hoping he'd get away himself during the confusion, but it wasn't looking too good. I could hear Sherrow calling for back up into his mike, and Krueger was exchanging the EMP for a long rifle that cracked and spat light. A close shot from Sherrow nearly got him and spoiled his aim and the burn gun sizzled the air past my ear and ate paint on the cruiser. Energy weapons again. And this looked higher tech than any I'd yet seen. That meant military for certain, like Canon had said, which meant Caulder wasn't the star on this Christmas tree unless he was importing again. It wasn't something I was happy to have confirmed. I had an idle hope that Sherrow had also figured it out and was even now, telling Skills via the dispatchers.

We could get lucky.

For a minute it looked like we would. Canon was up again and he broke from the car, to be followed by a slender young woman with long pale hair. The third person, the square Thug, got out of the driver's side to peg shots at us over the hood, and support Krueger's fire while Canon and the woman entered into unarmed combat like they were in the middle of a movie instead of the middle of a firefight.

There was no way to help Canon without risking hitting him, so we continued to trade fire with the others until Krueger's phone rang, and both me and the thug ran out of ammo. With a grin, Krueger ducked behind the sedan to answer it, and both Sherrow and I hit the ground running, Sherrow to get into a better position for cross-fire, clipping off shots to keep the thug's head down while he scrabbled in the front seat for something, and me to help Canon, who looked to be losing to the woman. She was some sort of Hong Kong demon from hell by her fighting skills and war vet Canon was having trouble with her. I was only glad it wasn't me up against her solo.

I came up to them and swung before I'd really stopped moving, not a good start, and while I contacted, I hit her off-center and she avoided most of the blow. Now Sherrow had the shotgun going to keep the thug's head down, but the shots were limited, and the woman slammed a kick into Canon, then turned 'em on me. I did my best, but I certainly wasn't trained against this sort of master ninja shit, and it took Canon to come at her from the other side to make opening enough for me to land a good solid blow.

The thug found what he was looking for and a baton came whizzing at us, glancing across Canon's back and ruining the hold he had.

The woman whooshed out some air when I kicked her, but not all of it, and there was a waltz while Canon and I jogged around, dodging punches and kicks while trying to find an opening to grapple her down and Sherrow expended the last rounds in the shotgun. Canon got a grip on our quarry's arm at one point, and I went in without finesse and body-slammed her sideways. He lost his hold, and the woman and I turned as we fell together, Canon missing his chamber on whatever move he'd been setting up and going down on three-point as we fell away from him.

She landed on the bottom, but managed to control the fall so I still took a good jolt of the impact in the elbows, shoulder and knee myself. There was a second of silent shock while fire passed overhead, high, so's not to hit his buddies, and Sherrow was wondering audibly where back up was while jogging back to the cruiser in a battle crouch to find more ammo. A baton sailed uselessly after him. I wondered briefly why Thug didn't get a burn gun, too, instead of a riot gun that only shot plastic plugs.

Canon was getting back up when the baton gun went 'sploot' again and Thug made a bull's eye. The PL went over like he was dead, and the woman squirmed free of me. We'd been out of the car maybe a minute and a half.

Krueger was still on the phone, like this was social hour, and I managed to land quite a respectable blow on the lovely lady. She went down, and didn't get up for a couple of seconds. She looked stunned, but I knew better than to trust that, and I was helping her up with a come-along that locked her arm bones into convenient handles when the Thug, apparently out of batons, came charging out like a prize-winning bull to grapple with me.

I lost my hold on the woman, and Sherrow was just emerging from the trunk with some impact grenades when Krueger finished his damn call. I was standing, in a lock with the Thug, and the woman was at our feet, having been unceremoniously tossed there by me in my rush to get my hands free. Krueger re-entered the fight unchivalrously by shooting at us.

He must not have cared so much for the Thug as he did for the woman, because the fire hit us both, and knocked us several feet back with its force. I came down on the bottom with Thug's blood all over me, but I was alive and he was a canoe, so who was complaining. Sherrow sent three grenades to Krueger and did enough damage to make the man yell, fall down and not get back up again.

I lay where I was for a moment, panting. Thug's head had come down on the woman's with a loud clock and she wasn't moving for the moment either. Sherrow came away from the cruiser in a battle rush, rattling off a report into his headset, sweeping the lot weapon first like a good soldier. I pushed the canoe off and hunched away from the mess.

Sherrow fetched up next to me, leaning wide to eyeball Krueger and the woman, and then turning his attention to me, jittery at the shadows and still speaking with crisp, radio-perfect urgency.

"901 ambulance, code 3 officer down. Also request coroner. Request clean-up crew. Friar, you okay?"

I was sitting up by then, saying yes like idiots do before they're sure if it's true or not, and Sherrow took my arm to help me to my feet. When he pulled back his hand, it was a hot sticky red.

"That's you," he said, meaning it wasn't the Thug's blood. "D'you wear your armor?"

"Yeah." I grunted as I became aware of the damage. "Too bad it doesn't come with sleeves." I tried to make a joke of it.

"Let's sit down again, Vic," He had my good arm and we went down in a controlled rush near the unmoving PL as my knees discovered once again the meaning of blood loss, and Sherrow was muttering into his headset some more.

I saw the woman move, but not soon enough to warn, even though I tried. She was on Sherrow even as he turned, and I tried to get to my knees to intercept or something, anything. She'd eat him alive.

Sherrow blocked the first blow, eyes wide, then something happened. His whole demeanor changed and he grabbed the woman in a totally unprofessional hold, taking everyone off guard by the unorthodox move.

"You!" He shouted into her face, giving her a shake in his outrage. Clearly, he'd just confirmed that she was indeed the cute little chick who'd drugged his drink.

But the next second she was free of him and they were engaged in furious fight, kicking and swinging and going for tournament gold.

I didn't really blame him for being pissed.

Anger wasn't enough to save him, though. She was so far superior, that she had him staggering in no time. Krueger came up to us, apparently recovered from whatever Sherrow's grenades had done to him and kicked me with a casual brutality I'd encountered only seldom before in such sociopathic purity and checked Canon's pulse. A grunt seemed to indicate that living was good, and he lifted Canon's shoulders to move him. Sirens started up in the distance.

"Silver, baby, we gotta go. Now."

"I'm not done playing." Her voice was musical and happy. She slapped Sherrow across the face like she would an impertinent boyfriend and he was too dazed to dodge it. She added another spinning kick for fun.

"We're out of time. Grab Canon's legs. We have to go now." Like Sherrow wasn't still on his feet, however groggy. Like I was furniture.

I felt like it, bent forward over the now burning torture of the wound. I couldn't even tell how bad it was. I tried again to get up. Krueger kicked me again, across the face this time, knocking me across Canon's legs in an untidy sprawl face down.

"Oh, alright." Silver produced a long silver knife of graceful proportions and stuck it into Sherrow like a girl pinning up a beloved's photo on the wall. He folded around it like he couldn't believe it was happening. The next second, his dead weight came down across my back, and I was kissing concrete, blood being squeezed out of my perforations and air through my teeth like a boiling kettle.

The scream was rage.

They rooted through the pile of fallen to get to Canon, kicking Sherrow over onto his back like an inconvenient corpse. Canon had come to enough to lock both arms around one of mine. Krueger and the woman tried for a minute to pull us apart, until Silver offered to cut my arm off to make it easier, but Krueger said she'd had enough fun for the day, and told her to just twist up my bad arm and see that I walked to the car on my own. Apparently a back up hostage was desired.

It was a lovely idea, but I wasn't going to cooperate with the sirens growing louder as they got closer, and Krueger had to nearly break Canon's fingers to separate us. Canon was put into the car with more reverence than I, so I assumed he was a special collection, which maybe explained the baton-gun. Me they hauled like 210lbs of pig shit and didn't bother protecting me from doorframes as they shoved me in after Canon. The door slammed behind me and I lurched myself upright to see if I could find the handle. I fumbled my blood-slick hands over the inside of the door and earned another blow across the jaw that drove my face into the window and dazed me enough to make me stop. Canon got his hands tied behind his back by the woman while Krueger fished on the floor for the keys the Thug had dropped.

In the parking lot, I could see Sherrow on his back in a corpse-like sprawl, hat three feet off with the badge facing me and kicking off sparks in the streetlights. It started to rain, misting down onto the shiny tarmac, reflecting the bubble gum flashers, red blue red blue, and the sirens were rising up in the next block, so close, our backup finally, too late.

The black sedan howled as Krueger revved her once into the high tachs and she leapt into mid-hover from 0 feet to 50 in 10.

The last thing I saw was a doll-sized Sherrow, generic officer down in the rain, with the cruiser and its party lights still flashing. Then even that sight was lost in the rain-shrouded maze of streets and buildings, the dark city cut through by the heavy black slash of river. We turned north, and Krueger blacked all the windows except his own.

I was bleeding all over the place and Canon was stirring, looking like a rejected hospital meal.

The silver woman was looking out her window as if she could still see the parking lot.

She asked idly,

"Wasn't baby cop the same kid we tested the first shot of Warp on? Y'know at that bar?"

"Yeah, I know. Maybe it was, so? Y' kill him?" Krueger sounded like he couldn't care less.

"I don't know. Didn't have time to confirm. Matthew might've hit him with the riot gun and I beat all kinds of hell outta him."

"Yeah, that's not a kill."

" So Mother Anne won't be pleased."

Beside me, Canon stiffened. Krueger saw it in the rearview but didn't comment. To Silver, he said,

"She won't care. He's dead, his own fault for being sloppy. Anne's outta time and patience for shoddy work. Told me so herself. Doesn't matter anyway. We got the one she wanted, and this cop'll make a good distraction or fodder, time comes. Hey, cop, you still alive?"

I could see his eyes in the rear-view, sociopath cold, but good-natured. He gave me the creeps.

"'M still bleedin'. You got a med kit, or would it be a waste of my time?"

'Here." He handed back his necktie. "Get Canon to give you his, too." He side-glanced Silver. "Baby, untie Mr. Canon so he can play medic."

She used one of her wicked knives to cut his hands free and I wondered if it was the one she'd used on Sherrow and thought how much I'd like to return the favor.

Krueger was still smiling, those icy sociopath eyes in the rearview watching everything.

"There's shop towels in the tool-kit," he told me helpfully.

Unfortunately, that was all that was in the tool-kit, that and some loose nuts and bolts. If I was special ops, maybe I could make a weapon out of those, but I wasn't. The woman untied Canon's hands and he removed his tie. He took the towels silently and proceeded to bind me up like a professional. Up front, Krueger was still talking.

"You police boys used to wear ties way back. Like the military. Nothing like a tie and a handful of table napkins to make a quick field dressing. Nowadays, what have you got? Not even a handkerchief. What good it that? You gonna go into combat, you should at least be prepared."

"Got a kit in the squad." I volunteered, mostly to keep myself from passing out as Canon cinched down on two lengths of silk and a stack of marginally clean rags.

"And where's yer car now?" Silver laughed her trademark cascade of tumbling mercury, the same sound I'd heard some of the officer's wives make when they were amused at the expense of someone else's pain.

"Parked next to his dying partner," Krueger said helpfully.

"That's enough," Canon spoke up suddenly, voice quiet, and sounding like the only adult in the car.

"Who the hell are you to order us around?" Blazing mad from 0 to 90, the woman rounded on Canon.

"I'm the target hostage, remember?" He didn't spare her more than a glance. "Mother Anne wants to talk to me, right? You two keep picking at my pal here like a couple a demented high-school junkies I may decide I don't wanna play anymore, jump out the window or asphyxiate myself on a safety strap. Put you right up shit creek."

"We'll tie your hands again." Silver declared hotly, much like a demented high school junky. I downscaled my guesstimate of her age to the early twenties.

"Won't make a difference," Canon shrugged, patting off the makeshift dressing and letting me slump back against the seat. I nodded thanks and shut my eyes.

"Probably wouldn't," Krueger argued. "He's a vet. He could suicide ten different ways before we could stop him. Better let the cop be, Silver, if Canon wants to play hero."

"You promised I could play." She sounded petulant now. She made me very nervous.

"You can play later. Maybe Anne will give you another hostage."

"Well, okay. If I have to." She subsided, but I opened one eye to look hard at the back of her silver-blonde head. Bitch.

Canon saw my snarl and grinned, looking like a death's head himself.

"Just a car full of soldiers," he said, with a little nod at Krueger for my benefit.

I raised an eyebrow, which hurt like charity and closed my eyes again. Somewhere along the dark, shuttered ride, I blinked out and either slept or was unconscious.

Nobody else cared enough to wake me to find out which it was until we arrived, and then I only woke up because my hands were being tied behind me with fiberglass link and they let my head drop forward to hit the window again. Krueger was more concerned with the window than my head.

*

Krueger was talking to Canon as we were moved by force and pain-control through a warehouse I thought I recognized and prayed Sherrow was alive enough to report.

"Some guy, Bart Something, found you first, oh, coupla months back. Her Highness wouldn't let him at ya, but he got annoying about it and when he went ahead at that bar, well, we had to scrag him then and hope you wouldn't remember much after you got hit with the bottle. Bart wanted you for himself and s'fars I could see you did likewise, but orders are orders. Messed up my coat, too, the lot of you."

Then we were being shoved into a concrete room with a serious door on it, maximum security serious. Krueger sent Silver off against her wishes by the sound of it, and came into the room to make sure our bonds were good. He was very careful about it, taking extra time over Canon's and giving him a smack or two just coz he was looking like moving.

"Howrya doin', cop?" He asked me when he got to me. He jerked on the ties hard enough to sting.

I looked over at Canon, saw him drag himself up looking dazed, and looked up at Krueger through a fish-eye.

"I been shot before," I said. "Feels about the same."

He grinned at that and produced a bottle from a pocket. He uncorked it and took a swig.

"Me, too, cop. Feels like everything's come loose and everything hurts." He looked over at Canon, swinging the bottle a little like he was showing it off. "This'll help, maybe." He offered the bottle to me.

Footsteps sounded in the hall, and his head turned ever so slightly. He added,

"Till we kill, ya, anyway. Might as well take it easy till then."

I'd been thinking about it, I'm no hero when it comes to pain, but I sat back at that.

"Yeah, well, fuck you anyway." Even that little took more breath than I really had, and I turned my face away since I couldn't walk off, and let him see one bruised cheek and the side with the badge on it.

"Over here," Canon said.

Krueger's shoes scraped on the concrete and I heard a faint slosh as Canon got his chance at the bottle. He tasted it and murmured 'gin' in a tone that sounded appreciative, though the mind boggled at anyone actually appreciating gin straight outta the bottle. Maybe it was high class synthetic. It smelled real to me.

"Humhmm," Krueger concurred, pulling the bottle back.

I squeezed my eyes shut, wondering if I was going to throw up or not. It'd been awhile since I'd hurt that bad. I hadn't missed much.

The low voices in the corridor got louder as they came around the door jam. I looked up and saw Max Canon go pale with something I couldn't begin to guess at. I followed his gaze. A woman I'd never ever seen before was sweeping into the room dressed full hilt in a ball gown that must've cost the original earth, dark hair swept up with something sparkling, jewelry on her neck, in her ears.

"Anne." Canon said.

The woman regally nodded to Krueger, who left without his usual cocky attitude in evidence. All I could be certain of was that everyone seemed to be afraid of this woman. Certainly, they were all respectful. That made me wonder if I should be afraid, too, and then I saw her eyes and I was.

I started twisting against my bonds again, even though it didn't do anything more than aggravate my pains and make me lie very very still with my ears roaring for the first part of the encounter. Whatever I missed, it was obvious that Canon and this woman knew each other. There was history. I tried to sit up, to concentrate and listen.

XXXII.

Canon

"I wasn't even in the Stalag when they bombed it: Not for weeks. The Hindeo had liked my record and thought I might be handy. I was pulled with three other women for psychological testing."

"Brainwashing." Max tested the fiberglass ties cutting into his wrists.

"Testing. I was trained, rated and given a job on an outer rim planet to see how I did. I did exceptionally well."

"I'm surprised, actually."

"Don't insult me, Max. I never did share your outdated sense of justice. I had a chance to get out of prison and into something where I could make good money and establish myself in high circles. All you wanted to do was marry me and settle down in that little dirt side town you called home, raise children and die poor and forgotten."

Anne leaned forward to impress her point on him. He could see the backs of her eyes. There was nothing there he recognized. The cop let out a breath that might've been a moan if it'd had any volume in it. Anne ignored it.

"Then I found you here. I was glad to see you again until I realized you'd actually decided to become a cop."

"A privately licensed detective."

"There's a difference? Not to me, Max. To me you're enemy."

"So why not kill me then?"

"You weren't a threat, really. You were too small time. You've always been small time, Max."

"Doesn't feel small time right now, sweetheart."

"It's not. You and him," the cop got a cold look, "and his baby brother partner, you're into things you cannot begin to comprehend. There's so much more than you can affect."

"Yeah? Like what?"

"Don't be stupid, Max. I like to hear myself talk, but I don't like to give away everything." She stood up and her dress whispered into place around her legs. Her head was up in an odd pose between dignity and preening. "It's much better if you die guessing. And this time, you will die."

"Why not give me a job offer, too? I'll kill the cop for you and you can fit me into your armed force in the spot Strindberg had."

"And replace a crooked cop with a badgeless one? I don't think so. Anyway, I know you better than that." She smiled, a touch of sadness on her features. Max was almost fooled. "It's part of why I fell in love with you."

"Is it part of why you had me nearly drowned, too?"

Anne turned away.

"You're getting petty, Max. You never would've mattered if you hadn't started spouting my name right and left while Krueger had you on the pentathol. Funny name for such a new drug, isn't it? I suppose tradition dies hard.

At any rate, I didn't really need you spreading history all over the ranks, now, did I?"

"Made you nervous?"

"You might've proved…inconvenient. So I decided you were already inconvenient and had them put you in the river. You were so doped up… But you were noisy and you could swim. Krueger underestimated your tolerances. His first mistake. So I hooked you up with little Noel. She talked a good talk, but when it came down to it, she couldn't pull the trigger. That was my mistake."

Another sound, tight and abruptly stifled, came from Friar's corner. Max glanced over. The look on the cop's face was something Max never wanted to see again on anybody, friend or foe. Friar saw Max looking his way and turned his face into the corner, effectively hiding the look of sudden, stunned trauma. It seemed to afford Anne a great deal of amusement and she laughed.

"I loved that little silver cop star she used to wear. So wonderful to have her in my employ, a police officer's wife. My little joke."

Friar's shoulders were in a rigid, painful line, and Max spoke again to draw Anne's attention back to himself.

"Was the bomb supposed to kill us both?"

Anne's smile at the officer's expense faded into a distempered frown.

"Another mistake. I'd employed an outsider for that job, and he proved disappointing. Never trust a cop to do a good job at real murder." She smiled again, adding, "They're only good for fighting amongst themselves." The new grin was feline and aimed at Friar. "With the proper provocation, of course."

He spared her a black glare out of a hate-twisted face, which she ignored, turning a raised, delicate eyebrow on Max.

"I chose a cop who couldn't even kill a couple of women properly. He certainly wasn't any good at blackmail, anyway. Another mistake. I employ idiots. Not by choice, but there are so few good people available on this desolate rock. Krueger is one of the better ones."

"Are all your people vets? The woman Silver doesn't seem the type."

"Oh, she's not. I hire from all walks. But with the mess that's been building up on this jaunt, I may have to dispose of them all and start over."

"Who's gonna dispose of 'em if they're all idiots?"

Both eyebrows lifted and her beautiful hazel eyes shone with delight.

"Why, darling, are you truly offering to join me?" But before Max could speak, she turned away abruptly to pace and went on, "I don't believe you. You were never the type to turn coat. It's why they left you in prison." She turned again on him and a slow smile spread over her face as she measured out her next words with obvious pleasure. "You were untenable." She came close enough for him to see the details of her tiny crystal earrings, but not close enough for him to endanger her. "And we had such high hopes, too, at first. There you were, my amateur pilot, all feral and vicious and strong. Now look at you."

A hand waved to encompass the picture he presented, slumped in a bloodstained, torn suit on a concrete floor next to a half-dead cop.

Max pulled a grin and dredged out a smart-ass phrase for old times' sake.

"I've been told I have the manners of an animal. That's not good enough for you?"

Anne ignored the attempt and went on with her monologue, glancing at the tiny sliver of watch on her wrist.

"Why did you choose to be a private license, Max? Why not be a career soldier or a police officer like that poor specimen next to you?"

"He was in better shape before your thugs got to him,"

"So were you, dear. So were you. No answer for me, then? I could make you answer, you know."

"And how much fun you would have, wouldn't you?" Max let contempt into his tone and watched her eyes spark.

"You'll answer me anyway, License. Shall I call Silver in? She was so disappointed earlier because we wouldn't let her play with the cop. I shall let her do so now."

"Wait." Max sat forward, not ready to sacrifice another just to cause Anne trouble.

She had known he would. It was her turn to display contempt.

"Soft. You're soft."

Like a rookie rattling off a report, rigid and monotone, Max said,

"I became a private detective because I was sick of uniforms, drilling and rules. And people like you." He paused and some life came into his face. "I'd forgotten there were people like you all over the army. But now I remember."

"But you still see people like me, don't you, Max."

He laughed at that, no humor in it.

"Only briefly, and usually behind bars or in the defendant's box. Or dead. I've always preferred dead."

"You wound me, Max. You hate me now?"

"You know I do. I imagine it's mutual. Are we talking so much to waste time, or are you planning on setting us free?"

"Now you're being stupid. Purely to waste time, dear. I have an appointment later and I thought we could do a little catching up before I leave you, and as long as I have you locked up, you're keeping out of mischief."

"So you're not going to kill us yourself? I'm shocked."

"And get my hands all dirty?" She delivered the remark in scathing tones and shook out the train of her gown to illustrate the ridiculousness of the suggestion. "I have people for that sort of thing. Besides, this dress was very expensive and Silver would never forgive me if I cheated her out of her fun."

"I don't merit personal attention?" Max shifted against the hard wall and tried to make her look him in the eye. Krueger had definitely made the ties on his wrists looser. When he wasn't so occupied with Anne, Max would think about why.

"Why, lover, what do you think you've been getting all these weeks? I would've had anybody else as interfering as you killed outright."

"What about Caulder? Didn't he interfere, or is he too in awe of you to protest while you mess up his good thing?"

"Daniel?" Anne looked mildly amused. "He was easy to control. Easier to kill, anyway. Now, he," she smiled archly, "got personal attention." The smile faded into indifference. "It was the least I could do for him after he'd proved so helpful, poor stupid man, trying so desperately to impress me by selling that ridiculous lower class drug for me. Of course, he might not have been so helpful if I hadn't put my own people into his ranks, causing trouble and making him feel all uncertain about his hold on this little backwater. Anyway," She waved a graceful hand towards Friar. "The police should find him in the river in a day or so, I imagine."

She looked at her watch again and straightened

"Time's up. Goodbye, Max," she said, and didn't wait for his response. She went to the door and called Krueger, instructing him as they walked out to wait an hour or two just in case she needed a hostage, then to give them both over to Silver. The minute her back was turned, Max started working on his bonds

"And don't leave them alone with her. Mr. Canon was well trained in his time. I don't want Silver getting hurt."

Their voices cut off as the door closed.

Max grimaced.

The cop turned a red eyed, blood-daubed face on Max and smiled horribly.

"Some cookie, man. You really wanted to marry that?"

"She looked better then."

"Better than that there? Yer kiddin'."

"I didn't know her as well then."

'That I understand." He put his head back against the stone, and closed his eyes, shuttering off weary grief and resignation.

"How y' doin'?" Max asked him.

"I'll live till they kill me, I guess. But it's gonna hurt for awhile, looks like."

"Be happy you got the extra breathing time."

"I am."

" I don't spose you told anybody where you were going and they'll send out a man hunt."

"My partner will, if he lives."

Max looked over to see the cop all hollow-jawed with blank pain in his eyes that could've been from the crack on the head or not. He chose not to comment.

They sat in silence until Krueger arrived, the slinky hit woman with him, making jokes and handing the bottle of gin back and forth between them.

Max noticed neither one of them actually drank much. They probably wanted to be fully alert.

Too bad.

Krueger looked at the cop then at Max. He grinned and took a hit off the bottle. Silver sidled in behind him and went directly over to Friar, who tried to lean away from her.

"What a party you gave us." Krueger said. "Too bad it couldn't've gone on longer. I never got to dance. At least Silver got to dance with your partner." The last was addressed to Friar, who lifted his head from the wall, leaving a faint blood mark.

He didn't currently have the breath to tell Krueger to fuck off, so like a dying dog he lifted his lip in a silent snarl.

Krueger thought that was funny. To Max, he said,

"That one'll bite after he's dead."

Friar glared feebly. Max spared him a cold evaluating look, and went back to staring blankly at Krueger.

"Huh," was all Max said. It earned him an amused glance.

"You will, too, I'll bet. Pardon me if I don't offer to shake hands with a fellow vet."

Over in the corner, Silver was hunkered down looking at Friar like he was an exhibit in a museum. A soft growl came from the corner and a round of bell-like laughter.

Max's eyes flickered, but he kept them on Krueger. Krueger glanced towards his companion with an expression Max wanted to call watchful or possibly guilty, and Krueger, shrugging massive shoulders, said in a tone that would've been defensive in anyone less sociopathically cold,

"Well, we can't let you out, even if we wanted to. M'lady wants you dead, but later, and since we won't be here, I thought maybe for old times' sake I'd say goodbye."

"Old times' sake?"

"Actually, Silver wanted to take a look at the cop. She's got a thing for cops. We're on our way out."

"Stopping by the safe on your way?" Max hazarded a guess.

Krueger's head rocked back in surprise, but a rough grin cracked across his face again and he nodded, swinging the bottle carelessly. Max barely avoided a knee-jerk reaction when his bonds suddenly parted under the continuous onslaught he'd been waging: He didn't want to show that his hands were free, not sure if they were supposed to be or not. Krueger didn't seem to notice the slight rocking and went on.

"You're smart. I forgot about that. I guess most of us still living aren't stupid." He looked over to where the woman was toying with the badge on Friar's ruined armor. "Gotta go, Sil. M'lady's waiting."

"Let her. Bitch." She had a hold of Friar's ear and tried to kiss him or bite him, her aim wasn't clear. He twisted his head away.

Silver didn't take rejection well, and she stood abruptly, tossing her hair and playing with one of the knives that she wore like other women wore jewelry.

"Bastard. You're no fun, cop."

"No one told me I had to be." Friar spit blood and gave her a squint eye.

"You could play nice. Might help you get free."

"I don't play with psychos."

"Well, what do you think M'lady hired her for? Of course, she's psycho." Krueger came over to grab her arm and pull her away. She was definitely fascinated by Friar in her own special way, and while Friar seemed to be aware that he was playing with fire, he didn't seem to care.

"Well, it's nice of you to stop by, but I'm not used to chatting with enemies," Max said, turning his attention back to Krueger.

"Are we enemies? I though maybe we were compatriots. I was on the colonies, too. Not the same unit, but the same battle."

"Yer too young."

"I was then, for certain. Anyway, now here we're both unhappy about Anne's little games. Doesn't that make us less than enemies?"

"You turning on your boss? You gonna set us free?"

Krueger shoot his head.

"I already told you we weren't. But I figure you can slow Anne down enough to give me and Silver a little head start."

"So while she's killin' us by inches, you'll be flying away with her cash."

"Something like. I didn't say we were friends. Take the rest of the liquor, how's that?"

They exchanged a long look in silence, then Max said,
"Okay."

Friar found a little air and gasped out,
"Don't put yourself out, asshole."

That made Krueger laugh again and he bowed a little as he backed out the door, pulling Silver with him and closing it behind them both with a heavy clang.

There was a silence.

Friar let his head drop back to the wall and tried not to feel the blood leaking slowly between his fingers.

"Special forces." Max said.

"Huh?" Friar opened his eyes and looked over at him.

"Krueger was special forces, too."

There was an odd little pause, then Max said,
"I just know."

After a moment, Max dragged himself up to collect the bottle of liquor and bring it back to his corner. Friar watched him with pain-squinted eyes and said nothing.

Friar

I'd forgotten there was a vet in the room. I'd never asked what Canon had done for the government and I didn't then, watching him break the bottle into two careful pieces, one holding the balance of the gin and the other a sharp-edged tool. He cut the ties on my hands then settled into scraping the heel of one of my boots into the liquor. I didn't ask how he'd gotten his own hands free. It was enough work to keep my head clear between the woozy blood-loss haloes everything was wearing and the sharp sting of gin filling my breathing space.

"That's breaking my heart," I told him conversationally, more to focus my wandering attention than to be talking.

"You and me both," he spared me a cool glance. "You holding up okay?"

"Yeah." I waved it off like my head wasn't about to explode into two messy pieces, left brain and right.

He nodded and went on with whatever he was doing. When the heel was gone, he took a little pellet out of an inside pocket and added it's powder carefully, carefully to the concoction.

"Suicide pill?" I asked, voice limp and idle.

"No. Something Krueger gave me. We're meant to escape, or at least try."

I thought about asking why, then didn't. Instead, I said,

"Spec forces, huh?"

"Spec forces, yeah," he agreed.

He tucked the mess behind me out of sight of the door, then joined me in my slouch against the wall.

"What now?" I asked, eyes squeezed shut to block out the glaring light and the mirror-reflection bruises he had that only reminded me of my own and made 'em hurt, too, along with everything else. I wanted to be sick, but my stomach was empty. I opened my eyes again when the room felt like it was slipping to the right.

"We wait." He closed his eyes like he was going to take a nap.

I sat and hurt and felt sorry for myself and wondered if Sherrow was still alive and could this guy's superspy tricks actually get us out, and would it be soon enough to matter, and why would the enemy want us to escape in the first place.

I don't know if he slept, but I didn't. All I could do was sit against the cold wall, think uselessly and keep track of how fast my temperature was going up. Eventually I slipped into a sort of comatose state that passed for sleep. God knew I needed it.

***

I was shoeless. Cold concrete, the smell of stone that had been wet for 1000 years, metal dust. I was shoeless in a river-side warehouse and I had been shot.

Funny thing to forget under the circumstances, but waking up can be like that sometimes.

Canon had borrowed my boots to destroy the soles. I hadn't really understood when he'd explained that his everyday shoes didn't have the right kind of soles, but I let him have the boots anyway.

Now, he was playing with the mess he'd made of gin and boot heel and mysterious powder, and I watched dumbly, listening to my pulse ring through the torn spots in my arm and shoulder. The vest was rubbing at it; if I thought I could get out of it without screaming, I would, but there was no way, so I sat and watched like a dead battery, while Canon, ex-spec op, war-vet, play with the plastique he'd made out of my boots and the bottle the enemy had thoughtfully left us. I wondered if Krueger's hope that we'd create a diversion for Boss Lady was even remotely valid. I wasn't sure I could stand, much less fight, and I had my doubts about the quality of explosive fabricated from materials the enemy provided.

"Who's this Anne, anyway?" I asked.

Canon looked at me with hollow, echoing eyes and I knew there was more to their past than just relationship, and that it still tormented him on bad nights when the city was the hungry haunted animal some writer once said it was, only it had a personal hate for you alone, and it was coming for you.

"I met Anne in the war." He said. There was a pause while he massaged the chunk of junk like it was play-dough. "You heard the rest of it."

I didn't nod because it would hurt me and I didn't say anything because it would hurt him. I let a space go by to let him know I'd heard, and then said,

"Think that'll do the trick?"

"You got a striker on you?"

I nodded; there was a striker strip on the back of my issue utility tool for use with the old style road flares. I offered it to the PL.

"It'll work."

I eyed the door with less enthusiasm than I probably should've, seeing as he was a trained professional, or had been in the day, and again kept my silence. If I'd spoken at that moment it would've been little more than a grunt anyway, because the room was swimming just then.

After a few minutes, he set his gunk aside again and helped me put my boots back on, the heels torn up and crooked, but it was better than the alternative. And he said we might have to run.

Like I could even stand.

I just nodded and let my head fall back against the cold hard wall. Canon went back to his plastique and his blank-faced meditations. I'm sure I had the better deal.

XXXIII.

Friar

I was dozing when Canon blew the door. One minute in blissful, pain-free heat haze, then next deafened and choking on noxious fumes. I didn't get to complain, either, because suddenly Canon had me on my feet and we were moving. There was a moment outside that involved shouting and the snap of breaking bones that apparently weren't Canon's because before I had a chance to really fall over properly, I was being hauled along again.

After a dozen feet I got the idea and started running on my own. I wasn't going to be able to fight, but it seemed I could run.

Canon had the duty guard's gun and that was all he really needed to get rolling. Down a long empty corridor and to main the intersection we went, a broken guard behind us and a brace of fresh ones ahead.

Of course, they knew what kind of door we'd been locked behind and they hadn't really thought the muffled 'crump' noise could be the helpless prisoners blowing the door off its heavy-duty hinges, so they were only looking our way out of curiosity, wondering where the smoke was coming from, when we charged out of the haze, swinging.

It was probably lucky that no guns were fired. By the time Canon had these two down, with little help from me beyond a sort of sandbag, bear hug approach that incapacitated one man long enough for Canon to knock him into next week, the little phone on the wall was ringing. I liberated the weapons they carried and gestured for Canon to lead on. Things were a little more focused now that adrenalin was my good friend again.

We ignored the phone and hurried along the corridor. It was door-less and blank, lined with stark tube lighting and marked with seams where the pour molds had stood when the multicrete was still damp, about a million years ago. We headed left, in the direction that smelled like fresh air and river water. The other way smelled like machinery and what we wanted was out, and that meant fresh air.

It wasn't to be, though. At the end of the corridor, we paused behind another heavy door, checking the loads on the guns, thankfully military beam weapons, newly charged and cleaned by the look of them. Canon took the lead and cracked the door open a tiny bit to have a look into the up-ahead.

He slammed it immediately and ran the primitive bolts into place, grabbing my arm and spinning me around the way we'd come.

"Okay, no," he said, running me back along the corridor. I followed, but managed a grunt in a questioning tone.

"There's about twenty armed people on the other side of that door. I think they saw me."

There was a ringing crash from down the way. Same somebody had also noticed the bolts were on and was battering at the door.

"They saw you," I agreed, shuffling along with a gun in one arm and another slung over my shoulder and digging into a sore spot. I didn't have a lot of use to my left arm, but I figured I could use it to steady the rifle maybe. I hoped I wasn't being stupidly optimistic.

"This way," Canon dragged me more rapidly towards the oily end of the hall.

Light fixtures became more scarce as we went and doors started showing up. Another crash echoed down the sealed hall and we came to a turn and skidded around it into near total darkness.

Canon produced a pin-light from somewhere. He ran it around and picked a door, hustling me into it and shutting it behind us. There was another out-of-place bolt and bar lock and he set it. I stood nearby watching. When I spotted the computer code lock box on the other side of the door, I started laughing. Canon followed my pointing rifle barrel, regarded it thoughtfully for a moment, then slagged it with a short sharp blast from his stolen gun. It glowed red and ran down the wall like jelly.

"Might as well see where we are…" He'd also found a light switch, which he hit briefly.

In the quick stab of light, I saw that we were in a motor pool area, with a full shop stretching away to our right and four or five vehicles out on the dim tarmac. To the left was an open revetment that currently housed two small water skimmers, one of which had its hood folded back and tools still laying around on the dock where an impatient technician had decided going home was better than cleaning up.

I hunched over to the oldest vehicle I could see with a clear shot to the exit doors and had a look.

Canon had found a full-sized flashlight on the workbench and brought it along to me. The car wasn't locked, which made me happy, but I couldn't get her started unless I could lie to the computer, and I didn't have the key or the codes. I handed Canon the unslung rifle and opened the door, telling him,

"See if you can find me a hammer and some screwdrivers and a pair of wire strippers."

He nodded, leaving the flashlight with me and tracking back to the bench with his pin-light. Faint shouting could be heard away behind the bolted door. Must've found the two cross guards.

Canon handed me a hammer and a posy of screwdrivers, three flathead and a set of Allen wrenches.

"No Phillips, sorry," he said. "And there's no strippers, just a pocket knife."

"Oh, don't matter," I could see the interface lock from my prone position across the seat and knew exactly how to get the engine to turn over. I hefted the hammer and said, "Go get the doors open, huh?"

It took three swings to bash the interface into shit, I was so wasted, but I got it, and when all the little circuits looked like confetti, with pieces of breadboard and plastic housing littering the floor and stuck in my hair, I could finally see the ignition wires. Thank God for retrofit.

There wasn't much left to do besides short circuiting the CPU, so I twisted this wire to that and the other to another and then laid one of the flatheads across the circuits yer expressly supposed to not do that to and got a gratifying flash and snap. Poof, lock-out computer gone. After that, it was cake and the engine turned over smoothly once I had the right wires hooked up.

Canon was running back by that time and shouting something I couldn't hear, but probably had to do with the bolted inside door coming unbolted under whatever onslaught the enemy was implementing. I could see stars through the opening exit doors which were neatly rolling back on their tracks, their motors purring only slightly louder than good maintenance would allow, and I imagined I could hear sirens, so who cared about the inside door. Freedom was nigh and justice was right behind.

Except that Canon and I were gonna have to wait for it. The inside door gave just as I was putting the car in gear and gunfire was suddenly splashing all around us. Madame Anne had liked her armor shielding, though, and even this older model was well provided with it, so the shots didn't do much more than smoke my rear window and smell nasty. I gave her gas and we accelerated out the door.

As we roared into the outside lot, I nearly ran down Krueger, who was jogging to the familiar long black car with the key-switch in his hand and Silver psycho behind him. They both spared startled glances our way, then were busy piling into the black car, a Defiant I could now see, or a customized version anyway. Bad guys spilled out of the garage behind us and I could see Krueger shouting like he was directing the posse and waving them on. Anne stalked out of the garage in a whip and sway of gown and seemed to be heading towards him. Another one of the garaged vehicles lifted off and came after us.

I applied more gas and we shot skyward in a brutal but effective arc of escape: The chase vehicle didn't have enough speed to copy us yet, and Krueger's car was following only reluctantly. I could spare breath to laugh at the expression I imagined must be on his face to have his getaway so badly spoiled, and with the Boss riding in his car, no less.

I leaned my head into the rest and tried to absorb the feel of the car, how it handled, what it was capable of, as rapidly as possible.

"Incidentally," I said casually, maneuvering the car around a sudden corner. "That substance you added to yer explosive? It's unusual, right? I just wanna be sure I won't blow up next time I'm policing in a bar and I run through a puddle of real gin."

The image seemed to amuse Canon very much, because he barked a laugh loud enough to make my ears ring.

"Yeah," he grinned. "And it has to be cured, like you saw. I doubt it's available outside the military."

"Like Krueger's fancy gun."

"Yup."

"And yours."

"Yup." His tone had years of memory behind it, unhappy memory, by the sound.

I jinked the car sharply to avoid a looming streetlight and eyed the rear-views, gauging how much head-start we had. It wasn't much.

Canon had two of the captured guns in his lap and was tinkering with one.

"Garbage, these are garbage," he was muttering. "What ya got there?"

He was looking my way at the rifle I had slung over my shoulder and which was giving me painful dents across my back.

I leaned so he could take it off me: no way was I lifting my arm that far. Not without crying anyway.

"Oh, better." He purred to the rifle when he had it, his hands running all over it and checking it out. He sighted it out the windscreen, checked the load and looked behind us. "I'm taking this one."

"And leaving me with garbage?" I managed to make the weak joke, scanning for the back-up cops so I could maybe lead the bad guys into 'em and save us at the same time. A blast of fire came from the pursuing vehicle, a blue sedan, looked like a Raider GL9, and my rear window hazed out for a second.

"They'll do the way you hose your fire around. I'm sharpshooter, I get the good gun. Anyway," he grinned at me and on his bruised face it looked manic. "Yer drivin'."

"That's true. And I only got one good arm."

"Until you pass out again, yeah." He said it like it was a given, and, from past experience, I figured he was probably right. The adrenalin would only get me so far.

Better to get there while I could still fight. I headed us back towards the river down a road I only half remembered.

The GL9 and the black Defiant were following, close enough to set off the proximity net's alert system, and I tried to ignore the flashing orange follow-close tags in my peripheral vision as I spun us in a screaming turn left down an alley way too tight for the Defiant. The GL9 followed, but the Defiant had to rise sharply above and fell back. I couldn't believe Krueger'd be upset, but I also doubted he'd come up with a convincing way to run with Anne in the car.

I fiddled with the radio set and got signal. Canon saw what I was after and fiddled some more and got dialog.

Enemy car, enemy radio. I wondered how long till they realized we might be listening in.

"...East towards Leary. We're still on the bumper. No return fire. Where the hell'd you get to?"

"Had to go high. Don't you lose them or you won't see next week."

"Yes'm." The reply wasn't happy, but listening to Boss Lady's tone, I could see why. She sounded grimly serious, and there wasn't much chance of her forgetting a fuck-up of that caliber.

"Where are you going?" Canon asked me finally, cycling the window and pegging a shot at the GL9 as it accelerated and closed fast. His shot was dead on and they fell back in a hurry.

"River. It's more open and the back up will be able to see us better."

"Yeah, well, so will everybody else."

"If they see where we go to, yeah. But we're gonna get there first." I cranked her over at the end of the alley, braked hard, and dropped.

The GL9 shot over our heads and began a shrieking turn, but I already had us going another direction and the Defiant didn't have a chance of matching me, so we were off free, at least for a few seconds. I hoped it'd be enough.

Canon pulled his head off the head support and gave me a look I'd most recently seen on Sherrow.

"You sure yer back up will know where to come?" he asked me idly, as if it didn't matter at all.

For answer, I punched in the station code on the radio and shouted towards the vocal-grill,

"Unit 312 requesting backup near Riverside and Kentucky Avenue. We have gunfire and are being pursued by two hover vehicles, armed and armored."

"Friar, is that you?" The radio squawked like a squished critter and sounded like Yarrow.

"Yeah, and I'm needing some help. You back me?"

"Yeah, yeah, units are already in the vicinity, looking for you. Sherrow said you might be dead."

"Is he okay?" I didn't know how much it meant to me till I heard his name on the radio, spun tinny and impersonal by the transmission.

"He was alive when they put him in the ambulance. Said you were shot."

"I am. Might be a good idea to send another bus when—wait a minute."

I broke off suddenly, seeing what I didn't really want to see. The road was about to end in a sudden deserted pier.

Must've taken a wrong turn.

I chopped the engine and hauled on the wheel, slewing us around in a squealing arc. The water rushed up on the right, like an invitation to jump. We came to a shuddering stop that rattled us from asshole to teakettle, settling mere inches from black wet with the starboard exhaust manifold dangling over the edge and puffing ozone out into a swirling cloud that sank over the water and dissipated slowly in the sudden smothering silence.

I could hear my own breath rasping in the cab. It sounded like it hurt. I was still too adrenalized to know for sure.

"Nice stop. Legal, even." Canon said, bailing out into a battle crouch beside the open door, facing back the way we'd come, gun trained thataway. He glanced over when I didn't answer.

"You okay?"

"I drive better without holes in me," I offered. My heartbeat was slowing and washing out the charge. That meant I was starting to feel again.

I leaned over to the radio and told it what's what.

"Yarrow, we're bailing out on the waterfront. Hurry, huh?"

I got his acknowledgment and shut the radio off.

"What next?" I asked Canon. In the distance, elusive sirens were wailing, but they weren't as close as the approaching engines.

"Come on," Canon shifted in his crouch, looking remarkably agile for a man who'd been knocked unconscious, karate-pummeled, pistol-whipped and bound in the past few hours. And he was older than me. Right now, I felt older. By about three hundred years.

I hauled myself out of the vehicle.

"Should we push this over?" I asked, thinking to hide the immediate proof of where we were. The words came out strangled as sensation came back. Like I'd missed it.

"No time. Gotta hide." Canon started over to a rack of storage barrels and looked back at me. "Hurry."

I nodded and shuffled after him, eyeing potential line-of-fire angles and trying not to puke.

I didn't have to sit down behind the barrels so much as just stop thinking about standing. The gun in my hands felt strangely plastic. My hands were strangely numb.

"You think Anne'll come after you now with cops coming all over?"

"She'll come."

"Why not just skip planet? Get away clean?"

Canon shifted to glance at me, then turned his eyes back towards the intersection where the streets converged. The engines were a whole lot louder now. I turned myself around painfully and propped the gun barrel up so I could shoot with one hand.

"It's personal now," he answered me. "She wants her revenge. This planet's ruined for her."

"And after all that hard work, too," I didn't have a lot of sympathy.

Canon grunted a laugh.

The engines turned somewhere and started fading down. For a wonderful and awful moment, I thought they'd lost us. Water lapped at the pier side, smelling like wet sewage. Canon looked over at me again, critically. I could imagine what he was looking at by the expression on his face.

"Look like something they feed the pigs, don't I?" I asked, slightly breathless.

His eyebrows crooked up at that in surprise.

"You a farm boy?" he asked with obvious delight. I wasn't sure if it was mockery, so I answered it like it was conversation.

"Was. Long time ago."

The engines started to get closer again, and we turned our attention back towards the road.

"You know anything about post holes?" he asked me.

I thought I might be hallucinating at that point, but I was game to go along with it.

"Sure. Dug my fair share."

"Is it hard?"

"Ah, no, easy. Just fuckin' dull, if you understand me."

"Does dull seem bad to you?"

I raised my eyes to the GL9 as it came spitting into the open, fire blazing from two windows and engine screaming as the driver pulled her around in an arc much more sloppy than mine had been. But the GL9 had never been much for tight turns.

"Not right now it doesn't," I had to admit.

XXXIV.

Canon

Max hadn't been bragging when he'd told Friar he was a sharp shooter. The driver of the GL9 pulled her out of the turn barely, nearly swapping paint with the abandoned hover on the water's edge. As it swung over their heads, spitting fire that couldn't get enough declination to hit them, Max took a careful bead, tracked, and led his target just enough. His shot hit the fuel reserve tank, much less effectively shielded than the main tank, and set it off. On the GL9, the main tank was close enough to the reserve that one going off acted as a detonator to the other.

There was a spectacular fireball and the pier side shook with the concussion. Friar ducked as shrapnel and fire rained down and didn't get back up.

Max didn't have time to spare for him. The black Defiant had come in on the heels of the GL9 and landed during the confusion to disgorge two figures, taking to the air again almost before they were clear. Max thought he recognized Krueger's large silhouette. The other moved so fast he couldn't make her out clearly, but instinct told him it was Silver.

He pegged a shot that direction and saw them duck, then the Defiant was overhead and angling for a shot. Max took a hasty shot at it, but had no time to make it good, and the beam splashed uselessly off the armored underside. Return fire was almost immediate.

Max rolled as the first shots ranged down, searching. Friar lay motionless, not much of a target, certainly not much of a threat to the hover, and the fire followed Max. He got behind the barrels, getting a brief moment of respite from the hover, but now open to Krueger and Silver.

But Krueger was firing high, Max suspected deliberately. Whatever he'd managed to steal from Anne was either small enough to be on his person or was more likely in the Defiant. Krueger couldn't want to have it shot down, but neither could he be happy about his current situation. He'd made no secret of the fact that he didn't like Anne, but a man in his profession didn't have the right to complain once he'd accepted the job. All he could do was leave, or terminate his employment.

Max watched a stray shot strike the door of the maneuvering hover and thought terminate might be the option Krueger was selecting. He didn't have any reason not to kill Max and Friar, so his reluctance to engage in proper combat must spring from a hope that they'd manage to kill Anne rather than any Christian feelings about sparing the fugitives. That, or he just wanted them to keep her busy while he figured out his next move.

Max took the opening created by Krueger's poor aim and bolted under the hover and out behind, making for a brick shed on the near side of the tarmac. Krueger bounced some fire around his feet, but nothing hit, and Silver was sprinting in the other direction. Too late, Max realized it was towards Friar, but he couldn't help that now.

The Defiant banked and turned, spinning neatly on its axis to come after Max. He could admire the driver's skill and thought Anne had learned to pilot after all. It wasn't a good memory to put in juxtaposition with current events and he flinched as a blast of energy and pulverized brick sang off the stock of his weapon and stung the side of his face. He could hear sirens coming fast and thought maybe they might even be in time.

He doubled back as the Defiant overshot the shed and fell into a kneeling fire position to send a shot after it. He hit too high, damaging a taillight and the outboard sensors package, but the hover was turning again in a long, graceful arc, much more like an aircraft than a car, which was why it cost the big money, and he'd done no appreciable damage.

Max had time for one more shot before it was on him. He could take a hasty one and run, or he could stand his ground and make it a good hit. Thinking of Friar, and the expression Silver had had on her face when she told him he could be fun, Max chose the idiot's way, sure Anne would laugh at him and call him soft, but the choices were bad either way.

He stood and braced himself on the corner of the shed, hoping that Krueger wouldn't have a change of mind and shoot him in the back. Energy cracked off the brick near him, but didn't hit. Max grinned.

The Defiant was at trim speed, needing maneuverability, and it gave Max plenty of time to put the sight over the starboard gun port. It was a difficult shot to land, but it was pretty much the only way he'd do damage with this weapon. He squeezed off three rounds in quick succession, knowing if the first one didn't hit, the second and third had decreasing chances of doing so, but he couldn't pin his hopes all on one shot.

He did hit, but it wasn't dead on. The starboard gun sputtered into flame and popped fireworks as the charge cartridge cooked off, but while it lurched and jerked, the hover didn't stop. Max ducked back around the shed as it pulled up, turning so the port side gun could come on him. He kept moving even though he knew he couldn't get out of line-of-fire in time. It was better than standing in one place letting her gun him down, and he would never ever give the bitch the satisfaction.

He put the shed between the hover and himself and brought up his weapon as the glossy black demon floated sideways over the roof to acquire him again. He sent two more shots into the underside, but they were rushed, and did only marginal damage, the first smoking more sensors and hazing the driver's side window, the second burning the back window black. With any luck, he'd cooked the scanners, and she'd have to roll the damn window down to find him.

Krueger laid down some half-hearted fire and managed to ping one off the Defiant. Anne gunned it away towards the city to circle and come back. Max heard the sirens keening down the echoing lanes of street at the same time he heard what might've been a noise from Friar. He certainly heard Silver's laugh, and he hit the ground running in that direction while the Defiant was in its turn.

Max could see the storage barrels, and one of Friar's feet. Silver stood over the officer, oblivious to the gun battle going on, with a knife in one hand and a happy smile on her face. As the angle of sight improved, Max could see Friar, propped on his one good elbow, fingers covering a new cut that bled freely into his right eye. There were cuts all along his forearms, as well. The woman was speaking to him, her smug purr too low to be heard across the distance. Friar looked up at her with a look of such rage and contempt that she laughed again, grabbed his ear and bent to whisper into it. Max clearly heard Friar's remark in what sounded like Spanish memorized by rote, saw him pull his head out of her grasp with a jerk that probably hurt like Hell, and spit in her face. Silver fell back, her sudden anger flaring and Max saw her bringing the knife up again just as Krueger sent off a warning shot. Max ignored it and charged on.

He was halfway to the rescue when many things happened at once.

Krueger, no matter what he thought about Anne, felt some sort of obligation to Silver and, when Max didn't heed his warning, sent a shot in earnest after the Private License. It singed across Max's back, setting his jacket smoldering, and spinning him around. Krueger stepped out of cover as the Defiant roared around and started back, and at the same time, the police cruisers came onto the scene from three different directions, sirens blaring and lights flashing.

The Defiant with its blackened rear view and crippled scanners, reacted late. Anne had been so focused on the running figure that she hadn't noticed the sirens. Now she jerked back on the controls in an attempt to get away as three police cruisers closed on her. She climbed at an abrupt angle, the engine wailing with effort, but it wasn't going to help. Max watched from where he lay breathless on the tarmac as she pushed the Defiant beyond its limits and brought it around towards the river. One of the cruisers sent a warning shot over her hood and she responded with angry return fire. Her retort hosed harmlessly across the windscreen of the squad, but it was enough that she'd fired and all three cruisers opened up with all weapons. In seconds, the Defiant joined the GL9 as raining garbage, and once again, concussion rocked the pier and deafened those on it. Max thought he might never hear again.

Krueger could be seen ducking away towards the water, so Max dragged himself up to go to Friar. One of the cruisers came down right in front of him and in a crazy Chinese fire drill, emptied itself of uniformed officers, who all pointed their guns at him and told him not to move, though not in so many words, or in nearly such polite terms. He put his hands up.

Silver had been staggered by the explosion and she looked around dazed for the split second it took to ascertain that Krueger was nowhere in sight and that there were cops everywhere. With a snarl, she hooked her fingers into Friar's vest and hauled him into a teetering stand as a human shield. He swayed drunkenly, threatening her balance, but she tucked that long silver knife under his chin and stared around wordlessly in threat.

A second hover landed at a discreet distance and disgorged more running cops, some of which went in the direction Krueger had gone. The third cruiser stayed in a holding pattern above, its carbon-arc beams lighting the scene in unreal harsh white light. Friar dripped blood and tried to steady his breath. He inhaled Silver's perfume and it made him feel nauseous.

"Give it up, girl," he said in tortured tones. "You can't win."

"I can kill you." Her tone was defiant and crazed, but very twentysomething young.

"Yeah, take me with you? But I don't wanna go anywhere with you. I don't like you that much." He realized he was rambling, and shut his mouth, trying to think rationally. Maybe...

Friar leaned a little harder against her, his weight overcoming her strength. She was lasting longer than he would've thought, but then he remembered her fighting skill. That took a lot of strength and discipline. He wondered how she managed to get that good when she obviously couldn't control any of her other impulses.

She reset her feet for better support and pressed the knife into the tender part of his throat right next to the jugular. He winced at the new pain and looked out at all the officers standing nearby, doing the hostage-wait pose.

He recognized more faces than he would've thought this far east. The blue-white light from the cruisers hurt his eyes.

"You okay, Friar?" Amplified Sergeant's voice, checking on the hostage.

Friar didn't dare nod, and he couldn't raise the one free arm he had since he couldn't feel it, so he said,

"I'm still breathing."

"Not for long," Silver Georgia Grau made her second mistake of the evening. The first had been when she chose Friar as her hostage.

"Is that so?" Friar said, with more steel in his voice than a hostage ought to have. He already felt like maybe he'd lost too much blood, so having his throat ripped open was a chance he'd be willing to take if it meant getting a chance to lie down. Later, he'd realize that he hadn't been thinking clearly, but everyone decided that was understandable. Crazy, but understandable.

Friar put more weight onto Silver and repeated himself. She shuffled to hold him in front of her and dug the point of the knife in a little more.

"Stop that," she snarled.

Friar lifted his right heel and brought it down as hard as he could on Silver's instep. It was the most basic of moves from defense class, but it worked because it hurt, and Silver's grip and attention broke for just long enough to allow Friar to push himself away in what was really a controlled fall. The gunfire started before he was halfway to the ground and one of the shots tore the shoulder of his shirt and spanged off the useless radio that had been clipped to him since his cruiser had been shot by Krueger. No one would admit to firing that shot, though, and he would later accuse them of trying to take him out, too, just to have a tidy ending. Sherrow would then point out that Friar wasn't a tidy man and the conversation would degenerate from there. But that was later, much later.

Friar lay where he'd fallen, definitely hors de combat. The impact of his two hundred pounds hitting the tarmac had been like another explosive concussion and the sensations produced were so intense he wondered if this was what it felt like to die. It was a minute before he could see again, and then somebody had turned him over and all he could see were boots and somebody's knees.

A confusion of voices came to him in clips and starts as audio faded in and out. Somebody pulled at his shoulder, cutting the straps of the armor, and burning pain knocked his head back and his breath out again.

"Careful, got it. It's a burn wound. Gimme the trimeth' gauze. How's that IV comin'?"

"Almost got it. That cut deep?"

"Nah, missed the artery. What's this, road rash? Guy's got gravel in his face."

"He still alive?"

Canon's voice, from the level of a standing man. One pair of boots turned and a voice said,

"Who the hell are you?"

"Canon, Max Canon. Frank Skills can give you an update."

"Is Skills here?"

And another voice, more distant,

"On his way,"

"No shit? Skills's comin' out on this one?"

"So I hear." There was a radio conversation too static-y to hear properly, then an added, "Oh, and hey, yer supposed to keep Friar alive and Canon on the scene till he gets here. His words."

Nearer by, Friar listened to the medics talk over him, saying things he was glad he didn't understand. He listened to officers taping off the scene and questioning Canon and comparing notes on the explosion of the Defiant, and conjecture on the wreckage of the Raider GL9. Visions of the last busy hour spun through his head in dizzy, hot waves.

When one of the medics addressed him, he was too disoriented at first to answer.

"Friar? I know you can hear me, just lie still. You're gonna be okay. Friar."

"How's Sherrow?" Medics made him think of ambulances, which made him think of Sherrow.

"Who's Sherrow?"

"His partner. Guy went in with the knife wound from West side few hours back. Dunno, Friar, we'll call it in, okay? Just take it easy now."

Friar could only nod at that and close his eyes again.

Max stood nearby, answering the rather angry questions from an officer who, by his attitude, thought he was going to be the one to have to clean this mess up. He kept his replies simple, since he figured he'd have it all to go over again when Frank Skills got here, and yet again when they had him down in the station house.

Max was very familiar with police procedure, and he was pretty sure this case would keep him in police company for some time to come.

Over the questioning officer's shoulder, he could see the medics working on Friar. With his shirt open, Friar looked even more damaged, and his eyes had the unfocused vacancy that usually meant extreme pain or heavy drugs. Another ambulance arrived right behind the coroner, and a brace of medics joined the first two, rolling a stretcher with them.

Max watched Friar be lifted like a dead man onto the stretcher and rolled into the ambulance, which lifted off at once and turned towards Alaman General with lights and sirens going full. He saw the coroner proclaim death over Georgia 'Silver' Grau's heavily perforated body; heard the unhappy swearing of the men who'd gone after Krueger and not caught him; watched Frank Skills' car touch down across the pier next to the abused brick shed.

The interrogating officer gave up on Max as hostile and seemed to want to read him his rights. Max returned his attention to the man half way through the Chucks and Mirandas and said,

"Chief Skills has just arrived. I'd like to talk to him."

"Yeah, right." The officer sneered, obviously unaware of who he was dealing with.

Skills got a good look at Max from halfway across the tarmac and checked for a brief moment before coming on and dismissing the surprised officer.

"Canon." He said, looking him up and down.

"Frank." Max nodded a greeting and fell silent.

Frank Skills looked at him for a long moment, then said,

"Do you need a doctor?"

"No. I could use a drink though."

Skills didn't return the grin.

"You'll get a doctor. Eddy's on his way. I'll hear about it if anything else happens to you."

"But you still wanna hear what has already happened, I assume?"

Skills took his arm and steered him towards the waiting car, dodging crime photographers, news choppers and documentation teams.

"You can tell me after someone's looked at you. C'mon, I'll give you a lift."

"You might wanna have someone check out Foghorn Maritime's warehouse," Max waved vaguely, unable to recall the street name off the top of his spinning head.

Skills nodded and kept walking.

Max let himself be put into Skills' car and put his head back. He shut his eyes. He was tired and hungry and his head hurt. He had a million bruises and aches, but he didn't have any holes, and for that he was grateful. Poor Friar.

Max turned his head to look out the window and thought about Anne.

Skills took one look at his expression and left him alone all the way to the hospital.

XXXV.

Friar

Sherrow was gonna be fine, I was told. I think they said that just to shut me up, because he'd given 'em a pretty hard time. They'd patched him in a quick surgery, but he was so upset over what might be going on with me that he'd tried to get out of bed as soon as the anesthetic wore off and had torn out all the good work they'd done and bled all over the recovery room floor.

They stapled him back together with him asking for Frank Skills the whole time, or Stephen Kay, and he wouldn't talk to anybody but who he asked for and he wouldn't stay calm or even sedated until they summoned them. Skills told me he was ripping out his I.V.s and cursing out the help when he got there, this on a load of sedatives that just wouldn't take, and the staff afraid to give him more until they knew why it wasn't working. It had to do, it turns out, with a resistance set up by the Warp cure my little doc pal had supplied.

Anyway, Sherrow remembered the warehouse and got the information to trustworthy people in time to get a hunt out for Canon and me and send all that lovely backup.

From there, it was down time in the hospital. They put Sherrow and me a bed apart in the curtained-off end of the Law Enforcement ward where the cases that have to be watched get put and gave us a brawny male nurse to make sure we stayed there.

The first bit went by in a sort of nightmare, waking up from being stitched back together to see Sherrow lying absolutely still down the row, grayish in the dawn light and looking like he wasn't going to make it. The absence of machines was my only consolation: If either of us were bad off, we'd be in ICU, not in the open ward.

Then there was that awful moment when his old man came to see if his son was dying. He stood at the foot of Sherrow's bed and stared at him, tight-faced and old, and looked like this was killing him. He'd brought Mrs. March with him because she wouldn't stay behind, and while she said all the right things, I guess, since all I can remember are her eyes, smiling, Mr. Sherrow stopped by my bed on his way out to give me a look that put all the blame for anything that ever happened to Sherrow on my head.

It made me so mad, I told him his son had the makings of a fine officer, one of the best I'd ever seen. He turned purple and stormed out. I thought Sherrow was gonna burst a lung, laughing like that.

A detective came in after that and we gave statements to the recorder, bruises and all. I saw the vid later and neither of us looked more than half alive. Some of the footage was actually released to the press and ran on the evening news, brave officers, bloodied but unbowed, cleaning up the Waterfront, and look at the reward they get. That was a little of the patented Frank Skills PR genius: it replaced the cover-up scandal instantly and suddenly there were heroes to talk about instead of villains.

It wouldn't last, but it never does, and I didn't want to be the guy having to talk to the press anyway. The hospital staff were fully cooperative on that front, and the press were denied us for long enough that I started hoping they'd lost interest.

I met Shelly for the first time flat on my back and breathless from a recent and rather rough checkup from my loving doctor, the same one's Mitchell had, turns out, and didn't we have notes to compare later. Sherrow was allowed to walk around by then and since I was finally allowed visitors, he brought her to meet me.

I think she'd been expecting someone more remarkable, certainly someone more impressive. She faked it well, though, and greeted me by embarrassing Sherrow, telling me how he talked about me all the time, me and Kay and some of the others. I didn't know what to say to that, so

I said I was glad to meet her and was Sherrow dragging her to the cops' picnic next month?

She said sure if he was well enough by then, which he and I both assured her he would be, since all he had to be able to do was drink beer and bullshit.

Then she left us alone, shooed out by an agitated nurse who said I looked pale, which was the doctor's fault, though he didn't believe me. Sherrow gave me a commiserating look and limped back to his own bed, the nurse flushing him ahead like a game-beater.

Skills came to see me with Canon, and fill me all in the bits I'd missed, which wasn't actually much. We compared notes, and I told Canon how bad he looked. He'd apparently heard it all already from various sources, coz he only grimaced at me, making all those lurid bruises dance. Skills said he'd like to knock our heads together and maybe he would first chance he could that wouldn't kill us both. Sherrow thought that was very funny, but the remark was followed by a silence where we all thought over the past few dangerous weeks. I knew Canon was thinking about Anne and Noel by the look in his eyes when he met mine and caught me thinking about the same thing. We traded forced smiles and they left me.

I had nightmares that night even after taking the medication they left me, or maybe because of it, and I ended up waking most of the ward when I fell over the side of the bed trying to run. After Simon Fraser, a motorcycle cop in for a broken leg, shouted up the night nurse, like the buzzer didn't work, everybody who hadn't been before was awake. Sherrow tried to get me up off the floor, nearly pulling out his Gore-text stitches, which pissed off the scowling nurse who arrived on the run. He seemed to think my dazed look was a dodge, and while he didn't lecture me, he clearly thought all police officers were idiots. After that, the staff were under specific orders to put up the rails on my bunk every night and they gave me a different medication.

And after all this, they let Sherrow out before me, which wouldn't've happened if I hadn't spent so much time sitting on concrete and bleeding. That was about four days along, though no way either of us was going back on duty for a coupla months, to hear the doctor talking. A fast walk was considered dangerous apparently, and I looked eagerly forward to freedom and testing this dictate, especially since, with Sherrow gone, I was at the mercy of the other officers in the ward who liked to spend any time we were all awake and undrugged teasing me about being a Media hero. The officers from the women's ward would occasionally come over to visit and join in in this shameless harassment, and since the only time I'd tried to walk away from it I'd strained something that didn't need to be strained and got the staff down my neck again, I usually had to sit and take it. The raised voices brought angry nurses our way more than once.

Ketchikian came to visit in a lull and brought me flowers. Inside the bouquet was a travel bottle of scotch and she sat on the edge of the bed and fed it to me when no one was looking. It was embarrassing and adolescent, but I enjoyed it immensely, and I didn't once think of Noel, though I did think of Crystal.

When Ketchikian asked me just how badly I'd been hurt and how was I coming along, there was so much innuendo in her voice that I know I turned bright red, and the duty nurse came and chased her away. He just didn't approve of any of my visitors. When he smelled the liquor on me, there was an explosion of outstanding caliber and not only was the doctor called to give me a lecture, but Captain Crocker was informed that I was drinking illicitly on top of everything else, and the rest of the ward were mad at me for not sharing.

Sherrow arrived right after the doctor finished his lecture and stormed out. My partner seated himself on the bedside chair with an unreadable expression on his face. He had the Satan eyebrows going, but I couldn't tell what had him in a knot.

We hadn't discussed anything important while we were prisoners together, and now that he was better enough for office work, but I was still on the casualty list, the balance of power was too weird to bring any of it up. For me, at least.

"So." He started, and stopped.

"So," I agreed, and cast around for a topic. "Press get ya?"

"Yeah, they sure did," Sherrow let a grin cross his face. "Snagged me the day I checked out. Shelly thought it was wonderful, cops getting recognition."

"But you thought otherwise."

"It sucked, man. Yer lucky yer still safe in here." That put him back in his tense mood. His eyebrows came down tight and his eyes went black.

After a moment of wrestling something, he said, "When I saw you go down, man..."

I could see it, the hollow look he'd had when he first came to me, the Randall look.

"I could say the same, kid. Leaving you in that parking lot looking dead, not a nice image, I promise."

It hadn't pulled him out of the Randall thing, though, so I went on.

"I was in much better shape than you," I told him, "If anyone gets to have nightmares, it gets to be me."

Which reminded him of Noel, which snapped him right out of it.

"I'm sorry, Vic." It was utterly sincere, with a touch of pity I pointedly ignored.

"Yeah, well, so'm I. It's done. Let's just go forward and try to stay outta warehouses while we're shot, shall we?" I joked it off with a shrug, torquing my arm with a sharp twinge that I ignored.

He laughed a little at that, looked up as Fraser swung past, then looked down at his hands.

"So, Crystal's been asking after you."

"Yeah?" That pleased me, so I said so. "That's great. How's she doing?"

Sherrow looked up and gave me the big kid eyes, but I could see he was serious, and oh, how he'd hate that description.

"She's worried about you. Doesn't say it, but I think she'd like to visit."

"Tell her to visit, I'd love to see her."

"Yeah, well, she doesn't think she has the right."

"Right?" I repeated blankly. "Ketchikian brought me liquor; Skills brought me Canon; You bring me grief. She'll make me happy. Of course, she has the right, pretty girl has the right to go anywhere she damn well wants."

Sherrow was grinning broadly by the time I'd finished this rant, and he said,

"Okay, I'll tell her to stop by."

"You do that." I put my head back and resisted the urge to close my eyes. I was tired but I didn't want him to leave yet.

He saw it anyway.

"Whyncha get some rest, Vic? I'll visit again tomorrow." He stood and patted my uninjured shoulder.

"Sherrow. Jerry." The use of his first name stopped him. It felt weird to use it, but if he was gonna call me Vic, I got to call him whatever I wanted, and right now 'kid' didn't seem right.

"Yeah, Vic." Standing perfectly still, and listening, I'd stopped him so good.

"About Noel."

There was a rigid, breathless pause from both of us, then I rushed on,

"You were right. About the roadhouse, about...everything. I just wanted to tell you that. Never ignore whatever instinct told you that." I turned my eyes on him so he could see I was real serious. "Never."

"Okay, Vic, I never will."

"Good. Maybe next time we can find out sooner and..."

I let it drag off, because I didn't want to ever hear it said out loud that we could've prevented Noel's death. I had to believe she'd gotten herself in so far I could never have gotten her out, that even if I'd known, I couldn't't've changed the inevitability of her death. If I thought otherwise, I'd never sleep again.

Sherrow let it die and patted my shoulder again, awkwardly fraternal.

"Yeah, maybe next time. You sleep now. Later."

I grunted to show I'd heard and he went away, leaving me to torture myself replaying scenarios and wondering if I could've actually saved Noel, by being in contact more, by paying more attention to what she said to me, by not letting her divorce me in the first place. I knew it was all useless conjecture, but it didn't keep me from thinking.

Kay came and told me I was an idiot.

It was the outer edge of visiting hours and I'd been dozing. Either Sherrow had talked to him or I'd been talking in my sleep.

He said all the right things about responsibility and adults making their own decisions, and when that didn't work, he said all the wrong things, like she'd left me a long, long time ago and even if she hadn't there was nothing I could've done to keep her from a course once she'd chosen it.

That worked, after all, and I felt much better that night. I took their damn medication, and didn't dream about Noel. Instead, I dreamt about my partner getting splattered all over a dockside warehouse, and this time woke up with Fraser sitting on my bed and trying to get me to shut up. I started thinking about going off the medication.

Crystal came the very next day and we talked. She weathered the rude and general nosiness of my fellow officers pretty well for a civi. We made a date, anyway, and when she got ready to go, she kissed me with her eyes tearing up and said she was glad I wasn't dead.

I like honesty in a woman, and I sat up to enjoy the view leaving as she hurried away down the aisle in her tight red skirt, me and all the other guys in the ward.

Canon

Still buzzing from adrenalin and overwhelmed by the dual assault of the night's violence and his own reopened past, Max was following Frank Skills and Eddy numbly down the hall, mind a blank, leaving Friar to the medics, when he looked up and who should be standing in the hallway ahead of them but Stephanie. March.

He was so shocked to see her out in public and unguarded that he stopped short and stared.

She did the same for other reasons. He hadn't had a chance to change clothes yet, and while the medical staff had cleaned him up some, he was still covered in cuts and bruises, scorch marks, dried blood and dirt.

Frank Skills stopped, too, and a grin crossed his face. Canon was relatively undamaged for all his adventures, so he didn't need Skills' escort, but the temptation to hear what Mrs. March said to him was too strong to pass up. He followed Max when he started up again.

Eddy cast a questioning look at them both, but came along. He seemed to recognize Mrs. March, but said nothing.

Mrs. March waited for them to come to her. She was wearing a short-skirted white dress that wrapped across the bosom in a V that showed just enough skin to make a man want to look closer.

"Hello, Frank," she said in her pleasant voice, "Officer," nodding to Eddy.

"Mrs. March," Skills gestured, "Eddy Archer. And you already know Mr. Canon, I understand?" He grinned again at her blank look at the wreck that was Max Canon.

"Yes, I...Are you alright, Max?" A worried frown creased her brow and drew her eyebrows down.

Skills could see she was holding back and sighed. Better to just leave them, then. He nudged Eddy, who started walking abstractedly, the frown on his face turning into a bemused, wry sort of smile as he started connecting the dots and got something other than the fluffy kitten picture.

"It was good to see you again, Mrs. March," Skills bobbed a head-and-shoulders bow. "I hope to have the pleasure again sometime."

She nodded in a distracted way, but uttered the proper civilities in a relatively convincing voice.

Skills caught up with Eddy, who pulled in close to say, "You'll be filling me in on a lot of this, Frank."

"Sure, Eddy, sure," Skills led him off down the antiseptic scented corridor, thinking about Mrs. March's lovely eyes and the even lovelier concern in them.

He'd once been the recipient of such concern.

A faint nostalgic smile crossed his face. Ah, those had been the days...Up all night with beautiful women, the excitement of the job, the challenge...And none of the report work.

The smile fled and the normal cross expression replaced it. By the time he was walking out of the hospital, his mind was entirely on the next stages of damage control and whether or not he should take the incriminating photograph Max had given him and march it into the office of the offending police official or leak it to the press first and make sure the bastard was drummed out of the department.

Or there was always the good cop-bad cop beat the confession outta'em method. But that was another loss to the good old days.

Frank Skills sighed deeply, startling his former partner, while unseen behind them, Mrs. March wrapped Max in her arms and tried not to cry from relief as he told her it was over and she was free.

"And you're really okay, Max?" she pulled back a little to look at him critically, as if he would be lying to her.

"I'm okay." He looked at her in some disbelief himself. "You were really that worried about me?" He couldn't help asking, he had to know, and something inside went very still waiting for the answer.

"Of course I was!" She looked angry that he'd doubted her. "I was terrified you'd be killed, you idiot! How dare you do that to me!"

She was holding his upper arms and her hands were clenched hard enough to hurt.

She gave him a little shake as she said this, and Max relaxed suddenly, still tired and hungry and aching, but suddenly content.

He detached one of her hands, drew her arm through his and started down the hall.

"Sorry. I wasn't thinking. Whaddaya expect? I'm just a man." He managed to put a twist on the last bit so it sounded just like it had when she'd said it to him so long ago.

The angry frown she held on him vanished and she smiled. It was a real smile, the library card smile, the smile he loved best.

"You are, aren't you?" She snuggled closer, and he breathed tropical paradise. "That's the way I like you."

* * * * *

Friar

I'm not ready to die. A drugged-out girl with a gun and a full load of Galaxy in her blood stream is seeing fireworks and aliens and pointing a great big hand cannon at my head. Sherrow is three blocks away in another pursuit and the back up unit is a siren in the five minute ETA distance. There's screaming and spittle on the woman's chin. Her hair is dyed a terrible red and her eyes are black with horror and hallucination.

Then her chest explodes and I breath again. I lean like an old man over a body—the girl's partner with my bullet in him, put there right before she showed up behind and silent like a cat to swat me with the hand cannon—to collect my gun and say thank you to Sherrow, no longer so far away after all. He's checking for pulse on the girl, then the guy, both wasted effort, then he looks at me sideways.

I slid into normal time as my adrenalin subsided.

"Your timing is excellent, man," I told him, checking my gun for damage.

"Yeah. S'one you owe me now."

"Sure." I thought for a second. "You say that like you owed me one before." I couldn't recall any before like that.

"The wife with the shotgun. Last week?" He prompted me, looking quizzical and waving the backup officers over.

"Oh, shit, yeah. Forgot about her. She wouldn't've wasted you, man."

"She fired on me, Friar."

"Yeah. After you'd moved out of the room. She was a suicide waiting to happen. I think we get points for takin' the pair of 'em alive."

"For as long as that lasted."

I shrugged at that.

"If the lawyers want to let their clients out to finish the job, that's nothing we can help."

"It turned into a murder-suicide," Sherrow was indignant with the convictions of justice we carry when we're young.

"Well, they waited until we filed our report, at least," I said, then heard how that sounded. "That's the way the law works, Sherrow. They made bail. If people want to kill and die badly enough, we can't stop 'em. I'm sorry," I told the look in his eyes. "We can't stop 'em."

"We can stop some of 'em," he said, grimly.

I nodded at that, agreeing.

"Some of 'em, yeah."

He shrugged off anger, then looked surprised.

"You okay?" Like he'd forgotten to ask me.

I nodded.

"Yeah. You?"

"Okay."

"Good. Let's go file reports."

The backups had radioed for the ME. One of 'em said he knew it would be necessary when he heard who the pursuing officers were. I didn't have the heart to ask who he thought would end up dead, the perps or one of us.

I let Sherrow drive us back to the station and didn't call him 'kid' once, the whole way.

T.A. Csorba